Somebody's Crying

Other books by Maureen McCarthy

Rose by any other name
When you wake and find me gone
Flash Jack
Chain of Hearts
Queen Kat, Carmel & St Jude get a life
Cross my heart
Ganglands
In Between series

maureen
McCARTHY

Somebody's Crying

ALLEN&UNWIN

Warmest thanks to Vince for his inspiration and support.

*And a big thank you to both Erica Wagner
and Susannah Chambers from Allen & Unwim
for their hard work.*

This edition first published in 2010
First published in 2008

Allen & Unwin
83 Alexander Street
Crows Nest NSW 2065
Australia
Phone (61 2) 8425 0100
Fax (61 2) 9906 2218
Email info@allenandunwin.com
Web www.allenandunwin.com

National Library of Australia
Cataloguing-in-Publication entry:

McCarthy, Maureen, 1953–

Somebody's crying
9781742370248

For secondary school students.

823.3

Cover design by Lisa White
Set in 12.5/15.5 pt Bembo by Midland Typesetters, Australia
Printed in Australia by McPherson's Printing Group

10 9 8 7 6 5 4 3 2 1

For my three sons, Tom, Joe and Paddy,
with much love.

Enid woke to a strange noise around four a.m. When she finally realised it wasn't a cat or a possum she shook her husband awake.

'Somebody's crying!' she told him.

Larry sat up, listened for a while and agreed that somebody was indeed crying. It sounded like a man, but neither of them could be sure.

Much to their later remorse, the old couple decided not to investigate for fear of being thought busybodies.

TOM

Hearing his voice after so long was weird to say the least.

Tom had been sitting at his mother's kitchen table, a squalling wind outside, rain pelting against the window. He'd been drinking tea and reading the paper, trying to summon up enthusiasm for what he had to do – go to the bank, return some calls, pack for the trip – the sort of stuff that could easy fill up the whole day if he didn't get himself into gear. Then . . . the phone started ringing. He sat there listening to it, oddly immobilised, letting his eyes drift out the back window to a pair of his own jeans being battered by the wind on the clothesline. It would just be someone wanting his mother, Anna, and she'd left for work already. Or else it would be for his sister, Nellie, who had a hot social life, if the number of phone calls was any indication. Tom's kid brother, Ned, was still in bed. He had a curriculum day, and instructions were to let him sleep. It was only after the phone had rung out and started again that Tom hauled himself out of his chair and picked it up.

'Tom Mullaney.' He is terse, wanting to give the impression that he has better things to do than talk to whoever has the bad manners to ring at this time of the morning.

There is a two-second silence from the other end and Tom's head jams into overdrive. *Amanda!* Nearly a month has passed since he broke up with her in Bali. The phone calls have eased off, but Tom can't discount the possibility that she is planning a fresh attack. She might need to tell him all over again how totally obnoxious he's become, how screwed up his ideas are, how hopeless his future is likely to be now that he's seen fit to proceed without her. Why did most girls like dragging out the painful stuff? It wasn't as though Tom had cheated on her or deliberately hurt her. He had nothing but respect for Amanda Cory. She was a fantastic girl and very pretty, too. Everybody thought he was crazy to break it off with her – including himself most of the time. The problem was, she seemed to want him to sign on for the rest of his life and . . . he couldn't do it.

'G'day, mate!'

It's a male voice, but his relief that it's not Amanda quickly turns to wariness. He half recognises the voice, but after a quick whirr his stagnant brain cells are unable to place it. What mate of his even knows he's staying with his mother?

'Yeah?' he says cautiously.

'It's me. Jonno!'

Jonno? Tom's whole body goes rigid. He slumps against the wall and slowly slides to the floor, squatting with one arm curled around his head as though he is warding off a monster or a pack of thugs. *Jonty van der Weihl!*

A cocktail of emotions floods through him, as if someone has opened the top of his head and poked a high-pressure hose in. There's shame, mostly, although that doesn't make any more sense than the rage that sparks to life as his brain clicks into gear.

2

Tom gulps a couple of times and tries to think of something to say. *You owe this guy . . .* the words ring through his head as clear as church bells. It wasn't true was it? But there it was again. *Tom Mullaney, you owe this guy big time . . .*

'G'day, Jonty.' Tom is surprised to hear himself sounding so normal.

'Yeah, it's me,' Jonty speaks fast. 'How are you, mate? You good?'

'Oh, you know. Pretty good. Yourself?'

'Well . . .' followed by a short laugh, 'I'm here, right?'

'Right.' Tom laughs, too, as though he knows exactly what Jonty is getting at. Is he meant to think that Jonty wouldn't be here? That he'd disappeared into the ether? Or necked himself? Tom is hanging onto the receiver with both hands now, but his brain is working slowly, shifting through the last three years with a weird, stiff, old-man's reluctance. The truth is, he's tried very hard not to think of Jonty van der Weihl. He has stuffed his former best friend away in the deep recesses of his brain, along with the rest of the crud from those years: the moods, the bad dreams and embarrassments. And the nightmare.

'Been a while, eh?' Tom mumbles stupidly.

'Yeah . . . just on three years.' Jonty clears his throat and laughs again, leaving all the unsaid accusations wafting in the air between them like poisonous gas.

Tom could hear them anyway. *Whose fault is that, Tom? I've been here all the time. When someone is in that kind of trouble you don't just say, 'See you later, mate.' You stick around, phone up and write. You give support.* Jonty was in that remand centre for five months and Tom never wrote to him or rang him once. Never went near him.

'So, what you been up to?' Tom settles down, trying to sound as if he's pleased to hear from Jonty, now that he is over the surprise.

'This and that.' Jonty pauses and takes a deep breath.

Tom has the distinct feeling he's about to be told something he doesn't want to hear. He looks at the phone, tempted to put the receiver down. *Seriously. Why not pull the whole thing out of the wall and tell his mother there had been a burglary? Anything to stop this . . .*

'So . . . you still living in Sydney?' Tom rushes in.

'Nah,' Jonty laughs edgily. 'Not for ages.'

'So where are you—'

'Hey, listen.' Jonty cuts Tom off. 'I'm ringing about something important.'

'Oh yeah?'

'I've got a few new leads,' he says quickly, breathlessly. 'Big ones.'

'Leads? What do you mean, *leads?*' Tom pretends not to know what he's talking about, just to give himself time to think and to plan a strategy to get out of this conversation, fast. If Jonty is the last person he wants to talk to, then the murder has to be the very last thing he wants to discuss.

Everyone knows Jonty is guilty, including Tom's own father, who got him off the charge by advising him to keep his mouth shut. *What more does he want from us?*

'On who killed her!'

Tom hears the recklessness in his former friend's voice and for a few seconds finds himself swept along with it, just like the old days. Jonty's enthusiasm had always been catching. He thrived on ideas and theories. Tom remembers how he'd loved the French Revolution back at school. *All those dudes wresting power from the rich and powerful. Awesome!* Year Ten science class. Jonty's eyes ablaze as he held up the dissected frog, begging Tom to appreciate the detailed beauty and intricacies of the limbs and tiny organs. He'd made Tom see the wonder of the world in that cold little dead green body.

Frogs, *Hamlet*, Leonardo da Vinci and the world economic order – Jonty was the only person Tom knew who used to get genuinely excited at school. It was hard keeping up with him, but fun, too. It had always been fun hanging out with Jonty van der Weihl.

Fun for everyone . . . *except Lillian Wishart.*

The whole town was stunned when police charged Jonty with the murder of his aunt. Sure, he was wild, but he was popular and personable, unlike his old man. Why would he murder his aunt, his mother's only sister?

Two days later he was found at the caves, a lonely tourist-site well off the main highway. He had spent two nights out there on his own and was reported to be in a semi-dazed state, stumbling about and talking to himself.

Jonty vehemently denied killing Lillian, but he couldn't remember why he'd visited her late on the night she was murdered. Nor could he remember leaving the house or how he got out to the caves.

So where had Tom been when all that shit was going down for Jonty? When the police had finished questioning him (mostly about Jonty, because Tom was the one who knew him best), Tom was off, taking up his place as a first-year student at RMIT. He couldn't wait to get away from that town. His parents were splitting up; his little brother, Ned, had some kind of speech condition that Tom found embarrassing; and there was the girlfriend he didn't even like. But it was the murder mainly. More than anything, Tom hadn't wanted to get caught up in all that sick shit. *Murder!* And his best mate the prime suspect. All through that last summer in Warrnambool, Tom used to wake up at night in a cold sweat. *Get me out of here!* was the mantra pumping through his head . . . *Get me out of here, fast!*

To be absolutely *fair*, a kind of wariness had been growing between them even before the murder. Their paths had began to diverge with neither of them wanting to admit it. Jonty was getting seriously hooked on dope, just as Tom was getting seriously hooked on the idea of a future for himself. The fact that they were both hooked on Lillian Wishart was never mentioned either.

'She was messing around with some weird types,' Jonty goes on breathlessly. 'It wasn't just us.'

'Us!' Tom explodes before he can think. 'Listen, Jonty, and listen hard – she wasn't *messing around* with me! So don't include me in your latest little theory, okay.'

'Okay. Cool it, mate. I didn't mean to suggest . . . anything. Sorry.' Jonty laughs sharply and stops talking. The silence between them is loud.

Tom suddenly finds he is breathing hard. Little red dots swim in front of his eyes, like brake lights in a heavy fog. The horror of it all is bubbling up again, making him want to puke. He puts a hand over his mouth to hold back the gagging.

Tom's father, Luke – who was also Jonty's lawyer – had the pictures in a manila folder, tucked away in a back file in his office. About a dozen colour photographs, taken from every angle. Police photographs. No one but the lawyers and coppers and medicos were meant to see that stuff, but Tom had found that file and . . . *he saw the way she died*.

A surge of blind rage fills him now. It makes him want to reach through the phone to grab Jonty by the scruff of the neck and smash his head against a brick wall, again and again and again. See *him* bleed. He puts his hand over the receiver so Jonty can't hear his ragged breath.

'Sorry,' Jonty says again, sounding genuinely contrite this time, although you never really knew. Jonty had always been a good actor. You had to see his eyes to see what was actually going on inside.

'That's okay,' Tom mutters. But it wasn't okay at all. He'd heard from his old man that Jonty'd done this once before. A year out of remand he rang Tom's father with some far-flung theory about who had committed the murder. Luke's advice then was the same as it had been when Jonty was first released: *just shut the fuck up.* He should put it behind him, count himself lucky that the prosecution's case had hit a stone wall and get on with his life. It was then that Tom had finally understood that his old man believed Jonty had committed the murder, just as the police did, although he never said it in so many words. There simply wasn't enough evidence to prosecute, and that was a common enough occurrence.

'I just mean that she was . . . seeing people,' Jonty persists quietly.

'Oh, yeah?' Tom sneers, determined that Jonty understands he isn't prepared to go along with the latest fantasy. No way. Being in cahoots with Jonty van der Weihl, even after all this time, could only mean trouble of one sort or another and Tom didn't need trouble in his life right now. 'You're saying the cops didn't know about these people . . . whoever they are?'

'That's right, Tom,' Jonty says softly.

'Bullshit, Jonty!' Tom's voice is way too loud. 'You know the cops went through every single person that *breathed* on her in the last five years.'

'Yeah, but—'

'You know it!' Tom cuts in again. 'They interviewed everybody! So let's cut the bullshit! They followed up on *every single person.*'

Tom suddenly hears himself. What is he saying? Cut the bullshit? Did he seriously want Jonty to start telling the truth? He didn't want to hear another word. The whole thing was over. Finished. Sometimes you just have to make the decision to shut the door on an aspect of your life or you go crazy, and this was one of those times. The woman was dead. Very sad and all the rest of it, but the fact remained . . . there was nothing he could do about it. Nothing. The other fact was that Tom was still very much alive, and planning to stay that way for a while yet. That's what he had to concentrate on.

'Well, maybe, Mulla,' Jonty says, quietly. 'And maybe not. Don't be so sure. They could have missed one or two.'

Tom winces at the use of *Mulla*, his old nickname. It makes him feel as though they are back there together, inside that terrible thing again.

'Don't you want to know more?' Jonty is baiting him now and the amusement in his voice makes anger flare in Tom all over again. *This isn't funny you drug-crazed weirdo! Her dying like that was not a game you . . . sick freak.*

'Not really.' Something thick is closing over Tom's throat. He is seeing the pictures again and thinking of her. Lillian. That lovely woman lying like a slain dog in her own backyard . . . all that springy dark hair matted with blood. She bled to death, but she would have died anyway because . . . Tom had seen the pictures and he'd read the coroner's report.

Of course he wants to know Jonty's latest theory, and Jonty knows he wants to know, which makes it worse.

'They tell me you're coming back here for a while,' Jonty continues, in an easier, more conversational tone.

'Where are you?' he asks, not able to mask his panic.

'I'm back here. In Warrnambool. Got a job.'

Tom takes a deep breath and closes his eyes, completely boxed in now. *No.* This has to be impossible. He will be there himself in a matter of hours and there is no way he can live in the same town as Jonty van der Weihl. He doesn't ever want to see him again or even *run the risk* of seeing him.

Tom looks wildly around the kitchen, as if there might be an answer to the dilemma in the photographs stuck on the fridge, or in the dust that flies up into the air when he smacks the slat blinds with his free hand. *How could he get out of it?* His old man had gone to a lot of trouble to get him three months work as a photographer on the *Chronicle*. Doing a stint on a suburban or regional newspaper was part of his course and, as far as country papers go, the *Chronicle* was definitely one of the better ones. He'd have to cancel, but how? What would he do instead?

'What's your job?' he asks dully.

'At Thistles,' Jonty replies quickly. 'Cooking.'

'Yeah?' Tom is surprised. Thistles is one of the classiest restaurants in the state. It overlooks the ocean and gets written up all the time as *the* place to drive to for *the* perfect meal. His father takes important clients there all the time. How could Jonty possibly get a job cooking there? 'You seen my old man?'

'Yeah, sure,' Jonty says. 'That's how I heard about you coming back.'

Tom shakes his head. *Thanks, Dad!* 'So, you work in the kitchen?'

'I cook,' Jonty says defensively, and then, when Tom doesn't respond, 'I've done the training.'

'Where did you do that?'

'TAFE in Sydney,' Jonty replies, adding matter-of-factly, 'I topped the year.'

'Well . . . good,' Tom mutters sourly.

'Yeah. I'm living with Mum.'

'What about your old man?'

'He never came back after the last trip. Mum and me live in town now.'

Tom has a moment of feeling glad. Jonty's old man is a pain in the arse. Jed van der Weihl was always a bit of a joke around town. Meant to be a farmer but never seen out of a smart suit and a snow-white shirt, the part in his hair as sharp as a blade. And the guy was always smiling. *Well, hello, Tom!* Eyes like fucking glaciers. His only child's natural cleverness was his own personal achievement. *Jonty will have a great future . . .* He'd actually taken Tom aside to tell him that, when the boys were both about fifteen years old. *My son is destined to lead.* Tom hadn't known what to say. Was he joking? *He has inherited the brains of my great-grand-father who lead the Dutch in the Boer War in 1899.* Tom had tried to look serious. Didn't this old fart know what a tosser he sounded? Jonty knew, of course. He'd been standing behind his father and winking wickedly at Tom throughout the speech. Once the old man left the room, they'd both snorted with laughter. Jonty was a great mimic and his father was his best subject.

Every other year Jed went back to visit relatives in South Africa, and that meant a holiday for Jonty and his mum. His mother hardly spoke when her husband was around. She was just there: ironing the great man's shirts, doing up his shoelaces and looking flustered when he complained about some small thing that was wrong with her cooking.

'How long has he been gone?'

'About eighteen months.' Jonty's voice remains flat. 'He pissed off not long after I finished my course. Didn't come back.'

Tom has no idea what to say to any of this. 'You hear from him?'

'A bit. Sometimes. Hardly ever.'

'Who looks after the farm?'

'We leased it out to neighbours.'

Tom is glad of that, too. Jonty's father had inherited a good little farm from an uncle but within a few years had managed to run it right down through over-stocking and neglecting the fences and animals. He was more interested in local politics and, in spite of his unpopularity, had got himself voted onto the local council a few times.

'So, what street do you and your mum live in?'

'Hobson Crescent.'

Tom shudders. Lillian used to live in a cottage only a few streets from there. Jonty would have to pass that house to get to work at Thistles.

'You work long hours?' Tom hopes Jonty can hear the question that he really wants to ask. *How do you feel when you pass her house, you sick fucker?*

'It's okay,' Jonty replies. 'Suits me okay.'

There is a few moments pause.

'So we'll catch up?' Jonty asks.

'Sure,' Tom replies shortly.

'Be good to see you, Mulla.'

'Yeah, okay . . . Jonty.'

Tom puts the phone down and goes straight for the bathroom. He turns on the taps and pulls off his clothes, his brain chopping from one possible scenario to another like an axe through a dead branch. *Jonty and me in the same town again? No way. Can't do it. Absolutely not on. So, back to uni? Nah. Overseas could be good? No money. Stay here in town living with Mum? No. So what will I do? What can I do?*

The hot water sloshes over his head and shoulders, and he lifts his face into its steady stream. *Nothing.* He can think of *nothing*. Photography positions are hard to get, and this one has been teed up for months. Apart from that, he's been looking forward to spending time with his old man. Since the split, he's only seen his dad for a quick meal or movie when he's been in the city for a court appearance, or when he dropped by to pick up Nellie and Ned. They talk on the phone, of course, but it's not the same. The truth is, Tom misses him.

Okay, he'd let Jonty down, no question. No matter how mad or stupid or downright *bad* a person is, they should be able to count on their friends. But does that mean that he, Tom, has to pay for the rest of his life? It's three years on for Christ's sake! He was just a kid then. Way out of his depth. Shocked, scared, confused. He didn't know *shit*.

So why should he put off his plans now? Let that drug-crazed jerk affect his life? No way. There are over thirty thousand people in Warrnambool. It has to be big enough for him and Jonty van der Weihl to miss each other. If they meet by chance he'll give him the message. Anyway, by next week Tom will be working in a busy newspaper office. There won't be time to think. All this shit will have taken care of itself.

He turns the taps off and vigorously rubs himself dry with the towel. In some weird way the phone conversation has energised him. His dull mood has given way to something sharper. He is in tune again: keen to get on with his day. This is good.

Tom met Jonty on the first day of Grade Six at Wattle Street Primary. Tom was bouncing a basketball on the grey concrete, about to join the other boys shooting baskets, when his attention was caught by a skinny blond kid about his own age. The kid was standing over near the fence talking to two tradesmen in overalls who were putting in a new gas pipe. Tom moved closer for a better look.

Wattle Street Primary didn't have a school uniform, but this kid was dressed in the full rig-out of a private school: short, grey, well-pressed pants; a grey short-sleeved shirt; long socks; black lace-up shoes and even a little yellow-and-grey striped tie. Part of Tom almost felt sorry for him. The poor geek didn't realise that the other kids were going to eat him alive.

Tom couldn't write him off completely though, because he was talking so easily to the workmen. Tom couldn't hear what the boy was saying but could see that the men were taken with him. He was making them laugh. *How come this new boy wasn't behaving like a new boy? How come he wasn't slinking around the fence feeling shy and awkward, waiting for someone to be friendly to him?* The workers had stopped for a smoke and were looking him up and down as he talked, as though they found him mightily amusing. Tom moved in closer still, curious to find out what he was saying. Too late. The bell went and the men waved the kid off to class. When the strange kid didn't seem inclined to move, one of workmen reached out and tousled his hair.

'Time for school, matey,' he said kindly.

'Okay,' Tom heard the kid say back in a weird posh accent, 'but at least think about it.' This made both men burst into hoots of laughter.

'Okay! We'll think about it!' one of them said. 'Now, off you go.'

By this stage everyone was streaming over to the main building to form lines, and although Tom was on the point of joining them – *wanted* to join them, in fact – he found that he was still standing there watching the new kid.

'Off you go, professor,' the younger workman said.

'Very well.' The kid shrugged, then he turned around and saw Tom looking at him. 'Fascinating, isn't it?' he said, pointing at the pipeline. 'That thing can hold eighty megawatts of gas at any one time.'

Tom didn't answer. For a start, he didn't like the weird accent, and he certainly had no idea what the kid was talking about. The strange boy stared at Tom thoughtfully for a moment or two. Then he held out his hands for Tom's ball, as though they were already mates and he was completely confident that Tom would oblige. *Bloody cheek!* Tom almost turned away. *Didn't he know he looked like a total loser in that get-up?*

13

But now that he was up close, Tom saw that the kid's tie was loose and his socks were down around his ankles, his hair was all messed up and he was chewing gum. The uniform clearly wasn't his idea. So Tom threw the ball to him, and the boy had it back so fast that Tom missed it. That had him on his toes! Only the year before, Tom had been voted Wattlebank's Sportsman of the Year. Having to go after a ball thrown from only two metres away was humiliating in the extreme. But there was no victory in the newcomer's eyes, nor any smart-arsed expression on his face. They moved off towards where the others were lining up, throwing the ball between them.

'I'm Jonty van der Weihl, by the way.' The boy stopped suddenly and stuck out his hand. 'And you are?'

What? Tom looked down at the outstretched hand. He'd never shaken hands with someone his own age before and he wanted to tell this sissy little dork where he could stick his hand and his stupid name. *Jonty?*

'As in Jonty Rhodes!' the boy said with a proud grin, and then, incredulously, when Tom made no reply, 'Great fielder. You don't like cricket?' The kid shrugged and took his hand away. 'Anyway, no matter.'

This was maddening. Tom *loved* cricket. He and his dad used to drive the rest of the family mad watching the tests all through the summer. He put his mind into overdrive. *Jonty Rhodes? Of course! Damn it!*

They were coming up behind all the other kids who were milling around trying to find their class groups. When Tom saw no one was looking, against all his better judgement, he decided to risk it.

'Tom,' he muttered, holding out his hand.

'All very well, Tom!' Jonty grinned as he took Tom's hand and shook it firmly, eyes blazing with good humour. 'But which

14

one are you? My bet is there are probably a dozen Toms in this school!'

What? 'I'm the only one in my class,' Tom replied sourly. *You dickhead.*

Jonty sighed, as though Tom's surly attitude was some tedious business that they both had to endure before they could get onto more important things.

'Mullaney,' Tom said, deciding then and there to give him the flick as soon as possible. *Here was a head case of the first order! Had to be. Better go find some old mates.* But since his best mate, Pete, had gone back to the UK with his family, and his next-best mate, Henry Rosen, had broken his leg over the holidays, Tom didn't feel quite as confident as usual about who he'd be mucking around with. He moved off to where Jason Searly and Murray Peters were teasing some poor girl about her plaits. Maybe they wouldn't be as boring as he thought they were going to be when he'd woken up that morning.

But when Tom went into class he found he was sitting next to Jonty van der Weihl and by morning recess he felt lucky. It was refreshing being with someone who didn't feel any need to hide the fact that they read history books for fun and knew every capital city of every country in the world. (At that stage Tom liked to study hard, too, although he didn't broadcast it.) Not only was Jonty a wealth of knowledge on any number of school subjects, but he could also rattle off Melbourne Cup winners back to 1975 and AFL premiership sides back to the sixties, and he seemed to be an authority on cricket scores and personalities.

On top of his cleverness, Jonty had a devilish sense of fun about him. What's more, his sense of humour didn't rely on belittling anyone else. Not even the truly pathetic Grade Six teacher, Miss Sue. Within the first two hours of school that day, it was obvious that Jonty had read more than she had, knew more geography and general knowledge, *and* could beat her at maths problems and crossword puzzles. In fact, the eleven-year-old ran rings around the teacher in every possible way, and yet . . . he didn't even bother to make her feel bad about it.

There was no one-upmanship in Jonty. He even made Jenny part of things in the most natural way. Jenny was the fat, disabled kid in the wheelchair who everyone ignored and who had trouble articulating her words clearly. Jonty chose *her* when they had to pick partners for the spelling bee. At recess he pushed her wheelchair up through the crowd of kids, right to the sideline of the basketball court so she could see all the action of the game the staff were playing against the Grade Sixers.

Within half a day of Jonty being there, Jenny was a person you could crack jokes with and say hello to without fear that anyone would think the worse of you for it. By the end of lunchtime, Jonty van der Weihl had become *Jonno*, and by the end of that first day everyone loved him. By the end of the week, he and Tom were best mates.

Tom throws his stuff – computer, clothes, phone – into his trusty backpack and tosses it, along with his camera case, into the back of the station wagon. He hurries back inside, writes a note to his mum reminding her to send on his mail, locks the windows and doors, crashes back outside onto the wet, quiet street and slumps into his car. The front seat looks, as usual, like a bombsite. He peers out the windscreen. The people walking by and the occasional passing car seem somehow unreal, distant, and as beside the point as some badly rendered charcoal sketch. *Nothing for it then. All systems go.* Tom slams shut the door, throws an apple core and two empty soft-drink bottles into the back seat, and starts the engine. *Why did it take me so long to get away?* He'd been piss-farting around for hours getting ready. Not hard to figure out that some part of him still doesn't want to go. But now that he is in the car he can't wait to be away. He needs to drive and drive and . . . *drive*.

Within an hour he's past Geelong, travelling down the Princes Highway to Colac, keeping to the speed limit and obeying all the rules. Seeing nothing, thinking nothing, feeling like an extension of the car: chugging forward, burning fuel, filling up space. He tries not to think of the conversation with Jonty. When odd snatches come back he refuses to let them take hold. Jonty is in the past. He has nothing to do with anything in Tom's life anymore.

Mostly he manages. But coming into Colac, Tom looks down at his hands. Even after two hours of driving, they are still gripping the wheel like claws, the knuckles almost white. He shakes one and then the other, willing himself to loosen up. Shit but he is glad to be out of that trendy plush Carlton pad! Everything from the walls to the curtains and furnishings are in muted shades of cream and white, with the occasional splash of charcoal. *Jeez, Mum, you swallow a copy of* Home Beautiful *or something*? He has a sudden image of the inside of his own head: big mounds of white dust, salt or sand, a never-ending desert just sitting there waiting to be blown away.

Three hours into his journey, almost out of petrol and starving, Tom stops to fill up in Camperdown and buys a pie, a jumbo, extra-strong coffee and a big custard bun from a nearby café. He leans his bum against the car and wolfs down the food. When the hot meat and pastry hit his stomach he begins to feel easier.

Apart from a steady trickle of women coming and going from the supermarket, a few men rolling to and from the corner pub and the ubiquitous half-dozen kids tooling around on their bikes, nothing much is happening. A group of chattering teenage girls wanders past, eyeing him up and down like he is something from Mars, before resuming their chatter. They are practising, no doubt, for the guys who'll roar up and down the street later doing their burnouts. *Nothing changes. These places are all the same, so what am I doing here?*

Tom drains his coffee, crushes up his paper bags and chucks them in the bin. Three years before, he'd left in a panic, a black cloud hanging over him. Not sure if people despised him or felt sorry for him. He's heading straight back into that. Tom pulls open the car door. Nothing will be different. What if he *can't hack it*?

He is belting out the other side of town when he catches sight of the *Old Cemetery* sign. The shock registers as a sudden lurch in his gut,s and his right foot goes for the brake, then eases off again almost as quickly. *What would be the point?*

This trip is about seeing his old man and furthering his professional experience. He can't afford to be distracted by *anything else*. Anyway, the radio said it was going to piss down sometime soon and big dark clouds have been building along the horizon since Geelong. His 1992 Commodore is a rust bucket; from a purely practical point of view it would be stupid to push his luck.

Even so, it seems somehow offensive to just *pass by*. Tom sighs, flips the indicator, brakes onto the gravel and waits for the road to clear.

The cemetery, about a kilometre up the dirt track, is just a couple of acres of land fenced off from the surrounding sheep-farming country. He pulls up beside the only other car and gets out. The breeze has turned into a rush of bitter wind, so he buttons up his coat and winds his scarf tight around his neck. Absurdly nervous now, he takes himself through the big new silver gate, past the elaborate nineteenth and early twentieth century headstones, into the modern section.

A line of pencil pines shelters one edge of the cemetery from the wind. They stand up sharply against the deepening green of the surrounding hills. A few other droopy black wattles and she-oaks are dotted among the graves, like sad relatives who have no idea of how to dress for a formal occasion. Tom stuffs his hands into his pockets and makes his way down the weed-lined path towards the far eastern corner.

Somewhere here. Gradually, his ears become attuned to the small sounds: the rustle of leaves in the wind, the tiny birds flittering about, far-off trucks on the highway and sheep and lambs baaing for each other.

At last he reaches it. *Lillian Joy Wishart (nee Hickey).* Right next to her father, Douglas John Hickey, who died thirty years before. They are lying side by side – a father and his daughter – under simple, polished-granite headstones that give only the basic facts: full name, the years of birth and death and *Rest in Peace.* She must have been about twelve when he died.

Tom stops hearing or even thinking. He is aware of a hollow space opening up right down inside: airy, spacious and slightly scary. He squats down, a rush of tears rising in his throat, and reaches out to touch the granite where her name has been gouged out so neatly. *Gone. This is all that is left of her.*

The first time Tom saw Lillian Wishart she was settling herself down in the back row of old Alan Murch's VCE history class, looking nervous. The class had been told the week before that an older woman was going to join them for the Friday morning double in European History and then for Literature in the afternoon. It was explained that this person couldn't take night classes because of work commitments, and that the class should do their best to make her welcome. No one thought anything of it until she arrived.

She was wearing a long black dress, embroidered with colourful flowers around the neck and sleeves. Her dark hair was all over the place. Curls sprang out from the clips and combs that were pushed in all over her head to keep them in place. Up to that point, Tom had never really *seen* an older woman. His mum was nice-looking he supposed. But she was normal and dressed in a pretty standard way for someone her age – straight skirts, pants and shirts from ordinary shops like David Jones and Myer, with well-cut, neat hair and subtle make-up. The other mothers were like that, too, and so were the female teachers.

But Lillian Wishart was something else. Every Friday she wore dresses that were flowing and frilled and sometimes old-fashioned. She wrapped herself in long shawls and bright belts and wore lace-up, chunky, black nurse's shoes almost always, unless it was very hot and then it was white rubber thongs, which showed her brightly painted toenails. She wore stuff in her hair: little combs, scarves, even weird bits of lace. No make-up except dark lipstick that made her mouth look as though she'd been eating beetroot. She carried her books around in an old scuffed-about leather briefcase that Tom secretly thought was very cool. There was something defiant about the very look of her, and something playful, too. She was using her clothes to say something about herself. But what exactly? Tom didn't know, but it interested him. He found himself wondering what her opinions might be about all kinds of different issues.

For the first few weeks she never said a word, just came into class, sat down and looked straight ahead to where old Murchy was writing notes on the board. Tom would sneak looks at her every now and again. He liked her profile: the long straight nose and well-defined mouth, skin like honey-blonde polished wood. In the early weeks she never gave anything away, but it was odd to have someone almost as old his parents and teachers sitting in class with them.

As first term progressed, before he'd even spoken a private word to her, he would find himself looking forward to Friday mornings.

And Jonty was the same. 'Wonder what the wacko aunt will be wearing today,' he sometimes mumbled on their way into class.

Tom had shrugged and changed the subject. He knew that the woman was Jonty's aunt but it somehow didn't seem credible. She was way too hip and interesting to be the sister of Jonty's fraught, shy and harried-looking mother. Besides, in those early weeks, Jonty rarely spoke to her, except for a polite smile and hello. No family chitchat between them. No easy familiarity. A cool understanding seemed to be in place. Tom was curious but didn't pry. Gradually, he learnt that there had been some kind of falling-out between the two families and that the sisters had only minimal contact with each other.

Tom could remember the first private conversation he'd had with Lillian. It was about midway through first term and it was hot. He was sitting in the library trying to complete a maths assignment that was not going well when he saw her walk in. The library was pretty busy, but by this stage people were used to Lillian being around the place in all her skirts and earrings and silk scarves, so no one took much notice of her. Tom found himself watching her walk around the shelves trying to locate a book. She couldn't seem to find it. He watched her look over at the librarian's station every now and then, as though on the verge of going to ask for help but then at the last minute chickening out. Eventually, he got up and asked her if she'd like some help. She was flustered at first, embarrassed about not knowing how to do such a simple thing, and then, once he'd shown her, she was overly grateful, which made him embarrassed. They stood by the stacks for maybe five minutes after they'd found the book, talking awkwardly about history and then in a more relaxed way about the literature course, which she obviously loved.

Tom never spoke about what touched him that day. Not to anyone, not even the police. It was one of those moments you mull over privately when you're walking home or sitting alone waiting for something to happen. There had been an essay on *Hamlet* due the next week and she'd obviously read and re-read the play and knew it well. But she seemed terrified of actually sitting down to write the essay, and wanted to know if he, Tom, had any tips on how to begin. She started raving on about the divergent points of view of the two main commentaries they'd been given. Professor *Blogs* said *blah*, but Doctor *Whatsisface* said something else and none of it was quite the same as what the teacher said, *so which one should I go with, Tom?*

He smiled, pleased that her problem was so easy to solve and went on to tell her that, because she knew the play so well and had thought about it, she should try to work out her own ideas and go with *them*. This suggestion threw her at first.

'But what would *I* know?' she said. Tom could tell she was being totally genuine, and for a few moments he didn't know what to say. It was almost embarrassing.

'But that's what all *this* is about,' he said, waving at the stacks of books and the computers and all the kids sitting down with their heads bent over books. She said nothing for a while but her face was pulled into a deep frown.

'How do you mean?' she asked politely.

'*Hamlet* and . . . the rest of it!' he laughed. 'History, politics and literature. You do the reading. You find out what other people say about it all. You think about it some, and then you write what *you* think.'

This seemed to shock her. She looked away, opened her

mouth to speak a couple of times and then turned back to Tom, a thoughtful frown clouding her features.

'You're sure about that?'

'I'm sure.' Her wariness had him smiling. Not often did he get the chance to give such good news to an older person.

'God! That makes it all . . .' The frown lifted and she looked over at the light flowing in through the window, smiling a slow delighted smile, as though something that had been murky and troubling was suddenly crystal-clear. 'Of course you're right. I see that now. And it makes it even better than I thought.' She turned the smile on him then, and something deep in his chest rushed up to meet it. 'I've been thinking a lot about this play, Tom! I've got some ideas about it. I really . . .' She paused and her eyes filled with tears. 'I really *love* it!' she whispered, looking straight into his eyes.

'So go for your life!' Tom said, feeling a hammering in his chest. 'Write 'em down!'

'Okay!' They were both laughing.

In spite of her carelessly thrown-together, flamboyant style of dress, Lillian was quiet and super-polite in class. She didn't give a lot away, which had the effect of making the rest of the class want to know more. Much later, when he got to know her better, Tom asked her seriously why she dressed the way she did, but Lillian's response was only to laugh and tell him that she didn't see why, after all the hard times she'd been through, she couldn't have a little fun. *Hard times?* She was open about the fact that she worked hard to make a living for herself and her daughter. Tom had done pub work himself and knew about long hours, bad money and no benefits. But of course he and Jonty wanted her to elaborate on the rest of it – they were both curious. Jonty had heard all kinds of stories about her husband, Mad Mal, over the years and he passed them all on to Tom, but Lillian wouldn't elaborate. Her previous life with her family, her mother and sister and then the husband and daughter was only ever mentioned in passing. What she was interested in, and what she liked to talk about, was the present, particularly her studies. And she loved Tom and Jonty introducing her to all their favourite music and films and books.

'I've been in a cage for the past twenty years,' she said once, when they played her one of Radiohead's early albums, marvelling that she'd never even heard of the band before. 'Now I'm out, and I don't want to look back.'

Those two VCE subjects were her first foray into formal learning in over twenty years. She'd left school when she was fifteen and had wanted to go back for years but hadn't been able to manage it. After a couple of months of being very quiet and tentative in class she gradually found her feet and would speak up and ask questions.

It wasn't just how to use the library and the net, Lillian needed help with a lot of the simple stuff. Together Tom and Jonty showed her how to set out essays and keep to word lengths, as well as more complicated stuff, like how to suss out the guts of an argument. Once she got the hang of it she began to do really well.

Jonty and Tom started to eat their lunch with her on Fridays. That was a lot of fun, too. They'd talk about what they'd learnt that morning in class. Lillian was friendly with other kids and everyone liked her, but she sought out Tom and Jonty because they were interested in the ideas behind what they were learning. Lillian did lots of extra reading for the class and that goaded Tom and Jonty to try harder. They wanted to keep up with her and it felt good to stretch their brains. The three of them topped both subjects in the exams at the end of first semester and that set the pace. For the first time in a long time it became cool to try really hard. After those mid-year results the whole class just got better and better. Even the teacher got excited. Alan Murch was on the verge of retirement but he made it plain that the threesome of Lillian, Tom and Jonty had made his last year of teaching really interesting.

Halfway back to the car, Tom sees the one other visitor – an old man, short and fat and balding, in old dungarees and rubber boots – standing on a grave not that far away, furiously polishing the headstone with a piece of cloth. Intrigued by the bizarre quality of the scene, Tom stops and pretends to read a nearby headstone. The guy has to be one of the seven dwarves. He is squat as an orange, and as round. Tom smiles as he watches the little guy pick a can from his pocket and carefully, almost reverentially, open it and dip the rag in. Then he starts rubbing the stuff along the angel wings in long slow movements, like he might be warding off evil spirits. *Shit!* In the low light one wing looks as though it's fastened to the guy's back. The image is funny, weird and tragic all at the same time. Tom makes a rough square with his hands and tries to frame it. With that big dark sky behind him and a hint of light catching the headstone it is so . . . nice! He has time to run back to the car, grab his Leica and catch it on film.

But at the car, camera in hand and about to head back, he stops. Amanda's mocking, angry voice in his head confuses him utterly. *All you care about is images, Tom! Real stuff is too much for you.* At the time he'd dismissed all she'd said as the crazy ravings of a jilted girl. But he puts the camera back in its case again. *What if she's right? Without my work, the photography, without that cold shimmering pylon of ambition holding me up, what do I amount to?*

He starts the car and drives back to the main road, thinking of how he'd first got hooked. Probably he was around thirteen, that first afternoon in the darkroom with his grandfather, watching images emerge in the bath of developer. Magic. Pa had shown him how the camera worked, shown him how to print and get the effects he wanted. There was always something new to learn, and Tom was keen.

Every picture tells a story, Tom! So you've got to make your pictures tell a story worth telling. His grandfather's respect for the power of the image made photography seem an almost *holy* thing to do. He knew all the technical stuff but he cared about the history, too, and introduced Tom to the images that had changed the way people saw and felt about the world.

By Year Twelve, Tom knew where he was headed. His heroes were those photographers in the thirties and the Second World War. People like Ansel Adams, Dorothea Lange, Henri Cartier-Bresson, and Robert Capa. They captured the important stuff: wars and famines, floods and earthquakes, births and deaths; but also the small moments between people: the funny, the bizarre, the sad and the ridiculous. That's the kind of photographer Tom wants to be.

The rain is really pouring down now and Tom has to concentrate. It's still light, but all the cars have their headlights on. Tom switches on his own and smiles, thinking of Pa taking him to that *Time Life* exhibition. The very first truly great photos he ever saw. How stunned he'd been, moved beyond words and not quite knowing why. Maybe that iconic one of Dorothea Lange's was the very first one. A head-and-shoulders shot of a woman holding a baby with a little kid pushed in close on either side of her. It was one of the key images that opened the eyes of the rest of America to what was really happening during the Depression. At fifteen years old, Tom had only a hazy idea of what the Depression was, he'd certainly never thought about what life had been like for a desperately poor mother with nowhere to go, but . . . that picture told him everything. His Pa hadn't said very much at all as they walked from one picture to another. It was as if they were in church.

The one of the little girl running naked down the road during the Vietnam War, screaming, the napalm sticking to her skin, burning her alive. The other of the handcuffed Vietcong prisoner being shot through the head. And the Buddhist monk setting himself on fire in protest against the war. They were all there. When those key images were reproduced all around the world they changed people's minds and they changed the course of history, too. *It all comes down to the one still image, Tom. One picture which makes whoever is seeing it just shut up because suddenly they understand something new.*

His grandfather had worked as a family doctor in the same practice all his life. Everyone around had loved him. He told Tom once that it was better to die doing something important than to live and do nothing. Driving west along that highway with the rain pelting down and the huge bleak grey sky above, Tom is moved all over again by the idea, but oddly unsettled by it, too. Part of him wants to protest. *Too extreme, Pa! Way too bloody extreme. What if you can't do something important? What if you don't have it in you? What if it's all too hard? Amanda could be right. What if I don't have what it takes?*

The wind has died down by the time Tom turns off the main highway. He takes the two familiar right-hand turns into the quiet, winding street that leads up to the old house where he'd been brought up. There are only five other houses in the street and his old family home is the only one not visible from the road. But the big shaggy front hedge is totally familiar to Tom.

He hasn't been back for eighteen months, but seeing the house in the dim grey light, he feels as though he's never been away. He gets out and stands in the lightly spitting rain, rubbing his hands for a few moments. Nearly four hours it has taken him, but he is glad to be there. He grabs his bag from the boot; kicks open the slightly rusty, wrought-iron gate; passes a few withered pot plants on his way up the front steps to the open front door and peers into the lighted hallway.

'Hey, Dad,' he yells through the flywire. 'It's me.'

No answer, so he walks straight in, drops his bag onto the polished floorboards and heads down the shabby strip of carpet to the living area at the back of the house. It is a big room with a television blaring the news in one corner. The smell of meat cooking in the oven in the adjoining kitchen gives him a sudden jolt of hunger. It has only been a couple of hours since he's eaten, and for the last month or two he hasn't had much of an appetite. It is back with a vengeance now and maybe that means something. 'There you are!' Bess, the ageing golden retriever, makes her way over from the heater to welcome him. 'What are you doing inside at this hour, old girl?' Tom bends to scratch her behind the ears, and she licks his hand to show that she understands exactly what he's saying. 'The privilege of old age, huh? I won't tell, promise.'

Tom snatches up a roll from the bench, breaks it open with his fingers, slathers it with butter and stuffs it into his mouth. Then he takes a long swig of milk from the half-empty plastic container on the sink. The table is covered in newspapers and dishes. Everything is untidy and worn, in just the way he remembers. Even the smell is familiar. Tom swallows more bread, feeling the ache that had gripped his throat outside settle in harder as he stands there taking it all in. He'd forgotten about the frayed floral curtains and the sagging brown leather sofa, the battered silk-and-velvet cushions on the couch and the heavy carved coffee table, stacked high with board games and a pile of newspapers. The fridge and cupboards are still stuck all over with drawings, some of them his own, all stained and greasy from the years of hanging there. Even the table is covered in a cloth he recognises – red berries with long green stems. *Christmas? Come on, Dad! What the hell is it doing here in July?*

Tom stands for a moment or two, breathing in the childhood that he left behind so abruptly three years ago. He can almost see the lot of them as they used to be – Mum, Dad, Nellie, Ned and Tom himself sitting around this old blackwood table; or on the big, comfortable, shabby chairs; or lying about on the sofa with its kicked-in cushions. How many times did he come bounding into this room to slump down to eat breakfast? He used to stick his feet up on the table and argue politics over dinner and tell Nellie to shut up when she insisted on reading out snippets from the newspaper. That sister of his had had attitude right from the time she was two! So much yelling had gone on here. All the years of stuffing his face, burping and fighting and laughing. This place was home in a way that his mother's house in Carlton, full of all her stylish stuff, would never be.

The night his team won the under-nineteen's footy premiership hits Tom right between the eyes. The First Eighteen came back to this room with their various parents, girlfriends and siblings, laughing and shouting at each other. All the team members kicking back in glory. Real men at last!

His mum and dad had been a united front, heating up pies and handing around chips and Cokes, laughing and pretending not to notice the guys going outside to take slugs from hipflasks. Tom had been so proud that night, of himself and the team, of course, but of the big generous ramshackle house too, and the family who inhabited it. His family. He knew his team-mates were envious of what he had. Who else had a good-looking mother like his who was also the town's most popular female doctor? (All their mothers went to Anna Mullaney's clinic.) Who else had an old man who not only ran the busiest, most prosperous law practice around, but who also made his own dry risqué jokes that had Tom's friends hooting with laughter? Luke could give them advice on which second-hand cars to buy, too, and could talk footy just as well as any of their fathers, who were mainly local tradesmen or farmers. He knew all their families. He'd presided over so many of their house sales and driving infringements, their divorces and petty disputes.

Jonty had been there that night, of course, stuffing the pies away with the rest. He was just another wild boy then, way brighter than everyone sitting around that table, for sure, but a hero as well that night because he'd played so brilliantly. The fact that he'd been off his face on a weed and tran binge two days before was conveniently forgotten. It was hard to pinpoint when the shift between them started, but by September Tom had well and truly decided that he was going to do well in his exams. A night off his face on grass, or whatever else Jonty was into, just didn't seem appealing anymore. That grand final night must have been three months before the murder.

'Hey, Dad,' he yells again. 'You around?'

Still no answer, so Tom walks through the glass sliding doors onto the back verandah and squints into the darkness. The night has come down while he's been inside. There is the familiar quietness, the smell of gum trees and mint. It isn't long before his eyes adjust and he sees the dark bulky shape of his father and the spark of his cigarette through the leaves of the lemon tree, right up the back near the fence.

'Hey, Dad,' he called. 'You there?'

'Tommo!' His father comes out from behind the tree. 'You made it at last!' He is grinning sheepishly as he walks back towards Tom, as though he's been caught in some illicit act. He takes one last deep drag of the cigarette before stamping it out in the wet grass. He holds out both arms and hugs Tom hard, then blows the last lungful of smoke out over his shoulder and shudders.

'You have trouble with the car?'

'Didn't leave till late,' Tom laughs. 'Still smoking, I see?'

Luke runs one of his big hands across Tom's head and grabs him for another bear hug. 'Jeez you've got thin, Tommy boy. You hungry?'

'Yeah.'

'Good. Come on then.' Luke flings an arm around his son's shoulders and pushes him towards the back door.

'Seriously, Dad. What you doing out here? It's bloody cold.'

'Not allowed to smoke on the verandah anymore,' his father sighs. 'Anyway, according to her, I gave up about three months ago, so . . .'

Her? Tom had forgotten about Nanette, the glamorous red-headed local businesswoman that his father is seeing.

'Is she here?' he asks anxiously.

'At some hospital board meeting,' his father grimaces. 'But she'll be around later.'

'Hey, Dad, is this going to be okay with her?' Tom pulls the sliding door shut behind them. 'I mean, me coming to stay.' He's wondering what the hell he'll do if it isn't okay with her, and why on earth he hadn't thought to ask before.

'Of course it is!' Luke heads over to check the oven, which has started blowing a bit of smoke, and then mutters to himself, 'It's my bloody house! She doesn't even live here, although you'd be forgiven for not knowing that. Anyway, she'll love having someone else to boss around.'

Nellie always comes back from her visits to Luke with horror stories about Nanette, how vain she is and how bossy. Tom figures his little sister needs to blame someone for their parents' break-up. But Luke had an affair with some *other* woman before Nanette and *that* was the reason that their mother left. It wasn't Nanette's fault. His father had never wanted the split, always maintaining that his 'fling' with the mystery woman was a stupid mistake

31

and meant nothing. He also made it plain to everyone, including Nanette, that he had no intention of ever marrying again.

'Right,' Tom nods awkwardly, 'but . . . you and her going okay?'

'Oh, sure,' Luke smiles in his doleful way and shrugs. 'You know how it is.'

'No, I don't, Dad,' Tom says, watching his father pull a couple of beers from the fridge, thinking he is looking older and tired, and heavier, too. 'That's why I asked.'

'Want one?'

'Thanks.'

Luke twists the beers open, gives one to Tom, chucks the tops in the vague direction of the rubbish bin, then leans back against the bench and holds up the bottle, looking at Tom and smiling.

'Tom! My firstborn boy, I've been looking forward to this!' He takes a deep swig, moves over and tousles Tom's hair. 'You coming to live here is going to be . . . bloody *fantastic*.'

'Yeah, well . . . thanks, old man.' Tom smiles, pleased by the obvious pleasure his father is taking in just *having him here*. He feels a stab of guilt, too, when he thinks of how he stayed away when his mother first left – even though he knew Luke was doing it hard. He holds up his bottle and meets his father's eye.

'I've been looking forward to it, too, Dad,' he says quietly.

'Yeah?'

'Of course.'

'Good man,' Luke says softly, and smiles before turning around to the cupboard. 'Now, some forks and knives.'

Tom watches his father bustling around putting out the plates and cutlery in a roughly organised way, feeling affection for him rise in his chest like a sweet soufflé. The three kids – Nellie, Ned and Tom himself – all take after their mother: tall and narrow. They all have her colouring, too – thick, curly, almost-black hair and dark-blue eyes. Although not short exactly, Luke has a stocky build and a tendency to stack on the weight. He is dressed, as usual, in a cheap crumpled suit, a loosened tie around his throat and his feet pushed into old slippers. His face is deeply lined, and his skin pallid from not enough sun and too many cigarettes. His sandy hair is thinning on top. Luke must feel Tom looking at him because he looks up and smiles.

Tom grins back, relieved. His father's light-blue eyes are the same as they've always been: bright and shrewd, like little gas lamps, lifting his ordinary, old-man's face into something else entirely. He's lost whatever looks he had as a young man, but those little lamps somehow get him across the line.

'Let's get some food into you,' Luke mutters, picking up one of the sharp knives and slicing into the meat. 'You look like you could do with a feed! Come on, kid, tell me the news. Heard that Bali wasn't such a success? But did you at least get a surf there?'

'A bit,' Tom muttered. His father has never been one to pry. Anna would probably have raved on to him about the weird state Tom had been in when he first came home – sleeping all day, not going out or seeing his mates and all the rest of it – but most of that would have rolled off Luke's back. He's never one to overreact.

'Mum says to say hello,' Tom tells him, 'and she wanted me to remind you to keep taking the iron tablets.'

They are sitting at the table eating the roast lamb. The football is on in the background. Luke has forgotten about most of the vegetables – they are still lined up, chopped but uncooked, on the bench – but Tom doesn't care. He couldn't have wished for anything more delicious than these hunks of meat, covered in mustard, pepper and salt, inside thick slices of fresh white bread, along with chopped-up fresh tomato.

'How is your mother?' Luke asks slowly.

33

'Good.'

'Still with Mr Universe?'

'Yeah,' Tom laughs, as his father gets up for another beer. His mother has been seeing a rich plastic surgeon called Heath for the last couple of years. He is a way better catch than his father, Tom supposes, at least on the surface. His mother is fifty, and Heath a couple of years younger. He has a silver Merc in the garage and a fancy pad down the coast. He keeps himself fit and doesn't smoke or drink too much, and he doesn't get around in suits from Target, either. She seems to like him well enough, although Tom finds the guy a bit straitlaced. Anna and Heath don't live together, so Tom hasn't had a chance to see evidence of really strong feeling. But then, he figures he wouldn't anyway, being her son and all. Anna tends to be more reticent than Tom's father.

But she always grills Tom about Luke, in just the way he does about her. *How are his spirits? Is he looking after himself? Still working too hard? Tom, you've got to convince him to have a proper break this year!* It is funny, almost as though they are still joined at the hip, even though they are divorced and live totally separate lives.

'Why don't you poison his soup for me?' Luke mutters as he gets up to turn off the TV.

'Righto,' Tom says with a wide yawn.

'I hate the way that bastard moved in on her life!'

'Okay,' Tom says slowly, thinking that his father is so far off the mark that it's laughable. But he doesn't contradict him. Tom has already decided he is too tired for anything but bed. The facts are that no one *moved in* on his mother unless she wanted it, and his father had to know it too, if he bothered to think about it.

'How could she go for a twerp like that?' Luke groans. 'The guy must have had a personality bypass!'

'You were the one at fault,' Tom reminds him savagely.

34

'It was a bloody midlife crisis!' Luke slumps back into his chair and groans again. 'Worst mistake I ever made. But I'm not Robinson Crusoe. A lot of men go crazy at fifty! There were no affairs before. Ask your mother.'

Tom has heard all this before so he sighs and says nothing.

'Do you like him?' Luke asks tentatively.

'You ask me this every time I see you, Dad.'

'Well, do you?'

'He's okay.' Tom shrugs. There is absolutely no mileage in any of this kind of talk as far as he is concerned. 'I don't see much of him.'

'Are they going to get married?'

'Well if they are, they haven't told me.' Tom watches his father throw a couple of cushions at an ugly picture on the back wall. For something to do, Tom follows suit with a few more, and they both laugh because Tom is first to get the picture and Luke doesn't even come close.

'I win!' Tom gives him a light punch on the arm and gets up. 'I've got to hit the sack. I'm bushed.'

'Yeah,' Luke sighs. 'God, I miss your mother, Tom.'

'I know,' Tom says, not bothering to stifle a yawn. His eyelids are starting to feel as though someone has injected them with lead. Besides that, he isn't really interested in hearing about the emotional life of old people, even if they are his parents. He has enough of his own shit to think about.

'You know what I miss most?' Luke grumbles on, throwing his head back and putting his feet up on the coffee table. 'Your mother likes to ease up and have a bit of fun. She gets a kick out of life in her own quiet way, doesn't she?'

Tom nods, trying not to look bored.

'So many women don't,' Luke goes on. 'They're always trying to improve themselves and everyone else around them.

35

I'm Nanette's latest project, you know. She sees it as her task to make me healthier, slimmer, kinder and richer . . .'

'What you mean is that Mum let you get away with all your vices,' Tom laughs.

'Yeah!' his father sighs longingly. 'Smoking, football, eating what I like! Nanette hates football. Can you believe it? If I even look at a pie or snag she has a fit. And there is no sex anymore.'

'Ah, shut up!' Tom gets up and goes to the sink for a glass of water. 'I don't want to hear about anyone's bloody sex life, much less yours!'

'Once a month if I'm good,' Luke chortles, throwing another cushion at the picture and then a last one straight at his son's head.

'Shut the fuck up, Dad!' Tom ducks and throws it back.

'Okay,' Luke sighs, 'let's hit the sack.' Then he smiles. 'I got things planned for you tomorrow.'

'Such as?'

'The hedge.' He nods, still smiling. 'And we might have a go at the garage.'

'Okay.' Tom shrugs and opens the door leading to the hallway. 'Whatever. I don't mind. Night then.'

'See you tomorrow, Tom,' Luke grins. Tom has walked out and is about to close the door on his father but something stops him.

'Jonty van der Weihl rang me today,' he says nonchalantly.

Luke is filling the dishwasher. He looks up with one raised eyebrow, waiting for Tom to go on.

'Reckons he's got some new lead on the case.'

Luke sighs and stands up straight, then picks up the roasting pan and begins to scrape the congealed fat into the rubbish bin, taking his time.

'He rang me, too.'

'When?'

'Last week.'

36

'What did he say?' Tom asks quickly. 'Has he got anything new?'

Luke settles the pan on the sink and yawns again, shaking his head. 'Poor Jonty,' he sighs. 'Poor bloody silly *sad* kid.'

'He's back here.'

'Yeah,' Luke nods. 'Saw him the other day. Working at Thistles. Good luck to him, too. It would be good if he could make something of himself after . . . all that business.'

Tom is on the point of asking him outright if he still thinks Jonty killed Lillian, but he can't quite manage to get the words out. Something in him baulks at bringing it all out into the open as though it is a *reasonable* thing to talk about when . . . even thinking about it makes his breathing go strange.

'I've got little Alice coming to work for me next week,' Luke suddenly says cheerfully.

'Alice?' Tom has no idea who he means.

'Lillian Wishart's daughter.' His father frowns. 'She's deferred university for this semester. I think the poor kid found it all a bit much. Some of the country kids find the city hard, you know. So she's taking a break and is going to go back next year.'

'Yeah?' Tom finds this news weirdly disconcerting. 'And she's coming to work for *you*?'

'What is so strange about that?' his dad yawns. 'The other gap-year kid was hopeless. I put an advertisement in the paper and young Alice was the best applicant by far. She seems to have her head screwed on.'

'What kind of job is it?'

'Just basic office work. Answering the phone, a bit of typing and sorting.'

'But . . .' the more Tom thinks about it the more it seems wrong, 'is that a good idea? I mean, you were Jonno's lawyer and . . . you got him off the murder charge.'

'It was over before it began!' his father contradicts him sharply. 'The prosecution's case was weak.'

'But you were his lawyer.'

'I told Jonty to shut up.' Luke looks at Tom as though he is refusing to understand a very simple fact. 'They couldn't pin anything definite on him.'

'So, you think Jonty might be . . .' but Tom's voice peters out. He is unable to meet his father's eyes so he looks away again. *Innocent?* But did he really want to know?

Luke was looking at him thoughtfully. 'Let's say Jonty is one lucky boy,' he says bluntly. With that, he puts the milk away and closes the fridge door. 'Now listen, Tom, Nanette said she'd change your sheets, but if she forgot then you know where to get clean ones.'

'Thanks.' Tom wishes like hell he hadn't brought Jonty up. It is his first night home and he doesn't want to have it churning away there in his subconscious while he sleeps. On the trip down he'd decided that the way to make the next three months work was to keep a lid on the whole business.

'Anyway, that little Alice came to me,' his father explains thoughtfully as he begins switching off the lights. 'She wanted the job. The business about her mother wasn't mentioned. That's all finished now.'

'Except it's not,' Tom says sharply. He is standing in the hall, one hand on the door, waiting for his father to finish.

'Oh,' Luke waves his hand dismissively, *'that's* all hot wind! Jonno is like a dog with a bone. Can't leave it alone. This Alice is a nice kid and I think she'll be good in the office.'

'How old is she now?' His father has deliberately missed the point. Last time Tom looked, when a person is murdered, it isn't finished until someone is doing time for the crime.

'About eighteen, I think,' Luke says. 'You wouldn't recognise her.'

Tom frowns, trying to picture Alice Wishart. She was a few years younger than he and Jonty, and had gone to the Catholic school. A shy kid, if Tom remembered rightly. She hadn't stood out in any way back then. When Jonty and Tom were around at Lillian's place she was just this quiet presence in the front room, reading her books and mucking around with girlfriends. Tom remembers that she used to draw a lot. There were always new paintings and drawings pinned up around the house.

'So what is she like now?' he asks his father.

'Well . . .' Luke says thoughtfully, 'I got a bit of a start when she first walked into my office. It was like seeing a younger version of her mother all over again.'

'Really?' A sharp chill runs down Tom's back. 'So . . . she looks like Lillian?' It gives him the creeps trying to imagine that.

'Well,' his father smiled, 'wider, I suppose, but . . . the face.'

'What do you mean *wider*?'

'Oh, the girl's got too much weight on her. But underneath she is a beauty. Like her mother.'

'Oh . . .'

'Go and sleep, Tom,' Luke waves, 'you look buggered.'

It doesn't look as though anyone has been inside Tom's bedroom since he last slept in it eighteen months ago. Football posters cover the door and a big U2 colour shot is on the wall. It is cold and smells musty. He opens the window to let in some fresh air and pulls back the sheets. Something tells him Nanette hasn't changed them, but he is too tired to care. He throws his case onto the spare bed and grabs an extra blanket out of the cupboard. Then he pulls on some old trackie daks from the drawer. After cleaning his teeth he crawls into bed and turns out the light.

She's a beauty . . . like her mother.

Tom and Jonty were sitting at Lillian's table laughing. They'd been there a couple of hours, getting stoned and listening to some wild old bluegrass singer called Stingray that Jonty liked. Lillian had made pizza and they were snorting with laughter because Jonty, who'd never eaten anchovies before, couldn't believe the other two actually liked them. He was carefully picking each one off his pizza slice and giving it a name and a history.

'And this is little Polly Waterlog. An angel until she started hanging out with a certain plankton high-flyer. After he dumped her she just went wild. You could hardly keep her in the water! She was scared of nothing and so,' here Jonty's voice became soft with mock radio-announcer concern, 'she came to an untimely end. About the same time as Sir Slimy Leak here, who . . .'

It was just your ordinary stupid stoned talk, but something else was happening too. Lillian seemed unusually agitated. It was nothing for her to get a bit charged up every now and again about something that was bugging her, but this night was different. She wouldn't let up about Jonty's mum.

Whenever Lillian saw Jonty she always asked after her sister. How was Marie's health? Had she been anywhere or done anything different? The worry in her voice was always there, but this night Tom could tell it was eating away at her. She kept coming back to it. How Marie used to be the sweetest girl. How clever she was when she got a little encouragement, and how much they loved each other as kids.

'You know, Jonty,' she said, while they were chewing away on the pizza, 'that father of yours is not just your ordinary, run of the mill bully-boy like my Mal.' She shuddered suddenly, her face tight with anger. 'Mal had some redeeming features, when he was sober. He had a sense of humour, and he could be really sweet when he felt like it and . . .' she frowned, 'he absolutely loved his daughter. But *your* father, Jonty! He is a total *monster*!'

'I know that.' Jonty's face immediately clouded over, the way it always did when his father was mentioned.

'He is downright *evil*,' Lillian added for good measure.

'Yeah, well . . .' Jonty tried to smile. 'What's new?'

'He shouldn't be alive!'

Tom wished Lillian would stop going on about Jonty's old man. What was the point of rubbing it in? Mostly their talk steered right away from families, and that made more sense. Tom had met Jed and Marie, had even been out to the farm a few times. It hadn't taken him long to work out that his friend's old man was a total head case.

'I just hate to think of the way that man is ruining her life!' Lillian went to the fridge for the vodka bottle. As Tom watched her half-fill a small glass then pop in a few ice cubes, it crossed his mind that she might be drunk. But there were no ragged edges or slurred words, and her voice was clear. 'My poor little sister,' she whispered to herself as she sat down.

'My poor little mother,' Jonty mumbled quietly in agreement.

'I used to protect her,' Lillian continued.

'She always tells me that!' Jonty smiled sadly. 'You were her best friend.'

'And what kind of a friend am I now?' Lillian muttered, frowning hard. 'I have been free of Mal for nearly four years and what have I done to help my little sister?'

'What can you do?' Tom didn't much like this twist in the conversation or the despairing note in Lillian's voice. Going back to laughing about anchovies would have been more in his line. Either that or something about the latest bit of music they'd been listening to. It was always better to leave families out.

'I feel like I've got to *do* something for her!' Lillian cried loudly. 'To get her away from him.'

'She'll never leave Dad,' Jonty said matter-of-factly.

'But why not?' Lillian stared hard at Jonty, her eyes glittering with anger. 'Why wouldn't she leave him?'

'She just . . . won't,' Jonty shrugged.

Lillian got up and turned off the dripping tap, then slumped down again and threw her head back to stare at the ceiling, arms folded across her chest, mouth grim.

'He's . . . abusive,' she whispered furiously. 'He bullies and . . . humiliates her. She is dressed in rags while he has the best. It's . . .'

'I know.'

'So why does she stay?'

'She says she . . . loves him.' Jonty threw his head back and closed his eyes. 'I don't know.'

There was so much sadness in Jonty's face that Tom didn't know where to look. This was his best mate and yet they'd never talked about any of this. Did *abuse* mean that Jed beat her up? Tom suddenly wanted to know but didn't like to ask.

'Your mother is wasting her life!' Lillian said sharply. Jonty shrugged and looked away. Sadness hung around his mouth and eyes, and his shoulders slumped, heavy as a pile of bricks on his back. It occurred to Tom that Jed was the only person who could make Jonty like this, pinched and sort of flattened out. *Totally reduced.*

'There is only one thing we can do, darling.' Lillian was rinsing the plates at the sink. 'Only one thing we can do. We have to get rid of him.'

'What?' Jonty stared at her in astonishment.

'Well . . .' she said, 'there is an obvious way of getting rid of someone around here.'

'Which is?' Tom said eventually.

'No,' she laughed, 'you tell me!' Her lovely bright eyes bored into Tom's mischievously and he felt himself suddenly helpless against her. '*Think!*' she said. 'You have a body that you don't want found. What would you do with it?'

A body? She couldn't be serious.

'I dunno,' Tom laughed nervously.

'The caves, sweetheart,' she whispered, 'the caves. Think about it. So damned obvious that it's a wonder they aren't used more for this kind of thing!'

'Assuming Jonty wants him dead, then how do we do it?'

'Oh that is the easy part!' Lillian said breathlessly. 'He's always fancied me. When the four of us used to mix socially he was always trying to hit on me.' She shuddered. 'He'll come and meet with me if I ask him. If nothing else, he'll come for the money.'

'Money?'

Lillian stood next to Jonty and put a hand on his shoulder.

'You must know that your grandmother has cut your parents out of her will because she loathes your father so much,' she said softly.

Jonty looked up at her but made no comment.

Lillian sighed and leaned over to pick up her glass. 'Your father is very interested in my mother's money. I could ask to meet him to talk about it. I could fix his drink and . . . it could all go from there.'

Jonty was staring blankly back at his aunt as though in complete shock. Tom broke the spell by getting up to pour himself a drink of water. Standing by the sink, he gulped it down and then went over to the window and stared out at the house next door. The old couple had forgotten to pull down their blind. He watched them moving around slowly in the yellow light, from the stove to the table and back again, getting their dinner maybe. Enid and Larry. He used to cut their lawns for them when he was about ten.

How come Lillian didn't understand that even though Jonty hated his father he also probably loved him? Most people do. You hate your parents and yet you love them. It's pretty standard stuff. When Jonty was mimicking Jed, or bitching about his bully tactics and crazy views, Tom could always see something else in his eyes.

'I gotta go now,' Tom said, without turning around.

'Me, too,' Jonty said, his voice soft with misery. 'My olds will wonder where the hell I am.'

Lillian saw them to the door, and put a hand on each of their shoulders, making them turn to look at her.

'I get silly sometimes,' she said apologetically.

'That's okay,' Jonty tried to smile, 'So do I.'

It was here in his bedroom, on the day before the VCE history exam, that Tom first heard that Lillian Wishart was dead. His father had come home midmorning – just walked into Tom's room without knocking, his face grim, mouth tight with distress. Tom was sitting at the desk, his head in his hands, staring at an etching of Napoleon leading his troops into battle. He knew immediately something serious was up because his father hardly ever came home during the day. Nor did he usually enter a room without knocking.

Luke didn't bother with preliminaries. 'Lillian Wishart was murdered last night,' he said, stony-faced.

Tom stared back at him. His father stood there motionless, waiting for Tom to say something, but Tom was so stunned that he literally couldn't swallow or move his mouth. They stared at each other for what seemed ages.

'I was here,' Tom managed to say at last, as though he'd been accused of something. Luke nodded, slumped down on Tom's narrow bed, threw his head back and closed his eyes, both hands gripped in front of him. He looked as though he were about to jump from a tall building or had just witnessed an execution.

'Okay,' he said in a hoarse voice, 'you were here and so . . . where was Jonty van der Weihl?'

Tom's face and neck had gone unaccountably stiff. How the hell would he know where Jonty had been last night? Probably off his face, the way he'd been a couple of days previously, when Tom had rung to ask him about a maths problem. *Where was Jonty?* Until that point, Tom had no idea his parents knew anything about the friendship he and Jonty had going with Lillian Wishart. *Murdered?* The word pounded in Tom's head like a series of rolling bomb blasts. *Lillian Wishart has been murdered. It couldn't be true! Could it? How?*

His father got up and left the room and that's when he finally *understood* the truth of it. *She's dead.* It came down like an icy avalanche, heavy and hard and cold, smashing everything in its way. It stayed with him for months, that feeling, like being held down under freezing water that flowed fast and furious above him. But at other times it was as still and quiet as a snake coiled up in the sun, seemingly asleep but alert and ready to strike. *Lillian Wishart is dead and . . . I killed her.*

Of course he didn't kill her! But . . . after his father had left his room he'd looked at that picture of Napoleon and been stunned to see that it was exactly the same image as before his father had told him the news. Ditto with the things on his desk and the view from his window. Somehow it didn't make sense because nothing was the same any more. Lillian Wishart was dead. *Murdered.* Life would never be the same again.

Tom lies in his old bedroom wondering if he should get up and move to his sister Nellie's room to get away from these sharp, cold memories. But it is too cold to get out from under the covers. He thinks of Amanda and the way they used to cuddle up together and whisper and laugh, before Tom ruined everything.

'Tell me the *real* reason,' she'd yelled at Tom, 'you arrogant, self-centred shit!'

What was the real reason? Why did he break it off with her?

He hadn't been ready to be in one of those full-on, cosy mini-marriages that everyone his age thought was so damned normal. No church and no ring, no kids and no house, no actual living together and splitting the bills, but you're as good as married. You're all tied up and every moment apart has to be accounted for. *Jeez!* All those frigging phone calls he had to make to keep things sweet. Call him a weirdo but he could do without sex if it meant that he didn't have to buy into all that.

Maybe . . .

He wishes he had Amanda with him now, though. He wishes that they were both under the covers, hanging onto each other. Or at the very least that he could go ring her, let her chuckling laugh calm the night fears that have hit without warning.

O what a rogue and peasant slave am I.

Lillian loved *Hamlet*. She learnt the big speeches off by heart and would sometimes quote bits and pieces with a twinkle in her eye that belied how deeply it moved her. Underneath the easy joyful surface there was such still sadness in her.

He tosses and turns trying to get comfortable but thoughts of Lillian Wishart lying cold in her grave fill the spaces between his thoughts . . .

So it will be the black skirt then – short with a kick-frill at the knee – and a pink floral blouse. The old bat won't approve but then, with luck, she won't see, will she? Sheer stockings? They look better. But no, it's too cold. Who cares if the thick ones do make her legs look fat? She *is* fat. She probably should wear heels, but it's a long walk, so the scuffed black-leather flats will do. What about a jumper? No. Alice doesn't feel the cold much and she loathes getting sweaty. Fat people with sweat marks under their arms are particularly disgusting. She will wear the light loose trench coat and bring a brolly in case it rains.

All set now, Alice will sneak out of the house before her grandmother wakes, make her way down to Main Street and grab a coffee and a couple of those big warm almond croissants at Lizzie's before she fronts for her first day at work at Mullaney Law Practice. Standing up straight now, she checks herself in the mirror. *Oh shit!* She looks like one of those hefty train conductors working the country line. *Ladies and gentlemen! Have your tickets ready, please.* Alice laughs as she mouths the words to herself in the mirror, pulls her long hair back into a ponytail and secures it with a pink velvet scrunchie to go with her blouse. She salutes herself and stands to attention. *Ladies and gentlemen, the buffet car is now open! Please do not leave your personal items unattended.* Maybe a job like that wouldn't be so bad. On the other hand what about a train *driver*? Or a pilot, or a floor sweeper or a people smuggler? Any of them would do.

'Alice!'

Oh, God no! She's awake! 'Yes?'

'Yes *what*? How many times have I told you?'

'Yes *Gran*!' She only just manages the fake-contrite note in her voice. 'Sorry!'

'That's better . . . Now, are you ready yet?'

Mind your own business. 'Not quite, Gran.'

'Well, don't forget I want to see you . . . and have you packed your lunch yet?'

Oh sure. It was my first priority. 'Yes, I have . . .'

'No point wasting money.'

'You're right!' *And when you're dead I'll waste every bloody cent you leave me, you old skinflint. I'll go out every night and eat in the poshest restaurants I can find. I'll stuff myself with caviar, and custard cream cake, and I'll drink French champagne until it's coming out my ears, and I'll bathe in asses' milk!*

Just being able to think these secret thoughts makes Alice feel better. Free somehow. Once out of the house she will think more of them in greater detail. She will let her imagination run wild with all the things she'll do with Grandma's money because . . . it will all be hers one day! Every sweet, shining little dollar. This beautiful house (fabulous garden, prime position on Snobs Hill overlooking town), plus the farm out west: five thousand acres of productive Western District pasture, complete with many thousands of fine-wool merino sheep! Not forgetting the two city investment properties and the shares in Western Mining and Rio Tinto. All of it owned by Mrs Phyllis Hickey, her grandmother. Ninety-two years old and, as might be expected, not exactly in the greatest of health!

Alice pictures herself in pale-blue silk pyjamas, lolling around on plump embroidered cushions doing crossword puzzles and sketches. She will invite people around for slumber parties and card soirees. *Just think! Long warm nights of French champagne in elegant crystal glasses, kissing people I don't really know, and don't even have to get to know because I'm not planning to marry any of them.*

In fact, Alice hasn't packed lunch. She doesn't much like sandwiches, would much rather go a large slice of pie or a delicious hot focaccia with lashings of ham, mushrooms and melted cheese. But on her way through the kitchen she picks a couple of pieces of fruit from the bowl and stuffs them into a brown paper bag and then into her leather shoulder bag, just in case she gets asked for proof that she's done what she was told. She doesn't much go for fruit either, although she might eat the banana.

'It's eight now. You don't want to be late,' her grandmother's imperious voice rings down the stairs.

'Okay.' Alice walks up the stairs and into her grandmother's room to find the old lady sitting up in bed in her pink quilted bedjacket reading that morning's broadsheet newspaper and sipping a cup of tea. *How come she's awake?* Her grandmother usually sleeps until the hired help comes at nine to bring in her paper and cup of tea. Alice stands in the doorway and waits as her grandmother slowly puts the paper down, takes off one pair of glasses, puts on another and then critically squints through them at Alice. 'Wherever did you get that skirt?' She shakes her head in disapproving wonder.

Here we go. 'Melbourne.'

'Frills are seldom a wise choice.'

'Black is slimming, Gran,' Alice protests mildly. 'The sales-girl told me.'

'Bah! What would those little flibbertigibbets know?' Her grandmother pushes the paper aside. 'It's too short, and you're too big for such a garment!'

Alice hates the fact that her face flushes as she feels those old crow-eyes raking over her body. But she is an expert at shifting her inner focus away from the present whenever she needs to. It is as though her brain has a number of rooms. When one room becomes uncomfortable she can get up and shift herself to another. Does it all the time. So, even as she's standing there, letting a cantankerous ninety-two-year-old boss and humiliate her, an important part of Alice *isn't even here*. She gives herself a secret smile as she acknowledges this fact and pats her own back, paying special attention to the itchy spot under her right shoulder. *Oh yes, and when I come into the money I'll have massages and beauty treatments, too.*

'I don't see what's funny, dear!'

Alice shakes her head. *Did I actually smile?* She puts on her mournful face. 'Sorry, Gran.'

'I am just trying to help, dear.' Her grandmother's cajoling tone grates on Alice's nerves even more than her bossy one. 'A little advice from someone who knows might save all sorts of embarrassments, disasters and dicky situations when one is growing up.'

Alice nods dutifully. *One? Why doesn't one just mind one's own business?* Her grandmother worked a year at *Vogue* in Paris as an office receptionist in 1953, which has naturally given her the right to tell everyone in the world what they should and shouldn't wear in any given situation.

'Your poor mother had no idea about clothing,' the old lady sniffs, as she folds and refolds the newspaper. 'Simply no idea.'

Alice stares back coldly. *You old bitch! Sometimes I hate you so very much.*

Little does Phyllis know that Alice's mother's clothes are all still boxed up in the locked back shed at Pitt Street. One day, in the not too distant future, Alice will magically lose all this excess weight and then . . . she'll wear them herself, because she loves her mother's clothes. If her grandmother disapproves, well, so much the better! Alice's mind shifts to the little kitchen in the old house where she lived with her mother. Life was good there. Well . . . good enough, anyway. On the whole it made sense, at least, which is more than anyone could say about life since. The Pitt Street house will become hers on her eighteenth birthday, less than a month away. In her mind she potters around the kitchen a bit – from the fridge back to the stove, to the shelf above, where her mother always had a vase of flowers, stopping to stare out the kitchen window.

The backyard was an ongoing project that Alice and her mother had been working on together. The pond had been dug only a week before the murder. Dug, filled and fitted out with a special pump and two beautiful goldfish. Lillian had wanted the pond to become home to all kinds of life: plants and waterlilies, fish and frogs. The newly planted semicircle of cherry trees was doing well, too. Her mother had visions of bricked paths, a miniature wooden bridge over the pond and a gazebo down the far corner. *All in good time, darling!* Planning the backyard used to comfort Lillian when she got lonely or dispirited. There was nothing she liked better than being out there in the sunshine, barefoot, in T-shirt and shorts, digging and planting.

Alice wonders if, by some miracle, the goldfish might have survived. The tenants were given instructions and a few packets of feed, but she knows it's probably too much to expect.

'Mullaney isn't paying me to look glamorous,' Alice says mildly.

'What rubbish!' Her grandmother waves one of her claws in the air as though directing servants. 'Every office needs an attractive girl at the front desk.'

Alice doesn't bother to tell her that Luke Mullaney made it very clear that he was not interested in some little show pony who took too long at lunch and spent half the time filing her nails and ringing up her girlfriends to chat. Alice had been thrilled when he rang to say that she had the job. She liked the cool marble floor, the leather lounges for the waiting clients, all those phones ringing and keyboards tapping. But most of all she liked the idea of herself behind a desk and *in charge* – instead of being behind a desk being told what to do by teachers and lecturers. *God, university was a drag from the word go. Worse than school!*

'And the blouse is too frivolous,' her grandmother adds.

'You liked this blouse last week.'

'You're in a lawyer's office, not an amusement parlour.'

A spurt of laughter builds up in Alice's throat, but she is also on the point of crying. How long does she have to put up with this? *How bloody long?*

'People don't go to amusement parlours any more, Gran,' she replies mildly. 'At least, I've never been to one.' As soon as she's said it, she thinks it probably isn't true. Not if those places on Elizabeth Street, down from the university, filled with the wild noisy slot games can be counted as amusement parlours. She used to go to them all the time with Eric Faltermaier, the one friend she'd made during her four-month stint as a uni student in Melbourne. She got to be just as good as Eric at some of those games and she was proud that he loved playing them with her.

'People certainly *do* go to amusement parlours!' the old lady declares. 'There's one down in the High Street arcade and I'm told it's full most nights.' The pink has hit the old woman's cheeks and Alice wants to scream with laughter, as well as knock the old girl on the head with the nearby Venetian vase. That thing would do the job. It must weigh a ton. *Oh shut up, you old bat!* Why don't doctors realise that this is what keeps old people alive? Forget about the operations and all those pills sitting on her side table, her gran never looks better than when she's in the middle of a nitpicking argument or driving someone else up the wall.

Alice is nodding carefully but she has already taken herself off to another room of her brain, lying flat on her back on a polished wooden floor, staring out of a doorway at a huge starry sky. A soft balmy breeze is fluttering through her hair. Sea and grass, trees and sky have always given Alice enormous pleasure. She got that from her mother. *Take the time to enjoy the simple things, Alice.*

'I have to go now or I'll be late,' she says abruptly.

'Oh, Alice,' Gran closes her eyes and shakes her head as though in great pain. 'At least change the blouse!'

'Okay, Gran.' Alice moves over to kiss the paper-thin skin of her grandmother's surprisingly unwrinkled cheek. 'Maybe I'll put on that white one you gave me last Christmas.'

'That would be much better, dear.' Her grandmother grabs her hand and squeezes it with her own liver-spotted one. Alice can feel all the bones under the withering flesh and thinks how easily they'd break.

'Off you go then, dear.'

Alice goes to the door.

'Did I tell you that your cousin is back?' the old lady calls after her just as Alice is about to shut the door.

Alice stops, turns back, her hand caught in midair. 'My *cousin*?' That can't be right. There is only one cousin.

'Yes, *the* cousin,' the old lady sighs.

'But . . . I thought he was in Sydney.'

'The boy is back,' her grandmother sniffs. 'Has some kind of job.'

'What job?'

Her grandmother is staring straight ahead now at the bright light coming in through the window, her cheeks still flushed. 'That boy had talent!' she hisses savagely. 'I heard it's said that he was bright. There was a time when I hoped he'd be a success.' The old women shakes her head to dislodge painful memories. 'But what else would you expect with a father like that?'

'What job?' Alice asks again. She has to know this. She figured that she'd never have to see her cousin again. Out of sight, out of mind, Jonty van der Weihl.

'I told you, I don't know!' her grandmother snaps.

'But why, Gran? Why would he come back *here*, of all places?'

'Calm yourself, dear,' the old lady snorts. 'It's nothing to get upset about. I certainly plan to avoid him and I'd advise you to also.' Phyllis folds her reading glasses into their case and snaps the lid sharply. 'No point overreacting.'

Overreacting? the small voice inside Alice is screaming. *But he murdered my mother!* She can't bring herself to say the words out loud because she doesn't even know if she believes them anymore. At one stage she did. When the police charged her cousin Jonty she had to believe it. She had to change focus from some unknown monster to . . . *him*, her cousin, Jonty. Then three months on they freed him! They let him out. Not enough evidence to go to trial. That didn't mean he was innocent but it didn't mean he was guilty, either.

'You should go, dear. Or you'll be late.'

'Okay,' Alice shuts the bedroom door quietly behind her and walks down to the front door.

Stuff the white blouse. Alice does up her coat and walks through the front gate and out onto the street. Luke Mullaney's office is in the middle of High Street. She tries to think of the day to come, but Jonty van der Weihl has invaded her head. She remembers him coming around to her house with that friend of his, the tall dark-haired quiet boy, the quiet boy with the nice smile. The one she used to like until . . . she saw the way he looked at her mother and she didn't like him at all after that.

Both of them used to sit at the kitchen table and talk to her mother for hours about all kinds of things that Alice wasn't interested in. At first she was tickled that this cousin that she hardly knew was visiting her home with his handsome friend, but she soon realised that she wasn't part of whatever they had going, so she tired of their visits. In fact, she came to dread finding them at the table looking at her mother with such admiration in their eyes. Those stupid boys with all their crap talk about *Hamlet* and Napoleon and boring foreign movies, their drinking and their smoking and all the rest of it. She remembers hating them both, her cousin and his friend.

At the end of the street she stands to cross at the lights. A man she vaguely knows, sitting behind the wheel of a stationary van, calls out to her, 'How's it going Alice?'

'Good, thanks.' *Was he the guy who fixed Grandma's hot water last year?* He is drumming his fingers on the steering wheel, smiling a bit, trying to catch her eye as she passes. But Alice doesn't stop, nor does she smile. She doesn't like talking to strange men. People viewed her differently afterwards. In the supermarket it would be, 'Hi Alice! How *are* you?' *Gush. Gush.* But almost before she was out of earshot they'd be whispering, nudging each other, pointing her out. *That's her! That's the girl whose mother was murdered.*

She's used to it now. No one mentions it directly any more, but it's in their eyes – curiosity, sympathy and even a strange kind of envy, because in a way she's a local celebrity and a lot of people would like that. They don't want their mothers murdered, but they want the notoriety and the attention that it brings; the pages in the newspapers, the name on radio and television and all the rest of it. Forget about fifteen minutes! Most people are so damned bored that they'd give anything for *five* minutes of fame.

That was a nice picture of your poor mother in the Chronicle, *Alice.* The local paper still runs the occasional article, usually with the same picture of Lillian alongside. It's a way of selling papers. People love a murder mystery. Alice understands all this now, but she avoids the articles if she can.

She stuffs her hands into her pockets and quickens her pace, enjoying the walk into town. In spite of everything, she's glad to be back. For the entire four months in the city she'd had a very strong feeling of being in the wrong place. She felt the pull back to Warrnambool, because the whole thing . . . wasn't over. Her life seemed to be caught in aspic somehow; on hold. She couldn't move.

One night in the city she'd flicked onto a TV program about mothers in Argentina whose children went 'missing' during the years of the military junta. Once a week the women would gather and walk silently around and around the central plaza in Buenos Aires, carrying placards depicting the faces of their loved ones. They wanted answers. Who took their children and why? At the end of the program Alice had switched off the television and wept for the first time since her mother's funeral. Then she'd rung her friend Eric Faltermaier and told him about the program and, for the first time, all about her mother and what had happened. He let her rave and although she couldn't see him she knew he was listening carefully.

'You have to go back there,' he said matter-of-factly, after she'd got it all out, 'and conduct your own vigil.'

Yes of course. A vigil. It was good to have a name for it.

Alice feels that she has more in common with those women

in South America than with anyone else she knows. There are vital things she needs to know before she can tackle . . . the rest of her life, for starters. She looks around at other people and notices that they are *solid* in a way that she is not. They think and talk and laugh in distinct ways. Compared to them she feels like a cardboard cut-out, a flim-flam girl, a piece of gauze in the shape of a human, blowing in the wind, changing colour all the time depending on the strength of the light. Her personality is cobbled together from all kinds of bits and pieces stolen from those around her. She tries on the pieces like articles of clothing. When she gets tired of one she tries another, sometimes almost in the same moment.

Only two blocks away from her destination, her mobile phone rings. Alice reaches into her shoulder bag and pulls it out without slowing down. She recognises the number and smiles.

'Leyla?'

'Sylvie, you idiot!'

'Sor-ry!'

Apart from Sylvie's odd-coloured eyes, Leyla and Sylvie Cassidy are identical down to their funny deep voices and the gap between their front teeth. Most people can't tell them apart, but Alice can.

'Whatcha doin'?'

'Walking to work.'

'*Work*?' Sylvie sounds indignant.

'The law office, remember. So what are you both doing?'

'Freaking.'

Alice grins. Sylvie's stern, impatient way of talking amuses her. The twins never call just to chat. There is always a purpose.

'Jonty's back.'

'I know.'

'He's working at Thistles.'

'Oh.' Alice tries to imagine it. 'Doing what?'

'Cooking.'

'Isn't that place meant to be . . . *classy*?'

'Yep,' Sylvie sniffs. 'So what is that *fucking goon* doing there?'

'Hmmm.'

'Want me to find out . . . stuff?'

'Yeah,' Alice isn't sure quite what Sylvie means, 'like what?'

'Any shit we can.'

'Okay.'

'Grannie carked it yet?'

'Nope,' Alice laughs.

'Bummer.'

'You said it. When do I see you both?'

'Soon. Bye. Have fun with the law.'

'Bye.'

She'd hardly known the twins before her mother was killed. They were just two skinny kids sitting down the back of her Year Ten classes. Oddballs. Always together. They didn't seem to need other friends. Alice had been moving through school at the edge of a crowd of good-natured, popular, noisy girls when the murder happened. Afterwards, she found she couldn't cope with the ordinary girls anymore – their curiosity and sympathy, their prayers and kind gestures only made her feel worse. The twins stepped in and filled the gap. Not straightaway of course. She didn't go back to school for weeks, and it was another month, at least, before she could face walking out into the playground at lunchtime. Mostly she sat in the library and doodled with a set of fancy pens that Mrs Hooper, the librarian, supplied. Then one day the twins came into the library, and Sylvie asked in her dry matter-of-fact manner if she'd like to walk down the street with them. From then on they were friends.

It's easy for Alice to tell them apart now. They *move* differently. Sylvie is the bubbly one, talkative and quick to smile. Her face shows it all, with twinkling eyes and a mouth that constantly teeters on the edge of a laugh. By contrast, Leyla is calm, a watcher rather than a participator. Her smiles are grave and often hesitant, as though she's not quite sure she should be doing such a frivolous thing. Actual laughing is done privately behind her hand or with her back turned. Leyla would rather stay silent (and often does) than give an ill-considered opinion.

Both twins are fair-haired and olive-skinned and, in spite of neither of them ever making even the slightest effort, they are pretty, with neat features and slim athletic bodies. Apart from school uniform, Alice has never seen either of them in a skirt or dress.

Their mother died in a car accident when they were two, and they live with their meatworker father in a small neat house out of town. Their idea of a good time is to go out on bird-watching hikes with their father on the weekends. Alice sometimes tags along with them, not really interested in birds but comfortable anyway. They have penfriends in all kinds of countries in Africa and Europe that Alice had never even heard of, and they make jam from the fruit trees in their backyard and sell it (quite shamelessly) in the middle of the street on Saturdays for pocket money, not caring if kids in their class see them. Alice knows the twins are a bit weird but she feels easy with them, which is more than she can say about most other people.

Alice pushes open the heavy door, walks into a large, expensively furnished lobby and looks around, liking the decor all over again. The marble floor is so impersonal and the original abstract painting hanging over the plush leather lounge in the waiting room is so nicely about nothing much in particular. *Yes, I could live with that.*

But when a well-dressed lady in her sixties looks up from the front desk and gives a professional smile, Alice wants to turn and walk straight back out the door. The expensive gold-rimmed glasses halfway down her nose, the two strings of pearls and the pale-green fine-wool sweater, the hair up in a stiff blonde chignon all give off an air of placid superiority. The woman looks exactly like a younger version of her grandmother! Alice makes herself cross the shiny floor to where the woman is waiting, her face upturned in a quizzical fashion.

'I'm here to see Mr Mullaney,' Alice says.

'And you are . . .?'

'Alice.' She tends not to give her surname unless someone asks for it, because she hates that jolt of recognition on people's faces when they realise exactly who she is. *Oh, you're the one whose mother . . .* But this woman's face relaxes into a smile.

'Alice!' she repeats. 'Of course.'

'I'm here . . . because I got the job.' Alice begins to fumble around in her bag looking for the letter offering the job, feeling heavy and awkward and unsure now if she should even be here. She's never had a job before. Not even babysitting or mowing lawns or selling ice-cream. Maybe she won't be able to cope, just as her grandmother predicted.

'Oh, don't bother about that,' the woman laughs. 'I know who you are. Luke is always late.' She points to one of the leather chairs. 'Have a seat over there, Alice. He won't be long.' She gives a small wave of apology and points to her screen. 'Just got to finish this before ten.'

'Okay.' Alice is filled with relief as she sits down. The woman is okay. *Maybe . . . the whole thing will be okay.*

'I'm Martha, by the way.' The lady peers over the counter and smiles again. 'Been with Luke a million years!'

Alice smiles and nods.

'And I knew your mother,' the woman declares matter-of-factly, not bothering to change her tone or expression. 'Enormously fond of her, too.'

Alice nods again and picks up a magazine and the woman goes back to her work. People are always telling her that. *I knew your mother.* It's the *way* they say it that makes all the difference. This woman's way is . . . fine. Alice can handle this. What she really hates is when they expect her to respond. When there is a question mark embedded at the end of their sentence. What do they expect her to say? *Oh did you? Shame she got murdered, isn't it? Gee, yeah . . . Hope it doesn't happen to us!*

'I'll make you coffee just as soon as I've done this,' Martha adds.

'Thanks.'

Luke rings in to say that he's been held up further and ten minutes pass. Martha finishes the urgent document and Alice is given coffee and shown the ropes. She will have her own desk in a separate room just off the main lobby, and the phone calls will go through her. Martha explains how to answer the phone. *Good morning. You've rung Mullaney Law Practice. This is Alice speaking. How may I help you?* Always be polite even if they are rude and stupid, the older woman tells her with a wry smile, and expect roughly half of them to be just that. Martha explains how to put a call on hold, how to switch it through to Luke or herself or the other lawyer working down the back of the building. She learns how to keep notes of the calls. To take down the matter in shorthand and to never forget to get a number to ring back. There will be more for her to learn, but Martha suggests she get the hang of the phones first up.

Luke finally hurries in, a briefcase in one hand and a thick document in the other. He doesn't see Alice sitting in her neat little office with the door open as he strides over to Martha.

'Got caught up down in the cells with a little cretin who thinks he can drive like an idiot, smash into someone's front fence, get out of the car, abuse the owner of the property *then* walk free as soon as he's sobered up!' He almost throws the document at Martha. 'Can you sort it?'

'Right,' she says calmly, picking it up, 'but you must ring that Shirley woman within the hour about her land settlement and . . .' She points to where Alice is sitting at her desk in the room opposite, 'Alice has arrived.'

'Alice?' He turns to where Martha is pointing.

Alice blushes awkwardly and stands up. She can see he has no idea who she is or why she might be sitting in one of his offices.

'I got the job,' she begins tentatively. 'Last week . . .'

'Oh, God yes!' Luke grins as it all finally crunches into place. He gives himself a playful punch in the head. 'Good on you, Alice!' he says, taking her hand warmly. 'Great to have you on board. Don't tell me she's got you working already?'

'Yeah,' Alice smiles back, surprised by a sudden spurt of happiness. She can feel his warmth rolling towards her. Luke and Martha are so . . . friendly and nice. *Maybe I will be able to do this.*

Alice spends a productive morning answering the phone and learning more of the ropes. Along with the phone, there is the mailing and case filing systems. None of what she has to do is too difficult and she finds herself enjoying the structured world of the office, the lists of clients, the ordered procedures and formalised way of going about things. First *this* and then *that* and always in a particular order. Martha's attention to detail and insistence on accuracy is fierce but she is also very kind and understanding if Alice asks a question or makes a mistake. The phone runs hot, and with each call Alice becomes more confident. At around one o'clock Martha comes in to congratu-late her on her voice and phone manner, wondering if she'd done this kind of work before because she has picked up so much in such a short space of time.

'No.' Alice shakes her head, hardly able to speak she is so pleased. 'I've never worked before.' And to think that her stupid grandmother thought she wouldn't be able to do it.

'Off to lunch with you then!' Martha declares with a big smile. 'Make sure you take the full hour.'

Alice takes her two cream buns and her banana up to the park bench overlooking the ocean at the end of the street. She begins to eat, staring out happily at the bobbing waves. Who would have thought she would be back here in this town only four months after she'd been so keen to get away? She can hardly believe it herself. When the phone in her pocket rings she is tempted to simply switch it off. Half an hour without phone calls is what she really wants. But when she sees the name in the window she changes her mind.

'Fawlty!'

'It's me. How are you?'

'Fine. Where are you right now?' For some reason she really needs to know this.

Eric is on his way back to his college room from the morning's lectures, and Alice is hit with a small pang as he describes exactly where he is, walking back from the library past the union building, through the sports complex and in through the back of Newman College. There is something lovely about the university grounds on a dull cloudy day, the fronds on the old trees shimmering in the light and wind, and the groups of students walking by, heads down, clutching their books and bags, scarves twisted around their necks. Alice loved that sense of being in a world within a world. Although Eric's well-heeled parents live in Malvern – a mere tram ride away from the university – his father insisted his only son have the full-on university experience of living in one of the beautiful old neo-Gothic colleges. And so Eric wears an academic gown to dinner every Sunday night, stands silently with the rest of the undergraduates as the head of college, his wife and half-a-dozen other senior people walk in and sit at high table. Grace is said, a bell rings and only when everyone is seated does conversation commence. Eric once told Alice that his father thinks Eric sits up all night in his room arguing philosophy and religion with other serious, like-minded students, and spends his free hours plotting student rebellion in the café. He has no idea that Eric actually spends most of his spare time down in the city in the virtual world of movies and computer games, or alone in his room trying to write film scripts.

'So how is the wage slave?' Fawlty's imperious accent comes down the phone line like warm treacle. 'It can't be good for your health?'

'Still alive,' Alice laughs. 'Did you have French this morning?'

'Emile was in full flight,' Fawlty chuckles. 'When Melissa and Sally started yawning about *The Outsider* being one big bore he spat the dummy.'

'What did he say?'

'That they were destined for dumb wifedom.'

'They get shitty?'

'Oh yes!'

Emile was the highly strung French tutor who had audacious, thickly accented opinions about everything. Half the class loathed him and the other half, including Alice and Eric, thought he was wonderful.

'They both walked? Tell me more,' Alice says greedily, beset with another sudden pang to be back there among it all. 'What did he say?'

'Oh, you know the way he raises his eyes?'

Alice had met Fawlty on the first day of enrolment, sitting by himself on the top step outside the Babel building, in the sun, smoking a roll-your-own cigarette and reading a thick science-fiction novel. He had flaming red hair, freckles, thick glasses, acne scars, really cheap terrible lace-up shoes and thin white fingers that reminded Alice of chicken feet.

But he looked up and smiled when she sat two steps down from him to eat her lunch (his teeth were okay, she noted with relief).

'You got enough room there?' he said in this deep, confident English-actor's voice, which totally threw her off guard.

'I'm fine, thank you,' she said huffily, picking up half her big salad, cheese and ham sandwich and biting into it. His easy, couldn't-give-a-shit attitude was initially confusing. *Don't you realise how very unattractive you are? Okay, I'm fat but in certain lights I am also quite beautiful. Whereas you've got seriously bad hair and awful shoes, and no one in a pink fit would call you even normal-looking.*

'Couldn't spare that, could you?' he went on mildly. Alice looked around and nearly keeled over with amazement when she realised he was addressing her.

'I forgot mine,' he went on, as though this was quite normal. 'Left it in my room.'

Is this guy asking for my lunch? Yep, the carrot-topped weirdo was staring at the other half of her sandwich. In the bottom of the clear plastic bag there was also a large chunk of wrapped fruit cake and a big red apple.

'Well . . .' Alice hesitated. She didn't want to give it to him but she didn't want to not give it to him either. What if he was poor and had no money for food? Wordlessly she handed him the rest of her sandwich.

'Thanks.' He unwrapped the sandwich and took a couple of bites. 'I left my wallet back in college, too.' He grinned at Alice. 'But I've got ten dollars in change. So I'll go buy us some coffee to go with the cake, shall I?'

So you're going to eat my cake too? Alice had been going to save the cake and apple for later but there was something about his unapologetic manner that she found intriguing. 'Okay,' she said.

They ate their food in silence for a while, then Eric got up. 'How do you have it?'

'Two sugars and very hot.'

'Consider it done.'

Alice frowned as she watched him loping towards the café. God he was thin . . . and so tall. He reminded her of the stick figures she used to draw in kinder.

'Very hot!' she called after him sharply, just in case he thought she was a complete sucker.

'Right.' He turned to grin at her and raise one hand in a mini salute. When he came back with two cups of good strong coffee, Eric got out a small knife and a tiny pocket tape measure and proceeded to measure up her cake. Alice watched as he found the exact halfway point before cutting it neatly. He then pulled out a big, brand new chemistry text from his battered bag, placed her coffee and share of the cake on it and handed it to her ceremoniously.

'Madam.'

'You're doing chemistry. Engineering or Science?' she guessed.

'Engineering/Arts,' he said. 'But I'm doing that to please my parents. I'm actually a screenwriter.'

'A screenwriter?'

'I finished another script last night,' he sighed.

'What's it about?'

'A *very* good question.' He frowned. 'I start off with one idea and end up somewhere else. Do it all the time.'

'What idea did you start off with?'

'A rich middle-aged woman who wants to transform her life,' he smiled wryly at Alice, 'based on my mother.'

'Your mother is rich?'

'Yes,' he said simply, 'very.'

'But I thought you were poor!' Alice wasn't joking. 'It was the only reason I gave you my lunch. You looked kind of shabby and bedraggled, like a down-and-out hobo, and I thought, well . . . he probably needs it more than I do.'

Eric's mouth fell open. He looked down at his clothing incredulously. 'Does all this really say *down-and-out hobo*?'

'Yep.'

'My God, I thought I looked . . . *cool*!'

'Sorry,' Alice laughed. 'Especially the shoes!'

'They don't cut it?'

'No.'

'Shit!' Eric gave a deep mortified sigh, then reached out to read her name on the outside flap of her bag of books. 'So it's Alice, is it?' He sighed again. 'You know I've always wanted to meet an Alice. *Alice in Wonderland* is my favourite book.'

'You've got no idea how many people say that to me,' Alice sniffed impatiently. 'So bloody tedious!' She figured that she was allowed to be honest. After all, she'd just given the guy her lunch.

'Really?' He was laughing at her now, and cutting her apple in half.

When it was time to go to their separate lectures they were both pleased to learn they'd be in the same French tute later in the day.

She misses Fawlty now. It had been nice to have such a nutty friend.

'So when am I coming?'

'Whenever you want.' Alice issued the invitation when she left university, not thinking he'd take her up on it, because it was impossible to think of Eric out of the city. He once admitted that he'd never been on school camp, and considered the elaborate excuses he'd made up each year from Grade Six onwards one of the finest creative achievements of his life. 'Any weekend you like,' she says weakly, 'but don't forget . . . there is my grandmother.'

'Ah yes, *the* grandmother,' Eric chuckles.

'Fawlty, I know you think I'm exaggerating,' Alice says, 'but believe me, she is *not* fun in any way, shape or form, and more than that she'll hate you.'

'Why?'

'She doesn't need *reasons*.' Alice stops. 'She'll have you wanting to slit your wrists within the hour.'

'Far out!' Eric sounds delighted.

'Well, don't say you weren't warned,' Alice sighs. 'What about the first weekend next month, then?'

'Great!' Eric hesitates. 'Oh, Alice, any chance of meeting . . . your father?'

'*What?*'

'Your daddy-o . . .'

'He lives in Darwin!'

'Sorry, you told me that,' Eric laughs. 'I forgot.'

'Why do you want to meet *him*?'

'Well,' Eric murmurs softly, 'he sounds like a weirdo.'

'So, why . . . ?'

'I want to see for myself.'

'For what purpose?'

'He sounds like a *character* I could use.'

'A character?' Alice frowns. 'Oh, you mean for your script? Well I suppose he is . . . a character,' she sighs grimly, 'but he's about three thousand kilometres away right now.'

'Point taken.'

'So, I'll call you soon and we'll arrange something.'

'You're on.'

Alice peels her banana slowly, thinking about her father and what it would be like to see him again. The last time was not long after her mother's funeral. Mal hadn't contacted Alice when Lillian died. Nor did he come to the funeral. Weeks later he turned up at the door of her grandmother's house. Alice had been excited to see him. But he only gave her a quick hug.

'She's my daughter,' Mal said to Phyllis, 'and I want her. We're going back up north today.'

Alice's grandmother didn't say anything. She walked past him down the steps to where Shaz, the girlfriend, was waiting in the Thunderbird. The old lady seemed to draw herself up into someone much bigger and taller as she looked from one to the other.

'Alice is my granddaughter,' she said stonily.

'That bitch turned her against me,' Mal burst out vehemently. But there was something missing in his voice. Some element of confidence was gone. Mal seemed more reduced, somehow, as each moment passed.

'It's up to you, Alice,' her grandmother said gravely. Alice loved her father, but she didn't want to live with him because that meant living with Shaz (who didn't like Alice one little bit) and all those dogs. It also meant horrible food, drunken brawls, not getting to school on time, and all the rest of it. So she shook her head.

Alice stood with her grandmother on the top step and watched him slowly turn around and head back to the Thunderbird. He got in, slammed the door and, without a wave or a smile, spun it around, backed out of the driveway and was on his way.

'Good riddance,' her grandmother muttered as she turned away.

That had been the last time she'd seen her father.

Alice watches the seagulls dip and soar in the wind. One of them hovers, wings outstretched, allowing itself to be buffeted about without moving its wings. *Do birds enjoy what they do?* There didn't seem any other purpose.

Mal wasn't a bad person. He could be unexpectedly kind and generous – she'd seen it often. And there were things he loved, like clay-bird shooting, racing cars and fishing and of course his precious Thunderbird. Alice can't think of much else except . . . her mother. Mal had adored his wife, Lillian, but he didn't know how to show it in any way that made sense. In fact, when she thinks back to her early life, together on the little farm, it seemed as though he resented the fact that he loved her so much and became intent on paying her out for this perceived weakness in his own character.

When Alice and her mother first moved away from the farm and into town, she worried about him out there by himself. Would he remember to feed the dogs and collect the eggs? Who would cook his tea and wash the dishes? Missing her dad was like heartburn back then. It would rise up from deep down in her, hot and unexpectedly bitter, and she'd have to swallow it because her mother didn't want to know. It wasn't true that he didn't care about them, she used to think angrily. When her mother had said she wanted to grow vegetables he'd dug up the garden for her and brought in special dirt that would make them grow. Her mother had hugged him when he'd put up a little fence to keep out stray animals. She said, *You're a good man, Mal.* And when Alice had wanted a fairy costume like Melissa Todd in Grade Three – one of those fancy lace-and-netting numbers with sparkles on the bodice – her mother had said, *No darling, it is too ridiculous,* but her father had laughed and said they'd go and buy one that afternoon. And they did too! Pink with little white flowers sprinkled all over it. And her father had whistled when she put it on at home.

From now on it's 'Your Royal Highness Princess Alice'. He'd kept it up all day. *Would Princess Alice like ice-cream on her potatoes?* Even her mother had laughed.

Does she miss him now? If asked she always says, *Of course,* but the truth is, she doesn't much. It's enough to get a phone call about nothing every now and again, a card around her birthday and some silly little present suitable for someone half her age at Christmas (if she's lucky). If she does miss him, then it's tucked away in a place so deep inside that she doesn't have to think about it often, if at all.

Lunch finished, Alice gets up and walks slowly back to the office. Some things are just too hard to work out. Better not to dwell on them. Better to just try and look forward.

'Do you know Tom?' Luke asks proudly. 'My son.'

Alice looks up and doesn't know what to say because suddenly panic is jolting through her. This was the thing she'd forgotten! *Forgotten? Or shoved out of her head the way you'd shove a dead rat into the bin if you found it behind the fridge?* Luke's son was the *friend,* her cousin Jonty's best mate. And here he is! A chill goes through her. How handsome he is with all that curly dark hair and how utterly unlike his heavy, world-weary, middle-aged father. How could she have blocked *him* out?

They nod to each other and murmur hello but time has suddenly contracted and it is all sitting there between them: the afternoons when Alice came home from school to find Tom and Jonty sitting with her mother at the table, talking and laughing. When Alice came in it all stopped, somehow. The three of them pretended that it hadn't, but she felt the way the puff went out of the air when she walked in. She wasn't part of whatever they had going. They were all wishing she'd go up to the front room and do her own thing. She didn't belong down there in the kitchen with them.

'Well, I'd better get back to it.' Luke can feel the awkwardness. 'Leave you two to catch up.'

Luke walks out and they are left looking at each other. A sudden thought hits Alice from left field. *If my cousin Jonty did it, you probably know.* She wonders where that idea came from and if it is fair to take it seriously – even if it did seem to come from deep in her bones.

'So, Alice.' His tone is light and easy, but he doesn't look at her directly. 'How are things?' Alice sees the slight quiver around his top lip and realises that he is shocked to see her, too. A spurt of sadistic pride goes through her. *Yes! I do look like her, don't I? Okay, I'm fatter, but my face is her face. It always was. How you going to deal with that, pretty boy?*

'Good,' she says curtly. How come he never noticed her three years ago? He'd been eighteen and she fifteen, and yet . . . she hadn't existed back then. Not for her cousin either, although they were both always polite.

Fifteen years old, shy, awkward and half in love with the cousin she didn't know and his cute friend, Alice had never even registered on their radar screens. They were too busy with her mother.

'Watch out for the old man,' Tom grins suddenly. 'Bit of a slave driver. You've got to call his bluff.'

She gives a tight smile, but she hates him now for being so clever at deflecting the awkwardness. She hates him for his charm. She knows what he's really trying to say. *Hey, all this is a little weird so let's just lighten up here!* The bold sureness of him with his clear eyes and even features, his thin tall body standing loose and easy in jeans and an old jumper, his feet in a pair of scuffed sneakers. So used to getting on with everyone. So used to everyone liking and admiring him. He'd probably never met a girl who didn't think he was a gift from heaven.

There are a few more uncomfortable moments. She wants to let him know that just because she likes his father – that she appreciates having the job and the rest of it – it doesn't follow that she has to like *him*. In fact, the good feelings do not extend to him. Not at all! She doesn't like him one little bit.

'Well, I'd better be going,' he says, backing towards the door.

She nods again and sits down behind the desk.

'See you around then, Alice.'

'Yeah, okay.' She doesn't look at him as she picks up the phone and pretends to be looking up a number. She can sense him hovering.

'You been out much since you've been back?'

What business is it of yours? 'Not really,' she murmurs, wishing that the phone would ring. She has to look up now. He is standing in the doorway, waiting for her to engage with him, to tell him with some small movement or smile that it's *all okay*. That after what's happened they can and definitely should make a fresh start. The past is the past and . . . all the rest of that bullshit.

Well, Tom Mullaney, you'll be waiting a long time . . . The past is not the past to me. The past is the present and the future as well. So stick that where the sun don't shine!

'Wouldn't be much fun living with your grandmother, I guess?' He tries his joking tone again. She glowers at him and says nothing, hoping he can sense what's on her mind. *What the hell do you know about my grandmother?* She suddenly can't wait to get with the twins to talk about this. Not only is Jonty back, but his sidekick is as well!

Then another shiver goes through her as she remembers that this guy was questioned by police, too, as Jonty's friend and as a friend of her mother's. How can she be sure that he told the police everything?

Alice, what exactly was the nature of this friendship your mother had with Tom Mullaney? It's the nice female detective back in Alice's head again, probing gently, as they drink their coffee down on the foreshore.

Alice grew to love Detective Becky Singer in the first few weeks after the murder. She wasn't sharp or brusque like the male detectives, nor did she ram information and questions down Alice's throat. She always spoke gently and calmly.

'Can you tell me anything that they talked about? How often he and your cousin Jonty were there?'

Alice did her best but she couldn't really because . . . she didn't understand it. And she was . . . ashamed. How did you explain that your mother, a forty-two-year-old woman, had no friends apart from two eighteen-year-old schoolboys? That in some subtle but fundamental way she had turned away from her only daughter as she'd got closer to them? That she saved her jokes and interesting stories for . . . them. That her maddest giggles – the ones Alice loved best, when she collapsed with laughter over some small incident or crazy thing – were kept for them.

Alice couldn't admit that. It was too humiliating.

Life on the outside continued as normal. Lillian went to work, continued to cook meals and do the washing, organised dentist appointments, bought Alice clothes and asked about her day. The drinking only began after Alice had gone to bed, but that was normal too. Everything was normal from the outside.

The drinking was another thing Alice never mentioned to anyone after her mother was killed. Her mother drank a lot, but she hid it well. She never drank with other people in a public place for example, and as far as Alice was concerned no one else knew about it. Except those two because they . . . were part of it.

But Alice wasn't actually sure about any of this. She wasn't sure about anything. All through her growing up she and her mother had been really close, more like sisters than mother and daughter. They'd stuck by each other through Mad Mal's bizarre schemes, his rants and rages, and they escaped together. They had been each other's best friends, until her mother went back to school and those two started coming around regularly. Did Alice tell the detectives any of that? No way! She didn't understand it herself, and at times she wondered if she'd simply imagined it.

What if this guy standing in the doorway had withheld similar, perhaps more vital, pieces of information? For example, he might be the one person on this earth who knows if her cousin Jonty van der Weihl is innocent . . . *or not*.

'Do you remember Josh Peters?' He is back in the room again, trying harder than ever.

'No.' She wants to swat him like a fly now. See him on the ground curling up with pain, screaming for mercy.

'I thought you might because he went to your school.' Tom hesitates. 'He's my age, but he was at the Catholic school like you. You went to the Catholic school, didn't you?'

Alice nods sourly. *You know I did!* In fact, she remembers Josh Peters well, a very short guy, five foot five at the most. When the murder first happened, all her friends kept their wary distance. They sent a joint note and a bunch of flowers, but they didn't come to see her and they didn't ring. Alice didn't blame them. As well as the horror of murder, she knew her grandmother and her huge secluded house were intimidating. Josh was one of the few people to make it up the front steps.

'Josh and me are going to go out tomorrow night to hear Pete's Revenge,' Tom says. 'Come if you want to.'

Alice has no idea who he means. She does not keep up with bands or modern music generally, so she lets his invitation hang in the air like the pathetic little gesture it is.

'My grandmother is old,' she says, still not meeting his eye. 'I've got to get home to her at night.'

'Okay.' He shrugs and then flushes, embarrassed that he asked, and she is glad that he feels stupid, really glad that she has hurt him. She wonders if he has any idea about how she used to hate those afternoons. Her mother used to belong to her until her horrible cousin started coming around with this guy. Whether they had anything to do with the murder or not, she associates them with the beginning of the end. As far as Alice is concerned she is entitled to hate both of them.

'Louisa took it all on board!'

Just home from school, fifteen-year-old Alice stopped outside the back door, her heart sinking. Her mother's excited tone meant those two boys were there. *Who the hell is Louisa?*

'Then life taught her that everything can't be reduced to a theory.'

'*Love* taught her that!'

'You're so romantic, Tom!'

'Why didn't she just . . . jump ship?'

76

'But how could she?'

'I know it was hard and everything but . . .'

'She was caught.'

Alice leant up against the wall near the door, feeling her heart beating like a hammer in her chest. *Who are they talking about? One day I'll come home and they'll be talking about me, instead of this* Louisa, *whoever she is.* Her mother would be telling them how *she* longed to jump ship away from her boring sulky plain daughter.

Of course Alice knew this was silly. Her mother loved her, told her so all the time, even when Alice was unreasonable and churlish. Even when she told her mother that she wished the boys wouldn't come around so often. *So what is she afraid of?* When she does go in she will only find the three of them sitting around the table talking. Not exactly a criminal offence is it? But there will be that distinctive sweet smell of dope in the air and her mother's face will be flushed and her eyes overly bright and she'll have her little glass close by. They'll all straighten up and pull themselves together when they see Alice. She . . . *hated that.* Because it made her feel as though she was different. Not one of them. Uncool.

'So, what is he trying to tell us?' Alice heard the serious enquiring tone in her mother's voice and hated it.

'He's dead.'

This response elicited much laughter and shouting about whether someone is able to come back from the dead. Soon after there was the sound of chairs being scraped back and exclamations about the time.

'He wrote it to warn us . . .'

'How could he have known?'

Oh, Alice sighed with relief, *they're only talking about a stupid old book!* Oddly enough, it didn't make her feel easier about those two being there. She had come home dying to show her mother the two essays in her bag both marked A. Mr Kelly had said her standard of work was way above her year level. But what she'd been so excited about only ten minutes before now seemed unimportant.

'We have our own "hard times"!' her mother was saying.

'Not the same.'

The back door suddenly opened and Tom tumbled out. When he turned to shut the door he saw Alice and stumbled backwards in surprise, the expression on his face changing into one of wariness and . . . *guilt*?

'Er . . . hello,' he said. He'd caught her listening and Alice was mortified. She'd never be able to look him in the face again.

'Hello.' Alice's face burned as she watched him head off down the path. *We live in hard times too.*

That night she goes to bed early. Tells her grandmother that she is tired after her first day at work and has a headache. The house-keeper has made Alice's favourite dish – a Mexican chilli – as a special treat after her first day, but Alice has to force it down. Meeting Tom Mullaney has made her remember that there was so much she didn't tell the police.

Those detectives wanted to know every little thing. But it just didn't seem right to tell. Not after . . . what had happened. If she'd told them certain things they might have judged her mother as cruel or weak or unsuitable as a mother, which was so far from the truth. Lillian was the best mother in the world. Truly the best!

Still it nags at Alice as she pulls the blinds and turns on the light.

'Hey, Buzz! Will I chuck it?' Jonty holds out the steel bowl full of whipped cream.

His boss, Buzz Critchley, looks up from one of the deep sinks where he is washing the last pan. He pulls the plug and motions Jonty over, wiping one hand on his apron. He dips his finger in the cream and brings it to his mouth, screwing up his face as he tastes it. Without saying anything he picks up a piece of leftover pecan pie from the bench, scoops up more cream with it and proceeds to eat that, too, while switching on the dishwasher with his other hand.

This all makes Jonty smile. The skinny old pig is always eating. He should look like a brick shithouse the way he stacks it away. Instead he reminds Jonty of one of those whippet dogs, lean and sleek and fast. The cream must be fine. Jonty shrugs and heads for the fridge to store it.

'No, chuck it,' Buzz calls gruffly. 'It's starting to sweat at the edges.'

'Like me.' Jonty takes an exaggerated sniff of his own sweaty armpit and Buzz laughs. He knows all about Jonty and he doesn't care. He reckons that the one thing he's learnt in life is to take people how you find them. Jonty has heard stories about some of the arseholes running kitchens and figures he got lucky. Buzz doesn't ask questions and he doesn't act like he knows everything either. Jonty scrapes the cream into the bin, rinses the bowl and goes back to covering the steel containers with cling wrap.

'You should be home by now.' Buzz points to the clock.

'Yeah, well.' Jonty puts the containers in the fridge, picks up a cloth and runs it over the smudge on the fridge door. Buzz is right. It's nearly midnight and the last customer is long gone. Jonty's hours are five to eleven-thirty, and he's stuffed. But he doesn't mind staying on a bit to help out.

Buzz – real name Bernard – is nearly sixty and he's worked in this place since it opened, near enough to twenty-five years ago. He's small and wiry, with a weird all-American-boy steel-grey crew cut and a sharp nasal New York accent to match. And he's gay. But Jonty likes him okay. He's a good enough guy.

'You doing anything on the weekend?' Buzz wants to know from inside the pantry, where he's probably measuring the distance between the sauce bottle and the flour bin with a tape measure. Jonty has never met a true perfectionist before and finds it kind of intriguing. When he was inside, some of the guards used to get off on making the inmates do things *properly*. That meant cleaning the floor three times, scraping plates until not a skerrick of food could be seen, even though they were going in the dishwasher – and a whole lot of other stupid shit. But they were just bored, needed some diversion. Buzz's fussiness is something else. It almost *hurts* him when a tea towel isn't folded exactly the right way, or the sink sponge isn't in the container exactly adjacent to the cleaning liquid.

'Nah.' Jonty slams shut the utensil drawer and goes for his coat hanging in a small alcove near the door. 'Nothing on.' This will be his first weekend off in six weeks of working this job, and he has no idea what to do with it. Hang about with his mother probably. *Jeez!* The mind boggles at the thought. He puts on his jacket and looks over as the older man wipes the spotless stainless-steel benches one last time.

Buzz sees Jonty laughing at him and gives one of his crooked, old-man smiles. 'Okay, I know I'm just a fussy old queen.'

'You said it, mate.'

The kitchen is big and modern, full of all the state-of-the-art appliances. There are mixers and blenders and grinders and juices, anything you can think of that opens or shuts or whirrs around. The dozen or so lights give the impression of a television studio. It was rebuilt from the ground up a year ago, transforming it from a grotty hard-to-clean dump. Jonty has never been to Buzz's house, but he'd bet anything that Buzz doesn't love the kitchen there near as much as he loves this one.

'You walking home?' Buzz asks, starting to switch off the lights one by one.

'Yep.' Jonty smiles. He walks home every night.

'I'll come with you.'

'Okay.'

Jonty is proud of how well he did in that cooking course. The whole hospitality industry is crying out for guys like him. Good cooks who can do quality food under pressure. He proved himself in the second week he was at Thistles. Buzz was laid off sick with some gay-man's disease (or that was what the owner told Jonty) and there was no one but Jonty to take over. He'd loved it. He didn't know Buzz at that stage, so he was hoping the guy might get worse and he could keep the top job. But Buzz was back in a week – he'd only had the flu – and by then Jonty had proved himself. The owner took him aside and told him that he had the talent to do really well.

'Whatever they say about you, Jonno, you're smart,' he'd said. 'You're quick and strong and you can keep a dozen things in your head at once. That's a gift. Stick at it and you could be very successful in this game.' Jonty went home and told his mum and they both cracked up. *Shit*, he couldn't warm up a meat pie when he was at school! His mum had had to poach his eggs in the morning because he always broke them and burnt the toast. You should see him now: a few basic ingredients and a good knife and he'd have a meal for you in seven minutes flat.

The insane hours in the kitchen suit him just fine. Who'd ever want to work nine to five? He likes working half the night and sleeping late. He likes the pressure, too. Figures it keeps him out of trouble.

Buzz and Jonty walk together out through the main part of the restaurant and onto the street. Jonty stops a moment to breathe in the salty air. He loves this moment after work, tired and sweaty, stepping into cold briny air and the roar of the ocean. Buzz turns to lock up and Jonty walks across the narrow road towards the sea to wait for him.

Thistles is built on a steep cliff. It's too dark now to see all the jagged rocks that cascade into the raging water below, but in the daytime . . . it's green and spumy-wild. People come from all over to eat the fancy food while they watch the sea crashing against the rocks below.

One of the local coppers told Jonty that eight people jumped from this point last year. *Eight!* Instant death. And that constituted a good year, the lowest number in a decade. The year before there had been eleven. He told Jonty it was a favourite spot, only beaten for numbers by the West Gate Bridge. He'd been almost proud when he said that, and Jonty had found it funny. Hearing about the council's proposal to put up a high fence to discourage people from using the *favourite spot* had him laughing harder. If you want to neck yourself, you do it. He should know, he's thought about it. Who hasn't? Ended up thinking that there had to be an easier way to go than jumping.

'I heard some famous band is going to be playing,' Buzz says, as Jonty falls into step with him.

'What band?' Jonty isn't really interested. The wind is sticking its fingers down his jacket. He should have worn more clothes.

'Can't remember.' Buzz pulls his thick scarf tightly around his neck. 'I don't listen to that kind of music,' he sniffs dismissively. 'But you really should go, Jonty.'

'Oh, so you don't listen to *that kind of music*?' Jonty mimics him. 'It's crap, and yet you want me to subject myself to it!'

'Look, I'm ancient,' Buzz laughs at himself, 'but you should be there, meeting people . . . enjoying yourself.'

Who with? Jonty thinks. Since getting back from Sydney, Jonty has kept his head right down. He doesn't take drugs anymore and he hardly drinks. But he knows what people are thinking. He can see it on their faces. They know more stuff about him than he knows himself. They think they do, anyway. *Well . . . hello, Jonno! You're back?* Their eyes dart away and then bounce to him again, like those dumb attached tennis balls people play with on the beach. *Yeah. I'm back.*

Anyway, going to hear a band completely straight probably wouldn't work. Last time he checked it was more or less mandatory to be off your face.

Jonty and Buzz walk home together along the coast road, the sea roaring along beside them like some tortured soul in purgatory. Jonty's house is only about ten minutes away, but Buzz lives on the other side of town. He lost his licence for drink-driving some months ago and Jonty feels sorry for him, wishes he had a car to drive him home. Poor old guy has got a bit of a limp from some shit that happened to him in Vietnam back in the sixties.

'Jeez, it's dead tonight,' Jonty says as they turn into James Street. Only two houses even have a light on.

'Yep, another wild Friday night in Warrnie town,' Buzz mutters in agreement. 'Always something going on.'

Jonty laughs.

'Pete's Revenge is the name of the band,' Buzz remembers suddenly. 'You like them?'

'I dunno.' Jonty hasn't listened to music seriously for ages. 'Might do. How come they're coming here?'

'Country tour before they go OS.'

'Yeah?' Jonty looks at Buzz. 'How come you know all this?'

'I keep my ear to the ground,' he laughs.

Three more blocks and Jonty's home. It's good walking past Pitt Street with Buzz. Just having the old guy there stops the ghosts walking into his head. Sometimes they come on hard and have his brain twisted up like a discarded chip-packet before he even makes it home.

'So when is it?'

'Tomorrow night.' Buzz gives Jonty a sly nudge. 'Apparently they're the next big thing, Jonty. Read it myself in the *Chronicle*! You'll kick yourself if you miss out.'

'Ah, I don't know,' Jonty sighs. 'Where's it on?'

'The new Arts Centre,' Buzz says. 'Good acoustics.'

'Right,' Jonty laughs softly, 'like I really need you to tell me this.' They stop outside the little house that Jonty shares with his mother. 'Farewell, Bernard.' Jonty flicks open the latch on the front gate.

'Go see that band or I'll have your guts for garters on Monday.' Buzz waves gruffly before heading up the road into the blackness.

'Okay!' Jonty calls after him. 'See ya Monday!'

'I'll want a full account then, remember.'

Jonty's mood shifts down a few notches when he sees the light is on in the front room. His mother is up and that could mean anything from a wall of stony silence because of the mess he left on the back porch, to a full-on neurotic drama about the state of the nation. Or she could just be watching a late-night movie. It's possible. She's been a lot better lately.

Marie is sitting in front of the television in her dressing-gown and slippers. The heater is on and the room is pretty tidy and clean.

'Hi there, Mum!'

Her face almost collapses with relief when she sees Jonty, but he pretends not to notice. She's still got a bit of pride left, which is good. Jonty wants to help her keep that.

'Hello!' Her voice is clear.

Things are so much better, he reminds himself. She's come a long way. For the first month they lived together he'd sometimes come home to find her sitting in the dark, in the cold, with only an old rug wrapped around her shoulders, shivering and panicky about where he'd been. Once, Jonty found her lying between the couch and the wall because she'd 'heard some noise'. He'd had to coax her out and more or less carry her to bed.

'You're late,' she says brightly. 'How was work?'

'Really good.' Jonty puts on a cheery voice. People who tell you to be honest at all times don't know shit about anything. The last thing most people want is honesty. 'We were packed out from six o'clock. So I stayed back a bit to help Buzz.'

'You're a good boy,' she says quietly, picking up the TV guide and pretending to read it. All this is good, he reminds himself again. Okay, she's acting too – probably been crawling up the walls all night – but she's not laying the trip on him now and that's some improvement. She's coping, sort of, and that's what matters.

'So, what have you been doing?' Jonty asks, taking off his coat and scarf, thinking that he'd give her ten minutes and then hit the sack. Late-night conversations with her can very quickly turn belly-up. She tends to sink into desperation really quickly at night.

'Oh, this and that,' she says, putting the TV guide down and fingering a notepad on her knee. 'Watching a bit of television and writing a bit . . . trying to work something out.'

'Writing what?' Jonty asks because he knows she wants him to, slipping off his wet shoes and walking over nearer to the heater. 'What are you trying to work out?'

She holds out the pad to Jonty.

'Have a look at this,' she says shyly. 'It's just a draft, but I'd like to know if you think it's worded . . . right.'

Jonty takes the pad from her and sits down on the floor. He doesn't want to do this. No way. He's too tired. It's too late, but . . . he will. His mother is the one person in his life he'll do anything for. She stuck by him, right through everything. She came to see him every single visiting-day when he was in remand. Wrote him letters, rang, badgered his defence lawyer . . . everything she could do, she did. The fact that she was having some kind of mini-breakdown at the same time makes it more amazing. When the old man cleared out it got really bad, but she's getting better now, starting to recover. He can see the changes. She'll be back to her old self soon.

His father never came to see him once, nor did anyone else. Jonty knows that if Lillian had been alive she would have come. She would have written letters and phoned him and told him that she believed in him, just like his mum did. Both of them are beautiful people in their own way. They're sisters, so it makes sense. It's not just the evil mad stuff that runs in families, least that's what Jonty thinks. Good stuff gets passed on too.

'Hang on just a minute,' he sighs. 'Just gotta get my wet socks off.'

Lillian will forgive me . . . everything. That sentence runs through his head, then slides away again like a bored guest at a birthday party, before he can even decide what it means. Out the door it goes and he's left wondering, did it even come in? Who invited it?

Lillian will forgive me . . .

His mother is not very much like her sister physically. Her *late* sister. *Christ!* Jonty keeps forgetting. It's too weird to admit to anyone, but he still thinks of Lillian as being alive. Someone like that can't just *die* . . . can they? His mum is much plainer, kind of dumpy and ordinary with her short, grey hair. But her eyes are like Lillian's: brown and, when she's happy, sparkling. Her face is very lined now, but Jonty supposes that's what comes from living with his old man. Jed was hard. His mum never had nice clothes or make-up or any of the other stuff women go for, but even so she is beautiful in her own way. Sometimes in the half-light Jonty catches her sitting quietly, her hands folded, looking out the window maybe. With her round dark eyes and bony face she is like one of those paintings of saints that Catholics carry around with them – a holy person living in some other realm. Sometimes he can imagine the two of them, his mother and his aunt, as young girls, looking out the window, up at the dark sky, waiting for the night to be over.

He sees that his mother has been working on a letter in her neat cramped writing. When he sees it is to his grandmother he groans inside. *Why is she writing to that old bat?*

Dear Mother,

I hope this finds you well. As you might have guessed from the address above, I have at last left the farm. I'm living in town with my son (your grandson!), Jonty, in this little house, which is very small but adequate for our needs, and I plan to divorce Jed as soon as I can – whether he turns up or not. Jonty is helping me. He has a job and I plan to get one myself just as soon as I get a bit stronger and something suitable comes up.

I still live in fear of Jed. Although he has rung a few times it doesn't appear that he's coming home anytime soon. Gut instinct tells me that he will fight the divorce every inch of the way. But I don't care. I'm prepared to do whatever I have to to free myself from his horrible clutches.

You were right, Mother. Since marrying him that April day when I was just twenty-two, I have paid dearly for the choice I made. At last it is over. I will never go back to him. I'd rather die.

On the bright side, I have Jonty. Since the big trouble of three years ago, he has turned his life around and is an enormous help and solace to me.

I'm writing now to beg your forgiveness and to ask that you treat me like a daughter again. I am your only living child. Your only close relative, apart from Lillian's daughter and my son, Jonty. That has got to mean something to someone who used to say that family was everything in life.

Hope you are feeling well these days and that the rheumatism isn't too bad in this cold weather.

Your loving daughter,
Marie

Jonty reads it through again.

'Good,' he says slowly, trying to put his finger on what it is that's definitely *not good* about it.

'You think so?' she asks eagerly.

'You want her talking to you again, right?' Jonty says matter-of-factly. 'To get back in her good books. Is that it?'

His mother flushes.

'I don't want it for *me*,' she says sharply. 'Why should *you* be punished? You weren't convicted, you've done nothing wrong.'

It's the first Jonty knows that *he's* got anything to do with it. He's been told that the source of the rift between the families was Grandma not approving of his old man. But he doesn't say this. Why rile her up or load her with more stuff? Not at this time of night, anyway.

'Listen, Mum, don't do this for me,' he says quickly. 'I'm not in jail. I've got a job. I'm okay.'

'I've seen the will; Lillian's girl is going to get everything!' his mother cuts in bitterly. 'Just because she has come back to live with her.'

Jonty shrugs, trying not to show his surprise. He didn't know his mother knew Alice was back living with Grandma. He hadn't said anything about it because he thought it might rub salt into the wound. He has seen Alice in the supermarket and the street a few times but purposely avoided her. What could he possibly say?

Grandma's money has never seemed real to Jonty. He isn't counting on getting his hands on any of it, nor is he losing sleep about it.

'Maybe the old lady is sick,' he says. 'Alice might have come home to look after her.'

'But that's my job! I'm her daughter!'

Then his mother starts laughing in this totally black, miserable, out-of-control way that gets Jonty's heart galloping in his rib cage.

Crazy! My old lady is crazy. On she goes like a wild bird caught in a trap, her arms flapping like wings. This kind of desperate stuff makes Jonty want to hightail it as far away as he can – from her, from this town, from this whole new life he's trying to build for himself. He should never have come back here. He'd rather be back inside the can. *No shit*, he'd rather be locked up with a pack of psychopathic morons who'd bust your head in as soon as look at you than listen to his mother laugh like this.

'Oh, Jonty.' She is wiping her eyes now, smiling at him as though they'd just shared a joke. 'My mother was always so difficult.'

The last time Jonty had seen his cousin Alice Wishart was two days before in the supermarket. He'd hidden behind the aisle and watched her wheeling her trolley around. She'd changed a lot, grown up. She seemed very serious. He couldn't explain the rush of sadness that passed through him when he watched her buying her things: soap and milk and bread. His throat choked up watching her roll off through that supermarket, her long hair swinging down her back, and wondered what it felt like to lose your one and only mother.

'We're talking millions of dollars, Jonty.' Marie is calm now, but when she looks around their little lounge room she grimaces. 'We live like *this* when she is sitting on all that money!'

'Yeah, I know, Mum,' Jonty says, wondering how long it will be before he can slope off to the cot. Jonty actually really likes the little house they're renting. It feels kind of manageable compared with that huge old farmhouse they used to live in. That joint was one of those National Trust numbers with big fireplaces and wood stoves and a wide verandah all around, full of fancy stuff passed down through the family from South Africa – china, silver cutlery, vases and glassware – that the family were never allowed to use in case it broke. But it's hard work living in a place like that with no modern appliances or heating. And anyhow, being out there had meant living with his father.

His mother goes out to the kitchen to get them both a cup of tea and Jonty stares into the red bar of the heater. Suddenly he is back there, or just a breath away . . .

'I had such hopes for you!'

Jonty opened his eyes. His father was standing by the door watching him sleep. *Oh jeez!* he groaned, and prayed that it was just an apparition. Hadn't his father gone to the livestock sales in Horsham? He hid his head under the covers. Not for long. The sheet and doona were pulled right off him and he was left lying in his boxer shorts and socks.

'It's cold,' he mumbled stupidly, looking around wildly before sitting up, bringing his knees up to his chin, shaking himself awake. There was no easy way out of his room. He knew he'd just have to deal with whatever was coming. He groaned again as a wave of nausea hit his guts and slid up into his throat. He tried to hide his face in his hands but they were pulled away, too.

'Give me a look at you!' His father had him tightly by one wrist and peered into his face. 'Where were you last night?'

'Just out.' Jonty looked up at his father.

'Out?' Those eyes were blazing, boring into his own, pinning him down.

'With friends!'

'*Friends*,' his father spat derisively.

'Yeah.' *Want me to explain what a friend is?*

'What friends?'

Jonty shrugged and tried to meet his father's eyes but it was impossible. *Who was there?* Jonty cleared his throat and tried very hard not to look as utterly trashed as he felt. He remembered they'd all been on the weed the night before and there'd been vodka, too, at the start of the night, and he knew his father could tell.

'What were you on?'

'Nothing.'

'Nothing, huh?' Jed panted, his face flooding with pink blotches. *Blood pressure.* Jonty hoped hard that it would get him one day soon. A massive brain bleed would do the job.

'Look at you squirming!' His father pulled his wrist backwards sharply, making Jonty yelp with pain, then suddenly Jonty's whole arm was being twisted up his back.

'Leave me alone!'

'Leave me alone,' his father mimics in a high voice. 'You weak little *girl*! If you had any guts you'd be fighting back!'

Jonty looked at the clock near his bed. Seven. He'd had two hours sleep and he wouldn't mind dying. He couldn't remember much about the night before, except that he and Tom had been down at the river with a whole lot of others. His head thumped, heavy as a load of concrete, and his mouth felt like the bottom of a rat cage. Then he suddenly saw Tom as he'd been the night before, standing on the bridge. Jonty knew it would be all right then. Let the old prick break his arm! He had something good to think about.

All of them had been down on the bank clapping slowly, egging Tom on, helpless with laughter. He'd stripped right down to his boxers, and just as the girls were screaming for him to take them off too, he'd jumped, straight as a die, right into the freezing river, surprising them all. There was silence on the bank. His head didn't appear for ages and even Jonty had a few moments' panic.

When that head did appear it was about forty metres downstream and travelling fast. They'd all gone running through the bush, spluttering with laughter, to help him out. Was there music of some sort? Who'd supplied the dope? Some girl went swimming, too, at some stage. Or maybe she just went in up to her knees. Jonty couldn't remember much else.

'Your head will never recover.' His father was squatting behind him now, his left arm around his throat, his mouth in Jonty's ear. The other hand was pushing Jonty's arm higher and higher up his back. Tears of pain formed in his eyes and his father hissed, 'You bring shame on my proud family. You hear me?'

Jonty gasped again.

There had been bark and weeds in Tommy's hair when he'd got out, water sloshing down his skin and such exhilaration in his eyes.

'Hey, Jonno.' The wet cold arm around his shoulder. 'Wanna do it?'

'Yeah.'

'Together man!'

'Let's die together!'

But Tom had left soon after that. He'd wandered off home mumbling something about needing to have his head clear for the next day. Whereas Jonty had stayed . . . right till dawn.

'You hear me?' Jonty's father shouted into his ear.

'Yes, I hear you.' The pain was even further away.

'What future will you have if you mix with cretins and degenerates?'

'No future,' Jonty mumbled, because that was the only answer he was allowed to give.

'So what were you on?'

Jonty can't remember that either. Had there been pills of some sort?

His father let him go suddenly and Jonty, weak with relief, scrambled off the bed and pulled on his jeans. But his father was a former boxer and could still move fast.

'Drugs are for degenerates,' he began again, softly. 'For people with no pride. You understand me?'

'Yes.' Jonty rubbed his wrist and shoulder. 'I understand you.'

Jed would have him on the floor with a knee in his chest if he tried anything.

'Pride! You hear me?'

Jonty nodded subserviently and readied himself for the full treatment.

But this time fate was on his side . . . The phone rang. It rang and rang. Loudly. Louder than Jonty could remember it ever ringing before.

'Marie!' Jed bellowed out. 'Phone! Get the phone.'

Still it rang. His mother must have been outside, maybe feeding the chooks or in the garden with her roses – the one pleasure in her life. His father gave him a last fleeting contemptuous look and was out the door.

Jonty's mother comes in with two cups of the cocoa he likes and some special chocolate biscuits he doesn't like but eats anyway just to please her.

'Sometimes there's nothing you can do, Mum,' Jonty mumbles, trying to sound calm.

'But she didn't earn it!' His mother has that hysterical sob in her voice. 'My father wanted it for *us*! Lillian and me. His girls. He used to tell us all the time. It was all for Lillian and me. *She* nagged him to an early grave!'

Oh jeez. All this again! What can you say when someone is on a roll like this? Nothing. Just sit and cop it sweet. As though he hadn't heard it before.

'Same way she nagged Lillian and me. We both ran like blind donkeys into completely senseless marriages just to get away from her. Oh my poor sister. To think what happened to my poor darling sister!' She falls down onto the sofa again and starts crying, searching around for a hanky in the pocket of her dressing-gown.

Jonty hands over his own and waits.

'Sweet *sweet* Lillian who never hurt a fly! She used to stick up for me all the time . . . when we were little.'

'Yeah, well,' Jonty keeps his voice steady, 'she's dead now.'

'I want *you* to be able to walk proudly in this town,' his mother says, 'in front of everyone, including your father when he comes back. One day you'll be a wealthy man, Jonty. I want that for you.'

'Hush, Mum,' he mutters softly. 'It's okay now, calm down.'

'As soon as the twelve months are up I'll divorce him and he won't get a penny!' She starts laughing again, and even though Jonty hasn't smoked anything in ages the laughter makes him roll into a kind of disconnected semi-stoned state. He feels like an actor being made to do weird things that make no sense but he has to do them because . . . it's his job. 'You get your share of her money and I'll die happy,' she is still raving. '*Her* wealth was the only reason he married me . . .'

'Listen, Mum, you've got to seem more *together* in this letter,' Jonty says patiently. 'Just tell her that Dad has gone and that you're never going back to him, and then maybe invite her to lunch or something.'

His mother frowns.

'You could bring her to Thistles so she can see me in action!' Jonty is only joking, but his mother looks so terrified by the suggestion that he smiles.

'I couldn't possibly . . . do that,' she whispers.

'Okay, but make it more upbeat anyway,' Jonty grabs the pad and biro from her and begins to rewrite and cross out bits and pieces. 'She won't want to see you *begging*.'

'Don't you believe it!' she whispers. 'She'll want me begging and I'll do it. I'll do and say whatever it takes!' But she finally agrees the tone should be lighter and more succinct. It should work as a bait to entice her mother into at least meeting for a talk. The overhaul takes about ten minutes. After she agrees on the finished draft, Jonty gets up, yawning.

'Got to sleep.'

'You go to bed then.' She touches his hand briefly. 'Did you know there is some big thing happening at the Centre tomorrow night?'

'Yeah, I know.' Jonty is edging for the door.

'You going?' She gives one of her wrecked hopeful smiles. 'You should. You've been stuck at home ever since you've been back. Don't hide away. You're young, Jonty. Get out and have some fun.'

'Yeah, well.' Jonty suddenly feels like a kid in kindergarten being urged not to hold back, to take his bag of lollies along with all the other kids. 'Maybe. Goodnight, Mum.'

'Goodnight, my darling boy.'

Jonty crawls into his unmade bed and switches off the bedside light.

How weird is this? His *mother* urging him to get out and have fun! Bizarre coming from someone who sits home most of the day looking at the wall – too freaked to phone anyone, too scared to go down to the shops in case she runs into her husband, who happens to be thousands of miles away. Too frightened of her own mother to knock on her door and say 'hi'.

Hey, Jonty, get out there and have fun! How do you have fun with no friends? The names of friends drift into his consciousness and then drift away again in just the way they did three years ago. But it was Tom Mullaney cutting him loose that really mattered. That one hurt! It all got too close for Tom. His old man being Jonty's defence lawyer and all but . . . *what kind of pissweak excuse is that?* One day he'll have it out with Tom Mullaney. He doesn't know when or where or how, but one day he'll make that prick face himself.

Those detectives! There was one guy Jonty had genuinely liked. Lloyd Hooper, a slow-talker, but quick to see the funny side of whatever was going on. He got Jonty's humour early on and they hit it off. Or it seemed that way. That guy could talk music. He'd lived in Europe for a few years and was interested in politics. Jonty liked talking to a kindred spirit who was older. Lloyd would take him out sometimes and they'd sit on the beach. The detective would buy coffees and they'd talk. Jonty told him about his old man, about his mum and about school, the trouble he'd been in. He told him about the afternoons he and Tommo spent with Lillian, too. Why not? There was nothing wrong there. It was just a close, unusual friendship. The detective was cool about them getting into dope. He took a real interest in the stuff the three of them used to talk about, too; the different views Lillian had about films and books and studying; what she was doing with her life and what Jonty and Tom thought about it all.

But then they'd brought Jonty in for a record of interview. Just Jonty on his own. *Anything you say may be used in a court of law against you.* And it had dawned on him that it was *him* they were after. That all the hours of pleasant talk had been a ruse. They had Jonty in their sights. *You are entitled to make a phone call.* 'Yeah,' Jonty had said to the bristly-faced, fat-bellied little prick, who was staring at him with his bulging eyes, like he could see right into Jonty's heart and didn't like what he saw one little bit. 'I want to make a phone call!' His *good mate* Lloyd seemed to have disappeared at that stage. And where was Tom?

Jonty rang his mother, and she got Luke Mullaney around to the police station within the hour.

'Say nothing,' Luke told Jonty. He said that constantly. Even when they charged Jonty and he was locked away in remand, Luke would come by and tell him the same thing over and over. Say nothing to nobody. It got so boring. Jonty had all kinds of ideas about how he was going to get himself out of that hole. But Luke's advice was always the same, like a broken record: *Say nothing, Jonty. Remember they've got to prove it against you!* It was hard remembering that because it got so lonely in there. After a while it was the *only* thing he wanted to talk about.

In remand he met up with a guy he knew in primary school. Bryce Collins. He'd been charged with petty larceny or some dumb thing. They'd been mates, so Jonty was glad to see him. But after a few weeks he started asking Jonty about Lillian and the murder. *Confide in no one*, Luke had told Jonty. *Coppers put stooges in to get information. Say nothing.* Jonty was totally freaked out by that stage, so lonely, with no smoke or pills to ease it either. But he stayed away from the guy after that.

Now, more than anything, Jonty wants whoever did it to be caught. He wants them put inside. And he wants the key thrown away. That's what he tells himself as he goes off to sleep, with his mother still rustling about in the living room. That's his prayer. *Whoever did it should be punished.*

Jonty ends up going to the concert. Anything to get away from his mother. The next morning she was still driving him nuts with all the talk about his grandmother's money. In the middle of it all she rings Luke Mullaney for advice. *So now Luke's their money guru as well? Fuck that!* Apparently you can contest a will if it's unfair *blah blah*. But it sometimes takes years *blah blah,* and you can't count on a favourable outcome. *Great!* Jonty knows that he's got to get out. He can manage small doses of her when he has work to go to at night, but actually hanging out with her *all day* makes him edgy, gives him an urge to do something wild and really stupid just to relieve the feeling that his heart is being dragged bumping and scraping along the road behind a utility truck.

So here he is, rugged up in coat and scarf, heading into town to see a band. *God! It feels like someone else.* But no . . . it's him all right. Jonty van der Weihl. Just another human being out in the spitting rain and the mean wind. Once he's down on Webber Street he becomes part of a whole throng of people around his own age, heading in the same direction. And it feels all right, it does. He's on his own A lot of ties came loose three years ago. He does recognise a few faces. Mostly they nod and say, *G'day, Jonty!* or, *You back, Jonty? How you doing?* Not overtly hostile exactly, more curious, like they didn't expect ever to see him again. But they don't hang around. Fair enough.

He lines up and buys his ticket. The good seats have gone already so he gets stuck right up the back, but he doesn't mind that much.

He finds himself next to a pack of sixteen-year-old girls, all of them dressed to kill in tight T-shirts and stilettos shoes, with studs and rings in their ears and eyebrows and mouths. A couple have rolls of fat spilling out over their skin-tight jeans, and they all stink of perfume and hair gunk. They gabble on excitedly about who is there and who isn't, and if some other dude will make the concert on time. Jonty hasn't heard this kind of breathless, babbling girl-talk for a long time. It's almost like another language, and it makes him smile.

'Hey, Skye!' the one next to him shouts. 'Over here!' She leans across Jonty to chuck something from her bag at whoever she wants to attract in a seat further down, and in the process swipes him in the face with her earring.

'Hey!' Jonty says, holding his cheek.

'Renee! You got him in the eye!' the one next to him giggles.

'Did not!' She turns to him. 'Did I?'

'Yeah,' Jonty shrugs. 'You got me.'

'Omigod!' she gasps and leans closer, peering into his face. 'Are you okay?'

Jonty nods. If there is one thing he hates it is being asked *Are you okay?*

Huddled up in the corner of the psychiatric ward of the local hospital having some sort of drug-induced psychotic episode, hallucinating like crazy, he thought he was in a helicopter during a war. The engine had been hit and was on fire. The whole thing was going to blow up any second. He was the only one without a parachute but his mates didn't know it, they were trying to push him out. The fields far below spread out like a green patchwork rug and the cars moved like little coloured meccano dots and he knew he was about to die. He was sweating like a pig, gasping and crying. He had ants crawling out his ears and up his arse and this young nurse came in, put a hand on his shoulder and said, 'Are you okay?'

'Oh sure,' Jonty sobbed, tears pouring down his face, 'just fantastic! What about you? Are *you* okay?'

The first band is a group of local guys and no one is interested. They get a bit of applause at the end of their set and a couple more bands come on. But when Pete's Revenge is introduced the atmosphere immediately belts up into a higher gear. Not silence exactly, just a heavy charge of excitement and expectation. The chatter stops. Even the girl who swiped him with her earring gets serious. Jonty takes a quick look at her face in the revolving red light and they share a smile. He suddenly wants to tell her that she looks good, so much better than she sounds. But he keeps his mouth shut because he knows she's likely to take it the wrong way.

Okay, here's the band! Five guys. They burst onto the stage like a pack of wild cats, half a minute tune-up and then – without a smile or a word or a wave – it's on. *So loud!* It crashes into his ears like a storm. He's not used to this. Fake smoke billows out from somewhere under the stage and the lights change from red to purple to yellow.

After the first few numbers, they sing the hit that got them known and the girls around Jonty go berserk. They squeal and clap and stand on their chairs. The earring girl hauls him up too.

'*Comeon!*' she screams, throwing an arm around his shoulders and kissing him on the ear. '*Whatchawaitinfor?*'

Jonty laughs and stands, too. He sees the number through with her hand clinging on to clumps of his hair and it feels all right.

At the end of the song she jumps down and edges nearer, and he kisses her in the dark because she wants him to. Her tongue immediately goes down his throat and he has to pull away because he's laughing so hard. She's obviously the leader of the group, the outrageous one who'd do anything. There is always one in a crowd. He knows because it used to be him. The others are watching and giggling and nudging her on.

'Whatsyaname?' she shouts up into his face,

'Jonno,' he laughs. 'You?'

'Renee!' she shouts. 'And this is Teagan and Mally and Skye.'

They all shake hands exuberantly and then turn back to the stage because the band has started a new number.

'Hey, *Jack*,' Renee declares boldly, so her friends hear. 'You're cool.'

'You too,' Jonty grins back. *Jack? Okay, Jack will do.*

After an hour of loud music, banter with the girls and a bit more touchy-feely in the dark, Jonty needs to take a piss. He's also got a thirst on him like a dead cat left out in the sun for five days. He and Renee have shared two more unsuccessful kisses and a lot of personal information like, *What star sign are you? What is your favourite CD ever? Can you surf?* It calls for a drink. Why didn't he bring in a bottle of water like the girlies around him, sucking on their bottles like babies? He excuses himself with promises to be back soon, ducks his way out to the end of the row and makes his exit past the security guys through the back door.

There are maybe fifty people in the foyer. Some of them are security, drifting around, chatting to each other or talking importantly into their phones. Others are lining up for drinks at a counter down the other end. There are more people out the front of the glass doors, smoking. Someone has a van out there selling doughnuts to a group of bikers who have obviously just pulled up. Jonty notes the half-a-dozen gleaming motorbikes parked on the footpath outside and wishes like crazy that he had one. The girls' toilet has the usual winding queue.

Jonty spots some guys he thinks are from his old school. Names he's mostly forgotten. They're larking around in the drinks line with a couple of girls he doesn't recognise. Before pushing the toilet door open he takes a second look. *Is one of them Tom Mullaney?* The tall guy with the black curly hair has his back turned. *It is him*, Jonty thinks as he ducks quickly into a cubicle. He takes a long piss and zips up his fly, feeling unaccountably nervous. *So . . . what do I say?* He feels like a loser here by himself. Jonty washes his hands and decides not to go back for the rest of the concert. Tom will keep. He takes a long slurp of water from the tap and puts on his coat for the walk home. If he cuts out now, with luck he'll be able to sneak in the back way and avoid his mother.

But when he walks out into the foyer again something is going on.

The bikers have come in from the cold and up close they look mean. They're older guys, most of them, in their thirties and forties, all decked out in tatts and leathers, beards and guts hanging over their belts. They're swaggering around, yelling out. But it's not until one of them stamps out his cigarette on the foyer carpet and the others start chucking doughnuts at each other that the two security guys come over to remonstrate – only to be totally ignored. The glassy eyes and loud voices tell Jonty that they're seriously out of it on some chemical or other. The two uniformed security guys start to confer, but they don't really seem to know what to do. The music has started up again in the main hall, so all noise in the foyer has been drowned out.

About to walk out into the cold, Jonty hesitates. There is something mesmerising about watching a group of idiots. He stands by the door and watches the bikers saunter up behind Tom and his group. There is a sharp exchange. At first it is just edgy aggressive talk and then one of the bikers starts screaming and pushing his way to the front of the queue. One of the girls topples over in her high heels. There is a bit of squealing and gasping and a few *are-you-okay* squawks. Jonty moves nearer.

'Careful, mate!' he hears Tom say loudly, helping the blonde girl up and giving the heavies a dirty look. A couple of them turn quickly to size him up.

'You got a problem?' the red-faced fat one says. The atmosphere is suddenly thick with hostility. Jonty stands well back, feeling a weird kind of excitement grow in him. He can tell what's going to happen. It's like a play he's seen before with everybody performing their designated roles. The leading moron figures that he's got the numbers so why not pick a fight for the hell of it.

'I don't have a problem,' he hears his old friend Tom snarl. 'Seems like you do, though.'

Oh shit, Tommo! Can he really have got that stupid in Jonty's absence? Must have been a while since he's dealt with a bunch of cretins. On cue, three of the heavies edge forward, singling Tom out. Jonty shakes his head. He's done it now.

'Hey, pansy!'

'You got something to say, pretty boy?'

All but one of Tom's mates pull back and merge in with the crowd. Unfortunately the guy sticking by him is too small to matter. *What is that guy's name?* Jonty recognises him but can't recall.

The cowardice of the others makes him want to crack up with laughter. He can almost hear what is going through their heads. *Please don't let me be associated with him. I don't want my face broken!* What pissants. Back at school, he and Tom used to hate guys like that. Occasionally he and Tom got into a fight. Never provoked one, but it would happen sometimes. Once Tom got his nose broken sticking up for Jonty. They both prided themselves on the way they never took shit from anyone. *So where are your new friends when it matters, buddy?* Jonty feels like jeering from the sidelines. *Looks like they don't want to know you!*

It suddenly hits him that he's going to see the shit kicked out of Tom Mullaney and the idea is . . . well, kind of appealing. Jonty leans back against the wall. Call it karma! This will go down better than the concert . . . It starts quickly with three onto Tom.

In spite of being off their faces, those heavy pricks know how to move into position when they want to. Jonty is still at the door so he doesn't quite hear what has been said, but the three surrounding Tom have pushed him into the middle of the crowd. There is a lot of scuffling and shouting. Jonty sees the security guys talking anxiously into their mobile phones. They must be calling for reinforcements from inside the concert hall. Jonty hopes one of them is ringing the police because they won't be able to handle these guys. Suddenly all the noise is drowned out by a particularly loud number from the band inside the main hall, but the excitement in the foyer has nothing to do with music.

The heavy one in front starts to push and shove Tom.

'Ah, fuck off, you fat bastard!' Tom yells. Jonty groans inwardly. *Not a good idea!*

A hard jab to the chest catches Tom unawares. He falls backwards – Jonty can see he's probably winded – almost onto the guy hovering behind, who uses the opportunity to smack Tom sharply around the head before he can even catch his breath. The little guy comes to Tom's aid but he's swatted off like a fly. Still, Jonty is impressed. *Full marks for trying, shortie!* The rest happens in a matter of seconds. Tom turns around and jabs a hard straight left to the fat prick's chin, and you can see the surprise on the heavyweight's face. Not a bad punch for someone who has been hit already. If it were just between him and this guy, Tom might have a chance, in spite of being half his weight. But the two sidekicks are standing by for such an emergency. They converge on Tom quickly and begin the clean-up. One grabs him by the hair and pulls his head back, while the other one punches into his ribs, then gets him fair in the face. *Crack!* You can hear his nose break. The gushing blood gets everyone screaming, as though they only now understand what is happening. To be fair, it has all happened very quickly.

A couple of fresh security guys run out from the hall.

'Okay now!' they're all yelling. 'Break it up!' But they're worse than useless, in their neat blue uniforms. Tom is still being pummelled, smacked around from one to the other of the cretins, as the guards try to fight their way through the crowd.

It is what happens next that Jonty can't handle. Tom is on his knees and that fucking fat prick starts kicking him, a couple of times in the back and the ribs, then in the arse and then Jonty reckons that he must have got him in the balls because Tom lets out a horrible scream. He curls over onto his side and the crazy shit-for-brains continues kicking him. While he's down! What a low dog.

Jonty loses it. He doesn't think at all, just runs full speed towards the fat guy and catches him completely unawares from behind. One in the side of the head, one in the eye, then one straight into his chin. *Shit but it hurts!* Jonty hasn't punched anyone in a long time and his knuckles feel broken. But the heavy guy is falling backwards, so Jonty is able to deliver two more hard ones. He's in luck, too, because by this stage, security have waylaid the moron's mates so for five seconds it's just Jonty and the fat prick, and Jonty is winning.

The adrenalin kicks in and there is no pain in his hands any more. He doesn't feel a thing except pure exultation. Boxing was the one useful thing his old man ever taught him. And Jonty passed on what he knew to Tom.

Even though Jonty is way lighter than this guy, he knows how to use the weight he has. Being completely sober is a big advantage as well. He manages to dodge a couple of wild punches and place another two sharp uppercuts into the slack fleshy gut, then another fast hard jab to the rib cage. The big guy's labouring breath is music to Jonty's ears. He'd like to kill him now. Finish him off.

Two security guys are pulling Jonty off when he gets in the best one yet, a truly beautiful left hook into the ugly fat mouth. It has the guy's head flipping back like a ball tied to rubber. When he raises his head, Jonty sees his lip is bleeding from a gash about three centimetres long. The guy shakes his head a couple of times and spits big globules of bloody saliva onto the carpet. Along with that comes – joy of joys – a tooth, bouncing out onto the floor. Jonty hears the police sirens outside. He turns to Tom, who is trying to get up from the floor.

'Can you walk?' Jonty says, hauling him up by the back of his bloody jumper.

Tom nods woozily and searches for a hanky to stem the blood from his nose.

'Don't worry about that,' Jonty says. 'Come on!' He pulls Tom back towards the side entrance he'd seen earlier. 'Let's get out before the coppers arrive, hey?'

'Yeah, okay.'

It's freezing outside, but Jonty is so pumped he barely notices. He feels amazing. He's walking on the moon. He's got one arm around Tom's shoulders helping him along but in his head he's reliving those punches. The wind is howling, the rain is spitting down like ice needles onto his face and he's really not thinking much about where they're headed. Main thing is to get away so they don't get caught up with the coppers, giving statements, being fined and all the rest of that crap. In spite of limping a bit and breathing hard, Tom's clearly doing his best to keep up. The gasps and stifled groans tell Jonty he isn't feeling too hot though.

When they come to the end of the main street Jonty takes the left turn up the hill, away from the centre of town, towards where Tom lives. Once they're out of the shopping precinct and into the quiet residential streets, he figures it's safe to slow down a bit.

'You okay?' Jonty asks.

'Yeah,' Tom says but it's obvious he's not. Jonty keeps his arm around his shoulders.

'I'll get you home,' he says. 'You can take it from there.'

'Thanks.'

They walk for a bit in silence. Gradually Jonty's high begins to drain away. He can feel the growing stiffness between them. Up Manning Street they go, past the swimming pool, then along Russell Crescent up into the nice area of town. Jonty takes his arm away and looks around at the big houses set well back from the road. He hasn't been up here for a while. His grandmother still lives somewhere around here, along with the doctors and lawyers and others with loot. Tom's old man being one of them. Jonty used to virtually live up here with the Mullaneys when they were mates.

Tom suddenly slows right down, then stops and bends over.

'Jeez, I'm crook,' he groans. He stumbles over to the edge of the road and then back again to the nearby fence.

Expecting him to start puking into the hedge any minute, Jonty retreats. But Tom just slumps onto the fence. When he turns back, Jonty sees his face in the street light, streaked with blood. Swollen eye closing over fast. Busted nose.

'Be okay now,' Tom says hoarsely, and then, as an afterthought, 'Thanks, Jonty.'

'I'll get you home,' Jonty says quickly.

'Nah. It's okay.' Tom waves him away, turns his back and starts walking off, as wobbly and out of control as a drunk. 'I'm just a few streets up. Thanks a lot though, Jonty.'

'Okay.' Jonty watches him teetering off, thinking that Luke's house is actually at least half a kilometre away and the last bit of the walk is uphill.

'You sure?' Jonty calls uneasily.

'I'll be okay,' Tom yells back, without turning around.

'Okay.' Jonty watches him walk away, wretchedness seeping through him like foul water. It keeps on coming, deep and bitter, filling him up. He leans back against the fence, totally overcome with it. *Tom doesn't want to know me, even after I saved his arse!* Jonty tries to shake the feeling, tells himself it doesn't matter, but it sits there like a thick, doughy and immovable growth in his gut. Cold. He feels cold. Goose bumps rise over his body and he clenches his teeth to stop them chattering. He is freezing hard against the wall. Worse, he knows he deserves it. He has lost his rightful place among other human beings. Has to be. If he could just *remember* then he'd go tell them all about it . . .

Ah shit. Not all that again. Got to move on or he'll go crazy. Got to get home and get warm then he'll feel better . . . Jonty walks off back the way they came. There is something vaguely familiar about the street, but he can't think what.

When he comes to the kerb, something makes him turn back to watch Tom stumbling up the hill like a drunk. Right at the moment he turns the corner, Tom topples and falls, first onto his knees and then lower, his head right down on the pavement.

Jonty hesitates only a moment then sprints back up the hill. Tom is lying curled up on the ground, spewing his guts out and groaning. Jonty grabs him under the armpits and hauls him into a sitting position against the fence. Tom sits gasping for a few moments, and then tries to stumble up onto his knees.

'You need a doctor. Got a phone?'

'Nah,' Tom groans. 'Didn't bring the friggin' thing.'

Jonty bends to look into Tom's face. It's only half visible in the poor street light but he sees enough.

'Should get you to the hospital,' he says, straightening up and looking around at the surrounding houses for any sign of life. But there is nothing doing. These joints are big, with long driveways winding back from the road, the houses hidden behind trees and hedges. It is hard to tell if anyone is up and about.

'I'll go knock on a door and ask to use the phone for an ambulance,' he suggests, not exactly relishing the prospect – rich pricks don't like being disturbed. 'They'll be here in a few minutes.'

'Nah,' Tom groans and waves off the idea irritably. 'Just give me a minute will you?'

'Don't play the hero.'

'Wait a minute,' Tom says again. So Jonty squats down next to him. They say nothing for a while and gradually Tom's heavy breathing eases a bit.

'You did good back there, Jonty,' Tom whispers at last. 'Didn't see you. Where did you come from?'

'I'd just been for a piss and saw what was happening.'

'Ah, right,' Tom laughs. 'That fat shit had lead in his boots.'

'Yeah.'

'Your old man had his uses, I reckon!'

'Yeah. Maybe.'

'One, anyway.'

Jonty smiles to himself in the darkness.

Suddenly a taxi turns the corner and pulls up outside the massive place opposite. A door opens, spilling yellow light out over the street. The three passengers, all female, confer in loud voices about who owes what for the ride and when they're going to see each other again.

Jonty finds the sound of the taxi radio weirdly comforting. Someone else is alive at least. Only one of the girls gets out. She stands on the footpath and waves to her friends as they roar off. Then the dark figure of the girl in a long heavy coat moves off towards the front gate of the mansion and Jonty is on his feet.

'Excuse me,' he calls loudly. She doesn't turn around, just

hurries faster towards the gate. So he runs halfway across the road to get her attention. 'Excuse me,' he calls again, louder this time.

She stops and turns around. He waits on the road, afraid if he goes any closer that she'll be scared. 'My mate is sick. Wondering if I could borrow your phone to ring an ambulance.'

She walks back towards the road and when she passes under a streetlight, Jonty finally sees her face.

Oh shit.

It's his cousin and that place opposite must be . . . *his grand-mother's joint.* That's why it seemed vaguely familiar! The last time he was here was when he was about twelve. Jonty pretends not to recognise her as she slowly walks across the road towards him.

'What's the matter with him?' Her voice is sharp and suspicious. She hasn't twigged who Jonty is yet, but she doesn't seem too nervous, which is a relief. If you approach some females in the street at night they act like you're about to rape them.

'He was attacked,' Jonty says. 'Don't really know how bad. Some moron was kicking into him.'

She moves forward and her jaw literally drops in shock when she sees Jonty up close. Her former confident expression changes into a blank, deer-in-the-headlights kind of stare before her eyes start flitting about this way and that, as though she's looking for some escape.

Jonty wants to laugh. *Yeah, it's your own personal nightmare, babe! Mine too.* But he doesn't. He keeps his face absolutely straight. He can see she is seriously freaked, but what can he do? 'He needs some kind of help,' his voice peters away.

Alice walks over to Tom – who is still sitting up against the fence, his head hidden between his knees – and bends over to take a look. She says something that Jonty doesn't hear and Tom looks up. His blood-streaked face in the street light is suitably impressive and she gasps. Alice looks from Tom to Jonty and then back again, her face slowly closing over, but she doesn't say anything.

'Think I'll be okay,' Tom manages to whisper hoarsely.

'Bring him inside,' she mutters. 'I'll call a doctor.'

So Jonty and Alice get on either side of Tom to help him up. He groans a bit but allows them to help him across the road and up through the huge wrought-iron gate, which opens easily. 'What about your grandmother?' Jonty say politely, on his best behaviour, trying to let her see she doesn't have to be afraid of her infamous cousin.

'*My* grandmother?' she sneers sarcastically.

'Yeah.' Jonty takes a confused look at her. She's angry as well as afraid. 'Will she mind?'

'She's *your* grandmother too,' is her sharp reply.

Jonty reels slightly in shock. *Fuck!* 'Will she mind?' He keeps his voice low and calm.

'Take a bombing raid to wake her up,' his cousin snaps back.

'Deep sleeper, huh?'

'Drugged to the eyeballs every night.' She gives a harsh laugh.

They have made it up the long drive and are almost at the house. Stone steps lead up to the front entrance but she takes them around the side to a wooden door set in the stone building blocks under the verandah.

A dim naked bulb spills light over a neat little room. A small square table and chairs, a sink, a stove and a couch. The low ceiling makes it seem as though it's in miniature proportions, even though everything is of a basic size.

'The slave quarters, huh?' Jonty quips dryly.

'Yeah.' A sudden small smile hovers briefly at the edge of Alice's pretty mouth, but she won't meet his eyes. 'You could say that.'

She leads Tom over to a single bed covered in a rug under

the window. He slumps down with a groan and curls up on his side.

'I'll call our doctor,' Alice tells Jonty, matter-of-factly.

Tom opens his eyes a bit and shakes his head. 'Nah, don't do that,' he groans. 'Can I just rest here a bit? I'll be okay soon, I reckon.'

Alice looks at Jonty but he can only shrug. They both know Tom should be checked out by someone – sooner rather than later. She looks at her watch. 'It's nearly midnight on a Saturday,' she says. 'Hospital Emergency will take forever. *Our* doctor will come anytime day or night. In fact, he *likes* coming at night.'

'How come?'

'More money in it for him.'

Tom looks up at this. He obviously finds the girl baffling, too.

'He likes keeping *her* alive,' Alice adds grimly as she heads for the door.

Jonty decides not to comment because he doesn't want to get her offside. 'Okay, then,' he says. It's the best solution. If Tom went to the hospital then he'd have to wait there with him and it could take all night. The police would probably get wind of everything, too. It could get very awkward for both of them.

'Clean him up a bit,' Alice orders, pointing at a door at the far end of the room. 'The bathroom is there. I'll have our doctor here soon.'

'Okay. The patient is Tom, by the way. Tom Mullaney.'

'I know who it is,' she says over her shoulder, then closes the door quietly behind her.

Jonty wants to go after her, tell her not to worry, that neither of them are people she should fear. Then the wretchedness is back, magnified by the small room and his cousin's quiet contempt.

He looks down at Tom, whose eyes are now open.

'God,' Tom mutters suddenly. 'This is very fucking *weird*, Jonno!'

'Yeah,' Jonty doesn't know whether to laugh or howl. 'Very fucking weird.'

'How did we get here?'

'Dunno.'

TOM

Tom opens his eyes. Where the hell is he? There are voices. Low. He looks around but sees no one. There is something hard on his face, spread out across his nose and cheeks. Feels like concrete. He raises one hand. It's some kind of plaster bandage. He tries to sit up but everything feels tight. His face. His chest. His arse and legs. Everything hurts. Nausea rides in on a wave, but after a few dry retches it recedes. He has no idea where he is. This room, the low ceilings and the funny little pieces of odd furniture – it's like a film set. Darkness, except for the hard bright slabs of sunlight shining through the blind slats and across the small table. Afternoon light, has to be. So how long has he been here? It's not a proper bed, more like a settee. He feels like he's been kidnapped. It's the kind of place they'd throw you if they wanted information. *What information have I got?* Are his interrogators going to walk in any minute?

Tom lies there waiting, trying to work out why he has a strong feeling that he's just been through something big and extraordinary. The mixture of pain and excitement is intoxicating. Was he dreaming about Jonty and Alice? *God!* She looked so much like Lillian that day in his dad's office.

Lillian. Ah! In spite of everything hurting, including his nuts, Tom notices suddenly that he's aroused, and not in your normal, easy-to-manage way either. His cock pushes like burning steel against the zip of his fly. Like it's got a life of its own, completely separate from the rest of him. There is nothing he can do about it. Even if he could use his hand without pain (which he can't) he senses there are people somewhere nearby, though he can't see them. What if they walked in to find him . . . *jerking off?* He squirms around a bit on the bed trying to ease the discomfort. *Think of cold things: avalanches of snow, ice cubes tumbling into a huge glass on a hot day.*

But it all rushes back. Lillian. He was dreaming of her. The way he used to. He had her in his arms. He was kissing her again and again, up and down her soft neck. She was pressing herself against him, laughing. He could feel those breasts, the hard little nipples against his chest. Her soft murmurs as he slid his hands over her arse and pulled her dress up. Oh, yeah. No stopping this time, because she wanted him just as he wanted her.

In your dreams, you moron!

When he and Jonty started going around to Lillian's place after school on a Thursday afternoon to discuss the class coming up, it was just Cokes or cups of coffee for a long time. Sometimes they'd be a little stoned before they got there. She knew, but she pretended she didn't.

'None of that!' she'd say, smiling, putting their little silver packets straight back into their pockets. 'I will not be an accomplice!'

But when they started going around there at night, usually ten or eleven on Friday or Saturday after they'd been out somewhere else and she'd got home from work, that's when things changed.

Alice was in bed by then, or out for the night staying with girlfriends. Tom and Jonty had usually been smoking already but they'd do more at her place or they'd all drink. Lillian liked vodka. She had this beautiful little crystal glass she always used. She took it very slowly and never seemed to get drunk, but on the other hand she didn't stop drinking for hour after hour.

Tom and Jonty would leave her place in the early morning. It was always quiet between them as they headed up the hill back to Tom's place.

Lillian loved Jonty because he was her sister's kid, and also because Jonty had the same kind of wildness in him that she had herself. But she was attracted to Tom. The physical pull was there all the time, but . . . way too dangerous to put into words. It was hidden under the surface for so long, he began to feel as though it would burst through of its own accord. *And isn't that what happened?*

Tom grimaces with pain as he tries to shift into a more comfortable position. He would never tell boastful lies about her. He would never desecrate her memory. He and Jonty were kids in their teens and she was in her forties. Tom was never her lover. Not in any normal sense anyway . . .

It took the cops three weeks to build up a case against Jonty. They were both interviewed by the police a number of times. At first Tom had no idea what suspicions they had. Somehow they'd picked up that he and Jonty had become friendly with her over the past year. At first they talked to them along with a whole lot of other people. Neither Tom nor Jonty had the feeling that they were being singled out.

The first chats with the coppers were friendly. Not held in the police station or anything like that. They teed it up with both sets of parents and came to the house to talk, or else agreed to meet in a café down in the main street.

There were two main guys from Melbourne Homicide. Detective Lloyd Hooper had this really easy laidback style that was kind of entrancing. Not much over thirty, he was tall and handsome and had one of those heavy moustaches that on anyone else would have been totally bizarre but on him was simply eccentric . . . in a good way. He was friendly and personable and his questions always seemed totally innocuous. 'Just need to get a picture of what was happening in her life, Tom,' he would say time and time again. 'We're talking to a lot of people, as you probably know. Hope you're fine with that?'

After the embarrassing business of having a close friendship with a forty-three-year-old woman was out of the way, it was all cool enough.

But Tom held back. Of course he did. He never came clean about his true feelings for Lillian, in spite of the detective telling him all kinds of shit that may or may not have even been true. 'Hey, Tom, I remember having a big crush on an older woman when I was around your age. Think I was nineteen and she was thirty-eight, and, well . . . she led me along a bit, I suppose. I didn't know what was happening really . . . and we ended up in bed a few times. She was my first and I'm not ashamed of it.' Just one of those things that happen in life. Did anything like that happen to you, Tom or was it . . . something else?'

'Well, something else, I guess,' Tom mumbled.

'Yeah?' Lloyd was so understanding. 'So what was it Tom?'

'Well, we were friends, and I . . .'

'You said *something else*, Tom. Can you explain?'

But Tom couldn't explain. He didn't want to and . . . he never did. So he'd come out with some bit of bullshit about them both getting off on history and Shakespeare and the rest of it. Which was true, too. But the detective wanted more and Tom held out.

The other detective was a quiet little guy. His name was Rowen Hill and he seemed to be Lloyd's sidekick even though he was quite a bit older. He wasn't half as easy to be with because his eyes darted around all the time. But he stayed in the background mostly, and hardly said anything, so Tom tended to forget about him. Looking back now, he understands they were working him hard for any detail that he might let slip.

Neither of those detectives blinked when Tom told them about him, Jonty and Lillian smoking dope and drinking and dancing together. Lloyd wanted to know all about the poetry sessions and their views about Dickens and Auden and Shakespeare. He never made Tom feel that there was anything odd about any of it.

By the end of the second week it began to dawn on Tom that they were talking to him and Jonty a lot more than to other people, and by the end of the third week he could see that they were really interested in Jonty.

'What kind of a guy is Jonno?' Rowen asked. His colourless darting eyes made Tom think of the ferrets that his uncle kept in cages. Lloyd wasn't there for some reason; maybe he'd gone out for a smoke. This guy was eyeballing Tom strangely, as though he knew about all the stuff that he was holding back.

'Well, he's my mate,' Tom said uncomfortably.

'Yeah, we know he's your mate,' ferret face snapped, 'so how would you describe him?'

'I dunno,' Tom shrugged awkwardly, 'he's a good guy.' But this was patently inadequate even to Tom's own ears. Hopeless. Jonty wasn't *a good guy*! Sure he was good-hearted, but he was also sharp and cool and funny and unpredictable and when they were together Tom sometimes felt as if he was living in a different realm to everyone else. It took up more energy being alive when you were around him. Jonty didn't just bumble along from one thing to another like other people. He was never content to stay bored.

'Tell me more about him.' The ferret was smiling now, trying to make up for snapping.

'Smart,' Tom said honestly. 'Very naturally smart.'

'You're close mates?'

'Well . . . yeah,' Tom was uneasy.

'So what does that involve?' the copper asked. 'What kind of things do you do?'

'Ordinary stuff,' Tom muttered. 'We just hang out together.'

'You two get up to a bit, though.' The ferret was laughing slyly.

'Not really.'

'How about that business in the local paper last year?'

'Yeah, well . . .' Tom shrugged. 'We were idiots.'

'Pretty dramatic!'

Tom nodded. Panic was rising in him at this point and he wasn't sure why. He'd already told Lloyd his version of that event and didn't want to go over it again. But Rowen was chewing his thumb, waiting for him to continue. When Tom turned around Lloyd was standing in the doorway with a sharp watchful expression on his face that Tom hadn't seen before.

Tom was suddenly absolutely freaked. In a police station, in his school uniform, answering questions about . . . his friends and his life because some woman had been murdered. This was no part of any plan he had for himself. This was . . . *shit! How did this happen to me?*

From then on he didn't trust either of them.

And it was at that point that Tom had begun to deliberately disengage from Jonty. It was an almost physical feeling, a bit like the painful peeling away of damaged skin. And it took ages. They still hung out together, they talked and laughed about it all. They rented DVDs and talked about sport. On the outside at least, things were normal until Jonty was charged and put away. But from that moment in the interview room, Tom had been looking for a way out.

'How about you tell us all over again?'

It was the end of Year Eleven – before they got to know Lillian – and very hot. Tom and Jonty had gone down to the river after school with the express purpose of getting stoned. After about an hour under the bridge they were both off their heads. They walked back into town laughing and kicking rocks, talking about movies they'd seen, singing lines of songs they loved and making plans for the summer holidays. There was a huge sheep transport truck parked on the highway, just outside the service station. The driver was obviously inside the roadhouse getting something to eat and drink.

Jonty stopped talking mid-sentence. He walked over to the back of the truck and peered in at the sheep, squashed together, their heads down, panting in the heat. Tom came up alongside him and peered in too. The smell of piss and shit and wool and misery was strong. Jonty was mumbling to himself as he circled around the truck, his face grim.

'We should let them out,' Tom joked weakly, wishing Jonty would hurry up so they could get out of the hot sun. But when Jonty came back around from the other side of the truck his eyes were ablaze with excitement.

'He left the keys in!'

'So,' Tom shrugged. 'I can't drive a truck, can you?'

'We'll take it anyway,' Jonty said.

'How?' Tom laughed uneasily.

'Can't be that difficult.'

But it was. It was very difficult. Crazily so. The bloody thing had fifteen gears! Neither of them had any idea at first, but of course it didn't take Jonty long to work out the basics. Within a few minutes they were moving, with Jonty driving and loving the whole gear business more with every second that passed. By the time they'd edged the monster out onto the main road, laughter was bubbling and buzzing and fizzing through them like lemonade. Tom's gut hurt, his eyes were streaming and for a while there he thought he was going to piss himself. Screaming like hyenas they headed straight into the centre of town. Luckily, it wasn't busy.

Sitting up next to Jonty in that huge monster was something else. Some part of Tom knew what they were doing was totally insane but they were too far gone now to stop.

Jonty was crunching inexpertly through the gears, his face a study of exhilaration. From high up in the cabin, Tom's home town looked different. Life was up for grabs. He wondered how far he could push out the edges of this boring schoolboy existence.

'Hey, Tommo,' Jonty turned to him with a grin as they passed the familiar bluestone town hall where they had speech night every year, 'wonder what this little town is called.'

'Slumberland,' Tom said, 'or maybe Yawning Hills!' They both cracked up again.

'We might skip it, then,' Jonty spluttered, sounding the horn recklessly as they thundered past the swimming pool and post office. 'Got to be more exciting places! Whaddya reckon?'

Heads turned to watch them but Tom didn't care. 'Reckon you might be right there, Jonno!'

Jonty hadn't quite mastered the brakes and at the corner of Miller and Poling Streets they almost collected a car. But once through that intersection they took the first left down a quiet street that led out to the highway, and were away.

'Where will we do it?' Tom said. 'Not too far, or we'll get caught.'

Jonty was getting used to the truck. Tom could see he was hell-bent on getting away from the rest of his life.

'A bit further,' Jonty grinned, 'see where we land up.'

The countryside out of town was pristine that day. Green paddocks full of peacefully grazing cows, hardly a cloud in the sky. It was hard for Tom to believe they were doing anything outrageous at all. They burned along the highway for eight kilometres to the Hobson Bridge, and directly after it Jonty made a sharp turn to the right, off onto a narrow lane full of cracks and potholes. *Oh jeez.* Tom felt his first pang of real concern as he bounced up, his head hitting the ceiling of the cabin. They were going way too fast.

'What's this road?'

'I dunno!' Jonty laughed. 'Let's see.'

'Slow down!' Tom said sharply as he was jolted up again.

'Once we let the sheep out we should just go on, Tommo.'

'With the truck?'

'Yeah. We could go north. Up to Darwin. Work it, you know?'

'*Work* it?'

'Hire it out!'

'It's registered, you stupid prick. They'd find us.'

'Not if we take the plates off and . . .'

'Paint it!' Tom chortled. 'Bright yellow!'

'Yeah!'

The truck hit a particularly deep pothole and they both bounced again to the roof of the cabin. Jonty was finding it hard to keep the thing on the track, he was laughing so hard.

Tom couldn't quite put his finger on when exactly reality kicked in, but when it did if was like being dipped in freezing liquid. They were two seventeen-year-olds, in their school uniforms, without even one driving licence between them but with a wad of strong dope in their pockets. And they were roaring along a dirt track in a huge truck with hundreds of sheep in the back.

'Hey, Jonty!' Tom shouted. 'Stop now.'

'Gotta get them to water.' Jonty was bending forward like a racing driver, gripping the steering wheel with both hands, staring straight ahead. The little track was heading through dense scrubland and getting narrower and rougher with each minute. Overhanging branches scraped the windscreen from all sides. Then suddenly, to Tom's relief, they were running alongside a creek. They came to a small bridge, and Jonty pulled up and opened his door.

'This will do.'

They both got out and walked around to the back of the truck.

'But how will we unload them?' Tom asked.

'Must be a ramp somewhere,' Jonty scrambled up onto the back gate of the truck.

Then Tom spied a ramp attached to the underneath of the chassis. They fitted the ramp to the back of the truck and Jonty got up and guided the first few sheep down. It worked brilliantly at first with just a trickle of sheep venturing out, Jonty escorting each animal down until it was safely aground. But when the rest smelled freedom at the other end of the ramp they started to bolt. Jonty was pushed out of the way in the stampede and fell heavily on his arse. There were no sides to the ramp and the truck was high. Most of the sheep made it, but too many didn't. By the time the last one was down, at least a dozen of them lay injured on either side of the ramp.

Tom wandered around trying to get the injured sheep up onto their legs again, but of course they couldn't stand; their legs, and sometimes their necks and backbones, were broken.

Jonty simply sat there amid the sheep, looking as though he'd landed on Mars.

It was very hot and there wasn't much to say. They simply looked at each other.

Tom, suddenly hit with a raging thirst, blundered off towards the creek with the rest of the sheep to look for water. He lay down on his belly to drink at the dirty trickle, feeling the full catastrophe creeping in around the edges of his consciousness like a dark shroud. The dope was wearing off fast. *This had to be some kind of nightmare!*

When he got back from the creek, Jonty was in the cabin frantically looking through the glove box and behind the seats, throwing all kinds of stuff out onto the grass as he did so. Papers and half-finished bottles of soft drink, a bag of tomatoes and about six greasy half-finished takeaway dinners. Tom wasn't much interested. He squatted in the shade against the truck and tried to think what to do next.

'You haven't got a pocketknife, have you?' Jonty called above the din of the distressed sheep.

'No.'

'Here we go!' Jonty jumped down from the cabin brandishing a large carving knife with a worn curved blade. 'This will have to do.' He jumped up again into the cabin and after another minute came down with a small black grinding-stone. He rubbed it vigorously on his jeans and then spat on it a few times.

'What are you doing?' Tom frowned.

'We can't leave 'em like this, Tommo,' Jonty replied, rubbing the blade in slow circular movements against the stone, first one side and then the other.

Tom stared at the bent head. The sound and smell of all those distressed sheep closed in around him; the stench was overpowering.

Jonty waved at the stricken sheep with his knife.

'We gotta put them out of their misery.'

'*What?*'

He was serious. Tom was filled with the urgent desire to simply walk away. To get as far away as he could, as fast as possible. He stood up, but panic made his legs shaky, so he squatted down next to Jonty.

'We can't do that, Jonno,' he said urgently.

'You think I *want* to?' Jonty snapped.

'Shit! They don't belong to us.'

Jonty's only response was to look at the poor bleating thing nearest to them. Wild-eyed with pain, she was panting and kicking uselessly. One leg was sticking out the wrong way, but her back might have been broken too, or maybe her neck, because she couldn't shift her position at all. It was a sickening sight. Jonty was right.

But Tom had never seen an animal killed. Just trying to imagine it made him dizzy. *Oh Christ!*

Jonty stood and tested the blade with his finger.

'We should try and get 'em back in to the truck, Jonno,' Tom shouted. 'Take them back into town and deal with it from there.'

'Don't be pissweak, Mulla.'

'There has to be some other way.'

'You got a gun?' Jonty said seriously.

'Of course I don't have a fucking gun.'

'Then we've gotta do it. Listen to them.'

Tom closed his eyes, hearing only the wild desperate bleating of the animals. *What jerks they were to do this! What complete and utter fuckwits!* He was almost crying as he counted the sheep. There were fourteen badly injured animals.

'Come on,' Jonty said sharply.

Tom stood up. *Time to cut throats.* He wasn't in a movie anymore. This was real. And he couldn't do it.

'You don't have to watch.' Jonty flashed Tom a grim smile. 'Being a lawyer's son and all.' It was the joke between them. Most of the time they were on a par. They prided themselves on not being scared of much. But Jonty lived out on the farm, so of course he'd had more experience with the basic stuff. Cows gave birth and sometimes died. He spoke of shooting wild dogs and poisoning rabbits, of dealing with sick sheep and chopping wood. And then of course there was his father . . .

'Fuck off!' Tom muttered angrily. There was nothing more to say.

Jonty had the first sheep between his knees now. Very matter-of-factly he bent over from the waist. Holding its chin with one hand, he pulled the head back so its neck was exposed. Then, he made a swift deep slice across the throat. The creature kicked frantically, its eyes big with terror, as the brilliant blood spurted out and frothed onto the ground. Jonty straightened up and stood waiting as the creature bled to death. It took about three minutes. Tom watched mutely from the sidelines, as the creature's life leaked away.

When the sheep was absolutely still, Jonty leant down and wiped the blade clean, back and forth on the sheep's back. Tom made himself keep looking at the almost completely severed head with the glazed-over eyes, the gash across its throat glistening red and raw in the sun. *Look at this*, he told himself, *learn something*.

'One down,' Jonty said.

'We don't have the right, Jonno.' Tom protested again weakly.

'We got the responsibility,' Jonty muttered and shooed away

some other sheep that were milling around the afflicted ones. 'Go on, piss off!' he yelled at them.

Tom had the feeling that Jonty was talking to him as well. He watched him move on to the next wide-eyed animal frantically kicking on the ground. Just before putting his knife to its neck, he looked up at Tom seriously. 'Life is a jungle, and you're kidding yourself if you think it isn't.'

A slow meditative dreaminess overtook Jonty at this point. As he moved on to the next sheep and then the next he seemed to be moving into a different space inside his head as well. He'd stopped being the wild, reckless guy that Tom had been mucking around with before. Tom looked at his watch. Only an hour before they'd been under the bridge, smoking, spluttering and giggling, raving on about music and getting stoned.

The *life-is-a-jungle* crap was what his father was always on about. He loved to rave on about the *survival of the fittest. Get used to it, buddy! What else had Jonty learnt from his father?* Tom watched his friend cut another throat. Jonty's feelings about his old man were way more complex than he ever admitted. Tom often heard the grudging admiration in Jonty's voice when he told the latest funny story about Jed.

Jonty had killed five sheep by the time the police arrived. The unmistakable high-pitched siren set alight Tom's most basic instinct to hide or run. *What will they say?* He watched Jonty's expression change as the police siren became louder. His wild green eyes gleamed with renewed excitement. He was going to enjoy whatever came next. At that moment, Tom truly admired him. He did. He was proud to have such an audacious and courageous friend. But it was at that moment, too, that Tom knew that he was different, and that their paths would eventually diverge.

If not today, then some time in the future.

'So how are you feeling?' A female voice breaks Tom's train of thought. He twists his head around but can't see who is talking. Gradually his eyes pick up the detail. A girl in jeans and a fitted black polo-neck jumper bends to put a tray onto the little coffee table. She flicks back a long loose ponytail and drags the table nearer to him. That's when he sees her face and the puzzle all falls into place.

'Alice?' Tom says warily.

'Yeah.' She pours hot tea into a mug.

It's all flooding back now: the concert, the fight and Jonty coming to his aid. Then Alice and her friends in the taxi. But lying on a bed in this room still doesn't quite make sense.

'How long have I been here?'

'It's nearly five now.' She looks at her watch.

'So have you been at work today?' Tom asks.

'It's Sunday,' she answers curtly.

'Is this where you live?'

'My grandmother's place.' She puts two spoonfuls of sugar in the steaming cup, without asking if Tom wants it or not, and then sits on the end of the bed holding it out for him to take. He sits up a bit trying to ignore the pain in his arse and side. 'I rang and told your dad about what happened. Told him I'd call him again when you woke up.'

'Jeez.' Tom shakes his head. 'Okay. Thanks.' Only home three weeks and he's already making a fool of himself! The old man will be fine about it all but that bloody Nanette will put it on him for sure. The woman is one big drag. Running after him all the time, making him feel like he's some little kid who needs a big sister called Nanette to sort out what he'll wear and eat that day – not to mention how he's going to plan the rest of his life! Tom doesn't know how his old man puts up with it. This little fiasco will play right into her fucking toolbox. Get her right in the groove she likes best.

'So my old man's gonna pick me up?' he asks grimly.

'Yeah, but you'll have to walk to the gate,' the girl tells him. 'I don't want *her* to know about you being here.'

'Your grandmother?' Tom takes the mug with two hands which are, much to his embarrassment, trembling. 'Why not?' He brings it to his mouth and the tea sloshes out onto his shirt, scalding his chest. He looks down. It's not his shirt. It's some old worn khaki thing about ten sizes too big. He is about to ask her about it but she is looking away blankly, frowning as though she's already thinking of something else far more important. The tea is fantastic, though, so Tom slurps it down thirstily.

'She goes berserk,' she explains at last, breaking open a packet of sweet biscuits and offering them to Tom, 'if she sees a strange car in the grounds.'

'My old man knows her.' Tom takes two biscuits and stuffs them into his mouth. It hurts to chew but he's starving. 'And you're working for him.'

She shrugs dismissively.

'The doctor is coming to check you again, then we'll go.'

'Again?' Tom says in surprise. 'I don't remember any doctor.'

'Who do you think bandaged your face?' she snaps.

Whoa! Her irritable tone startles Tom. *This chick doesn't like me one little bit, in spite of the nice-kind-nurse routine.*

'She'll see *his* car won't she?'

'He's in with her now . . . I told him to come down afterwards, and not to say anything.'

'Listen, I reckon I'll be okay.' Tom finishes off the tea. Alice takes the cup and refills it without asking if he wants more. In fact, another cup would go down very well, but Tom wants out, so he starts shifting himself around a bit testing to see how bad his injuries are. Apart from the face, it's just the ribs and bum and left shin that really hurt. He figures he'll be able to walk. He doesn't want to hang around with this girl. The little scene in the office where he was only trying to be friendly comes back and . . . sticks in his throat.

'Hey listen, Alice,' he says, shifting his legs gingerly onto the floor. 'Thanks, but I'll go get checked out by my own doctor.' He tries to stand up but the movement makes him dizzy. A wave of nausea floods over him again and he falls back against the pillows.

'Ah shit!' he whispers. His breath is really painful too.

'You had concussion,' she hands him the second mug of tea, 'two cracked ribs, a lot of bruising and . . .' She is frowning deeply as she folds her arms tightly across her chest, not looking at Tom.

'So?' He tries a smile on her with no results. 'I'm tough.'

She hands him two more biscuits with her fingers.

'Listen, I know you're sick and everything,' she says, ignoring his weak attempt at a joke, 'but I need to ask you something.' She gets up and stands a few feet away, looking down at him, arms still crossed, her long fingers playing up and down her arms nervously as though she's practising the piano. Her face swims a little in front of his eyes. *So much like her mother!* Younger of course and there is a whole different vibe about her too, more serious, whereas Lillian was always smiling. That's it. This girl is frowning so hard that her eyebrows nearly meet in the middle of her face. Underneath all his aches and pains, Tom feels wary.

'Fire away,' he says coolly, wishing like hell he had an easy escape. He curses his own idiocy and swears not to ever get caught in this kind of situation again. He couldn't give a shit if the wacko fat chick is Lillian's kid and working for his old man – maybe it is *because* of those things – but he doesn't want anything to do with her.

'Did Jonty van der Weihl kill my mother?'

Tom's head jerks up in shock and he's looking straight into her big dark eyes. They're like pools of water, two lakes on a calm day, so deep you can't see the bottom.

He is not sure if he's heard right. Maybe he imagined it.

Still frowning, she stares back at him, waiting. Then, when he doesn't say anything, she goes over to the window and pulls the blinds open. The room floods with soft winter light. No more the quaint little film set; the room is a simply furnished workman's flat.

He can see her properly now, too. *She's actually beautiful.* Tom shakes his head, about to say that he has no idea how to answer her question and that until the police charge someone and bring them to trial then no one should really speculate. But he doesn't say it. He can't somehow. There is something about this girl that demands the truth.

'I'm not sure,' he says, looking straight at her.

'You think it's possible?' she says quietly.

'Anything is possible.'

'You know him. Do you think he did it?'

Tom looks away. 'Yes,' he says calmly. 'I think he did it.'

He's not looking at her, so he can't see her face but he hears her sharp intake of breath.

'Will you help me, then?' she whispers.

Help her? What the hell does that mean?

But . . . he knows. He knows what she means and what's more he knows with everything in him that he doesn't want to have anything to do with it. He puts his cup down and tries again to sit up properly, this time with better results. He's sitting on the edge of the bed now, gingerly bringing his feet to the floor and he doesn't feel too bad. So far, so good.

The truth is, he doesn't want anything to do with either of them, Jonty or Alice. He doesn't want to see either of them again or have to think about the murder *ever again*! His feet are on the floor now and both his arms are propping him up. He just needs to stand and he'll be right. He manages to do this and then looks around for where his shoes might be.

Right near his feet as it turns out. He slowly slips one on and then the other. He'll walk home without doing them up.

'No,' he says, looking straight at her. 'I am very sorry about what happened to your mother . . . but the answer is no. It's all over as far as I'm concerned. I can't help you.'

*So it's all over. All over! I would laugh except I'm crying so hard. All over!
My mother is murdered and it doesn't matter to him that whoever did it is
walking around this town, free as a bird? It's all over for him. Finished. What
gives that skinny tall smartarse the right to look me in the eye and say that?
I wish I could kill him! I would too if I could get away with it . . . I'd come
around to his house and bash his head in with a brick if I could!*

   All over?

   *I don't believe him. Not for a minute. It's NOT all over . . . even for
him. It's not all over for anyone.*

It is not until three weeks after that weird night that Alice sees
Tom again.

   Alice loves her hands. Enjoys looking at the long pale
fingers and the perfectly oval cuticles. Like little half moons.
Unlike the rest of her body, which feels like someone else's half the
time, her hands truly belong to her. They are subtle and elegant
and quick, and they give her real pleasure.

Her job is good for perfectly tended, elegant hands. Sitting at the desk tapping away and then reaching out for the phone and taking a call, writing notes with one hand, drumming the desk with the other. Why, she could be anybody! That lovely clicking sound of nails on wood never fails to gives Alice courage, makes her feel older than her eighteen years, as though she might be able to direct the outcome of events, after all. Yes, it's her birthday today! From today the little cottage in Pitt Street is legally hers. Alice has all kinds of plans that she won't tell anyone about.

After three weeks in Luke's office, the whole sensation of working on a film set hasn't left Alice. She enjoys acting her part, typing letters neatly, along with answering the phone and putting people on hold. She enjoys opening the mail every day and arranging it into piles, and folding letters, putting them into envelopes and popping them in the post, then hurrying back to the office for the next task. It is so much better than hanging around at home or being at uni. She likes taking orders from the gently spoken Martha, who is always patient and kind, and knows how to have a joke too.

Sometimes Alice gets to knock quietly on Luke's door to see if he might be free to speak to someone important or to sign some papers, and she loves the way his face brightens when he sees her walk in.

'G'day there Alice!' he exclaims in a loud friendly voice, the concentrated frown rolling away as he holds out his blunt, middle-aged, nail-bitten hand. 'So what have you got for me today?' He might grin as he takes the papers from her, thump them down on the desk, and say something like, 'The usual crap, I take it?' which will have them both laughing. Or he might push his chair back and put his hands behind his head and give her some dry advice like, 'Get into some field that doesn't involve other people's problems, Alice. Take it from me!' Or he'll give her a quick run-through of his take on something. 'Real estate agents have to be the most rapacious greedy bastards on the face of this earth, Alice. Much worse than lawyers! Remember you heard that first here!'

Once, he waved for her to sit down opposite him. He finished his phone call and then asked her seriously if everything was okay. Was she happy working in his office? Alice became immediately wary, wondering if this was a prelude to telling her she'd done something wrong. Absolute panic set in when she thought he might be going to sack her! *Oh God!*

'Yes,' she gulped, and managed to mumble, 'very happy.'

'Well, that's good,' he said, eyeing her seriously, not having noticed any of her inner consternation, 'because we're very happy with you. Martha tells me you are an absolute pleasure to have in the office. No surprise to me, though; I knew you'd be good.' His mobile phone suddenly rang and he frowned and rolled his eyes when he checked who the caller was. 'Got to take this one I'm afraid, Alice,' he smiled at her. But before putting the phone to his ear he said warmly, 'You're a real asset to have around, Alice! I hope you'll stay with us for a while longer.'

Alice left his office walking on air, almost crying with happiness.

I wish you were my father! is the sentence that flies through her head. *Your son doesn't deserve you!*

Occasionally the younger staff members invite Alice out for a coffee at lunchtime, and once or twice they suggest she might like to go out with them to the pub on Friday night. She is polite, but she always declines. She has Sylvie and Leyla to go out with on the weekends, and at work Luke and Martha are more than enough.

Luke is regularly in court representing all kinds of clients. But this day is more serious, so he's briefed a city barrister to defend a client on aggravated assault and burglary charges. Late in the day he calls through to the office for some documents to be brought down to the court as soon as possible, and Martha suggests Alice take them.

The trial is upstairs in Courtroom Six. Alice pushes open the heavy silent door nervously, and bows to the judge in the way she's been told. She stands by the door looking around for Luke. Ah! There he is, sitting at a table under the judge's bench with about six other barristers and lawyers, all of them dressed in wigs and gowns. The jury of twelve is seated to the left of the judge and a pale-skinned middle-aged woman in a dark suit is in the dock giving evidence. Feeling self-conscious in her flat shoes and winter coat, Alice has to steel herself to walk past the public gallery, the security guards and the police. She hands over the file, feeling as though every eye is on her.

'Thanks, Alice,' Luke whispers, giving her one of his smiles. 'Hang around a bit if you want.'

'You sure that's okay?' she asks, pleased. The office is quiet and Martha has already told her she doesn't have to hurry back.

'Of course!' He points back to the public pews. 'Park yourself over there.'

There was no need to be self-conscious. These kinds of small interruptions happen all the time during a court case. Once settled, she looks around to see that no one has taken much notice of her at all. They're all paying attention to the woman in the dock, who is nervously giving an account of being attacked.

Mrs Susan Henley of 15 Miller Street, West Warrnambool, came home late one night to find her ex-husband in her kitchen, going through her cupboards. When she objected, he'd attacked her, held a knife to her throat, verbally abused her, then kicked and punched her, continually threatening her life. Alice finds herself leaning forward, her breath becoming short as she listens to the woman give her account of two terrible hours under the man's control before she managed to escape. The story proceeds at a halting pace, with questions from the woman's barrister prompting her for more details.

The accused's barrister stands up. 'Mrs Henley, would you say that your husband loved you?' The question seems to startle the woman. It is as if she's been slapped. One of her pale hands goes straight to her mouth and the mousy-blonde hair that she has pinned back from her face comes fractionally loose. What a question! Everyone in the courtroom takes a breath as they wait for her to respond.

'Mrs Henley. Let me repeat the question. Would you say that—'

'Objection, Your Honour!' Mrs Henley's lawyer stands to intervene. 'This has nothing to do—'

'Objection overruled.'

And so it goes on. 'I think he loves me,' Mrs Henley is barely audible, 'in his own way.'

'Mrs Henley, would you mind repeating that,' the crisp voice of the barrister interjects, 'I don't think the jury heard you.'

'He loves me . . . in his own way,' she whispers.

In his own way . . . Alice's eyes swim with tears as the soft hesitant voice of the woman in the dock drones on. Thoughts and memories of her own mother build in her chest, one on top of the other, like a pile of beautiful river stones made smooth by water and sun, each one so strong and warm and . . . *alive*.

Alice sits there in the public gallery of the local courthouse and the great shocking fact that her mother is dead hits her as forcefully and brutally as it did the very first time she knew it to be true. It's a semitrailer filled with bricks riding straight towards her, crushing her flat. *Dead.* Her mother is dead and buried in the ground and Alice will never see her again. Can it really be true . . .

She opened the back door in the early morning, a normal enough fifteen-year-old schoolgirl, and minutes later . . . she was somebody else entirely. Who exactly, she didn't know, but in some deep way she knew she would never again be that girl who came bounding out of the house to ask if she could buy her lunch that day, seeing as her mother had obviously forgotten to make it.

Her mother was there all right, but . . . she was lying in the grass under the clothes line down near the back fence. Her head was twisted to the side and her work dress was up above her knees, one arm was bent back almost under her head and the other was across her chest, as though she might have been simply resting. But she wasn't asleep. No. Alice could tell straight away. One of her eyes was open, glassy and lifeless. A stream of small black ants made their way to the blood around her head and in her hair.

And the necklace was missing. The necklace that her mother had taken to wearing all the time. Alice felt nothing at first. She hovered above the scene like a bird, watching, waiting for movement so she could dive once again into her real life. She wondered vaguely if she should listen for a heartbeat or feel for a pulse in the way she had learnt in First Aid at school. But she didn't. She stood there, rooted to the spot, breathing in and out and looking down at her mother who . . . *was no longer her mother.*

Silence, heavy and thick, had descended on the warm summer morning. Her ears felt blocked, as though she was underwater. Alice twisted her face away, up to the perfect blue sky, and wondered if she went inside and came out again, retraced that small journey from the back door to the clothes line, would this thing, whatever it was, undo itself? Like a few badly knitted rows on an otherwise perfect woollen jumper. Maybe she could just pull out the stitches and re-knit that section. And instead of *this*, if she came out again, she very well might find her mother pegging clothes to the line, or up behind the shed planting the new shrubs that she'd bought only the day before.

Alice knelt down beside her mother and began to search frantically in the long grass for the necklace. If only she could find that lovely thing, then her mother might spring to life again.

Back in the courtroom, Alice's eyes are awash with tears. She is trying like crazy to think of something else, because she is desperate not to break down in a public place. But she isn't hearing the woman's testimony any longer, she is hearing her own mother's voice, waking her in the morning. *Up and away, babe. It's a brand new day.* Too *incredible* that she will never hear that voice again.

Her face is hot now. She can hardly even breathe because the howl is building in her chest like a balloon getting bigger and bigger. This has always been the way tears come for Alice: without warning, like a freak storm in the middle of a pleasant day. If she'd had any idea, any warning that they would be about to make their grand entrance, she wouldn't have come. It's a courtroom for God's sake. If only she'd stayed away! She tries not to sniff as she fumbles about in her pocket for a hanky, then blows her nose in a bid to calm herself. But the tears have begun to seep from her eyes like fresh water from a spring. She takes a furtive look around but luckily no one seems to be paying her any attention.

Alice bites her lip, as the tears spill down her cheeks. She gulps and risks looking around again. And there, sitting just across from her, is . . . *Tom Mullaney! Oh God!* There he is, sitting in the space reserved for the press and the police, a pen in his hand, some kind of notebook in front of him and . . . he is not writing anything. He is not looking at the woman in the dock, nor trying to suss out the jury's reaction to the evidence. He is staring at Alice.

No! He has seen her helpless gulps and flushed cheeks. Seen the tears. She is coming undone in front of *him*!

Alice locks eyes with him for a flat three seconds before she turns away, overwhelmed with humiliation. She wishes she had Leyla's hunting rifle. If she did, she would shoot him right between the eyes. Stone dead. That's the way she'd like to see Tom Mullaney! Lying on the floor, quite still and unable to see inside her pain.

How dare you look at me!

There is nothing for it, Alice stands awkwardly and makes for the door. She remembers to bow towards the bench before she grabs the heavy handle, pulls it open and rushes out into the quiet lobby. There are a few straggling family groups and a hotchpotch of 'singles', waiting about on the rows of seats, most looking worried or bored. The younger guys, with their tatts and weird haircuts, look uncomfortable in their neat cheap suits, put on especially for their court appearances. They all look up when Alice comes rushing out, but she is so upset she hardly notices anything around her. She presses the button for the lift but when she sees it is stuck on the ground floor, she runs for the stairs.

Down two flights and then past the information desk, not crying now but panicking, because her breathing has become shallow. She knows she must look a fright with her tear-stained face and red eyes. A few police standing in front of the water fountain turn to watch her rushing past, but she is only barely aware of them. At last she is through the sliding glass door and out into the weak sunshine. She takes a few deep breaths, heads for the seat furthest away from the street, plonks down and blows her nose again. The terrible need to howl is slowly ebbing away, but her hands are trembling. Hopefully Luke didn't see her exit. Her enjoyment of the job is dependent on maintaining a certain formality between them. Things must stay on this even keel or she won't be able to manage the job at all. She throws her head back and shuts her eyes, as a shudder of shame passes through her. Tom Mullaney witnessed her sorrow and that makes her feel exposed, like he has seen her naked. Of all people! She doesn't want *anyone* to see her like that, but especially not him.

'Alice?'

Alice jerks into a sitting position, opens her eyes and looks around wildly. He is standing just a few feet away, in his jeans and sneakers, looking down at her. One eye is still a little swollen and there is a deep bruise on the other side of his face and around his neck. *Tom Mullaney.*

'Can I join you?'

She says nothing as he sits down on the far end of the seat. Alice is desperate to get up and walk off but can't seem to move. He pulls a packet of cigarettes out of his pocket.

'Smoke?' He holds the pack out to her, and Alice, who has never smoked in her life – in fact hates the smell and the whole idea of smoking – leans across and takes one with trembling fingers, noticing the cuts along his fingers. *Well I've got to do something!*

She puts it in her mouth. He leans across to light it for her and she takes a tentative puff. *Ugh! How revolting.* Worse than she thought. But it gives her something to do while she garners her courage to tell him . . . *what*? She can't remember. Her mind has gone blank. The pale sky above her is packed with dead, swollen clouds that might give way any minute with some ghastly secretion. Not water. No. What are clouds? These ones look like . . . *bags of pus*. She shudders, thinking of them oozing out over the world. They are just sitting up there with their disgusting contents, taking up space, and air. Tom doesn't say anything for a while, just crosses his stretched-out legs at the ankle and blows a thin stream of smoke into the air.

'Pretty gruelling in there, huh?' he says eventually.

But Alice doesn't answer. If she plays dead he might leave her alone. Moments pass and he continues to sit there as though he has every right.

In the end, it is Alice who opens the conversation. 'What do you want?' Her voice is hoarse.

'I saw you run out,' he mumbles, 'and I realised that I never thanked you for your . . . help that night. So thanks, Alice. Thanks a lot.'

'Okay,' Alice murmurs, taking another tentative puff. *Just go away will you. I don't need you or your thanks!* But she doesn't say that. She wonders if he's noticed the cylinder of grey ash at the end of her cigarette. She can't even smoke properly. *I'm a fake smoker.* Another thing to feel embarrassed about. If only the ground would open up.

'Just *okay*?' He gives a wry smile.

Alice meets his eye briefly but doesn't return the smile.

'Actually, I'm lying,' he says, more forcefully, as though he's only now decided on something important. He folds his arms across his chest. 'I didn't follow you out here to thank you at all,' he sighs, 'it's about something else.'

'What?' she sniffs coldly.

He shifts in his seat and clears his throat a couple of times.

'It's a bit . . . difficult,' he mutters. She flicks the ash onto the ground and takes a deep furious drag on the cigarette. Her throat immediately lights up and she begins to cough and splutter. *Oh, get on with it, you wanker, you pretty boy!* She wishes that she had the guts to tell him to stick his *difficult* right up his arse! The coughing fit over . . . she is still glued to her seat.

'I've been thinking a lot about . . . stuff,' he tries again.

'*Stuff?*' she mumbles sarcastically under her breath.

'About what you asked me . . . last time,' he replies, lifting both hands helplessly as though to say, *Come on, Alice, give me a break.*

But she won't. She won't! She *hates* him. Alice suddenly has the sensation of being caught in a mudslide, of being sucked down inch by inch from where she is sitting.

'I saw you crying in there.' He moves closer, waving his burning cigarette in front of him like some kind of divining rod. 'It made me feel—'

'None of your business,' she cuts in sharply. 'The way I feel is none of your business.'

'I know that, but . . .' he speaks fast, 'you asked me to help you. I just wondered what you had in mind.'

'Nothing!' Her tone is more unpleasant than she intends, but she can't seem to help that. To soften it now would be like a semi-apology and there is no way she is going to apologise to this handsome, skinny jerk. 'I had nothing in mind. Only that if he did it, if he killed my mother, then he shouldn't be just *walking around*!' Her voice catches in her throat.

'I agree,' he says quickly. 'He shouldn't be just walking around.'

'And he is.'

'I know . . . why you're angry.'

'No you don't!' she snaps.

'Well, I do, partly,' he says tentatively. 'I knew your mother and I refused to do what I can to help get justice for her death.'

'Her murder,' Alice cuts in ferociously, feeling her throat constrict and fresh tears rush up behind her eyes. She looks away, but she doesn't care that much any more if he does see her. 'Justice for her *murder*, you mean!'

'Her murder then,' he mutters.

'It's different to just dying.' She is almost choking as she speaks.

'Yes,' he agrees slowly, 'it is different.'

Tears begin to splash down her cheeks. Alice butts out the stupid cigarette, does up her coat and wraps the scarf more tightly around her neck. She stands up and walks off without saying goodbye.

TOM

No cameras are allowed in court, so when the editor of the newspaper found out that Tom could draw, he sent him down to get a likeness of the key players in the aggravated assault case. Tom had no idea that his old man was representing the accused. Since he has been home, they haven't talked much about Luke's work. Tom used to love hearing about different cases, all the stories about what was going down around town, the burglaries and the divorces, and who was suing who over what. Now he gets the feeling that Luke would rather leave work at the office. Whenever they do start some real talk at home, Nanette inevitably makes a grand entrance to complain about the cigarette smoke or the dog being inside, and the conversation is truncated.

When a girl carrying a bundle of documents walks into court, Tom doesn't take much notice. She's dressed in boring, old-woman clothes and her face is half-hidden by a scarf. But when she goes over to give the files to his father he recognises her. *Alice Wishart*. Before then, Tom had been doodling about with his pen trying to get a likeness of the woman on the witness stand, and idly wishing his father wasn't representing the smirking mongrel on the other side of the courtroom. But as soon as Alice Wishart sits down, he can't look anywhere else. He is drawn to her like a moth to a flame.

The way she leans forward to listen, so still and serious and concentrated, with her arms folded over her chest. Her face reminds Tom of one of those black-and-white portrait shots taken in the forties of Italian peasant woman at funerals or going about their tough work in the fields. Stolen images of grief and hardship and familial closeness. *Where are all those people now? Do they have any idea that their faces have made the photographic careers of strangers?* Her face seems to contain so much. It has seen a lot, and felt a lot, yet is still young and vibrant and . . . beautiful. The strong nose and chin and heavy eyebrows are almost masculine, but the delicacy of bone structure and the tenderness around her mouth and eyes belong to a woman.

Tom watches Alice Wishart as the other woman continues her testimony. Watches her frown clear, her mouth open and her cheeks become flushed. It's like watching the sky as a storm builds, those eyes widening and filling with tears. They glisten in the milky-pale light coming down from the narrow high windows of the courtroom. His own heart moves up into his throat, suddenly swollen with a weird grief. He wants to howl too, to shout and chuck his drawings, along with the rest of his life, right up in the air.

She blows her nose and tries to wipe her eyes without drawing attention to herself, but the tears continue to pour down her cheeks. And then, when she looks up and sees him looking at her, it is as though everything closes down around them and becomes very still. No one is breathing. No one else is in the room. They stare at each other for . . . *how long*? Tom has no idea, but for that time he seems to *know* her. Every single thing about her becomes clear. It feels as though he is looking right into the soul of Alice Wishart. It lies open before him like a wide, long pane of glittering glass. So delicate and beautiful and . . . ready to break.

At the same time, Tom can see that she doesn't like what is happening one little bit, that she is actually angry with him for watching her. He tries to smile to let her know that it's okay, but can't. He wants to look away. In fact, he wants to *get away* from the whole situation. But he can't. Instead he is drawn in, further and further into the turmoil that is . . . *her.* It's like some invisible rope is drawing him in against his will.

Tom watches her get up and rush out of the room and he can feel the deep wild strands of insanity coalesce inside him. *I love you,* is the sentence that runs through his head as he closes his sketchbook and packs it away. The words come to him with such force and defiance that he has the feeling that he's actually said them aloud when, of course, he hasn't. He has to speak to her.

But how crazy is that? *I love you! Fuck.* Nothing about it makes any sense. He has hardly exchanged a dozen sentences with Alice Wishart. He doesn't know her. Physically, she isn't his type and yet . . . *I want her. No one else. I love you, Alice Wishart, and I want to help you! We belong together . . .*

It takes all Tom's self-discipline not to break into a run as he makes his way out of the courtroom after her.

Alice

'You two have gotta help me with Eric!' Alice is walking the twins to the door of the office. 'Come up with a bright idea or two.'

'When does he arrive?'

'Tonight, for three days. What can I do with him?'

'Okay,' Sylvie sighs. 'Bring him out to the farm tomorrow and we'll take him shooting.'

Alice tries to imagine Eric standing at the back of a Land Rover with a shotgun in his skinny pale hands and she groans. 'This is a guy who has hardly ever touched an animal in his whole life!' she tries to explain.

'Then he'll probably *really* enjoy killing one,' Sylvie says dryly.

Alice thinks of the big round cow pats and lumps of chicken shit in the paddocks surrounding their little cottage, and of their father, Charlie, coming in from work, his overalls and hobnail boots bloody from a day at the meatworks. Like a lot of city people, Eric is fastidious about personal cleanliness. She bites her lip and frowns. How will he handle it?

'What sort of car does he drive?' Sylvie wants to know.

'He's coming by train.'

'I thought you said he was rich!'

'He is,' Alice sighs, 'but he tends to get lost driving.'

'Hasn't he heard of maps?'

Eric has an old BMW that had belonged to his mother, but Alice has never seen him drive it. It sits in his parking spot at college, like a king among all the Holdens and nifty little Japanese numbers, and never seems to be moved. Once, when they were running late for something, Alice asked him whether they should take the car instead of waiting for the tram. Eric was evasive. 'I enjoy my car,' he said dreamily. 'I just don't really like driving it very much.'

'So he's the full and utter geek, is he?' Sylvie says grimly.

'Well, not exactly—'

'Sounds like the complete package of pure nerd,' her sister cuts in.

'Just be prepared for a shock,' Alice tries to explain.

'A shock?'

'He's got carrot-coloured hair and big ears.'

'Oh!' Sylvie's face twists with disdain. 'Do they stick out?'

'Hmmm. Sort of.'

'I won't be able to take him seriously then,' she declares matter-of-factly. 'I've got a thing about *ears*.'

'You'll like him,' Alice laughs, 'I promise.'

'Sure,' Leyla sighs drolly as she leaves through the front door of Mullaney's Law office. 'I'm *in love* already.'

To make matters worse, her grandmother is insisting on a formal dinner to meet 'her young man'! When Alice tried to explain that Eric is just a friend, her grandmother gave one of her knowing little chuckles and said, 'Oh I've heard that before, young lady!' So what is Alice meant to do? Preparations are afoot for a formal meal! Helen, the housekeeper, has been asked to stay back to cook and wait on the table. Every time Alice thinks about it she feels sick.

Alice goes down to the railway station in her grandmother's silver Bentley with Colin, the gardener, driving. He is a quiet balding man of fifty, with a heavy gut and blunt features, who has been working for Phyllis for ten years. According to her grandmother, they've never had 'cross words' even once, and that makes him a certified saint as far as Alice is concerned. Either a saint or fundamentally flawed in some way. He is one of the very few of her grandmother's employees who've lasted more than a year.

Colin adores the car. He opens the door for Alice and insists that she sit in the back to be *chauffeured like a lady*. He positions himself behind the wheel, running his big rough hands reverentially over the leather seats and dashboard, whistling his appreciation under his breath. They get to the station early and when Alice suggests that they drive around for a while Colin's blank expression changes into one of total delight.

'You reckon she'd mind, love?'

'She won't know, will she?' Alice murmurs. So they drive around town with Colin giving Alice an animated account of the car's finer features. There is the purring gearbox and the oak dashboard, the quality leather seats and the second-to-none suspension.

'They don't make 'em like this any more, Alice.'

Glad to have made his day, Alice pretends to be interested, but she's heard it all before.

'So you reckon these old cars are better, Colin?'

'Well, of course the new cars have all the latest fandangles,' he sighs, 'but I'd pick this model any day over the new Jag XF, for example, or any of those Saabs or BMWs.'

'You should take this car out more often,' Alice says. She imagines herself swanning around in this grand old bomb, dressed in a fabulous shiny evening frock, jewels around her neck, a tall glass of bubbly in one hand and a long black cigarette-holder in the other. Maybe she could talk the twins into it for a lark.

'Feel free to take the keys and go for a spin, Colin. She'll never know. I promise you.'

'I'd never do that, love,' he sighs.

'Think of it as a perk!' Alice laughs.

'I'd never go behind her back.' Colin isn't laughing. 'She's been too good to me.' He catches Alice's questioning eye in the rear-vision mirror.

'Has she?' Alice is genuinely curious.

'Too right she has,' Colin says warmly.

'But doesn't she drive you absolutely nuts?'

He laughs. 'There is another side to her.'

They are pulling up in the railway car park now and Alice is already thinking about something else when Colin continues, 'I done ten years inside, missy. No one would touch me as soon as they knew. Couldn't get a job. Your grandma knew all about that. She just said if I mucked up, I'd be out on my ear, but that I could start the next day.'

'Really?'

'Yep. She's got guts that one!'

Ten years! What for? Alice studies the back of his neatly combed head and his big square clean hands with the bitten fingernails, and tries to guess. Burglaries, kidnapping, *murder*? It is on the tip of her tongue to ask but . . . she likes Colin. Better not to know.

The huge roaring train pulls up and Eric is one of the first of the small crowd to alight. Alice spots him immediately. It's not just his flaming red hair, he is also about a foot higher than everyone else on the platform. She'd forgotten how tall he is. And so very thin! What a beanpole. She smiles as she pushes her way through the chattering crowd towards him. With his heavy-framed glasses, dark loose clothes and small leather suitcase he could easily be mistaken for a geeky scientist twice his age, or the fall guy in some thirties movie. *Or*, Alice smiles to herself dryly, *a redheaded pencil!*

'Hey, Eric!'

He turns from where he is staring at the huge old weighing machine outside the parcels office and flashes one of his delighted smiles. Alice feels a rush of immediate warmth and remembers in an instant why she grew to like him so much.

'Well hello, Alice!'

There is an awkward moment before they hug each other. Then, as they make their way along the platform, the previous few months seem to collapse down into a couple of days. They fall into familiar companionable ease.

'It's so good to see you!' Alice says, meaning it.

'Likewise,' he says in his deep toffy accent. Before heading out into the car park, he stops, puts his case down and looks around the platform. 'Wow,' he says, shaking his head. 'What an amazing place!'

Alice smiles. Eric's capacity for delight is infectious. He is looking at the dreary old platform of a country station just as though he's arrived on Mars.

They sit in the back seat of the old car as Colin drives. Alice quietly tries to prepare him for her grandmother.

'She'll case you over.'

'What does that mean?' Eric ups his full-on BBC voice. 'Case me over indeed! Language my friend, language! Make yourself clear.'

'She'll want to know everything about . . . you.'

'Alice.' Eric squeezes her arm. 'Don't worry. I'm sure we'll get on.'

'Nobody *gets on* with my grandmother.' Alice remains grim. 'She doesn't *like* anybody, so don't expect her to like you or to get on with you. It's just not part of her *modus operandi*.'

'Alice! She'll absolutely *adore* me,' Eric cuts in dryly shaking his head. 'Just you wait.'

'Don't say you weren't warned.'

'Never!'

Dressed in a pale-blue silk blouse, heels and a pleated skirt, her hair newly styled, Phyllis is sitting waiting for them by the fire. When they come in the old lady looks up, opens her mouth and then, seeing Eric, closes it again in shock. But he seems not to notice. He glances appreciatively around the big beautiful room. After taking a casual peek out one of the nearby windows, he follows Alice over to where the old lady is waiting.

'Eric, this is my grandmother, Mrs Hickey.' Alice's inner antenna is whirring with a red alert danger signal, wishing like crazy now that she'd warned her grandmother that Eric was a little odd-looking. 'Gran, this is Eric. Remember I told you that we were at university together earlier this year? In the same tute actually . . .' she blunders on self-consciously, trying for a casual tone.

'Yes, yes.' Her grandmother shudders slightly as she steadies herself before standing up. 'How do you do, Eric?' She extends her bony right hand, her eyes raking mercilessly over the red-headed streak in front of her.

'How do you do, Mrs Hickey?' Eric takes her hand and gives a small respectful bow. 'So pleased to meet you at last.'

'Yes, well!' Phyllis replies sharply, then with another small involuntary shudder, her lips curled, she suddenly can't help herself.

'My goodness me!' she exclaims furiously. 'You're a very *unusual* looking young fellow, aren't you?'

Alice braces herself. The whole evening is going to descend into a barrage of similar, barely concealed rude comments.

'*That* has to be the understatement of the year!' Eric dismisses the old woman's disdain with an easy laugh. 'Unfortunately they ran out of oils when they were painting me.'

A thin smile appears slowly on her grandmother's face. *No mean feat!* Alice makes a thumbs-up sign behind her back, but Eric doesn't see. He points to a small porcelain figurine of a girl on the mantelpiece, 'That, however, is a very fine piece, if I may say so, Mrs Hickey.'

'You may indeed.' Alice's grandmother takes the time to smile again, before picking the thing up and putting it carefully into his hands. She begins to point out some of the features that make it one of the best of its kind. To Alice's astonishment, Eric can actually contribute to this conversation. He talks easily of the differences between work produced during separate eras in Europe. *Is Mrs Hickey familiar with Louis XIV miniatures produced in Leon?*

Of course the old bat knows everything, but Eric gives her a run for her money. The names of manufacturers roll off his tongue as though they were all close relatives, and he listens to her stories of similar pieces that were broken by incompetent servants as though the whole area is one of deep personal interest.

Alice looks on in bewilderment. She had no idea of his arcane interest in porcelain.

When they are seated in front of the fire and her grandmother turns her back to pour the sherry, Alice makes a *how come?* face, but Eric only raises one eyebrow and stretches out his long legs.

'A sherry!' he murmurs taking the tiny glass. 'Couldn't think of anything nicer after that trip.'

'How did you find the train journey?' the old lady asks, sitting down opposite him, her beady eyes raking over his body yet again.

'Delightful,' Eric replies enthusiastically, 'until I visited the dining car. The quality of the food was deplorable.'

'Oh, I know,' the old lady groans and shakes her head, sipping her sherry mournfully. 'So what on earth did you do?'

'Luckily I had thought to bring a sandwich and some fruit, but I could have done with more, to tell you the truth.'

Alice groans inside as her grandmother nods approvingly and gives another thin smile. *Another ten points to Eric!*

Alice hates sherry but she finishes the glass in one gulp and wonders how long she'll have to wait before she can pour another without drawing attention to herself.

'Then you'll be hungry now?' the old lady says sharply.

'Very.'

'Alice would you please go and tell Helen not to wait until eight, that we'll have dinner as soon as possible. Poor Eric is hungry.'

'Okay.' Alice gets up meekly.

'I hope roast beef will be to your liking, Eric?' Her grandmother isn't so much asking a question as declaring a fact. 'I rang the butcher myself and asked for his very best cut.'

There is a slight moment of hesitation as they wait for Eric to respond. Suddenly Alice remembers that he's actually a *vegetarian*! *Oh no.* How could she have forgotten? Eric eats fish but not meat. Something about Australian beef and sheep farming ruining our fragile soils. He didn't talk about it much and she never listened when he did. But Eric's moment of hesitation is short. 'Roast beef happens to be my favourite, Mrs Hickey,' he says, hardly blinking. 'And if by chance it's accompanied by gravy and roast potatoes, why then . . . I'm in heaven!'

'Then this is your lucky day,' Phyllis says with a dry smile.

By the time dinner is served Alice isn't just relieved, she's filled with awe. Eric is a master. Not just of small talk but of conversation generally. Why can't she be like this? From the very start he is totally at ease with her grandmother, immersed in the old lady's theories about growing roses. When the conversation moves on to her complaints about politicians and the local council he is equally involved, adding all kinds of amusing anecdotes and opinions of his own. Soup out of the way, Alice actually begins to relax. She can see that Eric knows intuitively that Phyllis will turn nasty if faced with serious dissent and so he doesn't stray too far away from her biased, eccentric, often self-inflated opinions. Even so . . . he manages to be himself, which says a lot for his ability to dodge and neutralise issues before they get out of hand. When Phyllis gets onto ailments and the side effects of different medicines, and Eric pulls a medico uncle out of his formidable box of tricks to impress her with inside information about prescription drugs, Alice almost starts laughing.

Phyllis is actually enjoying herself! Alice has never seen her so animated. Won over by Eric's charm, she even makes a joke or two. Which is not to say that she stops being blunt and caustic – she chides him about the shirt he is wearing and for not knowing the first thing about the importance of wearing wool next to his skin in the winter, then tells him that he should take a tonic to improve his pale colour and maybe think about joining a gym in order to *fill out a bit*.

Eric accepts, dodges or laughs off all the unasked-for advice with the grace and style of a chess champion. Rather than wait for the inevitable sly questions about where his family fits into the Melbourne class hierarchy, he implants small snippets of information into the conversation, all of which impress her grandmother greatly.

'You say your father is in business?'

'Yes.' Eric smiles warmly as though the mention of his father brings up pleasurable thoughts.

Easy now. Alice sits back to watch the performance. *Don't overdo it.* She knows Eric is bored witless by his father.

'He's the managing director of Alchemy International. That's a chemical company, you know. They make all manner of industrial cleaners, detergents and the like.'

'Sounds useful!' Phyllis says approvingly.

'Oh yes,' Eric smiles happily, 'my father is a very useful man!'

Alice starts biting her nails, remembering Eric's rants about his father's pugnacious attitude to everything, from his underlings at work to the man next door who wanted to lop off an overhanging branch. A gifted scientist, he'd sold out his passion to get into top management, purely for the money. Something that Eric swore he would never do.

'That must keep him very busy?'

'It's a German company so . . . he's overseas half the time.'

'So he's a German industrialist?' Alice's grandmother sits back, glowing with quiet approval.

'Well, yes, I suppose so.'

'And your mother?'

'She manages the house and—'

'Sensible woman.'

Eric eats everything, including a second serve of beef, which is, as far as Alice is concerned anyway, *definitely* overdoing things. By the time they are through with the lemon meringue pie, Alice is ready to scream, throw one of those prized ornaments at the wall, or stand on her head – *anything* to get away. Of course she's relieved that it has gone well, but she can't remember the last time she spent a whole hour with her grandmother, much less three! Surely Eric is starting to flag too. But no! Here he is launching into a description of some dreary uncle who is making a fortune selling rice into Asia.

'Ah, wonders will never cease, Eric!' her grandmother laughs, as though he's her best friend.

'When they do, we'll know we're dead,' Eric retorts with an aptly chosen aphorism that has the old lady chuckling with delight.

'Well, Alice, what have you got planned for Eric tomorrow?' The old lady tries to stifle a yawn.

'Not much,' Alice mumbles, not bothering to stifle hers. It is after eleven now and she is beyond politeness. 'Maybe look around the town in the morning.' She turns to Eric. 'Do you want to go out to the farm in the afternoon and meet the twins?' She has told him all about the twins and he has already expressed interest.

'The twins! Goodness,' her grandmother snaps, 'there must be more interesting people for Eric to meet!'

'Such as?' Alice is unable to keep the irritation out of her voice. Both Sylvie and Leyla are friendly and polite whenever they meet her grandmother. They put up with her grumpy, intrusive questions about their lives and rude comments about their Annie-Get-Your-Gun clothes and attitudes, and yet they still meet with her grandmother's disdain. Why? Because their father Charlie is a meatworker and they live in a small unimpressive house out of town. She has suggested a number of times that Alice should find more 'suitable' companions. *You snobby old bat! The twins are my best friends.*

'There is a rather good gallery down near the library,' Phyllis tells Eric pompously, ignoring Alice. 'I think you'll find it has an interesting little collection of nineteenth-century watercolours *and* of course there are some fascinating geographical features around this town. The caves for example are only a fifteen-minute drive. Do you drive?'

'Yes I do, Mrs Hickey.'

'Well, I have a rather good work vehicle. And it's at your disposal should you and Alice decide to do a bit of sightseeing.'

'Oh, how wonderful!' Eric's face lights up. Alice's mouth falls open. *Sightseeing!*

'Are you able to drive a four-wheel?'

'Oh, yes,' Eric says confidently.

Alice gives him a hard look. *Liar.* When she'd asked him that same question on the phone recently, he'd told her that he had no idea what gears were for.

'I keep encouraging Alice to get her licence but . . .'

'I've only just turned eighteen, Gran!'

'Well . . . you should have been down at the police station the next day, my dear. That would have been my attitude.' Phyllis smiles at Eric who smiles back in total agreement. Alice can't be bothered telling her that you don't go to the police station for your licence anymore.

'What age were you when you got your licence, Mrs Hickey?' Eric asks innocently.

'Well, I suppose I *was* over thirty, but . . .' she has grace to blush a little, 'things were totally different then!'

'Of course they were.'

'There was the war and . . . women were not encouraged the way they are now.' Phyllis stifles another yawn. 'I'm going to have to leave you now,' she smiles at Eric. 'I do hope you have a comfortable night.'

'I'm sure I shall.' He stands to help her up.

'I'm concerned that Alice won't entertain you properly tomorrow,' she grumbles, 'so I'll have a think tonight about some appropriate outings.'

'Please don't be concerned on my behalf!' Eric smiles at Alice behind her back. 'Those caves sound very interesting.'

After Phyllis has gone upstairs to bed, Alice and Eric don their coats and go for a walk. They say nothing for some time. Alice is enjoying the cool night air and the sense of escape. She strides out alongside her friend.

'You want to go down to the water?'

'What if I fall in?' Eric asks, half seriously.

'I'll save you.'

'Okay!' Eric squares his shoulders and sniffs the air. 'I'll risk it!'

They stride on. She will take Eric down to the beach and let the tang of the sea and the crashing of the waves do their work.

'So what did you think of Grandma?'

'Adorable!' Eric doesn't hesitate for a moment. 'Love her! *Christ!* What a museum piece! How old is she again?'

'Ninety-two!' Alice laughs softly. They are heading down Murtle Street now and Pitt Street is only a block away. *Will she show him the house?* The tiny bubble of panic that begins with the thought bounces around inside her chest, building strength and muscle. *No. Not tonight.* They will walk further along the beachfront, down to where that fancy restaurant sits perched out on the cliffs. Maybe they will get a glimpse of her cousin through the windows.

'So, Alice, are you going crazy here, or what?'

'What do you think?' Alice puts her arm through his.

'It's so very quiet,' Eric whispers, as if this is an extraordinary and unexpectedly freakish secret, 'and dark and . . . What do people do at night?'

Alice doesn't bother to answer. She takes the turn to the right that leads down to the ocean. *What do people do anywhere?* They go to bed at night and they get up in the morning, if they're lucky.

On they walk, along the dark quiet street, through the cold night and down to stand on a pile of rocks to look out over the raging sea. Eric slings one arm around her shoulders and she puts her arm around his waist. They say nothing as the wind bites into their faces. Eventually Eric moves away to stand by himself. He throws his head back and howls into the wind.

'Who brought you?' Alice laughs.

'I'm releasing my inner demons.'

They walk around the curve of the cliff and onto the jetty. Alice points out Thistles and ends up telling Eric everything about the run-in with Tom outside the courtroom. Eric listens carefully.

'So, what do you think?'

Eric sighs thoughtfully and remains silent.

'Come *on!*' Alice laughs impatiently, but in fact she has always liked Eric's reticence, the way he thinks things through before speaking.

'He could feel guilty and want to make amends,' Eric murmurs.

'Guilty?' Alice frowns, the thought alarms her.

'Well,' Eric says mildly, 'you don't really know much about him, do you?'

'No . . . I guess not.'

The restaurant looks wonderful at night. It is like a glass bubble suspended in the surrounding darkness. From this distance the people moving about inside make Alice think of tiny creatures inside a sack of liquid. Back and forth they swim like mosquito larvae, or fish, sliding around each other. She pulls her scarf tighter around her neck and stares out into the wind, momentarily forgetting Eric beside her, wondering about her cousin working in that glass bubble, trying to remember him from when she was small. Sometimes she'd see him in the street, a skinny blond-headed kid walking along beside his harried dowdy mother. *That is my aunt*, she would think to herself, *my mother's sister, and that one beside her is my cousin.* It's hard now to even summon up an image of what he looked like then.

'Can you see your cousin?' Eric is following her gaze. 'Shall we move closer?'

'No. Let's go now,' Alice says shortly, and turns away. She remembers her cousin on the night of the concert trying to find help for his hurt friend. He was quietly spoken and polite, deferential even, but in the fluorescent light . . . those eyes were there; the green, bright eyes. She shudders and takes Eric's arm. How often had she stared into his photograph in the local paper, those weird eyes that seemed to be looking straight at her. Accusing her, mocking her, filling her with rage! So often she'd thrown that photo out only to pick it out of the bin and put it back in her drawer. Her mother's murderer! What had he thought of her the night of the concert? How strange to think she'd been so close to him.

Sadness flies in from nowhere on a volley of arrows, unexpected, sharp and precise. Each one hits its mark. The first to her stomach, making her want to keel over as she walks along beside Eric. *Ping!* There goes another, straight to her heart, dropping its poison dart. The venom floods slowly outwards and upwards until her eyes sting with it. The black fog comes next, swirling over and around her, right into every hollow and crevice of her being, filling her with a helplessness she can't begin to explain. She could jump down from the jetty onto the sand, fill her pockets with stones – like Virginia Woolf – and just walk out slowly. Let the waves beat against her knees, her chest, and then cover her head. She would just . . . *sink* and it would all be over.

'Did Tom say why he's so sure Jonty did it?' Eric suddenly asks, as though reading her mind.

'He didn't say he was sure.'

'But he *thinks* he did it,' Eric says thoughtfully. 'He thinks he's capable of it. Why? Does he know something that other people don't?'

'I don't know.'

'So ask him, Alice. *Ask him!*'

Alice sighs. They head back to the house.

'You think those two are friends now?' Eric murmurs.

'How would I know?'

Once back inside the big gates, Eric stops to take a look at the house in front of them.

'So, all this will be yours one day?' he asks.

'Yep.' Alice hasn't thought much about her grandmother's money lately. 'Every single brick!' They look at each other for a moment or two before Eric begins to grin.

'I can see you up there,' he points to the small balcony on the second floor, 'overseeing your vast estates.'

'I know,' Alice laughs, 'it's going to be such fun!'

'Alice in her wonderland!' Eric puts an arm around her shoulders and they move off towards the front door. 'Will you marry me, Alice?'

'Why would I?'

'Your grandmother wants me as her grandson-in-law.'

'You think so?'

'I'm positive.'

'I guess that settles it then.'

'I can't believe you just got up and left him sitting there!' Sylvie whispers urgently as she drops the ammunition into the barrel, closes the gun, presses the cock shuttle and raises it to her shoulder.

Sylvie, Alice and Eric have been up on the back of the Land Rover for over an hour now, driving slowly through an open

166

paddock, rugged up in scarves and coats against the chilly night. Charlie is driving and Leyla is hanging out the passenger window looking into the vast dark night. Alice has just given a whispered account of her meeting with Tom Mullaney the week before, but she wishes she hadn't brought it up because she wants to stay quiet and just take in the night. The chill is making all their faces numb and each breath out blows like fine white dust into the surrounding dark air.

'What do you mean?' It's Alice's turn with the spotlight. She stands between the twins trying to keep it steady.

Sylvie leans forward – the barrel of the shotgun along the roof of the Land Rover, the butt held close to her shoulder – squinting through the sights, waiting for her moment.

'You should have asked him things! Or at least listened to what he had to say.'

Alice shrugs, hoping that no more rabbits will turn up and they can drive around like this for hours. How perfect this would be if they didn't have to shoot anything.

'But I hate him.' She tries to hold the light steady as she sweeps it over the land directly in front of the slowly moving vehicle. It is quite heavy and her arms ache, but she is proud of the way she is able to do it.

'Why?'

'He used to come around with my cousin and—'

'That was years ago!' Sylvie snorts. 'What do you think, Eric? Do you think she should have hung out to hear what he had to say?'

'I do,' Eric nods. 'He might have been going to tell you something important.'

'Exactly,' Sylvie sniffs.

'Maybe,' Alice murmurs, 'and maybe he's just full of shit!'

It all looks so different at night. Eerie. Every tree stands like a waiting ghost, the silver branches like skeleton fingers pointing into the abyss, calling her forward into some place she'd rather not go. It is a crisp clear night with the occasional heavy cloud drifting across the brilliant star-filled sky. She shivers, trying to imagine how she would feel out here on her own.

'What was your cousin *like*,' Sylvie suddenly asks, 'that night after the concert?'

'I don't know.' Alice shrugs. 'Normal enough, I guess.'

'Normal?' Sylvie says in a small voice. 'He can't be . . .'

'What if . . . he's innocent?' Eric says mildly.

The headlights are off and Charlie is crawling the vehicle over the small ruts and bumps, thistles and tussocks. Occasionally they hit a deep pothole, which makes the girls on the back lose their footing or bump into each other. They shriek and laugh and yell for Charlie to be more careful.

'Quiet, you lot,' he calls back sternly, 'you'll frighten them off!' Alice hears the tenderness in his voice and it grounds her. She can imagine his face as he sits behind the wheel listening to his girls, because she has watched it so many times before. More than anything, Charlie loves to hear his girls laughing. It is what he lives for. It is why he gets up every morning, why he goes to work with all the blood and dead animals. It is why he doesn't mind coming home at night stinking of death. The twins keep him alive.

'Okay. Number one, coming up!' Sylvie says under her breath. Alice holds the spotlight steady on the startled animal staring blind into the harsh light. She hears Sylvie's deep intake of breath as she squints over the rifle, taking aim. One second, two and then three before the whistling sharp crack of the bullet. A tiny squeal as the rabbit flips over in a crazy somersault and then lies still.

'Yes!' Sylvie declares triumphantly, handing the gun over to Eric who takes it awkwardly, too stunned to say no. He and Alice watch her jump down from the back of the vehicle and make for the slain rabbit.

'How's this?' she calls, holding it up. 'Straight through the head!' The blood dripping from its mouth and nose makes Eric gasp and turn away.

'Good one!' Charlie yells back. Any mark on the body makes the animal virtually worthless for either meat or skin. Only a shot through the head means it will sell.

Alice keeps the spotlight on Sylvie as she runs back over to the truck, grabs the pocketknife that her father is holding out the window. With the dead rabbit hanging between her knees, she makes a quick incision from the bottom of the rib cage straight down to the groin. Then she pushes her small hand straight into the body and pulls out the entrails, all bloody and glistening in the strange white light, and chucks them to the ground.

Alice swallows. She has seen this before but it never fails to amaze her. All of that done in one precise movement. And how quickly it happens! There was the rabbit – staring, frightened and alive – and now here it is, its tiny red liver and heart, and curling, wormlike intestines all warm and steaming on the cold grass. Finished. Alice nudges Eric who is staring open-mouthed.

'I warned you,' she says softly. In the shadows cast by the spotlight she can't really see his face. Still, she fancies that he's gone a lighter shade of pale.

'Are you okay?' she whispers.

'Of course I'm okay.' He grimaces. 'Loving it.'

They are back in the shed, sorting through the haul of dead rabbits. Skinning is done quickly and without fuss. Charlie cuts around the neck and four legs, grabs the neck with one hand and rips the skin off with the other. Alice, standing next to Eric, holds her breath in awe as each one comes off.

'Just like peeling off a coat,' Eric mutters to himself. And it's true. The skin rolls off and the body comes free, dark pink and nude. They watch as Charlie chops off the feet and what is left of the head with an axe. All in all they have netted two dozen rabbits for sale. The twins carry the bodies over to the freezer on the back verandah, and Alice follows them with the gun, which is always stored in the house for safety, leaving Charlie in the shed sorting the skins for drying the next day.

'I think you should ring Tom Mullaney,' Sylvie says suddenly.

'And say what?' Alice is appalled by the idea.

'Just ask him if he's changed his mind.'

'About what?'

'I think he wants to help you.'

Alice thinks of the night when she came across Jonty and Tom in the street. She wonders what her mother would say about the sheer coincidence of it happening that way it did. Lillian loved the whole idea of fate. Alice can hear her voice.

Hey listen, babe, maybe it was all meant to happen.

Jonty is walking home from work with Buzz one night when he decides he's got to cut the dramatics and deal with some of the shit that's been building up inside. It's time to go check out the house.

He's been holding his breath every time he passes Pitt Street, as though it's got some power over him, and he doesn't like that. Not one little bit.

He tells Buzz about his planned detour and the old guy's eyebrows shoot up into one disapproving line.

'Not a good idea,' he mumbles gruffly.

They stop under a streetlight, Jonty frowning as he wraps and rewraps his scarf around his neck.

'Why is that?'

'I'll come with you.'

Jonty shakes his head. He doesn't need company. He has never spoken to Buzz about what happened three years ago, but it seems the old bastard knows all about it anyway, which is kind of annoying and yet . . . *so what*?

He smiles at Buzz. Under the harsh streetlight the old guy's face is hollowed out with exhaustion. Dark shadows for eyes and carved-out cheeks under the bones. Earlier he was complaining about having to work so hard at his age and the rest of the staff – Jonty included – started ribbing him about funeral plans and who was going to get his money and his house. By the end, everyone was laughing, including Buzz.

'Go in the daytime, mate.' Buzz reaches out and puts a hand on Jonty's shoulder. 'It won't feel so good at night.'

'It's just a house, Buzz,' Jonty shrugs him off. 'No one lives in it now.'

'Yes, but . . .'

'What?'

'It will be full of . . . memories for you.'

'I'll be right.'

Half irritated, half amused, Jonty walks off into the night. *What the hell does Buzz know about my memories?*

Head down, hands thrust deep into the pockets of his jacket, trying to dampen down the chilly sense of expectation building in his chest, Jonty heads up dark, quiet Pitt Street.

When he reaches the house he sees that the front room is blazing with yellow light. Could he have made a mistake and come to the wrong house? But the number is written clearly on the letter box just as he remembers. *Twenty-one.* This is definitely his aunt's old house. *So who is in there at midnight?* He walks back and forth along the front fence a few times trying to catch a clue.

There is nothing for it. Jonty checks that no one is around before pushing the front gate open. He has to know. He walks down the path and up the three steps onto the familiar brickwork of the porch. About to ring the doorbell he hesitates, tries to caution himself. It's not as though he has the right to question whoever is in there! It isn't his place. What the hell is he doing here at all? None of this makes much sense.

The blinds are drawn but he sees there are gaps.

Jonty sneaks across the lawn and peers in through the front window. *Someone is moving around inside.* His heart begins to hammer in his chest. *Has she come back? It has to be her! Sure they put her body in the ground but . . . where did she really go? What is death anyway?*

He can hear music now. Some girl singer is wailing over a thumping rock beat. *It's her!*

But then the figure inside turns around and Jonty's excitement drops away. It's only his cousin dancing around the lounge room by herself. She has her eyes closed and she's waving her arms and hands around, singing along. Jonty wonders if she is drunk or stoned and feels vaguely guilty to be spying on her. But he keeps watching anyway.

He remembers the shock on her face when she realised it was him that night after the concert. Like he was a figure who'd walked straight out of some kind of horror flick.

She's your grandmother too. Her voice had been so cold!

He imagines walking in on her now. She'd soon get that dopey look off her face! He wouldn't have to do a thing. He'd just stand there in the doorway, cross his arms over his chest and wait for the embarrassment to kick in.

Hey, it's me, remember your cousin Jonty?

Imagining how her face would change from shock to embarrassment to outrage and fury makes him want to howl with laughter. All he has to do is tap on the window.

This night starts something new for Jonty. He finds himself walking past that house most nights after work. Sometimes she's there, but mostly not. When there are no lights on he sneaks around trying to see into other windows.

Once he climbs the side fence, goes right up the back and just stands for a while in the backyard. It is a bright clear night with a full moon. The grass has grown long and there is a bit of a breeze. He has the feeling that he is on a boat, looking out at a vast expanse of water, a sea of black choppy waves. There is this sensation of drifting in and out of a dream. He's on the verge of understanding something really important and then . . . it just slips away under the waves.

Okay. Jonty knows this is all pathetic in the extreme. Creeping around, looking in windows. *Hey, Jonty, get a life!* But it's become one of those things he can't help now. It's become a kind of addiction.

Mostly Alice just reads magazines or sits at the table sketching or writing. Sometimes she watches television. He stands there on the outside for maybe half an hour just watching, thinking and wondering about her. She shows no sign that she knows he's there, but strangely, Jonty feels that she does know, and that on some weird unconscious level they are getting to know each other at last.

Alice

Alice arrives at the Blazing Glory coffee lounge in Robertson's Road and stops to look inside before pushing open the glass door. She's heard about this place. Only last night Sylvie had said, *Oh but you can't wear that to the Blazing Glory*, and Leyla had smiled in secret agreement as she flipped Alice's hair about this way and that to see what suited her best. That made Alice feel anxious.

She hadn't rung Tom Mullaney in the end. They'd run into each other in the street and he'd invited her for coffee the following Saturday. So maybe it *was* meant to be. That's what her mother would say. Alice isn't so sure. No such thing as fate in a small town.

'We should talk,' he'd said, all serious, as though he had a perfect right to order her around. 'How about coffee?'

What makes you so sure we need to talk about anything? Alice had wanted to say. But it wasn't just Eric and the twins' advice that had stopped her; she couldn't shake the niggling thought that he must know something she needs to know.

She opens the door and steps inside. The place is big and busy, like a bustling railway station, with Art Deco trimmings. Reggae music plays loudly and waitresses flit about like bees. They stack plates and serve food, and smile constantly as though just being there is some kind of joke. Alice bites her lip and looks around.

She is wearing a new outfit for the occasion. It's a long mauve knitted top that covers her ample arse, over tight purple leggings and new black shoes that show off her small feet and nice ankles.

'You've got to look good,' the twins had commanded sternly. 'Get out of those dowdy skirts and old-lady blouses. Show him you're cool! Let your hair out for Christ's sake! Wear earrings. Lipstick. Keep the guy onside. *Use* him!'

'How?'

'Alice!' they'd laughed at her. 'Don't be so naive.' They took her shopping and fixed her hair, both of them unbelievably finicky and precise about what image she had to project, which was amusing seeing as neither of them cared two hoots about their own appearance.

Alice stands inside the doorway feeling ridiculous as she scans the room. She should have stuck to the boring skirts and blouses. At least she knows who she is when she's wearing them. Everyone else here seems to be in black of one sort or another.

It's eleven o'clock on a Saturday morning and heaps of the tables are full already. All these people eating breakfast and brunch, laughing and chattering – how come they have so much to talk about? When she's out, she often can't think of a single thing to say after the preliminaries. It would be a relief to step outside again into the fresh air and forget the whole exercise.

'Alice?' Tom is suddenly at her side. 'I was over there,' he points to a corner table near the window, 'reading the paper. Didn't see you come in. Sorry!'

'That's okay,' she gulps and follows him back to the table.

'This all right?' He pulls out the chair for her and, still standing himself, waits for her to sit. He dumps the paper on a nearby empty table. 'Want a coffee?'

'Thanks. A latte,' she mumbles, although she doesn't much like coffee.

'Anything else?' he asks, his eyes darting towards the nearby cake-counter for a moment. 'I'm definitely going to have something. A cake, maybe?' He smiles at her encouragingly.

'No thanks.' She would actually love something sticky and sweet. Too nervous to eat breakfast, her belly is suddenly responding to all the different delicious food smells. On tables all around her people are stuffing themselves. *How come none of them are fat?*

Tom rushes off to the counter to order and she stares after him. Tall and good-looking in his jeans and red striped sweatshirt, all that badly cut curly hair and blue soulful eyes. His movements are quick and easy. The dark growth on his chin has made him look older and more sophisticated than she remembers, and that unnerves her even as it adds to his charm.

'Thanks for coming, Alice.' He is sitting opposite her now, elbows on the table, both hands playing with the sugar sachets. Every now and again his face jerks up and he stares straight into her eyes as though waiting for her to say something important, before glancing back down to the sugar sachets. His nervousness makes her feel her own more keenly. How come he's so jumpy?

The waitress brings over a tray and puts their coffees down, followed by a plate with three big fresh almond croissants. Her favourite! *Damn.* She swallows hard, trying to think about something else. Is he going to eat *all three* of those things?

'I got extra,' Tom smiles, 'in case you changed your mind.'

Alice colours with embarrassment, but he's motioning to the passing waitress. 'Could we have another plate please?'

Should she be insulted? Does he just assume she'll eat them because she's fat? *Well then, I won't! Not even one little bite!*

'Do you see him . . . Jonty . . . regularly?' She jumps right in as a way to divert herself from looking at the food.

'No.' Tom shakes his head. 'You?'

'No.' She picks up her drink but her hand is trembling so much that the hot coffee sloshes out both sides onto the saucer before she can raise it to her mouth, so she settles it back down and turns to the window, trying to calm herself. *Stop watching me!* she wants to scream. He is studying her closely. She can feel it in every one of those sharp sneaky glances.

'But . . . are you still friends with him?' is her next question. She needs to know the score. Have some kind of picture of things so she can work out what to do.

'I haven't had anything to do with Jonty since it . . . happened.' His mouth tightens into a grimace. 'I . . . I wiped him three years ago.'

Wiped him? 'What about the night of the concert?' Alice counters suspiciously.

'I didn't know he was there until . . . I got attacked.'

'But he came to your aid?'

'Jonty was always . . .' He stops in mid-sentence as a sudden furious flush floods his face. 'He was always good like that.'

'You wiped him because you thought he was guilty?' she asks in a whisper.

'Yeah, I guess.'

Gutsy of you, Alice thinks. *Big-hearted*. And the clichés run through her head: Judas, turncoat, fair-weather friend. But she holds herself back. After all, he was *wiping* her mother's murderer! How can she despise him for that?

There is so much more she would like to find out. Does this guy sitting in front of her know a whole lot of things that she doesn't? Has he got *inside information* that he didn't tell the police? What was his friendship with her mother about? But asking those questions doesn't seem possible now. Not here, sitting across the table from him with all these chattering people around. Not while he's looking so awkward, gulping down coffee and stuffing croissant into his mouth.

'So how do I find out if he really did it?' she asks instead.

'I'm not sure,' Tom says slowly, looking straight into her eyes, 'but I'll help . . . if I can.'

'He's my cousin but . . . I don't know him.'

'Right.'

'What's he like?'

'Jonty?' He seems surprised by the question.

'Yes.'

Tom gulps down the rest of the coffee and stares into his empty glass. Then he motions to the waitress for another.

'Jonno was . . . is . . . a fantastic guy,' he says at last, weighing every word. 'A fantastic guy.'

'How could he be, if he—' Alice's voice falters.

'But . . . completely fucked up, you know,' Tom cuts in sharply.

'Fucked up?' Alice is sharp. 'What does that mean?'

'Drugs mainly.' Tom still isn't looking at her. There is a slight tremor around one corner of his mouth that makes her wonder if he has a tic or if it's just nerves. 'And his old man, of course.'

'Did you know his . . . old man?'

'A bit.'

'My mother hated Jed,' Alice whispers.

Tom nods and shrugs. 'No one likes Jed.'

They are quiet for a while. Alice can resist no longer. She breaks off a small piece of croissant. Tom immediately slides the whole thing onto the spare plate and pushes it towards her.

'Please. It's for you,' he says, then smiles shyly. 'I thought you might be just being polite.'

'Thanks . . .' The flaky sweet sensation in her mouth momentarily diverts her from the embarrassment of breaking her resolve not to eat in front of him.

'Nice, eh?' He smiles again. 'These are my all-time favourite.'

'Yeah,' Alice agrees with a small reluctant smile, 'me too.'

'I'll go you halves in the last one,' he says, breaking it in two and dumping the big half on her plate.

'Thanks . . . If you two became friends again then he might give something away,' Alice suddenly bursts out.

'Yes,' Tom nods, as though he'd considered it already.

'How would you feel about doing that?' she asks sharply, and then, when Tom shrugs and smiles wryly, she feels the anger rise in her. *This is way more important than any friendship. I don't care if you feel uncomfortable. My mother was murdered!*

'I want him caught,' Alice snaps, 'if he did it.' *And you can get that smile right off your face!* she wants to yell. 'We're not talking about some minor misdemeanour here.'

Tom nods seriously and leans forward.

'You know he calls my father every so often with some new theory?' Tom's voice fades as he begins an agitated tapping with his fingers on the table. 'Like it's eating away at him, too. Maybe he's ready to be found out.'

'New theory on *what*?'

'On who killed your mother.'

His words smack her in the face like an open palm. She gulps, searching her mind frantically for something else to think about so she doesn't keep hearing those words over and over again. *On who killed your mother.* Whenever *the fact of it* is spoken aloud there is this hard jarring *clang* deep down inside her. Just those few words! She breaks off more croissant and stuffs it in her mouth, then reaches out for the ragged big half that he'd just put on her plate.

'I'm sorry, Alice.'

She looks up to see that he is distressed that his words have upset her. But that only makes it worse! Now she is torn. What the hell is she doing here? Putting herself through this *for what*? This guy, Tom, was never her friend. He'll probably go back to her cousin and they'll both laugh about her!

'Why do you want to help?' she asks gruffly, tearing off another big piece of croissant. 'I mean, what is it to you?'

'A million reasons.'

'Such as?' she snaps, and gulps down the tears with the last bit of croissant.

'You want the full million do you?' He smiles broadly, and although she has to wipe her eyes with the back of her hand she does smile back.

'Yeah, start at the top!' she whispers. 'At number one.'

'For you, Alice.'

She stares back at him, not knowing what to say.

'You're lovely,' he says quietly, not smiling anymore. 'Do you know that? I think you're fantastic. That day in the courtroom I thought, *You are really . . . special*.'

She gives a nervous laugh as a rush of blood hits her face. *He didn't say that, did he? Did she hear right? No! Must have imagined it.* She stops smiling, picks up her coffee and tries to concentrate on the taste. *So bitter! How come people love this stuff? So strong. So bitter. So fucking horrible!* She empties another sachet of sugar into it. Number four at least.

'I could have a party,' Alice suggests quickly, more out of desperation to change the topic than anything else. 'Invite Jonty, and you might know some other people. Just to get the ball rolling,' she hesitates.

'But what about your grandmother?' Tom smiles.

'Not in her house!' Alice laughs at the thought. 'At my old place. You know, the Pitt Street house?'

'*Pitt Street!*' Tom sits back, startled. 'You mean . . . But that place is rented out, isn't it?'

Alice watches in astonishment as the colour drains from his face. His eyes are suddenly very dark and luminous against his pale skin. His mouth has become a thin straight line in his face, twitching a little in one corner.

'It's mine now.' She raises her chin defiantly. 'My mother left it to me. It's been mine since I turned eighteen. The renters have left. I've already been in there and worked out what I'm going to do with the place. I like it there. Sometimes I go for a walk down there in the evening and just sit about a bit.'

'You *like* it there?' he whispers, shaking his head.

'Yes, I do.'

'Why?

'Why not?' She is still outwardly defiant but his reaction has unnerved and humiliated her. 'I'm going to get it renovated soon. When I've got money. It would be fun to have people there and . . .' How can she explain what that little house meant to both her and her mother?

'No it *wouldn't!*' Tom says adamantly, shaking his head.

'Why not?'

'I couldn't handle it, Alice!'

'But why?'

'A party there would be . . . *ghoulish*,' he mumbles.

'I love that house!' she declares defensively.

'I'm sure you do, but it's where . . .'

'What have you got to hide?' she spits the words into his face before she can think. He gulps in shock and she watches appalled with herself as his expression closes over into one of cold discomfort, his mouth tight with tension.

'I didn't kill her, Alice, if that's what you're suggesting.'

'I'm not saying that!'

He sits back in his chair, fingers drumming the table, looking around as though trying to distance himself from where he is. To her dismay she sees he's really upset and is looking for a fast exit.

The waitress sidles over and begins to take their used dishes.

'Can I get you guys something else?' she asks cheerily. They both shake their heads. The croissants are all gone and Alice has eaten more than half of them.

'I need a smoke, actually.' Tom frowns, not looking at Alice 'Want to go now?'

Once outside he turns to her without smiling. 'I guess we both need to think about things then?'

'Yes.'

'Bye, then.'

Alice hurries off down the street, wishing like crazy that she hadn't listened to her stupid friends! Eric, Sylvie and Leyla. They meant well, but what do they know? It's just a game to them. He'd told her nothing and she'd made a fool of herself. *Jonty is your cousin!* Lillian had exclaimed that time Alice had tried to explain how she didn't want those two boys around all the time. *He's the nearest you'll ever have to a brother.* A brother! Alice always wanted a brother. From the time she was a little girl still living with her father it was, *When am I going to get a brother, Dad?*

Ask your mother, Mal used to grin.

Mum?

But what if we had another girl? Lillian used to tease.

No. Alice had been adamant. *I want a brother.*

Maybe the police didn't find the evidence because there *wasn't* any. What would that skinny pretty-boy know.

'Alice!'

'Yes, Gran.'

'Will you come here please, dear?'

'I'm in the shower.'

'Very well, but as soon as you're ready.'

Alice dries herself and looks in the mirror.

'Alice!'

'Coming, Gran.'

'Well, don't take all day!'

Alice dresses quickly in her jeans and favourite black jumper. Her long hair is still tangled from the shower but she doesn't want to annoy her grandmother any further so she starts up the stairs, still raking through it with her wide-toothed comb. Once outside her grandmother's bedroom she gives two sharp careful knocks on the door before pushing it open.

'Come in, for heavens sake!' the old lady barks irritably. Alice grits her teeth. If she had walked in without knocking her grandmother would be grumbling about her bad manners.

'Goodness me, Alice! Your hair! Never mind. But it's too long, don't you think, dear?'

'Yes, Gran.' Alice pulls the comb through, wondering what the latest *issue* is and how long it will be before she can get away.

'Needs a good few inches off.'

'Yeah, okay.'

Her grandmother is propped up against her pink satin pillows. There is a tray next to her with the breakfast leftovers. The latest maid, Sally, would have brought it to her over an hour ago and Alice wonders why it hasn't been taken away. Her grandmother is very particular about such things. Breakfast is at eight, lunch at twelve-thirty and dinner at seven. Dishes must be cleaned away minutes after food is served and eaten.

'Will I take the tray for you, Gran?' Alice goes around to the other side of the bed.

'Yes yes, please do!' Phyllis slumps irritably back against the pillows. 'But just put it down on the table for the time being.'

Alice glances again at her grandmother as she picks up the tray, noticing that she seems frailer than usual, and her skin more sallow.

'I'm not feeling too well today.' The sharp eyes have seen Alice's look. 'I'll rest here this morning. I should be right as rain by lunch.'

'Okay,' Alice mumbles. 'Is there anything you need down the street?' She is trying to think of some legitimate reason to cut short the conversation.

'No no,' the old lady sighs. 'That useless girl!'

'Who?' Alice looks up in surprise.

'That *Sally*,' Phyllis snaps. 'I just gave her marching orders!'

'Oh, Gran,' Alice sighs in exasperation, 'she's only been here a month!'

'Well, how many times do you have to tell someone how to set a tray?' the old lady explodes. 'I mean to say, it isn't rocket science! She was absolutely hopeless!' She points her crooked forefinger at the pretty cane chair in the corner. 'Pull that over, dear, and have a seat. There is something I need to talk to you about.'

Alice does what she's told, her spirits flagging. She can guess why she's been summoned now. *Damn.* Her grandmother will want her to write an advertisement for a new maid. Then when it's done, she will crawl over every word and end up writing the blasted thing herself.

'You know, your mother wore her hair long well after she should have,' Phyllis declares thoughtfully, leaning over to push Alice's hair back from her face. 'Now, don't you make the same mistake, will you?'

'What do you mean?' Alice stammers. Everyone knew that her mother had the most beautiful long dark hair.

'Everybody knows that women over forty should never have long hair,' her grandmother declares haughtily. 'It's just not flattering!'

'Well,' Alice smiles through gritted teeth, 'I'm only eighteen.'

'That's right! But you could do with some off.'

'Okay!' Alice can't keep the irritation out of her voice.

'Don't snap, dear.' Phyllis tries a weak smile. 'It's not that important, is it?'

'No, it isn't,' Alice sighs.

'I miss your mother, dear.' Her grandmother's eyes suddenly fill with tears. 'I miss her very much.'

'Yes,' Alice whispers, and looks away, out the window at the tops of the liquidambars along the front fence. The branches are bare now against the lead grey sky. In only a few months there will be masses of green leaves to flicker and shudder about in the wind. *Deciduous trees are the best*, Alice thinks. *They've got moods. Like me.*

'She was such a . . . sweet girl.'

Her grandmother hardly ever expresses any real sadness about Lillian's death, so Alice tends to forget how hard it must be for her. She turns back from the window, wanting to say something kind, but the moment is over. Phyllis is biting her lip, carefully marking articles in that morning's newspaper with a felt pen, for further reference. It makes Alice smile.

Her grandmother keeps up with what is going on in all spheres and has opinions on everything from federal politics to how one should conduct oneself at a Chinese New Year party. *Eric would adore this*, Alice thinks, *the precise way those elegantly manicured liver-spotted hands are turning back the pages.*

But it is much easier to deal with her grandmother downstairs, dressed in one of her classy pleated skirts and long-sleeved linen blouses, her hair properly pinned up and her lipstick plastered on, bossing everyone around. Inside the white lawn nightdress she is thin and wan and frail. Her scrawny old frame looks ninety per cent cadaver already, with the skin hanging lizard-like around her neck, and her eyes glassy and red-rimmed. Alice bites her lip and feels an unfamiliar pang of real sympathy.

'There is something I need to talk to you about, Alice,' her grandmother says again, picking up an envelope from her side table and pulling out the page inside.

'Okay,' Alice sighs.

'I've been sitting on this awhile,' she goes on, leaning across for her glasses, 'and I want your advice about how to proceed.'

'My advice?' Alice can hardly keep the incredulity out of her voice. Her grandmother has never asked her advice about anything before.

'It affects you,' Phyllis adds sharply, handing the piece of paper over to Alice. 'This is a letter from your Aunt Marie. She wants to come and visit me and bring that wretched boy with her!'

'What?'

'Yes . . . Exactly.'

'Jonty?' Alice is flabbergasted.

'Yes.'

Alice gulps and bends her head to read the note, feeling her grandmother's eyes on her. She reads it through twice and then folds it up carefully and hands it back, unable to meet her grandmother's searching eyes.

'What do you think?' the old lady wants to know.

'Why?' Alice whispers, the familiar dreamy sinking sensation pulling her into some other zone. She is being sucked into a vortex of hot ash and mud. *Must not panic.* Coming across her cousin the night of the concert was the beginning. Every time she thinks of him, and his friend, Tom, the sinking sensation returns. 'Why now?'

'Oh, well,' her grandmother gives a humourless laugh, 'I think we both know the answer to that question, don't we?'

'No.' Alice looks at her searchingly.

'The money, dear! Why else? It has to be the money.'

'Oh!'

'I'm over ninety!'

They are both quiet for some time. Alice knows she must think this through properly. She needs to talk to Sylvie and Leyla.

Her grandmother suddenly reaches out and grabs Alice's hand. 'Will you be with me, Alice?'

Alice stares back into the pale withered face in shock. 'What?'

The hand grabbing her own soft plump one feels as bony as a chook's claw, but Alice doesn't pull away. The desperation in the old woman's face is strangely riveting. *What is it that she wants? What is she trying to tell me?*

'What do you mean, Gran?' she whispers.

'When the time comes,' there are tears in the old woman's eyes now, 'will you stay with me? I . . . I don't want to die alone.'

'Oh.' Alice gulps, amazed by the naked fear she sees in the old face. She feels a sudden sharp jab of guilt for all the times she's wished her dead. 'I will, Gran,' she whispers. 'I will.'

'You promise?'

'I promise.'

'It won't be long now, dear.'

Alice doesn't know what to say to that.

Phyllis lets go of Alice's hand and they sit together for a while in silence. Alice watches the sun play in bright sparkling streams on the carpet.

'It is up to you, dear,' her grandmother says severely. 'It's up to you to decide about your aunt and your cousin.'

Alice wants to tell her no, that it most definitely shouldn't happen. Better not to meet her cousin ever again. And why meet her Aunt Marie at all? Alice barely knows her.

Phyllis is lying back on her pillows now, hands clasped on the sheet in front of her, eyes closed. Except for the slight fluttering under the lids she could be dead already. Who is this old woman? How did she feel when she found out that her daughter, her favourite daughter, had been murdered? How come she speaks of the other one, her only living child, Marie, as some kind of hindrance? But her grandmother was always hard to know. Even when Alice was little she never behaved like her friends' grandmothers, who turned up to school concerts and open days and sent presents for birthdays.

They'd stood together, Alice and her grandmother, by the grave, after the service in St Kieran's church. They'd watched the coffin being lowered as the final prayers were said, Alice and her grandmother on one side of that deep hole, and what seemed like the rest of the town, including Marie and Jonty, on the other. Jed was overseas and hadn't come home for the funeral.

They'd all watched as the shiny box went down into the earth. In reality, there had only been about sixty people, but they were a sea of faces that Alice didn't recognise, except for . . . yes, she does now remember . . . Luke Mullaney and his wife, Anna, standing there. Funny that she's never really thought about it before. *Who else came to my mother's funeral?* There must have been others she knew as well. Yes, there were those people from her mother's work who'd sent cards and flowers. Some of her teachers and fellow classmates must have been there. *What else happened that day?*

But she can't remember much at all – only that her grandmother did not invite anyone back to the house after the funeral. Nor did she put on an afternoon tea in the parish hall, the way so many people did. That much was spoken about widely, noticed around the town.

It was a hot day, and the old woman had been dressed in a black linen suit and a black wide-brimmed silk hat that made seeing her face almost impossible.

'I just need to think about it, Gran,' Alice says at last.

'Of course you do, dear,' the old lady whispers, without opening her eyes.

Alice has a clear memory of her cousin, outside a church, years before her mother's murder. Lillian and Marie were huddled close together having some kind of furtive conversation, and Alice and Jonty were standing about awkwardly waiting for them to finish.

'We're cousins,' Alice said at last, solemnly.

'I know,' Jonty replied stiffly in his weird accent, looking her up and down as though assessing if she was worthy of such a role, 'but we're not meant to be close, apparently.'

'Why not?' Alice had never heard a kid use the word *apparently* before and it both impressed and alarmed her.

'My father says . . .' His voice fell away and he frowned.

'What does your father say?' Alice was suddenly consumed with curiosity. *Why* weren't they meant to be friends? What was behind the shadowy unease between the two families?

But Jonty only shrugged and moved away to the stairs

leading up to where all the cars were parked. After a while he turned back, motioning for Alice to follow him. She did so very tentatively.

This cousin of hers was older than her by a good three years, and he was taller and a boy, all of which made talking to him a little fraught. She was unsure how to act. But then, when they were standing opposite each other and out of earshot of their mothers, Jonty suddenly grinned. That was when she noticed his eyes – so green and bright, with long soft lashes surrounding them. She'd read about people having green eyes but had never seen any before.

'I've decided I don't care what *he* says,' Jonty whispered. 'What about you?'

'I don't know.' Alice shook her head. Her cousin seemed to be asking something of her.

He shrugged, and then said something that thrilled Alice to her core. 'It's up to us,' he'd said, 'don't you think?'

'Okay,' Alice nodded eagerly.

'We could meet and talk about all kinds of stuff without them knowing. I could be like your big brother.'

'Okay!' Alice had been delighted. She had never been asked to be part of a secret alliance before. All the way home in the car she was dying to tell her mother about it, but she knew that if she did the whole plan would be in jeopardy, the magic of it all might disappear.

Oh, Mumma, she prays suddenly. *Give me some sign. Let me know if he is the one who* . . . She remembers that her mother had liked Jonty. She used to say he was a special kid who'd had a hard trot with that man. That he should be cut some slack when he got into trouble, and that he was extremely clever. *What else? What else did my mother say?*

'I think we should let them come,' Alice says finally.

'Very well then.' Her grandmother sighs deeply and opens her eyes. 'I'll invite them to afternoon tea next weekend.'

Alice suddenly panics, opens her mouth to renege on what she has just said. But no words come out.

'But, Alice . . .' Her grandmother is looking at her seriously.

'Yes, Gran?'

'I'll need you there.'

'I'll be there, Gran.'

TOM

No need for the alarm, Tom is awake at six anyway. He leans over and switches it off and lies there a moment, glad to be awake. He'd been dreaming of her again, some crazy stuff about running after her down a road at night, but he doesn't feel too bad now. Good really. Having something different to do helps get his mind away from it.

The truth is, since that day in the courthouse he can't stop thinking about Alice Wishart. He shuts his eyes at night and it's her face he sees. He wakes up in the morning and it's there. That lovely *sad* face! The awkward hour in the café only made it worse. His dreams are wild and murky and always about being lost and trying to find her, or else about chasing after her into some unknown dangerous territory. He still doesn't understand what happened in that courtroom. All he knows is something *did* happen. Since that day her face is in his head, she is *breathing* under everything else going on in his life.

Tom throws off the blankets, jacks up the blind and looks out.

But there is nothing to see. The darkness is as thick as a blanket. He gets into a shirt, jumper, jeans, socks and boots, then grabs his jacket from the cupboard. Only takes a minute. September now. The days are starting to get light earlier. It will be dawn in twenty minutes. Mustn't wake his dad or Nanette. Sneak out of the bedroom. Tiptoe down the passage to the kitchen. Fill the kettle, switch it on. A quick coffee and he'll be awake.

'How about getting me something fancy for the weekend front page?' his boss had suggested the night before, as they were leaving.

'What do you want?' Tom had tried to hide his surprise. His pleasure, too. Steve is a nice guy, easy to get along with and good for a laugh. But there are four photographers on staff and Tom is the most junior, so he never expected to be given anything interesting. He assumed the others were busting their guts for something other than weddings and kids' sports days, Farmer Ted's prize bull and the latest local to make a name for himself in the big bad world.

'Sunday is the first day of spring.' Steve, a tall heavy bloke with a loud voice to match, was easing his bulky frame into his car. 'How about early morning down on the coast?' He slammed the door shut and wound down the window of his Holden Commodore. 'Let's see what they're teaching you in that fancy course.' He grinned at Tom as he backed the car out of his space.

'You're on,' Tom calls after him. 'Might even take the old Minolta out for a run.'

'Good man,' Steve yells as he roars off. 'I'll leave it to you then.'

So that's the plan: head out to East Beach to catch the sun coming up, with the lovely battered old 35mm single-lens reflex camera that his grandfather owned when he was about Tom's age. A couple of rolls of slow film and a tripod ought to do it. Of course, actual film isn't used much anymore. At the *Chronicle*, and even back at college, it's all digital. The images are there on the computer as soon as you get back to the office. Every device on his old camera has been superseded a thousand times over. But the lens still happens to be among the best ever made, and if you know how, there are things you can do with these old cameras that the digital technology can't. For all its efficiency, the equipment Tom works with at the *Chronicle* doesn't come anywhere near this heavy old girl for subtlety. Besides, he loves handling it. He loves its weight and the clicking of the shutter. He loves taking light readings manually and working out the aperture and speeds and . . . all the rest of it, because it reminds him of his grandfather.

There is a thermos on top of the fridge. He pulls it down and fills it with instant coffee, grabs a banana from the bowl and heads out to the trusty rust bucket.

'Hey, Tom!' It's his old man at the back door. Probably come out for a leak. Not a real pretty sight in his jocks with his gut hanging out under the grubby T-shirt he slept in, grey hair sticking up all over like a porcupine. 'Where you going at this hour?' he says, all gruff and bleary-eyed.

'Gotta shoot the ocean,' Tom calls back. 'Sorry if I woke you.'

'You're going to *shoot* the ocean?' Luke smiles and shakes his head.

'Shoot it to bits!' Tom gives him the thumbs-up before opening the door of the old bomb and climbing in. Luke walks over with a look on his face that tells Tom he'd like to come along too, if he could.

'This for work?'

'Yeah.' Tom slips the key in and starts the engine. 'So, Dad, what's up with you and Nanette?' He'd walked in on them having one of their rows again the night before.

But Luke only shrugs as he lights up a fag. 'Ah, dunno.' He takes a deep drag.

'Something about Mum?' Tom asks curiously. He was only half-listening but Nanette was raving on about not having dignity in front of Anna. Something like that anyway.

'Your mum is bringing Nellie and Ned down this weekend.'

'So?' Tom sighs in exasperation. 'Nanette objects?'

'She wants to move in properly and get married.' Luke sighs. 'Suppose that's at the bottom of it.'

Tom waits but Luke doesn't expand on this. He feels for his old man and wishes he could say something helpful to him like, *So tell her what she wants to hear.* But the fact is, he actually doesn't like Nanette much and hopes Luke *doesn't* marry her. Tom revs up the rust bucket, turns on the lights and give his father a quick toot. Then he backs out of the yard and heads off down the street.

Once he's at the beach he locks the car, walks down onto the sand and starts looking about. Not much is happening, but he doesn't care too much. He loves waiting for the moment. Sometimes he thinks it was what he was born for. The sky is mottled, mostly heavy grey, and the sea is a black monster roaring back and forth as he walks along the sand. A sharp wind makes him wish he'd remembered his beanie.

Half a kilometre along, Tom stops to load film into the camera. Then he screws the camera to the tripod and keeps walking. It won't be long now. He's praying for the clouds to break a bit so there will be something to see. He breathes in the cold salty air, thinking of his father and then his mother. Neither of them is happy anymore and he wonders why. What really pulled them apart?

Ah, here we go! His prayers have been answered. The sky is breaking up, leaving tiny patches of pale translucent blue between the long threaded beads of dark cloud. The light comes through them like long straight spikes of gold. Slowly, very slowly, it gets stronger and the tops of the black waves start to come alive too, shimmering with gold and pink bubbles of light. Moments pass. Or is it minutes? The clouds are cracking now and the big red sun is coming through like a victory flag. *Wow! Where is the music to go with this? A majestic drumbeat, maybe, or some famous singer belting out a Verdi aria.* The water is on fire with a million glowing flames. Tom sets up the tripod quickly, parks his eye at the viewfinder and begins to shoot.

Corny? Of course it's bloody corny. It's a sunrise for Christ's sake! If you've seen one, you've seen a million. But at the beginning of any shoot you've got to get the obvious out of the way before you can go on to anything else. It's a way of settling down, of getting into a rhythm. You're out there hunting for images, but you're hunting for what's inside too. It doesn't come all at once. It happens on a deeper level than words. If you wait for the perfect shot to come along then odds-on nothing will happen. But by setting up the camera and shooting a bit here and there you gradually move into another place in your head. It happens by degrees, ever so slowly, and after a while it's like being in a trance. Nothing else exists except the light and the form between the four sides of the viewfinder. The camera becomes an extension of his hands and eyes. Tom is in another realm entirely.

He keeps walking for a bit and then stops to watch a van pull up. Three guys get out and pull on wetsuits. Tom laughs, imagining how freezing the water will be in that cold Southern Ocean at this hour. Their idle chat and spurts of laughter come back to him on the wind as he lines up the shot. A jogger suddenly pulls into frame in front of the surfers, making her way towards Tom. Against the sea she looks good, blonde hair blowing back, absolute determination on her face. Now she is on her own and behind her, against the amazing sky, three gulls wheel and spin in the wind. Tom catches all of them facing different directions in the frame; the woman's face down in the left-hand corner looks spooky with those weird birds above her.

Once up in the car park, he sees the surfers better. Three older guys and one little kid about ten, someone's kid brother. He's standing apart, looking on longingly as the others organise their boards. He wants to be part of it, but he knows he's too young. One of the older guys moves across to talk with him. The big brother? Tom snaps them from behind, two black silhouettes against that bright streaky sky. The tall one puts his arm around the kid's shoulders, and Tom catches the moment.

None of this is what he's after, but he's still trying to get into the rhythm. The little guy gets him thinking of his own brother, Ned, and the fact that he hasn't seen him for two months. Ned took the brunt of their parents' bust-up. Just twelve years old, he sort of closed up around that time, his speech impediment got worse and his friends stopped coming over. By the beginning of the next year he was living a new life in the city . . . No one was paying him enough attention. Luke was walking around like a shell-shock victim. His mother, Anna, couldn't talk normally to anyone without shouting and/or crying, and Nellie ignored the whole situation by spending every waking minute out with her friends. Tom wasn't any better, except that it wasn't the divorce on his mind, but Lillian's murder . . .

But you can always find some excuse to behave like a shabby mean selfish prick. Tom never asked Ned how he found his new school, or if he missed his hometown and his old mates. He was too keen on getting away himself.

Tom catches the surfers as they are about to hit the water. He introduces himself and tells them the paper might use a shot of them on the front page the following weekend. They are immediately enthusiastic, so he takes down their names and a few other bits and pieces about where they work and why they surf, then leaves them laughing and jostling with each other about who'll look the best in the photo. After all that, he moves on down the beach to see if he can catch them on a wave to complete the series.

Surfers on the water: black insects against the red and gold sky. The shots he gets are *nice* enough. In fact, he knows they're just the kind of thing Steve wants. They'll sit well on the front page. But Tom hankers to go better. It's the way he's always been. He's running out of time this morning, but he'll have another go tomorrow. He wants to get something really special.

A pile of scattered black rocks marks the end of the beach. Further around are the cliffs, steep and craggy and impossible to get to at high tide. He walks up from the beach, along the winding tracks through the grass and over to the old disused bridge across the river.

He and Jonty lit a fire here once at the beginning of Year Eleven, when they were both about sixteen. It was hot and they'd come down to the river with a couple of girls from another school that they'd debated against. The topic that day had been 'Australia needs the American Alliance more than ever', and Tom and Jonty had argued the affirmative. But the girls' team had won and they teased Tom and Jonty about that mercilessly. *Females are just so much superior, why don't you admit it!* They were nice girls, though, and the four of them had had a lot of fun, laughing and mucking about. Jonty had a small flask of Jack Daniels which they passed around. Then Tom had made a fire while the girls ran over to the supermarket and bought sausages and tomato sauce and a loaf of sliced white bread. Tom and Jonty stuck long sticks up the snags and held them over the flames to cook. The girls moaned and complained but in the end they all ate them, burnt on the outside and half raw inside. In fact, they all stuffed themselves, then took off their shoes and waded in the river.

Tom remembers how exciting it was to have girls to do things with. At about nine, the girls had had to leave, and Tom fell into bed that night mad keen to meet up again with the one he'd fallen for. *Louise.* She had dark hair and blue eyes that danced when she smiled. But within a week he'd forgotten all about her. And they never saw either of them again.

That was before they'd even met Lillian. It is sometimes hard now for Tom to remember what life was like back then. Eight o'clock already. Shit, he's been out on the beach for over an hour. Better get back, have a shower, change his clothes and get to work. But he doesn't move. He sits on one of the rocks wishing the out-of-sync feeling that seems to have set up camp in his head since the courtroom would just piss off.

It's not until he gets to the office that he sees that day's edition of the *Chronicle*. There is a small article on page two, with a picture of Lillian's face alongside the headline *New lead on Wishart murder.* There is a brief summary of the known details of the case and then a police spokesman claiming that the police 'might only be days away from making an arrest'.

Tom's heart jumps in his chest and his mouth goes dry. *What the hell does that mean?*

Tom gets home at about six that night to find his father already in his work clothes, covered in dust and grime, clearing out the shed. Unusual. Luke is usually not home until seven or eight, and he hardly ever gets around to cleaning anything. Tom calls hello, goes inside to put his camera away, then comes out again.

'So what brought this on?' he asks.

'Ned is bringing his bike and surfboard,' Luke grins. 'Thought I'd better make some room for him.'

The place is packed full of rubbish: rusty bikes, cans of paint, packets of unopened tools (every so often Luke likes to pretend he's a tradesman), three old lawnmowers and piles of cardboard boxes. There is also a 1958 DeSoto car that Luke plans to restore one day and about a dozen model aeroplanes, many with wings off or broken, scattered about like disintegrating dead insects.

'When are they coming?' Tom asks, throwing an old bottle in the bin.

'Tomorrow at about midday.'

'Will Nanette be here?'

'No.' Luke raises his eyes to heaven. 'She's staging a protest.'

'What about?'

'Not being married, especially in front of my ex-wife!'

'Jeez, Dad,' Tom shakes his head, 'sounds like you two are really made for each other!'

'Yep,' Luke laughs, 'getting on like the proverbial house on fire.'

'So who is the house and who is the fire?'

'What do you reckon?'

Tom doesn't question him any more. His mother and Nanette are always civil to each other, because Anna knows she wasn't *the other woman*. Even so, it's usually pretty strained.

'Flatten these out for me, will you?' Luke hands him a pile of boxes. 'Then take them down to the drum.'

'Okay.'

The drum is where Luke burns stuff at the end of the yard. Apparently it's against the law, but that doesn't worry him. He gets the cleaning bug about once every two years and it's usually a matter of keeping out of his way until it's over. Tom begins pulling the boxes apart.

'You see the paper today?'

His father stops hurling small cans of old paint into a metal rubbish bin. 'All piss and wind,' he says shortly.

'How do you know that?'

'Well, I don't, but . . . I'd bet on it.' Luke picks up another can and aims it at the bin. He misses and the can clatters along the concrete floor of the shed.

'So why are they doing it?'

'Jonty will have rung them the way he rang you and me,' Luke says. 'He can't leave it alone.'

'But if there is nothing in it . . .'

'Look, Tom, they want Jonty,' Luke says matter-of-factly. 'They believe he's guilty and want to haul him in like a fish on a line.'

'What's that mean?'

'Get him talking and maybe he'll give something away.'

'They want him to confess?'

But the old man won't answer that. He just shrugs, hands Tom some more boxes, then heads off down to the other end of the shed, making loud sniffing noises.

'Has Jonno rung you again, Dad?'

'Nope.'

'Are you going to ring him?'

'Nope.'

'You're his lawyer!'

'That's right. I'm not his mother! He'll call when he needs me.' Luke sniffs dramatically a few more times and opens one of the side windows. 'This place has got stuffy.'

'Did Alice say anything?' Tom asks after a while.

'Nope,' his dad says.

'Did you talk to her about it?'

'Not my place.'

Tom feels like asking his father if he's having second thoughts now about employing Alice, but doubts he'd admit it if he did.

As far as Tom's concerned, this turn of events proves his own instinct was correct. Luke is Jonty's lawyer and so Alice Wishart shouldn't be working in his office. End of story.

'Can't be much fun living with old Phyllis,' his father mutters conversationally. 'Cantankerous old bitch!'

'Why do you say that?'

'I used to do all her legal work,' Luke stops to laugh, as he shoves a full wheelbarrow towards the door. 'Jeez, that old bird has got a head on her for money! No two ways about it. She's canny. She moved to another firm when I started representing Jonno, and I was bloody glad she did. More trouble than she was worth.'

'How come?'

'She was in and out of my office every week, changing her will!'

'Yeah?'

'And she queried every bill I sent.'

'Did she pay them in the end?'

'Too right she paid!' Luke laughs again. 'I once held over an important document until she paid three or four unpaid accounts, and she didn't like that one little bit.'

'What happened?'

'We understood each other after that,' he said, smiling at the memory. 'She stopped playing games with me when she knew I meant business.'

'So what is Alice like . . . at work?' Tom asks, trying to sound as though he doesn't care one way or the other, when in fact his heart has begun to pound just saying her name.

'Very good,' Luke sighs, and looks around for the next job. 'Methodical, bright and hardworking, but she must be lonely living up there in that great big mausoleum.' He stops and looks at his son, frowning. 'It'd be nice if you befriended her a bit, Tom.

That kid has had a tough time. When you go out with your mates, you could ask her to come along. I get the impression she doesn't get out much.'

'I already have,' Tom says bluntly. 'I invited her to come with us to that concert.'

'And?'

'She wasn't interested.'

'Why not?'

'How do I know?' Tom snaps. 'She's not exactly friendly.'

'Oh, I wouldn't say that!' His father frowns. 'She's very friendly at work. Seems to really enjoy it and . . .' He chucks down one of the model planes. 'Why don't we go and have something to eat now? We've made a bit of room. I'll come back out again later and finish up.' He throws the broom aside and winds up the side window. 'What do you feel like for tea? There's steak and eggs, steak and potatoes or steak and onions.'

'All of the above,' Tom smiles, 'with tomatoes!'

'What? You want steak with eggs, potatoes, onions *and* tomatoes?'

'Yeah.'

'Demanding brat!' On the way into the house he puts a hand on Tom's shoulder. 'Something is worrying you. I can tell.' Tom shrugs. 'It's the Wishart thing, isn't it?'

Tom shrugs again and moves away from his father into the kitchen.

Luke washes his hands at the sink and dries them on a tea towel. 'Try not to worry,' he says conversationally, 'this business will come to nothing. You won't have to be embroiled in it all over again.'

'What makes you so sure?' Tom slumps down in a chair at the table and flips the *Age* back to the front page. Another gangland murder and four Iranians found with explosives on their way to a London airport. The world goes on.

'It will be Jonno up to his old tricks,' Luke continues quietly. 'There'll be no evidence, no trial. He can get on with his life and same goes for you.'

'What about Alice, Dad?'

'What about Alice?'

'She needs to know who killed her mother!'

Luke sighs and goes to the fridge, pulls out the eggs and some salad things and then two huge pieces of choice rump. 'Can you eat all that?' he asks, holding one of them up.

'Half,' Tom says, thinking that they must teach *dodging the issue* in Law School. His old man would have come top of the class. He watches his father cut the meat and switch on the griller.

'I don't know about all that stuff,' Luke muses, 'really I don't. The Yanks are into this "victim vengeance" caper and where does it get them? What good will it do for her to know who killed her mother? It's hardly likely to bring the poor woman back, is it?'

'*What?*' Tom lets his mouth fall open for effect, but Luke only laughs. Tom can see that his father knows he's committed a clanger and is trying to laugh it off. 'I fucking can't believe you just said that!' Tom shakes his head to underline the point. 'I really can't.'

'Language, Thomas, language.' Luke is slightly more shamefaced now. 'Well, *you* tell me why I'm wrong?'

'So *justice* doesn't matter anymore?' Tom declares derisively, as he starts breaking up lettuce for the salad. 'That's truly pathetic! You're a lawyer and you think justice doesn't matter!'

'Hmmmm.' Luke rubs his chin then bends to re-position the meat under the grill. That done, he looks up at Tom. 'Yeah, of course justice matters, Tom,' he says seriously, 'but you get older and you care less about the big ideas. Somehow even doing the right thing by the people around you is hard enough.' His apologetic smile tells Tom that he doesn't want a serious argument. 'That kid has to have a lawyer. It might as well be me.'

'Oh, right.' Tom juggles a couple of tomatoes in the air before putting them down on the chopping board. He picks up a sharp knife and begins to chop them. 'And those Jews are going to die anyway, so it might as well be me who switches on the gas. And someone is going to torture some poor bastard in jail in Iran or Chile or China, so it might as well be me. I get the drift. Nice one, Dad!'

'What are you saying?' his father looks up sharply.

'I don't know,' Tom sighs.

'Everyone has a right to legal representation in our system of justice,' Luke continues sternly. 'Everyone is innocent until proven guilty. You say you don't believe in that?'

'I'm saying that someone accused of murder should not be able to just sit there and say . . . nothing! They should have to account for themselves at the very least!'

'So, no right to silence?'

But Tom is unsure now. All those cop shows where they're handcuffing some innocent guy and at the same time shouting, *I'm duty bound to inform you that you have the right to remain silent and that anything you say might be used in a court of law*, start playing over in his mind.

'Well,' his father shrugs, 'I work within the system we've got.'

'Even if you know someone is guilty?' Tom shoots back at him.

There is a slight pause. Luke stands up from where he is bending to turn the meat and looks straight at Tom. 'Jonty van der Weihl has never admitted guilt to me!' Luke says, stabbing the air with his finger, 'and if he did tell me he was guilty, I would not defend him on a *not guilty* plea, anyway. Simple as that! It would *not* be ethical, so I wouldn't do it.'

'But you've got a fair idea!' Tom hits right back. 'Just because he hasn't said the words!'

'A hunch is worth nothing. It's bullshit.'

'Why?' Tom thinks of all the films where the protagonist has only a hunch to go on. And how often it turns out to be right.

'It is up to a jury to decide on the basis of evidence!' Luke says. 'That's our system and it's a good one.'

'But how will the jury decide?' Tom sneers. '*You're* going to make bloody sure that he never goes near a court!'

Luke says nothing, but he is frowning as he goes to the cupboard and gets out plates, knives and forks. Tom finishes off the basic salad with way too much Paul Newman dressing – the lettuce looks like strips of dripping wallpaper – and places it in the middle of the table. He is sorry to have upset his old man. The meat smells good and he's really hungry.

'What about the eggs?'

'You want eggs?' Luke asks blandly.

'Yeah.'

Luke heats up oil in the frypan.

'Listen, Tom, I can only do my best for that kid,' Luke continues evenly. 'He used to be a mate of yours. Surely you wouldn't deny him a lawyer?'

Ah! That's below the belt! Tom has never talked to his father about the way he and Jonty fell out three years ago. *The way he dropped Jonty* . . . He watches the eggs spitting and sizzling in the pan and wonders if other people noticed the way he slid away like a . . . *coward*.

'I'm getting old, Tom.' Luke throws the eggshells one at a time into the rubbish bin over the other side of the room. He gets all four in and they grin at each other.

'That's your excuse, is it?' Tom says lightly.

'Yep.' Luke forks the meat onto the plates.

'Well I suppose we all tell ourselves bullshit in order to keep the wolf from the door, eh?' Tom is dismayed by his own judgemental attitude but can't seem to help it.

'Jeez! What's got into you?' His father suddenly laughs. 'Give an old codger a break, will you!'

They eat companionably in front of the television, then Luke goes to finish off the shed. After watching a football panel show and then half of a sexy European movie, Tom decides to go to bed. He finds his father making up the spare bed downstairs.

'What are you doing that for?'

'I thought your mother might like to stay tomorrow night,' Luke says casually, without looking up. He is taking great care to make the sheet corners absolutely straight, and it strikes Tom that this is probably the first time he's ever seen his father make a bed in his life. 'After the long drive. What do you think?'

'Oh, yeah.' Tom shrugs as though this is a perfectly reasonable, thoughtful and kind suggestion. But he knows the whole idea of his mum staying the night is simply wishful thinking on his father's part, and *that* makes him feel sad.

Tom's mother, sister and brother arrive at about midday the next day. It's only been a couple of months, but Nellie and Ned have both changed for the better. Nellie looks good in her short grubby denim skirt, black jumper with holes in both elbows and hot pink leggings complete with a few runs up the back. The heavy Doc Martins could do with a clean – there's dried mud encircling both heels – but even so she manages to look ultra cool. She's always had a great sense of style, but now, at eighteen, any awkwardness she had seems to have gone. The carelessly worn red scarf around her neck, and the jet-black hair pulled straight back into a knot at the back of her head, make her look like a cool French student off to a philosophy lecture. Tom grins, thinking that she'll go well with the sharp crowd at uni next year.

'G'day, Ned!' Tom gives his fourteen-year-old brother a hug. 'You takin' growth pills, or what?' Ned's skin is spotty, but his eyes are clear and bright. He's also not hanging his head and looking like he'd rather be somewhere else, which is a big improvement. Even before they get inside he backs up against Tom so their father can measure them. Tom is just over six feet and Ned is delighted when Luke tells him that he's only a couple of inches shorter.

'You'll be bossing *him* around soon, Kel!' Their mum laughs, as she hugs Tom.

'When have I ever bossed him around?'

'Don't call me Kel!'

'Sorry!' Kel is Ned's pet name, from Ned Kelly.

'Well if it isn't lover boy!' Nellie smirks. 'Broken any hearts since you've been here?' They clap hands, then a quick hard hug, glad to see each other. Nellie was in on some of the stuff that went down when he split with Amanda, so she feels she's entitled to hang it on Tom about his love life.

'Only three or four.' Tom grabs one end of the red scarf and tries to unwind it before his sister can slip away. 'So you've been hanging out in St Vinnies again, have you, Sis?'

'At least I have *some* idea!' Nellie steps away for a long cool look at what he's wearing. 'Same old baggy jeans, I see, and this has to be,' she plucks at his chest and makes a disgusted face, 'one of Dad's cast-off jumpers!' She hugs her father, pats Tom on the head disdainfully and walks past him into the house. 'Thought you'd have a whole new wardrobe for the big lights of Woobie by now, Tommy boy!'

Woobie is the name Nellie and Tom gave their home town when they moved to the city. Nellie had pretended to be totally glad to have left, but Tom knows she missed everything a lot. He

209

can see in her eyes that she's glad to be back, even for a visit. Ned wasn't old enough to pretend. He was really homesick for the first two years.

Nellie and Ned are first inside. Tom follows his parents, who are talking quietly about the way Ned's speech impediment has improved dramatically over the last few months. It's true, Tom thinks. From the little bit he's heard, the stutter is almost gone.

Once they realise that Nanette isn't there, his brother and sister immediately begin snooping around their old house, commenting on changes and reliving past triumphs and mishaps.

'Hey, Nellie, remember when you cut your foot trying to escape out the window?'

'I wasn't escaping; I was—'

'You sooked for ages!'

'I did not!'

'Who gave you this dorky painting, Dad?'

They open windows, poke in cupboards, loll about on the furniture and make rude comments. Although Anna is being super-polite, it amuses Tom to see that she's dying to have a poke around, too. It's her old house after all, and she hasn't seen it for over a year and then only with Nanette around. Tom watches his mother looking at everything, smiling at the photos that Luke has pinned up and even running her hands over the furniture – most of which she chose herself.

'Love this chair,' she mumbles to herself as she sits down in the huge old leather club with a glass of wine. 'They don't make them like this anymore.'

'Take it, if you want,' Luke immediately responds. 'I don't need it.' He waves around the room, which probably *is* too full of furniture, although its cluttered comfortable feel is nice.

Anna smiles at him a bit sadly. Luke has always erred on the side of being overly generous. 'Thanks, Luke, but I knew when I bought my apartment that I wouldn't have room for this kind of stuff.'

Luke cooks the barbeque outside and Tom helps his mother make the salad. Nellie and Ned are meant to set the table but basically just stand around stuffing themselves with slices of the fresh bread, packed up high with dips and olives and whatever else they can get their hands on, while teasing Tom about his dorky taste in music. Years ago they'd caught him listening to a country album and they've never let him forget it.

Eventually, the five of them are sitting around the table and it's just like old times on a good day. Nellie isn't snaking around like a viper, hitting out with nasty comments about everything from someone's bad breath to the state of the nation under the present government. And Ned seems to have gained a whole lot of new opinions, along with his renewed ease in speaking. Ned is probably the major factor that puts the rest of them in such a good mood. He's not sitting back with the blank doltish look on his face that he'd worn for most of last three years, letting everything happen around him. He's getting in there with his own comments and jokes and put-downs.

It's pretty rare for the five of them to be together these days, and Tom can see it means a lot to his parents to see everyone happy. Luke and Anna don't say much, but they laugh and smile and obviously love the banter.

'Saw Amanda the other day.' Nellie has a look in her eye that tells Tom she might well be lying, but he couldn't care less.

'Yeah?' Tom acts interested just to get her going. 'So how is she?'

'Amanda is *sooo* hot!' Ned cuts in, pointing his fork across the table at Tom. 'You were the biggest friggin' *idiot* in the world to break up with her!'

'Yeah, well.' Tom gives his little brother a kick in the shins. 'My business, isn't it? You want to have a kick of the footy later?'

'Yeah!'

'She had a guy with her.' Nellie waits for everyone to take in this information. 'Older dude in a really cool leather jacket.'

'Probably her personal trainer,' Tom quips. Amanda was a complete perfectionist. If she put on an ounce it was all systems go at the gym for the next week. All that *perfect body* stuff bored Tom after a while, so many times they'd go out to eat and she'd have about three bites and say she wasn't hungry when Tom knew she was.

'Wanted to know how you were,' Nellie goes on.

'So, what did you say?'

'I said as far as I knew you were the same complete loser you've always been.'

'Gee, thanks, Nellie! Good to know I've got someone to put out the good word about me!'

'She wanted to know about your new girlfriend.'

'No go on that front,' Tom shoots her a wry look, 'unfortunately.'

'Dad?' Nellie turns to him.

'How would I know?' Luke grins.

'I bet he's panting after some hot little local Barbie doll!'

'I did see two girls outside my office checking him over the other day,' Luke adds mildly, 'but I have no idea if—'

'Who?' Tom cuts in. *What if it was Alice?*

'Didn't know them.' Luke laughs at his quick response and looks around at the others. 'He's interested, though, isn't he?'

'So what did they look like?' Tom asks, more to keep the ball rolling than because he really wants to know.

Luke frowns, trying to think. 'Ah well . . .' He looks at his ex-wife down at the other end of the table. 'Everyone under forty looks eighteen to me these days.'

'I know what you mean!' Anna grimaces. 'We had a locum in at work the other day and I thought he was my partner Rob's son, so I asked him how school was going!'

'*Mum!*' they all chorus.

'That is truly fucking pathetic, Mum,' Nellie almost shouts as she serves herself more meat. 'There is no excuse for being so completely stupid.'

'Watch your language, missy!' Anna slaps Nellie's hand. 'It's just not appropriate to speak like that . . .'

'But it is so insulting!'

'Mum *is* blind!' Ned says solemnly and everyone nods, including Luke. She is too vain to wear her glasses most of the time.

'Honestly, Mum,' Nellie lectures with a full mouth, 'you can't just go around humiliating people like that because you're too proud to wear glasses!'

'Humiliating!' Luke comments dryly. 'Wish someone would ask *me* how school is going!'

Suddenly Ned is spluttering with laughter, his face red with it as he rocks helplessly on his chair, pointing one finger at his father. It's so good to see Ned like this that the rest of them crack up laughing before they've even heard the joke.

'Imagine Dad in a school uniform!' he shouts, and they all hoot away picturing poor old fat Luke in grey shorts and tie . . .

Not that funny at all, Tom thinks wryly, *but so what? You had to be there. It was just really good.*

After the lunch dishes have been put away, Tom has a kick outside with Ned. When he comes back inside, he finds Nellie trying to cajole Luke into taking the boat out for a fishing trip. Tom can see his father would rather just stay home and catch up with his ex-wife, but he ends up agreeing.

'Will you come, Tom? Help me lift the boat?'

'Sure.' Tom had been planning to head off in the car for a couple of hours with his camera, but he doesn't want to be the spoiler.

'Anna, you want to come?' Luke asks.

'I'll come and watch,' she smiles. 'I get sick, remember.'

The old man immediately gets into Chief Commander mode, working out what tackle to take, telling Ned how to lift his end of the boat and Nellie how to hook bait. Everyone starts fighting about who will wear what coat and if the life jackets are seaworthy. Nellie tries hers on and starts screaming because there's a spider.

Part of Tom is looking on all this a bit cynically. *A family outing? Wow!* Been a while since he's been on one of these! But he can see that Ned is so thrilled by everything that he thinks, *What the hell. Just get into it.* He grabs his coat and the old Minolta. Might as well catch a few happy snaps on the boat while he's at it. They all pile into the grunge-filled four-wheel drive and head off.

It takes less than five minutes to get down to the pier. Tom helps his father start the motor, which takes a bit of doing. They're both cursing and yelling and kicking it in the side by the time it splutters to life, but at last the whole circus is ready to launch. It's a bit cramped in the boat with four so Tom elects to stay back with his mother, who is sitting up on the grassy embankment in the sunshine, watching them all.

He grabs his camera and runs back down to the water to snap the three of them: Nellie, Ned and Luke, all laughing and waving as the crappy little tin dinghy roars out over the water.

It's a good day for it. Slight breeze, but the slate-grey water is calm enough. It shimmers like flat steel under the overcast sky. Tom walks back from the water to where his mother is sitting on a long bench, both arms extended across the back, her head back, face turned up to the sky.

'Hey, Mum!' Tom calls out as he gets nearer.

He catches her look of confusion and surprise as she opens her eyes and sits up, dazed; then her warm smile as she sees him walking towards her, still clicking away.

'Not too many! I haven't got my lipstick on.'

'You look fine.'

'Okay, Tom,' she teases as he sits down beside her, 'what's going on in your life? You've got that faraway look in your eye.'

'Nothing,' Tom shrugs, looking out over the water. The little boat is now just a silver speck racing towards the horizon.

'You're preoccupied,' she insists.

'No, I'm not!'

'What is happening?'

'Not much at all,' Tom says shortly, 'apart from working on the paper.'

'So . . . good living with Dad?'

'Yep.' What is it with mothers? He'd seen her watching him through lunch, looking for any clues about what was going through his head. He'd had to work hard to keep up the carefree front. The idea of anyone, much less his parents, knowing anything about his preoccupation with Alice Wishart would be horror territory of the first order.

'What about Nanette?' she asks casually.

'Nanette is . . . Nanette,' Tom sighs. He could mouth off about the way the woman annoys him but decides not to.

'You get along with her okay?'

'Fine.' Tom smiles at his mother and she smiles back wryly. She knows what is going down on that front without being told, anyway.

They're quiet for a while, watching small groups of tourists wander by, looking at the boats and eating ice-cream. It's very picturesque down here. The clouds clear for a bit and his mother takes off her heavy jacket.

'I just love watching the sky,' she mumbles, pushing her face up into the light again. Tom looks up. Clouds are skidding past in the wind, but every now and again the sun makes a brief appearance. It's ages since he's just sat about with his mother. They used to do stuff like this all the time. Tom slides over and puts his arm around her shoulders.

'How is Heath?'

'Oh, he's terrific,' she says, without much interest.

'You really like him?'

'Sure thing.'

'Going to get married?' Tom asks.

The question obviously surprises her because she sits up properly and looks at him. 'Goodness!' she laughs, a little defensively. 'That might be a little extreme, don't you think?'

'Has he asked you?'

'Well, yes, but . . .' Tom can tell by her eyes that she is being evasive. 'I'm just not sure if I want . . . to marry again.'

'Why not?'

'Well . . . been there, done that. We're going to Europe and that's going to be *soooo* very lovely!' she suddenly says enthusiastically. 'I haven't been since I was in my twenties! I'm so looking forward to it!' She links her arm through Tom's, smiles again and then pushes her face back up into the sun. 'He's terrific.' She sounds as though she is trying to convince herself. 'A very nice man.'

'Do you love him, Mum?' Tom knows he shouldn't ask his mother such intrusive questions, but he's thinking, *What the hell.* He suddenly wants to know the score. *What is love? Is what I feel about Alice Wishart love or . . . something else?*

'Ah, what's love?' Anna murmurs quietly.

'So you don't love him?' The thing Tom has for Alice feels

216

more like an illness than love. It's a physical condition that won't leave him alone. It doesn't seem to matter what he *should* feel about her. He can sometimes forget for a little while. The family lunch was fine; he got stuck into what was happening for a couple of hours, but then *wham*! It's back. *I want to see her. Alice Wishart. No one else will do.* The feeling, the yearning, the wanting invades without warning. Not pleasant at all.

'I didn't say that!'

'Okay then . . . what are you saying?'

She gives a deep sigh, but Tom is buggered if he'll let her off the hook so easily. Some stuff you've got to know.

'Look, we get on,' she explains, not meeting his eyes. 'We are great friends. We like doing things together. Concerts and plays. He's considerate and kind and absolutely understanding and very . . . undemanding. If I go to his place after work there is a meal ready for me.' She turns to Tom with an apologetic smile. 'What I'm saying is that I have a good life with him.'

'So why don't you live with him?'

'There are Nellie and Ned to consider.' She is defensive now. 'And yes, I need my space sometimes. I do like having my own place.'

'So you *don't* love him?' Tom continues ruthlessly.

His mother has clearly had enough. She jumps up, grabs Tom by both shoulders and looks into his eyes.

'I loved your father, Tom,' she says, 'and look where that got me!'

'What are you saying?'

'That love is overrated.'

Tom doesn't say anything to that. But he's surprised by her vehemence after all this time. He owes it to the old man to at least try to put another point of view. 'Dad is sorry about all that stuff, Mum,' he says eventually.

'All that *stuff*?' Anna repeats incredulously. 'Listen, Tom, once trust has been broken it's gone, okay? There is no getting away from that!'

'But do you still love Dad?' Tom cuts in.

She hesitates a moment, open-mouthed at the suggestion.

'*We're divorced, Tom!*' she says sharply. 'Have been for nearly three years. I thought you understood that?'

'Of course I understand it, but—'

'You don't love people who betray you!'

'Don't you?'

'No, you don't, Tom. You don't.'

Do you have any choice? he wants to ask. Tom never did get his parents' split. Everyone makes mistakes, why should all trust be obliterated by his dad's one big blunder? Then again, everyone is different. His mother has always been tough. Maybe it's her job: always being the one in charge, telling everyone what the score is. No one messes with her.

Luke, Nellie and Ned stay out for over two hours. They come in full of excitement, the bucket full of two quite large bream. They put the boat back onto the trailer and head for home. In the car, Anna takes a look at her watch. 'Should really be on the road,' she says worriedly from the back seat. 'It's a four-hour drive.'

'I made up the back room for you in case you wanted to stay,' his dad says lightly, but Anna doesn't answer. Tom takes a glance at her serious profile. She is frowning. He reckons the idea might be attractive to her but that she doesn't want to admit it. He also knows that his father is probably hanging on her response.

'Be a lot of traffic on the roads tonight,' Luke adds casually.

Don't beg, Dad! Tom pleads under his breath. Luke has caught on that she doesn't seem keen on going back that night and is trying to push her buttons without it seeming so. Hasn't he learnt by now that his mother hates being manipulated?

'Why is that?'

'Racing in Dunkeld.'

'Right.'

But, amazingly, against all Tom's previous assumptions she does decide to stay. Luke orders in pizzas for tea and the five of them sit in front of the television to eat. Tom hasn't seen his father so cheery for years. He's in his element, cracking jokes, telling stories and making everyone laugh. Tom ends up ringing his mate Josh. He comes along with a good DVD and Craig, a guy Tom knew at high school. After the movie, Craig and Josh, Tom and Luke sit around playing cards till about two in the morning. All in all, it turns into a good night.

His mother leaves after lunch the next day. She gives everyone a hug, including a circumspect one for Luke. Tom, Nellie, Ned and Luke head out onto the verandah, to wave her goodbye. She unlocks the car, gets in and backs quickly out of the driveway into the street. Everyone is yelling the usual crap, 'See you, Mum' and 'Safe trip!' She waves back. She's smiling but her mouth is tight. She's feeling it. Tom doesn't dare turn to see if his dad has noticed. Tom hopes, in a way, that he hasn't. It is Ned who sees her anorak lying on the verandah. She has only gone a few metres, so everyone screams out for her to stop. Luckily she hears and Tom runs over to the car with it. Anna winds down the window to take it from him, and that's when he sees his mother's eyes are glassy with tears. He waits there, shielding her from the others, as a few escape and roll down her cheeks. Not knowing what to say, he hands her the coat and waits.

'It's okay, Tom,' she mutters, tucking the coat onto the seat alongside her and fumbling in her handbag for tissues. She blows her nose loudly, clears her throat and squeezes his hand briefly.

'You sure, Mum?' Tom puts his other hand on her shoulder. His mother doesn't cry often or easily.

'Sure.' She clears her throat and smiles. 'Just feeling a bit *thingo* about leaving everyone.' She laughs at herself and rams the stick into gear. 'You know how it is.'

'Okay, Mum.' Tom watches as she shoots off. He walks back to the others wondering what the hell *thingo* means. But he knows.

His father's mood remains buoyant for the rest of the evening, until poor old Nanette gets back the next day, in fact. Tom wants to caution him. *Mum left for a good reason, at least as far as she was concerned*. And Tom has seen up close the way she is with Heath. They do get on very well. But Tom doesn't say anything.

On Sunday night after the big family weekend, Tom is in bed by eleven, but once he's there he can't sleep. He tosses and turns, thinking about what he is doing with his life. As thirty minutes turns into an hour and then two, his outlook gets bleaker . . . and more desperate.

His father is having a relationship with a woman he doesn't even like much and he doesn't want to talk about ideas anymore. His mother is sticking with a guy because it's convenient and they have a *good life* together. *Shit! What does all that amount to? Not much of fuck all. No passion for anything except for a comfortable life.*

Tom sits up, suddenly angry, and switches the light on. Is this what happens to everyone when they hit thirty or forty or fifty? He's not suggesting everyone should be saving the world. But what about living with a smidgeon of integrity?

He stares up at the ceiling, then at the cobwebs in the corner and his old schoolboy stuff. He is almost twenty-two years old and what is he doing that is any different? Nothing. He has his old Minolta and his comfy little job at the local rag. He has his neat, lefty opinions and his secret ambitions. Is that what it's all about?

He gets up and opens the window, letting the gusty wind blast in. Freezing. A smattering of tiny rain bullets come straight at him, but he doesn't flinch. He leans out further into the night and watches his hands go blue with the cold.

She asked for his help not long ago, and he refused her. Okay they'd met up again, but that time in the café he was playing it safe, too. He didn't give away much. And he dismissed her one suggestion without coming up with anything himself. What did he offer her? Nothing. Same as always! His gut reaction has always been to look after number one. *And now?* There is something about that girl! Something about her that makes him sick of himself. Sick of who he is and how he operates in the world. *Crap.* He can't stand the idea of being just another wimpy shit who ducks the hard stuff. He wants to show her. Yeah, he wants to show that he'll put himself out on a limb for her. Do whatever has to be done. He'll go the whole way. Whatever it entails.

Tom goes out to the kitchen. He picks up the phone. He must commit himself before the temptation to stay cool and comfortable takes over. He dials three numbers and then . . . stops.

It's after midnight and he doesn't have her mobile number. What if he wakes the old lady? No one calls anyone at midnight! Tom puts the phone down again. Maybe he should get his clothes on, walk out into the wet cold night and simply knock on the door. But what if she's out? Maybe she'll come home late again in a taxi. His mind jumps from one improbable scenario to another.

Suddenly the phone rings. Startled, Tom stares at it stupidly. Who would call the house at this time on a Sunday night? His father is in bed. Anyway, clients always ring his mobile. No one would ring this house at this time . . . except *Jonty.* Jonty has seen the article in the paper. He probably needs to ease whatever is going on in that sick head of his by talking about it. Tom feels himself being dragged the other way. Isn't it enough to have rejected Jonty? *Do I have to orchestrate his ruin as well?*

Tom tries to steady himself and picks up the phone. 'Hello.'

'Tom?'

'Yeah. That you, Mum?'

'It's Alice Wishart.'

What? Tom grips the receiver harder and presses his other hand up against the wall. He watches the knuckles go white as he clenches his fist.

'Alice Wishart,' she says again.

'Oh, yeah,' Tom keeps his voice flat as a pancake. 'G'day, Alice.'

'Sorry to ring at this time,' she mutters in this hoarse, semi-whisper, 'but I thought you should know.'

'That's okay.' *Know what?* Tom's heart is pounding. There is silence for a while. Tom fancies that he can hear her heartbeat.

'Tom?'

'Yeah.'

But she doesn't say anything. He can picture her lovely face frowning. Maybe she's biting her lip. Maybe she is twisting a lock of dark hair around one of her long white fingers.

'Sorry,' she whispers at last.

'Don't worry, Alice,' Tom stammers and then mouths off the standard counsellor/cop line. 'Just . . . take your time.' He hates himself for doing it.

'Okay,' she whispers.

When she does pick up courage the words come rolling out like heavy bowling balls, one after another, knocking everything down in their path. 'You should know that Jed van der Weihl has come home and admitted guilt for my mother's murder,' Alice says, her voice a monotone. 'He has given himself up to police and is now in custody.'

'Whoa, hang on!' Tom breaks in with a sharp laugh. 'Sorry, Alice, I didn't hear you properly. What did you say?'

'Jed murdered my mother!'

'What?'

'Jed, *not* Jonty!' she cries loudly and angrily, then her voice breaks and he can hear that she is sobbing. 'You were wrong Tom! Everybody was wrong. They all thought it was Jonty, but it wasn't. It was . . . his father.'

'His father?'

'Yes.'

Shock hits Tom like a sudden gust of icy wind.

'How do you know this?'

'I've been with the police . . . for hours.' Her voice breaks again. 'He came in and they've been questioning him for days and now he's made a sworn statement. Everyone was accusing my cousin, including you and . . . I believed it,' she gasps through tears. 'But Jonty had nothing to do with it. My uncle Jed was the one and now he's come clean. Everyone thought he was out of the country but he came back early to talk my mother into convincing Grandma to change the will and . . . anyhow that's how it happened. The police have checked out his story. There is evidence,' she gasps, 'that he did it and let his son take the blame.'

Tom gulps and tries to think. 'But he's been *away* for over a year.'

'He came back last week,' Alice says bluntly. 'He didn't tell anybody. He snuck back and went straight to the police in Melbourne, and then they brought him down here. He's been here for days.'

'But Alice, I . . .' Tom stops. Panic and dismay are driving through him like sharp nails, each one hitting its mark. 'Jed was away in South Africa when your mother was killed. He left well before—'

'No,' she snaps.

'No?'

'That is what everyone thought! But he sneaked back into the country. Hung out in Melbourne a while and then came back here secretly. He went around that night to try to persuade her to . . . A fight broke out and he . . . he is saying he didn't mean to do it. It was an accident, but he killed her!' She begins to sob again.

'But . . . do you believe that?'

'Yes!' she says hoarsely.

'Well!' Tom's whole mouth has gone dry. His throat feels jammed with some kind of foreign material.

'Anyway, I thought you should know. It will be . . . all over the papers tomorrow.'

'Alice.' He can feel that he will lose her any minute and it will be the end of him and her and everything else besides. He takes a breath, about to suggest that he come around to see her immediately. They could talk things through, try to understand it together, comprehend what it means for everyone, all the ramifications. But the line has gone dead. Alice has hung up. *Jed van der Weihl.* Tom stands numb as a statue in the kitchen, still holding the phone, trying to gather his thoughts into one coherent picture.

But not so unbelievable. Jed was the first person Tom thought of when he heard about the murder. Then when he found out that Jed had left for South Africa two weeks before, well . . . *what a relief.* It meant he didn't have to tell the police of his suspicions. He didn't have to come clean about all the rest of that *personal stuff.*

Eventually, Tom goes outside into the cold, sits on the back step and lights a cigarette. *Jonty.* The way he flew in to help that night of the concert. *What's mine is yours, mate!* Always. His bright eyes and generous grin.

Tom leans his back against the verandah post and lights another cigarette. *Jonno did three months inside that detention centre with a great fucking murder charge strung around his neck! Not knowing what was going to happen to him or where he'd end up. Three months on a hard little bed, locked up at eight each night, one phone call a week and visitors once a month.*

This very night Tom had been preparing to betray him in order to win the affection of some girl that he didn't even know! Tom is freezing now but he doesn't care. He stays out on the back step for a long time, smokes another cigarette and then another. By the time he's ready to come back inside he can hardly stand. His limbs are like blocks of ice.

Midyear exams were over. Instead of heading off down to the oval with the others in his class, Tom went by the Pitt Street house. Lillian had finished her exams the week before and he hadn't seen her since. She opened the door with a smile and asked him in, but Tom could tell she'd been crying. Her eyes were red-rimmed and glassy, her face swollen.

'We'll have a drink while you tell me about the maths exam!' she declared, pushing him onto a kitchen chair and going over to fill the kettle. He could see she was determined to act as if everything was fine, but her manner was forced, overly animated and bright. Something was up.

It was while they were sipping their coffees at opposite sides of the table that she broke down again. She just turned away, slumped down in her chair, buried her face in her hands and started sobbing. Tom got up and went around to the other side of the table. He knelt beside her and put both arms around her shuddering shoulders.

'What's wrong, Lillian?'

'Oh, Tom,' she said, 'you don't want to know.'

'I do. Tell me.'

'It's my sister,' she blew her nose and wiped her eyes, trying to pull herself together. 'Her life is just too awful. *Too sad!* That man is getting worse. She might as well be chained up like a dog. I have got to do something for her!' She pulled away and looked into Tom's face. 'I have to help her!'

'What can you do?' Tom was holding her with one arm and kneading her shoulder with the other, concerned but enjoying the physical proximity. After a few stiff moments she seemed to melt into his embrace as though it was the most natural thing in the world.

'Why don't you get your sister to see my old man?' Tom suggested, still caressing her shoulder. 'He deals with people splitting up all the time,' he smiled. 'Divorce is his bread and butter.'

She pulled away a little, wiped her tears away with the back of her hand and shook her head. 'That is the sensible solution, of course,' she said, 'but it wouldn't work in this case, because my sister hasn't the confidence to leave and, well . . . there is all the money.'

'What money?'

'My mother's money,' Lillian sighed. 'While he's around, my sister won't get any of it and . . . she needs it. Oh boy does she need it! If she is going to have any kind of life then she needs money.'

'What if they're divorced?'

'She won't leave him!' Lillian shook her head. 'Even though she is miserable. My mother is nearly ninety and not well. She could die any day now. She figures he'll find a way to get his hands on the money, and I think she's right. So Mum is entrusting all of it to me but . . . God, I don't want the responsibility!'

'So you give it to your sister when . . .?'

She nodded. 'My mother insists that I'm to get Marie into an independent situation, away from him, and then give her half.'

'How are you meant to do that if she won't . . . leave?'

'Exactly.' Lillian smiled sadly. 'But I've got to try.'

'So what's the plan?'

Lillian didn't answer.

Tom got up and sat on a chair next to her, and they sat there awhile, sipping their drinks. Lillian suddenly reached across and touched his arm, giving him a nudge.

'Get that frown off your face, Tom Mullaney,' she laughed. 'Don't go worrying about my problems.' She turned herself around to face him, put her hands on both sides of his face, pulled it down to hers and began rubbing his nose with her own. She was still sniffling a bit but smiling through her sadness as she kissed him first on each cheek and then . . . after a moment's hesitation, quickly on the mouth.

The only way to describe that kiss from her is that it was like an electric shock. The feel of her mouth sent a pulse of wild electricity straight through Tom, setting him alight, making him reckless and crazy for more. She was about to turn away but he clutched her upper arms and pulled her back. Then he kissed her, clumsy but passionate. She resisted, but when she stood up, he stood up too and kissed her again. At first she squirmed and laughed a bit and shook her head, but then she seemed to give herself up to it and let him hold her tightly, caress her and kiss her.

The feel of her, the smell of her hair and skin was intoxicating. He couldn't say how long they stood there by the window. Tom the eighteen-year-old schoolboy who'd never really kissed anyone before, with the lovely, dark-haired, warm, passionate forty-two-year-old, Lillian. It was the most wonderful sensation he'd ever known. All the pent-up passion for her that he'd been holding inside for months was suddenly and overwhelmingly coming out in that kiss.

'Oh, Tom,' she murmured at one point, 'this is so silly, darling.'

'No, it's not,' he managed to say. But he really had no idea. It never crossed his mind to think that it was so very *inappropriate*, if not dead *wrong*! He didn't think of Jonty or his parents or anything else. All the love and lust he'd been feeling for months made absolute sense. He was dizzy with it.

'Tom,' she laughed, 'stop this now, please.'

'Okay.' But the feelings racing through his blood were so powerful that he couldn't let go. He kept kissing her, and running his hands up and down her body, revelling in the shape and softness of her, the way her back tapered down into her waist and then flared out again to make that beautiful bottom, which, until now, he'd only secretly fantasised about touching.

It was then that Tom sensed a shadow cross the window. The light in the room briefly darkened. He looked over and it was gone. He could remember thinking it was probably just a cloud as he clumsily tried to undo her blouse, desperate to touch more of the creamy skin around her neck and chest. All the while she was laughing and saying that it wasn't a good idea, but he kept holding her and kissing her.

'Tom, you must go home,' she said, her voice hoarse and more serious. She sounded as though she might mean it this time, but because she didn't actually push him away or disentangle herself, Tom didn't take much notice. But in the middle of their next embrace she suddenly went stiff and started pushing him away frantically, before letting out a shrill laugh. Or was it a scream? Tom jerked backwards into reality and saw that her eyes were staring, wide with shock, at something behind him.

Tom turned around.

Jonty's father, Jed van der Weihl, was standing in the doorway holding a huge bunch of beautiful flowers in his hands and staring at Lillian. The shadow must have been him coming down the side of the house to the back door. Whether he saw them embracing through the window Tom didn't know, but he must have quietly slipped in without knocking. Jed van der Weihl in his snappy tailored suit with his cold eyes, carrying flowers, his face frozen in shock, staring at them. Tom gulped. He was in his school uniform.

'You bitch.' Jed began to laugh, softly and venomously. He moved across to the table and put his bunch of flowers down, as though he had all the time in the world, never taking his eyes off her.

Blushing furiously, Lillian tried to hold his look as she fumbled clumsily with the front buttons of her blouse.

'Just go, Jed!' she cried angrily. 'Just take your flowers and get out of *my* house!' It was a desperate ploy to bring a little dignity into a situation where there was none, but it was all Jed needed to unleash his unspent fury. He swiped the flowers to the floor in one movement of his arm and came towards her, grabbing her tightly by both wrists and pushing her up against the wall.

'You bitch!' His voice was low with anger as he tore at her blouse, making the buttons come popping off onto the floor. 'Leading me on!' Gripping her long hair he started to bang her head back against the wall in dull sickening thuds as he tried lifting her dress with his other hand. 'I'll have you anyway . . .' he breathed into her face. 'We'll forget the nice stuff, eh?' His voice was coarse and he was gasping between the words like someone at the onset of a heart attack.

Lillian was not screaming but panting and gasping, doing her best to fight him off. She didn't have a chance.

After the initial shock, Tom swung into action but there was nothing he could do either. He tried pushing and shoving Jed away, but the older man was much heavier and stronger and swatted Tom off. Tom looked around frantically for a weapon. Some part of him must have been thinking sensibly because he went for the breadboard instead of the long knife on the kitchen table. He smashed it down as hard as he could on the back of Jed's head. Jed gave an almighty roar, like some wild animal, then staggered a bit, momentarily stunned. But it didn't last long. He grabbed Tom around the neck and held him up against the wall by his school shirt and tie.

'You little punk!' he breathed in Tom's face, before kneeing him sharply in the groin. Tom collapsed to the floor, crying in agony.

'Leave him alone!' Lillian yelled.

Jed turned to find she was brandishing the knife. He sneered contemptuously but didn't move. Tom could almost hear his brain ticking over. Lillian did look riled up enough to use it. They stood there awhile, panting heavily and staring at each other.

'Now get out of my house!' Lillian said in a low voice, the knife held out in front of her with both trembling hands. 'Or I swear I'll use this!'

Jed took a couple of steps backwards, still staring at her.

Most of Lillian's hair had come out of the bun, the curls bouncing around her shoulders, and her blouse was flapping open, showing her lace bra. Even through the crippling pain, Tom could see Jed was crazy for her, as well as furious. *He is in love with her too.*

'A schoolboy?' The man sounded as though he was being strangled. 'Why would you lower yourself to . . .' he waved at Tom on the floor, 'some bloody *kid*?' The steam was ebbing out of him. You could almost see it. He was still angry but truly bewildered as well. From Tom's position on the floor he could see that underneath the fury Jed was actually begging her.

'Do you actually think that I would *willingly* have anything to do with *you*?' Lillian jeered at him from her position on the opposite side of the table. 'You gross, horrible man! Do you honestly think I would cultivate my own sister's nightmare of a husband for anything other than my own ends?'

Jed's shoulders slumped and his eyes jerked this way and that. His expression was one of raw desire and sick shock.

'You seemed happy enough to go to dinner . . .' he gulped in a soft voice, quite pathetic now. 'You liked all that if I recall.'

Once he'd gone, Lillian put the knife down and collapsed into a corner of the room. Tom propped himself up against the wall on the other side of the table. They sat there without speaking, just looking at the beautiful flowers lying on the floor between them. Perfect blue irises and yellow roses and all this lovely white stuff that looked like snowflakes, still wrapped so nicely. Lillian got to her feet eventually and picked up the flowers.

'Well,' she said, her voice still shaking as she tried unsuccessfully to smile. She put the flowers on the table, went to the cupboard under the sink and pulled out a couple of vases, 'better put these in water.'

'Were you going to *kill* him?' Tom couldn't help asking. He was deeply curious. Jed had come assuming . . . something.

'Oh, Tom,' she groaned, and threw her head back shutting her eyes for a couple of moments. 'Oh Tom, I'm such a fool!'

It surprised Tom that she was going to accept the flowers. After all, they'd come from someone she loathed. But she only laughed when he told her to throw them out.

'Why would I do that, Tom?' she said, filling the two biggest vases with water. 'Such beautiful flowers! Who cares who bought them? Come on! Help me split them up.'

So Tom began to take off the wrapping paper and ribbon. To his surprise he found a long, narrow, expensively wrapped box nestling down among the flowers.

'Look what I found,' Tom said, holding it out for her. But she didn't take it immediately. She brought the vases over to the table, and without speaking they set about arranging the flowers together. Tom pretended to be interested but he couldn't have given a rat's arse about flowers. What he wanted to do was ask her how far things had progressed with Jed, and what she had planned. But more than that, he wanted to hold her again. He wanted to go straight back to how they'd been before Jed arrived on the scene.

Lillian positioned the vases carefully – one in the middle of the table and the other on the sideboard – wiped her hands down her dress and sighed as she picked up the box.

'Let's have a look, then,' she said softly. Inside, nestled in plush red-velvet lining, was a gold necklace with a heart made of tiny sapphires and diamonds at its centre.

'Oh, wow!' She laughed with delight as she held it out for Tom to admire. 'Isn't it beautiful?' Then she began to examine the box carefully, checking out the plush lining and the gold lettering.

'Eighteen-carat!' she whispered in awe. 'Wow!' She looked at Tom. 'Real quality!'

'Nice,' Tom murmured sourly. It was no cheapo number, that was for sure. The knotted deep gold rings were pink-tinged, and the stones twinkled in the late afternoon light from the window.

'Help me put it on,' Lillian said, putting the necklace up around her throat and turning around. Tom's hands shook as he brushed away her hair and opened the clasp. This finicky task took a while. And all the time his clumsy hands were trying to position the two parts of the clasp together he was thinking about bending down a little further to kiss her neck and then her lovely little ears. But he didn't. Once the necklace was secure he stepped back, and she moved over to the mirror near the window.

Bemused, fascinated and aching with love, Tom watched her admiring herself. The necklace sat perfectly on her neck. Against her olive skin and dark hair, the deep gold and bright stones caught and accentuated the sparkle in her eyes. Tom came up behind her and put both hands on her shoulders for a moment, then wrapped his arms tightly around her waist, looking at her in the mirror.

'You're so beautiful,' he said, awestruck by her lovely image. Tom wished passionately that he was old enough and rich enough to buy something like it to take this one's place. He longed to give her this kind of pleasure, and make her smile in this special dreamy way. 'But you can't keep it.'

'But I can!' she laughed, without taking her eyes off her reflection. 'I've never had *anything* as lovely as this before!'

Tom let go of her and backed away. *For Christ's sake! She had to be joking.* After the previous acrimonious scene it was *unbeliev-able* for her to think of keeping it.

'Marie and I never had anything beautiful,' Lillian explained, moving closer to the mirror, her long pretty fingers moving up and down the chain. 'My mother is so wealthy, but always so tight-fisted!' She turned to Tom. 'Wouldn't you think that we'd at least have had what other kids had?'

'Why was she like that?' Tom asked, but he wasn't really interested in her childhood. Of course she wouldn't keep the necklace! She'd see sense any moment now and he'd help her return it.

'Said it would do us good. Toughen us up,' Lillian said bitterly. 'Build our characters.' The light seemed to go out of her eyes. 'When we were little, Marie and I used to fantasise about having plastic lunch boxes and cordial bottles like everyone else!'

'But you'll probably see him again,' Tom protested hotly. 'How embarrassing will that be?'

But Lillian only laughed one of her throaty laughs that caught Tom in the guts and lower, and turned briefly to ruffle his hair in a way he didn't much like. She was treating him like a kid again. She turned back to the mirror, fingered the necklace lightly, and laughed again.

'It will be my revenge,' she whispered, 'and there will be nothing he can do about it!' She turned to look at Tom, still smiling. 'He gave it to me, didn't he? The risk would be that I'd tell everyone if he asked for it back. He wouldn't want that kind of humiliation.'

'But Lillian!' Tom's mouth opened in protest.

'It's mine now,' she said firmly.

Tom went home soon after that, downhearted and confused. He could tell she wanted to be alone.

From then on she wore the bloody thing all the time. She never took it off. Tom sometimes heard people ask her about the necklace. Where had she got it? Was it a gift or an heirloom? She told a different story each time. First she'd inherited it from her mother and had only just decided to *drag it out of the closet*, then it had been a gift from a past boyfriend, and finally she said she'd saved for it herself. It was *my little gift to me for having the courage to go back to school*. Tom never knew where to look when she told these stories. It wasn't so much the lies that confused him as the way she told them. It just seemed too easy for her. She didn't blush or hesitate at all. It was as though she'd forgotten how she came to have it. And it made Tom doubt her. It made him question who she actually was deep down.

How well do you ever know another person?

But it didn't stop him loving her. Far from it. That afternoon was the only time things ever got out of hand between him and

Lillian, but . . . it wasn't for want of trying on Tom's part. The whole necklace episode made him even more crazy about her. After that day she filled every waking hour. He was desperate to kiss her again and to feel her in his arms. He woke in a sweat most nights from dreams of making love with her.

But . . . it never happened.

Tom gets up and leaves for work while his father is in the shower. A rolled-up copy of the *Chronicle* is lying on the doorstep when he steps out into the cold air, but he decides to wait till he gets to the office. Let his father read it by himself.

He is pulling up in front of the office when he sees the front page in the wire billboard out the front of the *Chronicle* building.

Brother-in-law admits guilt, with a small photo of Lillian underneath. Tom turns off the engine and sits there behind the wheel, letting the cold feeling pass through his arms and legs.

He gets out of the car and walks into the office, says good morning to cheery middle-aged Margaret at the front desk and picks up a copy of the paper on his way through to the back room, where the photographers hang out with all the equipment. His boss, Steve, is alone, sitting at one of the computers, going through shots. He looks up when Tom comes in.

'G'day, Tom!' He takes a moment to register Tom's rumpled appearance and smiles. 'Hard night on the turps, eh?'

'Yeah.' Tom manages to sound jocular. He slumps down at the little table with his paper.

'Got a bit on today,' Steve continues, conversationally, 'and I'll need you down at the golf club at eleven. Some old dear is leaving the committee.' He notices Tom reading the article and frowns thoughtfully. 'You went to school with that van der Weihl kid, didn't you?'

'Yeah,' Tom's heart has already started to quicken as he scans the article.

'Seems it was his old man all along.' Steve is scathing. 'Imagine letting your own kid do time for some crime you committed!'

'Hmmm.'

'I'll let you read it then.' Steve goes to the fridge for milk. 'You want a coffee?'

'Thanks.'

There is not much more in the article than Alice told him the night before. Details of the murder are described again, along with the photo and a brief rundown of Lillian's life. Jonty is mentioned as the one initially charged. The police spokesman admits that they were shocked when Jed van der Weihl came home recently from South Africa to admit guilt for the murder.

Alice. Her face comes to Tom without warning. What will this be like for her? He closes his eyes and tries to imagine her picking up the local rag to find her mother's photo on the front page, *again.*

Tom takes a few slurps of coffee and suddenly he's woozy and dazed. He feels as though he's been hit by a truck that he didn't see coming. His father will have heard the news by now.

'Hey, mate.' Steve is concerned. 'You've gone pale. Feel all right?'

Tom nods and tries to breathe deeply. But he knows he's going to chuck.

'Ate something weird last night,' Tom lies as he makes his way to the back bathroom.

After throwing up his guts he feels better. It will be lunchtime after the golf club assignment, so he'll call the office and hear his old man's take on it all. Tom washes his hands and has a long drink of water from the tap. When he heads out again, Steve is checking a list of names.

'You okay?'

'Yeah, thanks.'

'It's South Primary School first up,' Steve says casually, pointing to the Nikon on the bench. 'They've got some special multicultural day happening. You can go out there with Leanne.'

'Okay.' Tom picks up the camera and slips it into its case, checking first to see if the right lenses are there. 'Just got to make a phone call first.'

'Hurry then,' Steve says, going back to the computer. 'She's waiting for you with the car out the front.'

Tom rings his dad's office, hoping that he'll be able to meet up with Luke for lunch. Maybe Alice will be there too. Maybe the three of them will be able to sit down together and talk things through.

The phone is picked up after only two rings.

'Good morning! You've rung Mullaney Law Practice. It's Alice speaking. How may I help you?'

Oh shit! 'G'day, Alice!' Tom tries to sound cheery. 'It's Tom here.' He gulps and waits for her to say something. 'Tom Mullaney.'

You rang me last night, remember!

Silence. Even a murmured 'hello' would do. She doesn't have to use his name. But there is only silence. She says absolutely nothing. He can't even hear her breathe. He is about to blather on about how grateful he is that she rang him the night before and how sorry he is to see the *Chronicle* that morning. Sorry, too, that she has to live through it all again. *Sorry about everything, Alice.* 'Is Dad there?' *Don't hate me, Alice, please, because . . .*

'Sorry, Tom,' she says in that special singsong style that all secretaries seem to manage. 'Luke is in court all morning and he has been called out to another matter for the afternoon. He won't be back in the office before four, but you can try him on his mobile.'

'Okay,' Tom gulps again. 'Thanks, Alice.'

She hangs up without saying goodbye.

Tom rushes out the front with his camera case. Leanne is leaning on the car, scowling.

'Sorry, sorry!' Tom runs over. She is one of the senior reporters and she's obviously irritated at being kept waiting. She stubs out her cigarette on the pavement and unlocks the work car.

'You know anything about that?' She points to the *Guilty* billboard.

'No.' Tom gets into the car and slams the door. 'Why would I?'

'I thought you and his kid Jonty were *best* friends.' Is there sarcasm in her tone or is he imagining it?

'Well, yeah.' Tom starts to feel sick all over again. 'We used to be.' *How would she know that?* It was three years ago. Leanne is in her thirties. He never knew her or her family before coming back to work here.

'You know the old man?'

'A bit.'

'What's he like?'

'Bit of a nutcase.'

'You think he might be trying to take the flak for his son?'

'He isn't the kind of guy to take the flak for anyone.'

'Even his son?'

'Especially his son.'

She doesn't say anything else. Just starts the car and heads off to the primary school. Tom's forehead is damp and he feels a trickle rolling down his back. He'll be having conversations like this every day from now on. Everyone he meets in the street will ask his opinion of Jed van der Weihl and whether Tom thinks Jonty was involved too. They all know he was close to the action so the tone will be curious, suspicious, as though he might be hiding stuff. *Well they won't be wrong there, will they?* Three years ago he was sharp enough to know that certain things could be taken out of context. He'd told himself then that none of what he withheld was relevant to the murder. Now he knows that's not true. But it's too late now.

It's not until evening that he gets to talk to his father, who turns out to be just as stunned and curious as everyone else around town, although he doesn't say much.

At around ten, Tom summons up every bit of courage he has and rings Jonty. 'Jonno, it's me.'

'Yeah?'

'Tom Mullaney.'

'I know who you are.'

And the line goes dead.

'Something wrong?' Buzz asks.

'Nah.' Jonty tips a plate of expensive leftovers into the slop bucket, wondering how he managed to get two orders wrong *and* mess up that pumpkin risotto that he can usually do to perfection with his eyes closed.

'Go home, mate.' Buzz puts a hand on his shoulder. 'I'll finish here.'

'I'm okay.' Jonty hands a garden salad to the new waitress, Lou-Mai, who is waiting with one of her dreamy little smiles playing at the corners of her mouth and eyes. *God, if only I could get it on with her, all my troubles would be over!*

Everyone has the hots for Lou-Mai, Buzz included. She has coal-black hair hanging to her waist, and her smiles are so slow that you'd swear she knew exactly what you were thinking. Jonty turns back to the stove. So what would she think of him? An ex-drugged-up Aussie loser with a weird past! Christ, he's feeling mad tonight, crazy with something. Everything seems wrong.

He's wondering why the hell he's doing what he's doing. *What is he doing back in this town? Working in this kitchen? Making food for rich people? Shit. What's that all about? Who decided that's what he should be doing with his life? What will it prove?*

'Listen, this whole business must be traumatic for you.' Buzz takes the bowl out of Jonty's hand. 'So off you go, mate! Have a break. See you Monday.'

Jonty is left standing with his hands hanging empty by his sides, watching Buzz's skinny arse slinking off towards the sinks, and he can hardly see because he is suddenly so pissed off. He wants to kick Buzz's legs out from under him, hammer his head against the floor and hold a knife at his throat. The moment passes, leaves his head reeling. *Jeez! Where did that come from?* Jonty has an hour left of his shift and Buzz is telling him to go home? *Home? Okay, but what then? What do I do at home?*

Since he'd got up that morning and seen the local paper with his old man's face plastered across the front page, the ground under Jonty had felt slippery, as though it might give way any moment. Three years ago Detective Lloyd Hooper used to lean across the table and tell him that it was only a matter of time before he would start to unravel. *Sooner or later everyone has got to tell someone Jonty, otherwise they come undone. One way or another they start to unravel.* Well his old man had proved that true, hadn't he? Old Jed unravelled good and proper. *Took him long enough, but . . . he did it!*

Jonty collects his jacket, winds the scarf around his neck and steps out into the dark night. *Now it's my turn.*

He'll go straight home now, make some tea and watch a movie. His mother is taking it all pretty hard, so with luck she'll be out of it on the pills the doctor gave her.

Jonty had been expecting something since his father had turned up outside their house just before midnight a few days previously. Jonty had known in his bones it was just a matter of time. Something was going to explode.

The knock at the door came at about 11.30. Luckily it happened to be his night off work, so it wasn't his mother who answered. For a second or two he didn't know who was standing there because he'd forgotten to turn on the porch light. Even so, the shape of the head, the wide shoulders and blocky build were immediately *familiar.* Jonty blinked a couple of times. It was his father standing there holding out his hand! Jonty didn't move, not even a muscle in his face.

'Is your mother in?'

Jonty stared back. It didn't occur to him to answer.

'Jonty,' Jed said in a low voice. 'Get your mother, please.'

'She's asleep,' Jonty said, quite clearly. He was on auto now.

So they stood there facing each other, saying nothing, for however long.

'I'll come again in the morning,' Jed said. 'Will you tell her that?'

Jonty didn't answer.

'God bless you, Jonty.'

'*What?*'

'God bless you, son.'

'Yeah!' Jonty snarled. 'Whatever!'

'Just give me a chance.' His father extended both hands in a helpless gesture. 'You're my only son. Please give me a chance!'

'*What* do you want?'

'I've come home for you, Jonty. I want to set things right. None of it was your fault,' his father pleads softly, 'none of it.'

'None of *what*?'

'I've come home to beg forgiveness. For all I put you and your mother through. I want to make up for everything. I've seen the light now Jonty, and . . . I want to save you too!'

Jonty closed the door on him. He went into the kitchen and grabbed a knife. When he came out again, his father was gone. Jonty ran to the front gate but the street was empty. He went back to the house and sat on the front step, listening to the strange night sounds and the beating of his own heart. His mother need not know of this. *Never.* He would protect her always. Even so, part of him knew something would blow – sooner rather than later, probably. His father was back. There would be no keeping it from her.

Tomorrow is Sunday. His old lady has been building up to it all week. Trying on different outfits, asking Jonty if this suits her or if something else looks better. Should she try to be young and breezy, or more demure and old-fashioned? *Yeah, whatever, Mum!* How the hell would he know what middle-aged women should look like? But he tries not to let on what he's thinking because . . . she hasn't got anyone else.

'That's it, Mum,' he says when she comes out in some pink thing with flowers on it. 'That one looks good.'

Standing at the door in their best clothes. Ringing the bell. Jumpy. Been like it all morning. Jonty is trying to picture his grandmother but all he sees is this thin, stick-like black shape walking away from him – black hat, black coat and a kind of mesh veil over her face. A spider, tiny but reeking with some kind of weird *power.*

That's Jonty's one big memory of his aunt's funeral: his grandmother. Apart from then, he doesn't reckon he's seen her up-close since he was about ten. Not properly. He pushes the hair out of his eyes. His clothes are clean and his boots are polished – all organised by his mother. He's wearing a new white T-shirt and black jeans. His mother has an orange mouth and black stuff around her eyes. It pulls at his heartstrings. But Jonty says nothing.

He doesn't want to hurt her feelings. The long and the short of it is that they're here for the old bird's loot and he doesn't feel too comfortable about that. Grovelling is the one thing he doesn't do. Money was never his problem.

Alice opens the door, in jeans and a dark striped shirt. Her hair is pulled back from her face with a velvet band and . . . Jonty's eyes flick away in surprise. *Jeez! She looks so much like . . . yeah well, her mother! Lillian. She used to pull her hair back like that too.* His heart is suddenly pounding. He'd been getting so uptight about meeting the old lady that he'd forgotten he'd have to deal with his cousin. Guilt washes over him as he remembers watching her dancing alone in that house.

'Hello,' she says with a tight smile for his mother. 'Aunt Marie?'

'Alice!' His mother smiles nervously and steps forward for the obligatory kiss, but his cousin steps away sharply and pretends not to see the extended hand. Instead she turns to Jonty.

'Hello, Jonty,' she says carefully, trying to smile. Holding the door open wider she motions them inside. 'Gran is ready for you.'

Jonty and his mother follow her into this big draughty hallway with dark wooden panelling halfway up the walls and a huge staircase at the end. They follow her past a carved polished-wood hallstand, and Jonty sees his face in the mirror above it. Yeah, that's him. Sometimes he has to look twice to make sure. In spite of all the clean clothes, he looks like Kurt Cobain's little brother on a bender – pale and edgy. As though he's on a massive dose of speed. His eyes glitter in his head like green marbles.

'So, this where you grew up, Mum?' he asks, looking around.

'Lillian and I used to slide down those banisters!' his mother points, then pulls her hand away so he can't see her trembling.

'Hey, just relax,' Jonty grabs her shoulders briefly, 'everything will be okay.' But he's nervous now too. This old joint is so big and dark and quiet. It's creaking with money and class, and he knows how much his mother wants it all. After heading through a heavy wooden door they are suddenly standing in a wonderful room. Jonty looks around admiringly: it's so big and full of light and air and blue carpet and bits and pieces of polished furniture. You hardly finish looking at one thing before something else demands your attention. There's a big vase of real flowers on the sideboard – Jonty can smell them from where he's standing at the door – and a carved ivory chess set on the round polished table in the middle of the room. The main window has a view over the whole town. This place even smells different from an ordinary house. It's got that deep sweet whiff about it, nicer than a fancy hotel. Jonty has stopped to take it all in, but his cousin motions him towards the fire at the other end of the room.

His grandmother is sitting by an open fire in a blue velvet chair, staring as they approach. *Jeez the old bird is ancient! Did Mum say over ninety?*

'At last!' the old woman barks in a surprisingly strong voice. 'You're here at last, Marie!' She doesn't stand up or even try to smile.

'Hello, Mother.' It hurts Jonty to hear the tremble in his mother's voice. He watches her hesitate a couple of feet from the old girl, and his heart is suddenly breaking for her, willing her forward. One of the scrawny arms reaches out and his mum goes forward to kiss the withered bark of her cheek. The claw-like hand lingers on Marie's shoulder for maybe two seconds before retreating to the arm of the chair. His mum immediately jerks back, grabs Jonty's arm and tries to drag him towards the old bird.

'Jonty is here too, Mother.' Marie sounds like one of those TV sales guys trying to flog a dud washing machine.

'As I can see.' The old girl squints at Jonty without smiling. 'They tell me you have a job?'

'Yeah,' he nods, feeling even more weirdly nervous now. *Fuck. She hasn't even said sit down yet.* He didn't know what he expected, but this is totally outside anything normal as far as he's concerned. *Who does this old biddy think she is? The queen, or what?*

'Pull up a chair, both of you,' his grandmother orders and then sighs as though she's bored already but has to go through the motions. She reaches for her glasses from a nearby side table. 'Let me have a proper look at you both.'

Jonty pulls up a comfortable chair for his mum, then sits himself down next to her on a hard little number with a straight back and no sides. He waits as the old girl checks them over without comment. His cousin Alice is hovering somewhere in the background, but he doesn't turn around. The truth is, Jonty is pretty intrigued by this decrepit old duck. *So this is my grandmother. In a weird way, she's perfect. Tom should take a few shots of that bony little head. He'd be able to catch those bright fast eyes flicking up and down, here and there, taking everything in.* The old lady reminds him of a crow, that cold hard way they have of sitting up in the tree, surveying everything, waiting for the main chance. Crows are mean bastards, but you have to give it to them: they know what they're doing and they don't muck around. He likes her pressed linen shirt, the pearl brooch and the grey hair pinned back into a bun. She belongs in a movie or a painting.

Everyone is seated now and Jonty is waiting for the conversation to begin with the usual inane comments about the weather and a question or two about how everyone's doing in the aches and pains and fatal diseases department. But this old girl isn't having any of that. She cuts straight to the chase.

'So, why are you here, Marie?'

His mother stares back for a moment or two, flummoxed, moving her mouth, but not speaking.

'I'm your daughter,' she mumbles eventually. Jonty sighs, wishing she'd remember that being subservient won't work. 'I really thought it was time we reconciled our differences,' she adds lamely.

The old lady gives an impatient snort. 'You were my daughter twenty-five years ago!' she snaps. 'And it didn't mean a thing then, so why now?'

'I was . . . very young then, Mother.'

'You'd reached your maturity, hadn't you?' his grandmother barks, waving one hand dismissively. 'If I remember correctly, Marie, you were a fully functioning adult!' She looks across to where Alice is standing by the chess table, watching all this, playing with one of the porcelain pieces at the same time. 'For goodness sake, Alice! Pull up a chair.'

'I wasn't sure if you wanted me to stay,' Alice mumbles.

'Well, of course I want you to stay!' His grandmother points to a chair. 'Why wouldn't I want you to stay? Pull that one over and sit next to your cousin.'

'Okay.'

So it's the three of them now, sitting alongside each other in front of the old girl, like they've been pulled into the Headmistress's office for a telling-off. Jonty badly wants to laugh. This is unreal! He has never been in a situation like this. If any teacher tried to pull this kind of stunt when he was at school he'd have been out the window by now.

Hey, come on, Grannie, cut us some slack! Jonty wants to joke.

'Youth is no excuse!' The old lady looks straight at Jonty.

Youth is no excuse . . . Wow. Okay, so she's having a go at him already! Those glittering dark eyes are like stones boring into his skull. He stares straight back into them and holds tight. He knows instinctively that she is waiting for him to look away, but he won't and . . . doesn't. Jonty can beat anyone at this game. Being able to hold someone's eyes can be the difference between being taken for a weak know-nothing idiot or someone worthy of respect. When you're inside, it can actually mean the difference between *surviving* or . . . not. So he holds that look until it is she who turns away. A spurt of excitement runs through him. This is starting to feel like a BBC thriller. He's not quite sure what part he's playing yet, but the plot is hotting up.

'Your father and I knew what that man was like as soon as we met him! And we forbade you to see him again!'

Jeez, give us a break! His poor old mum is being hauled over the coals for something she did twenty-five years ago! This has to be bloody ridiculous in anybody's language.

'I know.' Marie is close to tears. 'It was a terrible mistake.'

'And you were so wilful and stupid that you actually *married that monster*!'

'Mother, I had no idea . . . what he was like. He . . .'

'A psychopath with next to nothing in his favour except a farm he inherited from his grandparents. And from what I've heard, he systematically ruined that over the years!'

Poor Mum. The old bitch is on a roll now and part of Jonty wants to get up and walk out, tell her to go *get fucked*. But he can't do that. He's got to stick it out for his mum. She told him that he wasn't, under any circumstances, to take offence on her behalf. So he knows he's got to stay cool. He has to support her. That's why he's here, after all.

'You let him bully and torment you for twenty years before he deserted you. And now,' his grandmother shudders, '*now* it turns out he has *murdered* your sister! And this whole terrible business begins all over again. It's all over the papers, *again*. I've lived with respect in this town all my life, Marie, and I deserve some peace in my final years. What in heavens were you thinking? Where was your gumption, girl?'

'But he's gone now, Mother,' his mum pleads, trying to smile. 'He's in jail. There will be a sentencing hearing soon. He'll be given many years in jail. Jonty and I are living in town now. Getting on just fine without him for the past year. I think I told you.'

'Did he contact you when he came back?'

'I wouldn't see him. I refused to speak to him.'

Jonty looks at his mother for signs she might be lying. It's the first he's heard that his father had contacted her too.

'Did he tell you anything?' The old lady's voice is shaking a little now. 'Any reason for . . . this, this absolutely *terrible crime*?'

His mother shakes her head vigorously.

'I refused to talk to him. I put . . . the phone down. I found out . . . from the police.'

'What about you?' Phyllis turns to Jonty sharply.

'Nope,' Jonty shakes his head, thinking of his old man that night at the gate. *I've come to beg for forgiveness. I want to save you too!*

'Will you go and see him in jail?'

'Of course not!' Marie shudders, and then adds with real conviction, 'He killed my sister!'

'Quite!' His grandmother gulps and turns away. She takes a sharply pressed hanky out from her sleeve, blows her nose and dabs her eyes. No one says anything for some time. Then the old lady sniffs and turns to Alice. 'Could you organise afternoon tea, please, dear?'

'Sure.' Alice gets up hurriedly, turning to her aunt and cousin. 'Tea? Or would you like coffee?'

'We'll have *tea*, thank you, Alice!' the old lady cuts in. 'I believe there is a fresh sponge cake in the pantry.' She turns to Jonty with an icy stare. 'Perhaps you could help your cousin while I talk to your mother?'

'No, no, I'll be right.' Alice heads for the door. 'Don't need any help.'

'Alice will need help to carry everything.' Phyllis gives Jonty a dismissive flick of her fingers. 'Off you go.'

Something about the flicking gesture gets to Jonty. Before he can think, he stands slowly, leans both hands on the back of the chair and stares at the old girl until she has to turn back to see what is keeping him.

'I've got a name,' is all he says, quite politely.

She stares at him in surprise for a few moments.

'*I beg your pardon?*' Her top lip is quivering with anger.

'I've got a name,' he says again.

'Believe me, young man,' his grandmother says in a low, very slow whisper, the vitriol seeping through the words like dirty old sump oil from a car engine, 'I *know* your name!'

'Good.' Jonty ignores his mother's pleading look and adds, 'So there will be no problem when you want to talk to me next.'

'*Your name*, young man, has been the cause of enormous suffering to me over these last few years,' his grandmother continues angrily. 'It was plastered all over the papers, just in case you've forgotten!'

'I haven't forgotten,' he says, following Alice to the door.

'Nor have I!' she shouts after him. 'How could anybody *forget* such humiliation?'

Jonty walks out of the room breathing hard.

'But, Mother, Jonty was acquitted!' He hears his own mother pleading. 'He was wrongly accused. You know that now. It was his father all along!' *Oh Jeez! Shut up Mum.*

Jonty follows his cousin down the passage towards the back of the house.

'Like father, like son!' he hears the old girl declare triumphantly. Jonty stops and closes his eyes. *Like father, like son!* His breath is short and his heart is pounding. Her words have pierced through the thick skin he has cultivated around himself since coming back to this town. They have torn great gaping holes right through it and the icy wind is blowing in. *She is right.* His grandmother is right.

Like father, like son.

The big old-fashioned kitchen has all the modern appliances – microwaves and toasters and fridges – but there's a worn wooden table in the middle of the room and two funny little windows surrounded by old yellow tiles on either side of a huge cast-iron oven. It's something to look at anyway. Jonty feels jumpy. He walks around the kitchen from the fridge to the stove to the little windows, trying to calm down, trying not to flip out. His cousin disappears into the pantry, finds a big silver tray, puts a little cloth on it and then starts piling on crockery. She fills the kettle, puts milk into a little jug and rinses out the teapot.

'She's one tough old lady,' Alice gives him a tentative smile, 'but she's not as bad as she seems. Honestly. Try not to take it personally.'

Jonty can tell that Alice wants to put him at ease, but he is feeling so edgy that he can't think of what to reply. The inability to talk makes him feel like an idiot, so he diverts himself by snooping about. He opens canisters and checks out their contents – cocoa, tea, flour – then he tries out the microwave. *Yeah, it works.* He peers closely into a glass-fronted cupboard where a million crystal glasses sit polished and shining. He feels Alice watching him so he stops, looks up and meets her eyes. Her expression is bewildered more than anything else, as though she doesn't know what to make of him hopping about her kitchen.

'I'm so sorry about . . . everything, Jonty,' she says.

He nods and gulps.

'You didn't deserve . . . all you went through.'

Jonty slumps, unsure what to say, or how to take it. He wishes they could talk about why she goes to the old house. And he would like to ask her what her life is like now that her mother is gone and she lives in this big old joint.

'It must be terrible to be accused of something you didn't do,' she continues awkwardly.

'Do you ever see Tom Mullaney?' Jonty suddenly asks, and then laughs when she shakes her head. 'It was pretty weird that night we landed up here a few weeks back, wasn't it?' She nods carefully. 'Hey, you were pretty cool that night, Alice. You did well to look after him the way you did. Bit of a trooper! I haven't seen him since. Was he okay? You work for his old man, don't you? He's a good guy, old Luke. I got a lot of time for Luke . . .'

Jonty knows he's blathering, filling in the silence, but he doesn't know how to stop. He *really* wants to talk now. He feels as though he hasn't spoken to anyone for years. He turns around to check out the knives lined up on the magnetic strip above the bench and pulls down the biggest one. What a beauty! Top brand, too. He runs the blade across his hand. It's more of a cleaver than a knife. The ones at work are nowhere near as big as this one. He holds it up to the nearby window to watch the light sparkling along the blade and tip, musing about onions and frying meat and the last meal he'd prepared where he used a big knife. Maybe he should ask his cousin round to dinner at his mum's place. He could cook up something impressive and the three of them could just hang out. No pressure, just good food. *Would she come?* he wonders.

'What are you doing?' Alice's shout breaks his reverie.

Jonty looks up. Her face is taut and distressed.

'Nothing,' he says, dumbfounded. 'I'm not doing anything.'

'So put it down!'

He lets the knife drop to the floor. It clatters on the stones, making a lonely sound. When that stops there is nothing. Just air. They look at each other; neither of them speak. He can see she's really upset. He wants to apologise but doesn't know what for exactly. He picked up a friggin' kitchen knife! *So what?*

'Go back . . . to the others,' she stammers. 'I'll bring the things in.'

'I'll help you.'

'I can manage!' And when Jonty doesn't move or say anything she gulps and adds, '*Please.*'

'Okay.' Jonty doesn't move, but he gets it. They stand, locked eyeball to eyeball, before she lurches forward, puts the cake on the tray with the other things, and hurries out with it.

As soon as she's gone, Jonty heads out the back door, cuts across the lawn, jumps over the fence and heads home. It was the *please* that brought him undone, and the way her eyes flicked down to the knife on the floor. *Please.* No point trying to tell her that he's harmless, is it? The very idea makes him want to laugh! *Me? Harmless?* No. He doesn't think so either. He thinks of his father outside the house. *I've come home to set things right. None of it was your fault.* The words play in his head like a stuck record, over and over.

Like father, like son.

The next few days go by in a blur. Jonty rings in sick and sneaks sleeping pills from his mother. He sleeps most of the day and then goes out at night. It's hard to remember how he's been filling in the hours. Mainly it's just walking around. Around midnight, he looks for somewhere to plonk himself for a rest. The all-night café on the highway does the job one night. His old high school is the go the next. It's a weird feeling, sitting outside the school gates at three in the morning, trying to work out who he was back then.

Another night he ends up at the hospital. He makes his way around to the side gate, slips in and sits in the little garden outside Ward Nine for a while. He remembers this joint. God, does he ever! He was admitted here once with drug-induced psychosis. The lights are on in a couple of rooms and he sees the occasional shadow of a figure moving about inside. He wonders what's going on in there and tries to remember what it felt like. It was only for a few days but slivers and fragments come to mind and then fade away. There was an Indian doctor with a great big white smile. Jonty remembers asking him what toothpaste he used, and he didn't take offence. And he was real easy in the way he gave Jonty that injection in the arse once, told him that it was his great joy to stick needles into bums. Jonty had always hated injections but somehow having the guy joke about it made it easier to handle. When he'd finished, Jonty heard him talking to someone outside the door. *Another fried brain*, was what he said. Was he talking about Jonty? He'd sat up at that point. *Have I fried my brain?*

And he remembers his mother coming in with some of his favourite pancakes, telling him that she was looking forward to having him home soon.

Another fried brain.

Nothing much comes when Jonty tries to remember bigger sequences. In fact, the longer, more useful memories usually arrive when he's thinking about something else entirely.

One afternoon he walks all the way out to the caves by himself. Something is pulling him there. He half expects to see his father, even though he knows Jed is tucked away *inside*, by this stage. Jed has found God! Jonty laughs at the thought. He tries to imagine his father behind those walls, doing what he's told, but . . . it's too difficult. His imagination won't reach that far. The whole idea of Jed bedding down in a little cell every night and lining up for rollcall is just too sad. Jonty wanders from one cave to another, listening for the hollow sounds of the tunnels underneath the earth, feeling the light breeze against his skin. Even in the middle of this quiet grey afternoon the place is spooky. The few other people out there don't seem to feel it though. English and Japanese tourists chatter to each other and pose for photos as though it's somewhere ordinary. Jonty stands on the rim of one deep cavern, thinking, trying to remember. When nothing gives, he moves on to another and another.

He hasn't spoken properly to his mother since that afternoon tea. He doesn't even know how the meeting ended up for her. Whenever she tries to talk to him about anything now, Jonty tells her to stick it. He doesn't want to talk to loopies who go crawling up the arses of people they hate, begging for money. If she persists, he goes to bed or leaves the house. He hears her crying in her room at night. He feels bad about that, but he stays away. She's too crazy, and Jonty is scared he's headed the same way. He either takes another sleeping pill or turns on the radio to cut out her noise. Sometimes he sinks right back down under the blanket of sleep with the radio going loudly and when he wakes he thinks this might be it. Finally, he might be unravelling.

Alice

'Look, I know you don't want to talk to me, but you should know that your cousin Jonno is in a bad way.'

Alice swivels around to find Tom Mullaney standing in the doorway of her office. He's in loose jeans and a jumper. His tousled hair could do with a comb and he's moving from one foot to the other, crossing and recrossing his arms as though he's warming up for a race. She stares at him, her mind jamming. *What did he say?* For the last ten minutes she'd been wholly taken up with finding an important file for Luke, and now, at last, she has. She sets it down on her desk.

'What?'

'His mother, your aunt, rang me.'

'And?'

Tom moves a few steps further into the room. Alice gulps. He is fiddling around with his shirtsleeves now. First he hides them under the cuff of his jumper and then he pulls them out again. His focus shifts from her, to the desk, to his hands. Alice feels cornered but . . . intrigued too. She likes his unkempt appearance. There are holes in the sleeves of his jumper and his old muddy gym boots have pink laces with silver spangles on the end that make her want to smile.

'Your aunt rang me about Jonno.' He pushes his hair back and half closes his eyes. 'He's gone AWOL from work and won't talk to anyone. He's just wandering around like a nutter. She's worried about him. Thinks he's on some kind of downward spiral. I mean, I don't know. Maybe she's overreacting but . . . she's scared he's going to get back on the dope and . . . the rest of it.'

'Why did she ring *you*?'

Tom stops moving about and looks up at her in surprise.

'I dunno,' he says, 'I'm a mate, I guess.'

'*Used* to be.' Alice is being too sharp, but he was the one who busted in here with no warning. He didn't even knock.

'Yeah,' Tom gulps awkwardly, 'used to be.'

Alice doesn't know whether to ask him to sit down or to piss off. She doesn't know whether she wants this conversation at all. Work has been her only relief over the last few days. All the phone calls and letters and appointment times, all the real estate, petty crime and divorces have kept her sane. Jed van der Weihl's confession has the whole town talking. The local paper is full of it and the twins tell her the hotels, cafés and pubs are seething with gossip. *Was he having an affair with Lillian? Why did he let his kid take the flak? Did he really do it? Was his kid part of it?* Even walking down the street for lunch makes her self-conscious. Phyllis has gone to ground, and that makes it all doubly difficult. She won't go to her weekly hair appointment or play cards with her cronies. Worse still, she's become unusually compliant, lost some of her sting. The vitriolic outburst she dished out to Marie and Jonty the previous week was the last sighting of pugnacious Phyllis. Since then, she's become increasingly subdued, hardly bothers to tell Alice anything about anything. Alice finds herself longing for her usual feisty, stubborn, demanding grandmother, who has views on everything from boiling an egg to solving the country's water shortage. At least she knew where she was with that one, and she didn't have to feel sorry for her.

'I thought Jonty would be relieved,' Alice says curtly.

'*Relieved?*' Tom repeats incredulously.

'Well . . .' Alice feels a little silly now, 'he's off the hook isn't he?'

Tom doesn't say anything to that for some time.

'It wouldn't be easy knowing *that* about your old man, Alice,' he says softly. 'Nothing about that would be easy.'

'I suppose not.' Alice turns from his gaze.

Tom is fiddling with a bunch of papers on the bench now and looking out the window. She has a sudden longing for him, a sharp edgy *pang* that makes her want to go over to where he is standing and draw close against the heat of his skin. It's like a river rushing through her, impossible to stop. She longs to sink her face into his neck, run her hands through his curly hair, feel that bony body pressed hard against hers and . . . *smell* him.

You're lovely Alice. You know that? That strange hour they'd spent together in the café. She never told anyone about what he'd said, but she often thinks of it.

'I rang him a few times but he wouldn't talk to me,' Tom continues as he straightens a pile of already straight files, 'so I went up to the house.'

'And?'

'He said he was busy. But he was just hanging out in his room. He was doing nothing. The only way I could get him to agree to go to the pub tomorrow night was by saying I'd ask you too.'

'*Me?*' Alice stares back at him, dumbfounded. 'Why me?'

Tom shrugs.

'Said he'd come and have a drink with me if you did too.'

He is looking at her steadily now, waiting for an answer. Alice takes a deep breath and looks away.

'My grandmother is very upset about all this. It's so horrible for us . . .'

'I realise that.'

'What does he want to talk to me about?' Alice wishes she didn't sound so damn desperate. 'Is it going to be all about his father and why he's confessing to it now and . . . all the rest of it?' She shudders.

'I don't know. I just wanted to get him out of the house. Get him talking.'

'So where are you going to meet?'

'At the Vine, tomorrow night at six. Just for a couple of drinks?' He is pleading with her now. 'Please come, Alice?'

She takes a deep breath and frowns. She hates that place. It will be full of her old schoolfriends on a Saturday night. All those girls she has avoided since coming back home, getting drunk *en masse*, screeching at each other, lolling all over their boyfriends. Then she remembers Eric.

'I'll have a friend staying,' she says, relieved to have an excuse, 'from Melbourne.'

'Who is she?' Tom demands.

'It's a guy,' Alice explains hurriedly. 'He's coming tomorrow. I can't just . . . leave him at home.'

'A guy?' Tom repeats suspiciously. He is standing in the doorway again.

'Right.'

'Does he . . . know about all this stuff?'

'A bit.'

'Well, bring him too, then,' he mumbles, anxiously.

'Really?'

'Sure. Why not? Just a drink to . . . you know, *break the ice.*'

Alice is suddenly curious. 'Why do you care what happens to Jonno?' she asks. Tom sighs and leans his shoulder against the doorway, looking down at his feet. One of his pink laces is loose so he bends to retie it. Standing again he folds his arms and looks at Alice.

'I betrayed him,' he says softly.

Betrayed? Such a heavy word. It's in the air between them, like a huge mysterious box that has landed on the doorstep, waiting to be unpacked. She's not sure she wants to see what, if anything, is inside. But there is something raw in his eyes as they shift from her to the window to his own hands. Pain flickers around the corner of his tight mouth. He's not faking.

'I'll be there, then,' she replies shortly.

'Thanks, Alice.'

She goes back to her filing. Her mother wanted her to be friends with Jonty. *He's the nearest you'll ever have to a brother.*

'Oh my dear boy! What a relief to have you back here!'

Alice's grandmother comes into the lounge room, dressed for dinner. Ignoring the others sitting by the fire, the old lady only has eyes for Eric as she totters into the room. She is wearing a red dress and black pumps. Her hair has been done properly, too, and she's wearing bright lipstick.

'Mrs Hickey, it's wonderful to be back!' Eric rises and greets the old lady warmly. 'I've been so looking forward to seeing you.'

After kissing him on both cheeks Phyllis takes both his hands in her own and looks into his face. 'You've heard of the recent developments, I take it?'

'Yes, yes,' Eric says quietly.

'I don't know how much longer I'll last,' Phyllis shakes her head dramatically. 'The strain! How much more can one person take?'

'Now don't say that!' Eric deflects the morbid moment beautifully. He squeezes her hands. 'You promised to take me to the local show next year, remember!'

'I did too,' Phyllis chuckles.

'And you're a woman of your word.'

'I am indeed!' Phyllis smiles.

'So that means you must be here.'

'You're right, of course,' she actually laughs, 'and you must be hungry?'

'Of course,' Eric replies.

Alice hasn't seen her grandmother downstairs for dinner in over two weeks. Seeing her animated again is good, but it's downright embarrassing that she has ignored Sylvie and Leyla who have also been invited to dinner and are sitting right alongside Eric, dressed in their best. That they don't seem to have taken offence and are watching the greeting of golden-boy Eric with obvious amusement, is beside the point.

'Gran!' Alice calls sharply.

'Yes, dear?' Her grandmother is leading Eric over to the table and speaking confidentially. 'Alice has been absolutely marvellous throughout it all. I don't know what I'd do without her. She's like her mother, you know, Eric. For a while there I thought I could see the father in her, you understand?' Phyllis stops to shudder. 'But no . . . she is just like my darling Lillian. She was always absolutely wonderful if I was in any kind of trouble.'

'It doesn't surprise me,' Eric murmurs and then turns around to wink at the others.

'Gran, the twins are here, too!' Alice says quickly, motioning to Sylvie and Leyla, who get up and walk over shyly.

'Hello, Mrs Hickey! Thanks for inviting us.'

'Oh, you're both so welcome, my dears,' Phyllis says distractedly.

'Welcome!' She kisses first Sylvie and then her sister. 'When did you come in? I didn't see you.'

'They were sitting right next to Eric, Gran,' Alice says dryly.

'Were they now?' Her grandmother has the grace to give a wry self-deprecating smile before starting to look the twins up and down critically in just the way Alice loathes.

'You're both still in the *cowgirl* phase, I see.' Phyllis is eyeing Sylvie's plain pink cotton shirt and cord pants and Leyla's jeans. 'Jeans! Goodness me, everyone is in jeans!'

Alice gives the twins a mortified look. *Sorry!* But the twins' eyes are bright with suppressed laughter.

'Thanks, Mrs Hickey!' Sylvie manages.

'Have either of you got a boyfriend yet?'

'No,' they answer demurely. 'Not yet.'

'Well, I think it's time you did.' Phyllis is first to sit down at the table, and she motions for the rest of them to follow suit. 'As you can see, it's done Alice the world of good.' Alice opens her mouth to protest . . . then closes it again. What is the point? It will only get more embarrassing. They are all looking at her now, her friends nodding and pretending to be serious.

'Alice does look well, doesn't she?' her grandmother mumbles approvingly.

'Yes, she does!' Sylvie and Leyla chorus.

Eric picks up his knife and fork and cuts into his meat. 'She looks wonderful.'

'All thanks to Eric,' Phyllis declares, picking up her soup spoon. 'Now, please begin, everyone! We don't want it to get cold.'

'Thank God for Eric, you gorgeous thing!' Leyla mutters under her breath, kicking Alice's foot.

'Is it hard being her boyfriend?' Sylvie asks innocently, nudging Eric in the ribs.

'I'm sure it is quite difficult.' Phyllis hasn't missed the exchange. 'Alice can be quite determined when she wants.'

'I have an idea where she might have got that from, Mrs Hickey!' Eric quips and Phyllis gives a small pleased smile.

'Well, Eric,' she replies demurely, 'I've always operated on the principle that if I didn't stick up for myself then no one else would.'

'Quite!' Eric nods approvingly.

Later, when the twins have gone, Alice tells Eric about her strange visit from Tom and the invitation to the pub.

'He might well be keen on you,' is Eric's thoughtful response. 'I'll be able to tell you when I meet him.'

'How?' Alice smiles.

'I can tell by the eyes.'

'Really!'

'They'll go drifty whenever you say anything.'

'Oh, stop bullshitting me!'

The whole idea of someone, *anyone*, being keen on her seems totally outside the realm of possibility. *Especially him!* It's a preposterous idea and yet it pleases her, it's a nice fantasy. Later that night it expands in her head, tripping about like an inflated balloon-figure flapping outside a second-hand car dealership. What would it be like to touch Tom Mullaney? To feel the skin of his arms and back under her hands?

TOM

Tom turns up at on time but neither of the others is there. That's cool. Not to worry. He'll go get a drink. On the way to the bar he chats to a few local girls he used to know at high school. They want to know all about his course and where he lives and what it's like being home again. Okay for twenty minutes. Still no show. So where are they?

He's looking at his watch when Alice comes in, all flustered, followed by this amazingly tall geeky-looking guy, dressed in black, with a long nose and high forehead. *God, he is really something! In the right gear he'd fit one of those princes from the Renaissance. Either that or a praying mantis.*

'Sorry. We were waiting in the other bar,' she explains breathlessly, looking around. 'Jonty not here?'

'No.' Tom tries hard not to notice that she looks different. Her dark hair is spilling in curls around her face. He hasn't seen it out like that. And she's wearing a red shirt, the buttons open to the top of her breasts. Some lacy thing peeps out from underneath and he has to force himself to look away. She introduces the guy and they find a table.

The guy, Eric, goes to buy the first round, and Alice sits down opposite Tom and folds her hands carefully in front of her. Then she looks up seriously and steadily as though accusing him of something. Her eyes in the yellow bar light are like pools of dark clear water.

'So where is Jonty?' she wants to know.

'No idea,' Tom says. 'I don't have his mobile. Not sure he's even got one.'

Tom tries to calm down but he is revved up just being here with her. Those eyes! The sweet oval cut of her face, all angles and planes. Every time she turns her head it's different. Tom thinks he would like to put one hand under her chin and make her look at him. He'd like to reach out and run the thumb of his other hand along the soft shadows under her eyes. He wants to *learn* her face, commit it to memory. This is how far gone he is. The spell breaks when the tall guy gets back with the drinks.

'Hey, a band is setting up over there,' Eric says in this very assured toffy voice. 'We could move nearer.'

'Later,' Alice says. 'We've got to wait for Jonty, remember?'

'Okay.'

After that they have a go at polite small talk as they wait. Eric is cheery and sociable, looking around and making smart comments about the rest of the clientele. Alice is laughing and making nervous chitchat about him being so much the city boy that she can't believe he's game enough to come back after the rabbit shooting.

As though Tom cares! He hates dudes who act all wide-eyed as soon as they're a few kilometres out of the burbs. It's just another excuse to be superior as far as he's concerned. The guy is looking around now as though he's in a circus instead of an ordinary pub, and it suddenly gets Tom right offside, makes him want to smash his face in.

'I might leave you two to catch up.' Eric gets up eventually. 'See if I can find a pool table.'

'Okay.' Tom tries one of his fake smiles. *Hey, Eric, why don't you fuck right off home?* 'We'll come find you soon.'

Alice watches Eric wander off into another room of the hotel. Tom wants to tell her she can do way better than him.

Give me a chance, Alice! Come on, look at me! We could be good together. We've got so much to talk about. We got . . . history, baby. Okay, it's a sad history, but . . .

The band has started at the other end of the room and the crowd is building up quickly. A few people come by and shake Tom's hand and say hello, but he makes it plain that he doesn't want them to linger. A girl at another table asks if she can have their spare chairs and Tom says *sure*, because he doesn't want anyone else sitting with them and it means he can move nearer to Alice.

He's jumpy, nervous.

Her hand is playing with a cardboard coaster. Long white fingers, tapering off into these polished oval nails. He wonders what would happen if he reached out and took that hand.

She looks around, her eyes flitting from the group of girls at the nearby table, to the doorway where her friend has gone and then back to Tom.

'I know those girls,' she says at last. 'I went to school with them.'

Tom nods and looks over, vaguely recognising a few faces. It's his cue now to say, *Do you want to ask them to join us?* But he can't bring himself to. It would ruin everything.

'Hope they don't see *me*!' Alice gives a sudden girlish laugh and pulls her hair over her face to hide.

'You didn't like them?' The laugh has undone Tom. He's had no more than three sips of his beer, but everything suddenly feels like liquid, as if they're both swimming underwater. He does his best to smile back.

'They're okay,' she wrinkles up her nose, 'but too much like hard work.'

'Yeah, some people *are* hard work.' Tom says, too carefully. After that, he's weirdly tongue-tied. It's his turn to chime in with some snippet of his own along the same lines, but he can't think what. Not like him. He has never had a problem talking to girls before. He's heard guys giving each other hints about how to open up a conversation with a female and always felt secretly superior. Now he's in exactly the same boat. He needs to be impressive but . . . what about?

Added to this, Tom has an insane sense that he has to hurry. That he doesn't have much time. That he has to let her know how he feels soon or all will be lost. Jonty might turn up any minute, and the geek will probably be back soon, too. But what can he say?

'You're doing photography, right?' she asks suddenly.

'Yep,' Tom nods.

'So where do I go to print up some old negatives?'

'How old are they?'

'I don't know, but they're big square things.' She makes the shape with her hand. 'I don't think they use cameras like that any more.'

'That doesn't matter,' Tom says quickly, 'as long as you have the negs.'

'I asked the photo shop in town and they said they didn't do that sort of work anymore, that I'd have to send them away, but they weren't exactly sure where to.'

'I could do them for you. I've got a little darkroom at the old man's place.' He is suddenly drunk with the possibilities of such a scenario. It will give them an excuse to spend time together, for . . . all kinds of things to happen. *Yes.*

'These are . . . black-and-white,' she adds cautiously.

'Yeah,' Tom smiles, 'I got that kind of old-fashioned set-up. You could come and help, if you like.'

'Well . . . I don't know.' Her face closes warily, as though he's just overstepped the mark and suggested something way too familiar.

Tom immediately backtracks. 'I can do them. Be no trouble. Just drop off the negatives.'

'But you must be busy.' He can tell she's just filling in time trying to work out what she thinks about the idea.

'I have spare time.' Tom drains his glass and tries to make light of it. 'Actually, I've been looking for an excuse to get into the old darkroom again. I enjoy it.'

She nods and his mind goes into overdrive. He's imagining himself with her in that little cramped room, teaching her how to print up her photos under the red light. The smell of chemicals, their hands brushing over the fixer tray.

'I think one of them is of . . . my mother and her sister, Marie, as little girls.' She is frowning. 'There might be a few like that.'

Is she telling Tom she doesn't want him to see those images? 'Would that be a problem?' he asks carefully.

She turns back to him. Those pools of water are extra bright now. They make him think of rivers and rock springs, and the clear drops left on leaves after rain.

'I'm not sure,' she says sternly. 'I'll have to think about it.'

'Okay then.' He looks up to see Eric making his way across the room towards them, and adds lamely, 'I'm happy to do it, if you want.'

'Thanks, Tom.'

Is that a yes or a no?

The redhead sits down next to Tom and starts raving on about being off his form, and one of his pool opponents being amazingly good. Then it turns out he won anyway. Is Tom meant to be impressed? Interested? Alice's phone rings and Tom tries to think of a way to get rid of him again. Pity he's so ugly. The local girls aren't going to be lining up.

'Okay,' Alice mutters into the phone, frowning. 'Okay, I'll be there.'

She switches the phone off and slips it into her pocket before turning to Tom and Eric.

'I've got to go,' she says. 'My grandmother has had some kind of turn. The doctor is there already.'

'What does that mean?' Eric is genuinely concerned.

What do you think it means, you twerp!

'Who knows, but I guess I'd better go.'

'I'll come with you.' Tom stands up.

But Alice doesn't hear him. She's putting on her coat, picking up her bag and making for the door.

'It's okay.' Eric takes keys from his pocket. 'I'll drive her home.'

Outside in the cold air, Alice turns to Tom. 'I guess Jonno forgot?' she says.

'Yeah.' He looks at his watch. 'He's over an hour late, anyway.'

'You sure he said he'd come?'

'Of course,' he sighs. *You think I made it up?*

'Well, bye then, Tom.'

'Bye, Alice. I hope your gran is . . . hope everything is all right.' Tom stands alone, one foot up against the side of the pub watching the two of them walk off towards Eric's car, feeling like absolute . . . *shit. So that's it! The big night out where everything gets off to a new start. Blah Blah.*

'Hey, Tom!'

Tom turns in the direction of the voice. Someone is waving madly on the other side of the road. *Jonty!* Alice sees him too just as she's getting into the car. Tom watches her hesitate, then bend to say something to Eric. His heart lifts when he sees her coming back.

'Hey, he's come!' she smiles. 'You weren't lying!'

Tom laughs, and wishes he could plant a kiss on her shiny face.

'I don't lie.'

'Don't you?' She looks at him, amused.

'No,' he says. 'Do you?'

'Sometimes.'

'I'll remember that, Alice Wishart!' He grins and suddenly they are both laughing.

Jonty takes his time negotiating the traffic. He lopes across to them in a half-distracted way and stands under the streetlight, shifting about from one foot to the other. He looks oddly young, and ill-equipped for the cold night. His face is pale, he is wearing no jacket or jumper and his shirt is thin. His feet are grubby in worn thongs. The long red hand-knitted scarf dangling around his neck is his only bit of warm clothing. About to hold out his hand, Tom decides that playing cool was never what this meeting was going to be about, so impulsively he grabs the two ends of the long scarf and wraps them quickly around Jonty's head and neck.

'Hey, Jonno!'

Caught by surprise, Jonty tries to dodge and slip out of Tom's grasp but can't. Tom can tell that under the awkward *Piss off, can't ya*, he's laughing a bit.

'You guys drunk yet?' Jonty asks, unwinding the scarf.

'We were waiting for you,' Tom quips. 'You look like you've

just come back from a blizzard.' Jonty laughs as he rewinds the scarf around his neck. 'Or from committing a burglary!'

'Yeah, well.' Jonty sniffs a couple of times, pulls out a hanky and blows his nose, then looks quizzically from Alice to Tom and back again.

'So,' he chuckles. 'We're here.'

'The three of us.'

'Why are you late?'

'My old lady,' Jonty grimaces, 'that's why I'm late.' His voice is steady enough but his movements are jerky. He half turns and takes a step away as though he is going to leave altogether. On impulse, Tom grabs him again, this time by the shoulders, pushes him up against the wall of the pub and looks into his face.

'You okay?' he asks gently.

'Yeah,' Jonty laughs softly. 'I'm okay, Tommy boy.'

'It's good to see you then.' Tom doesn't trust himself to say anything else. Being up so close to Jonty drags him through some kind of time warp and he feels like bawling.

'Thanks.'

Tom lets him go and clears his throat. Jonty smiles at Alice who is leaning up on the wall alongside him.

'So, cousin,' he jokes, 'you know Tom, huh?'

'Sort of.' She smiles uncertainly. 'Not really.'

'Don't worry,' Jonty throws an arm around Tom's shoulder, 'not much to know.'

'You want to go inside?' Tom waves towards the pub.

Jonty looks over at the crowd of young people spilling from one of the doorways and shakes his head.

'What about a coffee, then? We could walk around to the Angry Cat.'

'No.' Jonty screws up his face. 'I drink way too much coffee.'

'And I should get home,' Alice says.

But none of them move.

The usual late-night yelling and excited pissed talk of people deciding what to do next swells around them. Cars roar up and down the road and it begins to spit with rain. Tom isn't sure what's happening, but he is aware of their cocoon-like separateness from the rest of the crowd. If anyone bothered to look, they'd see the three leading actors in the current local drama.

'So, we just stand out here in the rain?' Tom asks wryly. 'Is that the idea?'

'Hmmm.' Jonty is looking around edgily, frowning as though his mind is already concentrating on something else, humming a bit, then scratching his head.

Tom glances at Alice. She shrugs as though she doesn't know what's going on either. Tom gives him a light punch on the arm and suddenly Jonty refocuses. He's back on board with them.

'So?' He smiles. 'What's happening, man? You working at the local rag?'

'Yep. Holding the whole place together.'

'Of course!' Jonty fumbles around in the front pocket of his shirt for a cigarette. 'The place would fall apart without ya, huh?'

'That's right,' Tom laughs uneasily.

Jonty is so shaky that he only just manages to pick a cigarette out of the pack. He gets it into his mouth but his hands are trembling so violently he can't get it lit.

Tom takes the lighter from him, does the job then waits as Jonty takes a couple of deep drags. 'You don't seem too good, mate,' Tom says softly.

'I'm okay,' Jonty laughs, and makes a tight fist with one of his hands. He puts it on Tom's shoulder. 'Just bit *unco* at the moment, you know? Things are . . . have been . . . pretty *full on*, you know? Everything is . . . so bloody weird.'

'Yeah,' Tom says. 'I can guess.'

'My old man wrote to me today.'

'From prison?'

'Yeah.' Jonty looks at Tom and then at Alice. 'He's found God.'

'*Jeez!*' Tom's mouth falls open.

'Exactly.'

'So where did he find him?'

'Dunno.'

'Where *does* God hang out?'

'We always wanted to know that, didn't we?'

They grin darkly at each other in the wet yellow light from the streetlamp. It strikes Tom that the old Jonty – the one he knew years ago – would be killing himself laughing by this stage. The old Jonty wouldn't be looking so anxious about his old man *finding* God. He'd be spluttering with derision, laying bets maybe on how it happened and how long it would last. They'd be joking about where God had been hiding all this time – under a bush, in the wall cabinet, or in some celebrity's coat pocket? And the question would be, did God want to be *found*?

Alice knots her hair up at the back of her head and buttons up her coat, then takes a worried backwards glace at Eric, who is still waiting in the car. A taxi pulls up and they all watch a young guy in a sharp suit and a skinny girl in ridiculously high heels argue about who should pay the fare.

'So, what do we talk about?' Jonty asks suddenly. 'Nobody is saying nothin'!'

Tom laughs. *This* at least is like the old Jonty. *So much* to talk about and no one can find a word. Tom, for one, wants to clear the decks big time. He wants to apologise and make amends in some real way. He also wants to talk to Alice. He wants to walk home with her. Tell that geek in the car to piss off. He'd rehearsed

274

all of the above a million times over from every angle but now, *now* he's got both of them here and he's *on the spot*, he can't think of a single thing to say or do. The other two must be thinking along the same lines because Alice suddenly giggles.

'We're here though!' She smacks Jonty on the arm. 'My one and only cousin!'

'Only the two of us.' Jonty puts his arm briefly around her. 'We should . . . you know, stick together!'

'Yeah!' Alice agrees warmly.

Tom grabs Jonty again and pulls him closer. Then he grabs Alice with the other arm and pulls her in. A spurt of elation goes through him when her arm slides easily around his waist. It's the three of them in close now, arms around each other, their heads touching, all breathing hard, laughing a bit. Tom has a moment of being aware of not wanting or needing anything else. *These two*, he thinks. Apart from his family it's just *these two*, really, in the whole wide world.

'Jeez!' Jonty is the first to pull away. He rubs two hands through his hair. 'What's all this about? . . . You're both fucking idiots!'

'I've got to go back home now, anyway.' Alice backs away, pointing at Eric waiting in the car. 'My grandmother is sick. I mean . . . *our* grandmother is sick.'

'What's wrong with her?'

Alice shrugs. 'Had some kind of turn.'

'A turn?' Jonty grins. 'I want one of them.'

'Good luck, then, again,' Tom tells her. 'I hope everything is okay.'

'Thanks!' Alice gives him a sudden wide warm smile that makes him feel dizzy with hope. 'Bye, Tom. Bye, Jonno.'

'Yeah, bye, Alice.' Jonty waves. 'Tell that old lady I *like* her.'

'You *like* her?' Alice yells back incredulously from the open car door.

275

'Yeah!' Jonty is quite serious until he sees Alice break up into laughter and then his own face splits open. Tom watches them both, loving the way the laughter rolls out of her as though she can't help it.

'I really like her,' Jonty yells again, 'I mean it.'

'I know you do!'

'Tell her I think she's great!'

'I will!' Alice shouts back as she gets in and slams the door, 'I'll tell her you *like* her. Promise!'

Tom and Jonty wave as Alice speeds off with Eric.

'I gotta piss off, too,' Jonty mumbles. 'Gotta get home.'

'Okay.' Tom grasps his hand. 'You take it easy, okay?'

'Okay.'

'Come around any time.'

'Okay. I will.'

On the way home Tom feels the beginnings of a cold setting in. His head feels stuffed up and there is a raspy tight soreness in his throat. The glands in his throat are swollen too. *Damn!* He knows the signs. When his phone rings his voice is slightly croaky.

It's Amanda. Weird. It takes a while before Tom recognises her voice.

'Happy birthday for tomorrow,' she says, with one of her short bright laughs.

'Thanks, Amanda!' He is genuinely touched that she has remembered. 'How are you?'

'I'm good,' she says. 'So what are you going to do?'

'You mean tomorrow?'

'Yeah.'

'I dunno.' It's true, he hasn't given it a thought. After all the fuss and fanfare of turning twenty-one last year he's kind of glad it will be quiet. 'I'll probably end up having a few beers with the old man,' Tom jokes. 'Should be *really* exciting.'

'Why don't you come down to town?' she suggests lightly. 'I could get a few of the old crowd together or we . . . I mean you and me, could do something?'

Oh jeez, don't, Amanda, please. The false carelessness in her voice makes Tom feel really bad. He doesn't want to hear that yearning sad note, but . . . it's there all right.

'Ah . . . I don't think so. It's just that I'm . . .' he stumbles on, making it worse, 'I mean that is a *really* nice idea, Amanda, but . . .'

'It's okay,' she cuts in crisply, 'don't worry about it. I just thought you might like to do something.'

'Yeah, well, it's so nice of you to ask,' he adds sincerely, 'and really nice of you to remember.'

'Yeah, well, I'm a *nice* person, Tom,' she says sarcastically. 'You used to think so, anyway. Have a good one, won't you?'

'I will, thanks, Amanda.'

Tom clicks off, feeling absolutely shithouse. Getting knocked back is hard for anyone, but for Amanda it will be *agony*. He knows how proud she is. He knows how much it would have taken for her to make the call. Tom remembers his last birthday. They were so much *the couple*! Everyone was saying they were made for each other. She bought all that bullshit, hook, line and sinker, and he almost did too.

Tom wakes to a raging head, a sore throat and the sound of things being slammed around the kitchen. He groans and covers his head with a pillow. *What's going on?* Is some kind of renovation happening that no one bothered to tell him about? The noise eases off a bit and he lies on his back for a while, thinking about

Alice the night before – the way her hair fell in waves around her face, and those deep and shining eyes. What was she thinking? How was she feeling about him? Pity that Eric guy was there. If not for him, Tom could have driven Alice home in his car, and been part of whatever was going on with the old duck. What will happen to Alice if the old lady dies?

The noises start again and Tom gets up to see what's happening.

It's only Nanette, dressed in a new set of designer weekend gear – pink tracksuit with a white shirt collar sticking out like cardboard, hair teased up into a perfect natty little roll. She is up on a stool clearing out the high shelves of the pantry, chucking stuff down.

Tom sighs. It's eight o'clock on Saturday morning. She must have stayed overnight. How come this woman never relaxes in an old T-shirt and jeans, or dressing-gown and slippers, like other people? She's furiously chucking jars and bottles and plastic containers into two separate cardboard boxes. As she wipes down surfaces, clouds of dust and flour and bits of paper and other rubbish fly out around her. Something stinks, too.

Tom heads for the medicine cupboard to get himself some Panadol, thinking that no one would have cleaned the pantry out for at least five years. He's always finding bottles full of weird mouldy stuff in there.

'G'day, Nanette,' Tom says. 'Feeling energetic, are we?'

She nods sharply but doesn't answer. Tom switches on the kettle as his father comes in holding the weekend papers, stinking of stale cigarettes. Luke stands back to regard Nanette with a kind of fuddled bewilderment before he speaks.

'I thought you were heading off early to the sales?' he says meekly.

'I am,' she snaps.

'Well,' he says guiltily, 'don't . . . bother with all this.'

'But it's disgusting!' She continues to pull stuff out and throw it at the boxes. 'Weevils and mice and see *this*?' She shoves an opened packet of flour in Luke's face. 'The *use by* date is eighteen months ago!'

'I know,' Luke looks genuinely shamefaced, 'but I'll do it.'

'When?'

'Today. This weekend. Sometime soon.'

'You say you'll do things, Luke, but you . . . *don't*!'

'Well, I will this time. Tom and I will finish it, Nanette! Really. You don't have to bother with this. It's not your responsibility. Just get going. Your sister will be waiting.'

She gives a deep sigh and gets off the stool, throwing down the cloth she's been using.

'Hang on!' Tom sees the brightly coloured box on the bench. 'This for me?'

Tom opens the card first, knowing it will be from her – his old man never remembers birthdays – and then he starts his *gush and suck* routine.

'Hey! Thanks a lot, Nanette!'

She gulps down her irritation and pecks him on the cheek.

To a special young man, it says on the front, next to a picture of a tennis racquet and beer glass. And then inside: *Happy Birthday, Tom, with love from Nanette.*

Tom suddenly feels so sorry for her. She hasn't got the faintest idea. *Poor bloody woman!*

'That's so nice of you.' He tries to be sincere. *Well, it is nice of her!*

'Open your present,' she orders, smiling now.

'Okay.' He puts on an enthusiastic face and rips off the paper. 'You shouldn't have bothered with a present! You know me, Nanette. I tend to lose everything anyway.' This is a vague reference to the horrible present she gave him last year, which he conveniently lost. It was a really vomitous print of two people holding hands and looking down into a stream with the sun behind them – absolutely gut-wrenchingly terrible. It got worse when Luke and Nanette had called in at the student house two weeks later, and she saw that it wasn't pride of place on his bedroom wall. Tom had hurriedly lied about someone pinching it at a party.

'Hope you like it,' she mumbles, coming over.

'I'm sure I will.'

This year it's a striped business shirt, a purple silk tie and a pair of cufflinks. *Christ!* Tom is completely gobsmacked and so is his father. He turns to see if it's a joke, but no, of course it isn't. Nanette is smiling proudly. She's deadly serious. Not only does Tom not *own* a suit, but more importantly he never wants to own one. *Ever. Period.* In fact he has made it known generally that one of the biggest ambitions of his life is *never to own a suit.* What could have been going through that well-coiffed head of hers?

'Gee, thanks a heap, Nanette!' He kisses on the cheek. 'They're *really* great!'

'You like the cufflinks?'

'I sure do,' he says, picking them out of the box and flipping them from one hand to the other, pretending to be impressed by the weight. Heavy, gold, oval jobs with a tiny little bit of opal in one corner. They were probably really expensive. No one has ever been able to explain the point of cufflinks to Tom but *shit,* what does he know? Maybe he'll be able to sell them.

'Thought you needed smartening up,' she says happily, looking pointedly at his old jeans and T-shirt. 'Getting older now and all that.'

'Yeah, well,' Tom tries to laugh, 'I guess this will do the trick!'

Nanette pulls the shirt out of its box and holds it up against his shoulders.

'You think the size will be right?'

'Perfect,' Tom says and begins undoing the buttons. *Why not try it on? It will probably look great.*

They chitchat for a while. Tom sits at the table in his new shirt, chattering on about the exact colour of suit that will 'go' nicely with the shirt, until Nanette's sister rings and she goes to have her shower.

When she is out of the room, Tom and his dad look at each other. Luke shrugs and shakes his head, then goes into the kitchen to turn off the whistling kettle. 'You want tea?' he asks.

'Yeah,' Tom replies, flipping on the television, 'after you give me your present.'

'It's coming!' Luke grins.

'So is Christmas!'

They sit down together at the table and flip through the papers. Luke suddenly stops, leans over, picks up the little velvet box and stares down at the cufflinks.

'What am I going to *do*, Tommo?' he sighs. 'What the *hell* am I going to do?'

'I see what you mean.' Tom turns around to stare pointedly at the pantry and all the stuff on the floor. 'Not looking too good, is it?'

'But what can I *do*?' Luke shrugs. 'I mean, she is a nice woman.'

'Tell her,' Tom says.

'I have!'

'So tell her again!'

Luke nods and goes back to the paper. 'I don't like hurting people,' he mumbles. Then grins wryly, 'God I wish I'd never let her race me off.'

Tom snorts at the very idea. 'Sometimes you've gotta be cruel to be kind,' he says as he gets up and brings over the kettle to refill the pot.

This is met with a deep groan from Luke. 'You think you can give me lectures!' Then he laughs and slaps one hand on Tom's shoulder. 'Happy birthday, Tommo! God, the day you were born seems about five years ago to me. That trip to the hospital was the scariest ride I've ever done. Your mother was doing her best, but she was terrified! Everything,' he sighs, 'I remember everything about it.'

'Thanks, Dad!' Tom laughs.

'What for?'

'Getting there on time.'

'They're home, Mum!'

'Both of them? Oh goody! Hey there, Birthday Boy!'

'Congratulations, dickhead!'

'Come here you skinny streak! Let me hug you!'

It's just on noon when Mum and Ned burst in unexpectedly, full of greetings and presents and smart-arsed comments. Luke and Tom are still sitting around reading the papers in the middle of the same untidy kitchen that Nanette had left them with four hours before. Tom is pleased of course, but his father is *really* pleased. Luke's whole expression loosens as he jumps up and busies himself welcoming them.

'So you had nothing planned for today?' Anna asks tentatively, looking around at the mess. There are dishes all over the sink and newspapers everywhere. The pantry has been virtually emptied and there are half-empty packets and jars all over the floor. 'We thought we'd make it a surprise.'

'Not a thing.' Luke grins happily as he takes her coat and asks about the trip and whether he should turn up the heating. It's weird: even the lines in his face seem to have disappeared.

Hang on a minute, Tom opens his mouth to protest. For one thing he was going to set up the darkroom so that if Alice did want him to do the prints for her he'd be ready, and that could take the rest of the day. But Ned is on his case before he has a chance to say any of it.

'Nothing happening, eh?' He shoves Tom in the back.

'Watch your mouth, *bubs*.' Tom twists his arm up his back. He's still stronger but not by much.

'So you're the *total* loser now, huh?' Ned gasps through laughter. 'It's Saturday *and* your birthday and you've got nothing on! I guess your true nature had to come out sometime!'

'Shut your mouth *little Mr Sunshine*.' Tom pushes the arm up a bit further to make his little brother howl.

Anna laughs at them, rubs her cold hands and tells Luke that yes, a cup of tea would be just what the doctor ordered. Tom watches his father laugh at their old joke – she being the doctor and all that *ha ha* – and become ten years younger in the process. All within the space of five minutes.

Ned prowls the room, from the new television, to the window, then to the fridge for a plate of leftover meat and potatoes. The kid looks happy. His skin has cleared up even more and he's starting to lose a lot of his gawkiness. Funny how you notice stuff like that when you haven't seen someone for a while.

'Ned!' Anna grabs the plate from him and puts it back in the fridge. 'You had a burger on the way and we'll have a proper lunch soon!'

Ned scowls. He is wearing baggy daks that hang from his bum, a jumper that is too small and a hat that is way too big. He is already sizing Tom up for a fresh bout. But first things first, he pushes Tom up against the wall to check out who is the tallest. Much to his disappointment it is still Tom, but not by much.

'Who threw the bomb?' Ned asks disinterestedly, as he surveys all the pantry junk all over the floor.

Mum's only comment is to raise her eyebrows and look at Tom as she steps around it.

'Wasn't us,' Dad says ruefully, winking at Tom.

'No, it wasn't us.'

After all the birthday hugs, the personal comments on how thin Tom is (from his mum) and how much he stank (from Ned), Anna goes back out to the car and comes in with two big baskets. Luke and Tom watch guiltily as she unpacks them on the bench. Apart from tea, half a bottle of milk and a loaf of plastic bread there is no food in the house. Tom had been trying to write a shopping list when his mother and brother arrived, so this is like manna from heaven: a beef casserole, fresh rolls and packets of ham and cheese. From the other basket appear fruit and biscuits and a big homemade cake.

'Anna this is very good of you,' Luke says formally, trying to look contrite. 'I'm afraid we're a bit light-on here. I can go down the street now and—'

'I've got everything,' Anna laughs, 'just put that bottle in the fridge!' Suddenly Tom is starving. He reaches out for a roll but his mother shoves him away.

'Go have a shower, Birthday Boy,' she orders, 'then we'll have a proper lunch.'

So Tom leaves them to it and heads for the bathroom. He takes a few more Panadol for his cold, closes his eyes under the hot water and thinks of Alice and Jonty the night before. The way she smiled as she said goodbye. The way Jonty put his fist on Tom's shoulder. *I'm all right, Tommo.* A strange rush of heat rises in Tom when he thinks of that trembling fist. What is happening in Jonty's life right now? The poor bastard looks as though he's being eaten away from the inside.

Tom comes back into the kitchen to find the table laid with all his mother's stuff and his parents well into their first glass of champagne. 'I thought it was *my* birthday!'

'We couldn't wait forever,' his mother teases.

'So, how are you two going to fix all that if you're drunk?' Tom points at the pantry junk on the floor. 'I thought you'd have it done by now!'

His mum frowns at the mess as she reaches over to fill his glass.

'Did one of you have a bright idea in the middle of the night or something?'

'That's it,' Tom and Luke grin at each other and clink glasses, 'right on the money, Anna!'

'As usual.'

'It seemed like a good idea at the time, did it?' she asks dryly. *She knows*, Tom realises, *but she's not going to comment.* For whatever reason his mum always makes a point of being nice about Nanette.

'Yeah, that's about it,' Dad sighs.

'Then it all just got a bit too hard,' Tom laughs.

'Well cheers, Tommo.' His mum gets up to give him another hug. 'Love you, darling. Happy birthday!'

'Thanks, Mum. Hey, why didn't Nellie come?'

'There's a young man on the scene,' Anna whispers, leaning over to put a hand across Ned's mouth, 'and no comments from the peanut gallery, thank you!'

'A complete and utter wanker,' Ned growls, pulling away, then starts mimicking the guy: *My name is Julian Francis Austin-Barton and I'm going to be an airline pilot and . . . I know everything!*

'Ned he's *not* that bad!' Anna is laughing.

'He's an arsehole!' Ned looks at Tom and shakes his head. 'You'd really hate him, Tom!'

'He's okay, Ned!' Mum insists. 'He's just a little . . .'

'What?' Tom smiles at her. She always stops mid-sentence when she doesn't want to say something derogatory.

'Well . . . a little *pompous*.'

'So why would I hate him?' Tom laughs at his brother's furious face and reaches for the bottle. The first glass of champers has gone down very well on his empty stomach and sore throat.

'There is not one thing to like about him!'

'Fair enough,' he takes a forkful of meat and almost swoons. God he hasn't tasted anything this good in ages! He looks at his father. 'This is good, eh?'

'Very good.'

'So why can't you make things like this?'

'You're the one who should be doing it!' Luke says mildly. 'The young can learn anything.'

Anna smiles. 'Thought you might need something substantial.'

'You thought right.'

'I approve without having met this Julian whatever-his-name-is,' Luke says, 'because I like the idea of a pilot for a son-in-law.'

And so it goes on. The banter is warm and easy between them all. The cold of the early spring day stays outside. Inside it's warm with laughter. Nellie is the only missing element.

They're messing around trying to find candles for the cake when the doorbell rings. Anna throws the three mingy candles she's managed to find on the table in exasperation.

'For God's sake, Luke, you must have a candle or two in this house! Off you go Ned. Get the door!'

Ned slinks off up the hallway and Tom is left sitting at the table on his own, watching his mother and father flirting with each other on the other side of the bench. *Jeez, what is this!* His dad is opening one cupboard after another making out there are mountains of candles somewhere just out of reach, and his mum is laughing and flipping him with a tea towel yelling, 'Find them for me . . . you hopeless man!' Luke turns around, snatches the tea towel from her and starts flipping her with it, then they're both giggling like maniacs and shoving each other around. *Seriously!* Tom shakes his head. They're both over fifty! The four of them have just had a leisurely two-hour meal and he can't remember what happened to get things quite this jolly.

The high jinks stop abruptly when Ned walks in followed by *Jonty*. Anna and Luke stop mid-laugh. Tom is surprised, too, but also strangely moved. Moved because it has been three years at least since Jonty set foot in the house, and before that he used to just about live there.

'G'day, Jonno,' he says, getting up from the table awkwardly.

'Hi, Tom.' Jonty comes into the middle of the room, dressed as he'd been the night before. He stands there a moment, looking around, biting his lip, hands dug deep in his pockets, as though unsure what to do with himself, eyes flitting from one to the other of them, taking everything in.

'So last night wasn't enough for you then?' Tom jokes.

'You said come around,' Jonty smiles hesitantly.

'It's great to see you,' Tom says, suddenly not sure if he means it. The old jeans, thongs and shirt, and the hair falling over his forehead are exactly the same as the night before, but in the daylight Jonty looks older, more battered, somehow; way harder than when he was last here, that's for sure.

It's Anna who breaks the ice. She jumps into welcome mode, hurries over to where Jonty is standing and pulls him into a warm hug.

'Jonty van der Weihl!' she laughs. 'Long time no see. How are you?'

'Okay. Thanks, Anna. Okay.' A tinge of pink floods briefly across his cheeks. He's embarrassed by her display of affection but pleased too. 'I thought you didn't live here anymore?'

'I don't,' she smiles and ruffles his hair briefly. 'Just here for the day.' She pauses and then says gently, 'I was so sorry to hear of the latest business with your . . . father.'

'Yeah, well.' Jonty looks at his feet.

'It must be terrible for your mum and for you,' she continues kindly. Jonty says nothing. No one else speaks. But Tom is proud. His mother always knows the right thing to say.

Luke pulls out a chair. 'Sit down and have some cake with us. It's Tom's birthday.'

'Ah!' Jonty looks at Tom properly for the first time and frowns. 'So it is. September the fifteenth.' Then he grins, and Tom can see the old Jonty sitting there under the surface of this new tougher version.

'My present is out in the car,' Jonty quips, his green eyes suddenly bright with humour.

'Right.' Tom nods. 'Too heavy to bring in is it?'

'Cost so much, I'm scared it will break.'

At first the heavy stuff that happened three years before is there in the room with them. Jonty remains standing as though he might have to make a quick getaway. He rests both hands on the back of the chair, looking around uneasily while the rest of the family try to make him feel welcome. It takes Tom a while to twig that Jonty is waiting for *him* to say it's okay to sit down with the family. A dart of sorrow flies in from left field, settling in Tom's chest like a stone. Sorrow for Jonty, for how things have changed and for this strange great gaping *hole* in all their lives.

'Come on, Jonty,' he says, 'sit down. Have some cake, *please*.' So Jonty does and he sings Happy Birthday with the rest of them, too.

'Have a glass of champagne, Jonno?' Anna wants to know.

'No thanks.' He shakes his head.

'Tea?'

'That would be good.'

He accepts the plate of cake from Anna and examines it carefully before he takes a bite.

Her eyes are noting that one foot jigs about constantly, that his right hand trembles and that his eyes can't stay still on any one thing or person for more than a moment.

'Meet with your approval?'

'It's good.' He gives a shy smile and blushes again.

'Jonty cooks for a living now, Anna,' Luke tells her.

'I know that,' she says huffily. 'What I want to know is if my cake is up to Thistles standard!'

Jonty's expression becomes instantly boyish again. 'Way better! You always made the best cakes.'

'Well, I'm glad someone remembers!'

Tom watches the way his mother gets this kind of stuff *right*. No wonder his father misses her so much. After all the cake and tea, Ned slopes off to the couch to read car magazines, and Anna and Luke start doing the dishes together in the nearby kitchen, leaving Tom and Jonty at the table. Anna occasionally directs a comment or question to Jonty as she tidies up and puts away dishes.

Tom's back is to the window, and the light coming in gives him a clearer view of Jonty. It's not only the new scar on his chin and the twitch around his mouth, there is also a new watchfulness in his eyes.

'Sorry I couldn't hang around last night.' Jonty's voice is tight and low.

'So, what is going on with your mum?' Tom tries to sound easy.

'I dunno.' Jonty shrugs.

Tom offers him another slice of cake but Jonty shakes his head. He remembers that Jonty never was that interested in food. It's strange to think of him working as a cook.

'I think of her a lot, you know,' Jonty says.

'Your mum?'

'No no,' Jonty laughs darkly. '*Her*, you know. She's never that far from my thoughts. What about you?'

Tom stops eating as Lillian's face drops into view. Smiling and lovely, sitting at her kitchen table, sipping from her little glass. And then . . . those pictures! Lying dead in the grass outside her house. After that comes Alice as she was last night in the pub. The two faces merge together in Tom's head and he suddenly feels like he can't cope with any of it anymore.

'Yeah.' He gets up, turns his back on Jonty and looks out the window.

'Not right she's dead, is it?' Jonty says softly behind him.

'No.' Tom is still looking out the window. He feels itchy suddenly. It's like he's got tiny insects running around under his T-shirt, up the back of his neck and into his hair. He starts rubbing his neck trying to stay calm. *Shit!* He turns around suddenly.

'But it's over now, Jonno,' he says urgently. 'You've got to believe that.'

Jonty shrugs and looks away.

'So what else did your father say?' Tom says desperately. 'You said he's found God?'

'Yeah,' Jonty smiles sadly, 'he's crazy, I guess.'

'What kind of crazy though?' Tom cuts in sharply. 'I mean, there is crazy and crazy and then . . . there is fucking mad-dog-howling-at-the-moon *crazy*.'

This makes Jonty's mouth split open into a wide grin. 'Is that a fact?'

'Yeah.'

'I guess you'd know, Mullaney!'

'Actually mate, I seem to remember you're the expert in that department!'

They both start laughing then and somehow everything eases up a bit between them. Ned asks them both outside for a kick of the footy before the rain comes.

The backyard is big enough for them to spread out. Tom positions himself up the house end, and Ned and Jonty go down near the fence. It's getting on for four by this stage, and rain is well and truly in the air. Clouds are building overhead and the breeze is nippy.

There is a lot of shouting and laughing and bad kicking at first, as they get into the swing of it. It is easier for Tom watching Jonty with this distance between them. Not so intense. Ned seems to have taken a real shine to him, and Tom smiles as he hears them pour shit on each other's marking and crap kicking as they jostle for the ball. It turns out they both barrack for Carlton, so their conversation is smattered with stuff about the upcoming grand final. Tom is surprised to hear Jonty so on top of it all. He knows the players and makes intelligent comments about the coach and the training. Over the last couple of years Tom has let all that stuff drop.

'You reckon Kellot will play?' Ned asks.

'Yeah.'

'But his knee is stuffed!'

'He played last week.'

'He wasn't any good, but they'll play him. He cost them so much.' Tom's little brother says matter-of-factly.

'How did this kid get so cynical?' Jonty asks pointing the finger at Ned as he sends down another kick. Tom misses another easy mark. *Shit!* And the other two are openly scathing.

'Grease on ya fingers, Mullaney!' Jonty shouts.

'Still pissed from lunch,' from his little brother.

'Just warming up,' Tom shouts back.

When Tom sends down another bad kick, Ned loses patience. 'You're hopeless!' he roars furiously. 'Concentrate!'

Anna pokes her head through the back door. 'Ned!' she growls loudly. 'Tone it down.'

'Sorry!'

'So how is working at the restaurant, Jonno?' Tom yells down the yard.

'I've . . . cut loose for a bit.'

'Oh, right. Good people though?'

'The owner is a moron who knows everything about *everything*.' Jonty calls back. 'I'm in love with the Vietnamese waitress who won't even say hello and my best mate is an ageing fag who suffers from memory blackouts about Vietnam. So they're all terrific.'

Tom nods and smiles.

At fifteen, Ned finds the 'ageing fag' business fascinating. His face squints with curiosity as he lines up the ball.

'What's the *fag* like?'

'Great guy.'

'You're joking?' Ned sneers.

'He's a good guy,' Jonty repeats.

'What's his name?' Tom asks.

'Buzz,' Jonty smiles, 'short for Bernard.'

Ned shakes his head, confounded all over again. 'Does he . . . ever try to . . . hit on *you*?'

'Can't turn around,' Jonty winks at Tom, 'but he's at me!'

The rain starts to come down seriously and they move up to the verandah. The sky is brilliant, huge and inky-black with shafts of transparent yellow light pouring out of the cracks like gold streamers. Tom handballs to Ned, thinking of his grandfather. He'd have the tripod out now. He'd be screwing on the old camera, looking for an angle. Never let an opportunity pass, he used to say, the next shot might be the one that makes your career.

'You want to come in and have a drink, Jonty?' Tom asks.

'Okay.'

They find Anna and Luke watching a DVD of *Henry V*. His dad is looking way too relaxed for his own good, lying on the couch, his head propped up with cushions. Anna is sitting in one of the club chairs with her legs on the footstool, eating an orange. It's the Kenneth Branagh version, and Tom knows for a fact they've both seen it at least six times already.

His mum is leaning forward, mouth open, taking it all in. Tom gets caught up himself and so does Jonty. They rest their elbows on the backs of chairs and gawk at the telly for full-on five minutes, while Ned scoots off to meet his friend. At the very end Anna turns to Luke with tears in her eyes and gives three big claps.

'Ah! Wasn't that something!'

'Beats *Home and Away*,' Luke laughs fondly, and picks up his packet of smokes. 'Anyone mind if I smoke?'

'Yes,' Anna says, 'go out to the verandah.'

'Okay,' Luke laughs. But he puts the cigarettes down again as they start discussing some of the minor actors in the play.

Tom walks around all the pantry junk still spread out over the floor and gets drinks from the fridge, thinking how good it is to see his old man so *engaged*. His father's big bushy eyebrows are flying around his face and his sudden loud laughs are easy and unforced . . .

'Well, I'll be seeing you all,' Jonty says to Tom's parents, after gulping down the drink. 'Thanks for the cake and everything.' When they finally twig that he's going they stop talking and Luke stands up.

'Don't feel you have to go, Jonty,' he says. 'Stay for a meal.'

'I don't think so.' Jonty looks embarrassed.

'Stay for tea, Jonty,' Anna chimes in. 'Ned and I will be going after that. We can drop you home.'

'No,' he declares more firmly, 'I'll get going now.'

The rain has eased off but it's still cold outside when Tom walks with Jonty out to the front gate. He offers to run back in and fetch him a coat but Jonty refuses.

'Well, thanks,' Jonty says awkwardly, but once he's out the gate he spins around again and grasps Tom's hand impulsively.

'Bye, Tom!'

'See you, Jonno.'

'I often think of how things were back then . . . you and me,' Jonty says. 'We were great mates, eh?'

Tom nods.

'My old man wrote to me, you know?' Jonty is exuding a soft, troubled mood that makes Tom wary.

'Yeah?' Tom replies impatiently. 'So what is he on about?'

'Saving me,' Jonty says simply.

'Saving you? You mean he wants you to find God, too?'

'He says that him being in there will . . .' Jonty gives a small anguished laugh, 'help me discover the truth.'

It's getting really cold now and Tom wants to get back inside. The Panadol is wearing off and his throat is on fire.

'Listen, Jonno, try not to worry about what he says. Forget the fucker. Don't read his letters. Get on with your own life! He's crazy, Jonno. You said so yourself.'

'Yeah,' Jonty looks away thoughtfully, 'one crazy bastard. Well I better go now.' He walks off, yelling, 'We'll have that beer, hey?' over his shoulder without turning around.

'Okay,' Tom shouts after him. 'You're on, mate!'

By early evening the cold that has been threatening Tom all day gets serious. His nose starts dripping and he's coughing up yellow gunk, so he decides he might as well go to bed. But first he rings Alice. He knows he shouldn't push things but he can't help himself. He needs to keep some kind of connection happening.

Or maybe it's just that he needs to hear her voice, make real that smile of the night before.

'How is your gran?'

'Would you believe she's sitting up eating toast and drinking tea?'

'You're kidding!' Tom is momentarily flummoxed. He's been expecting bad news. 'Well that's good, eh?'

'I guess so,' she gives a deep sigh.

'You don't sound exactly elated!'

'Oh well,' she sighs again and this makes Tom laugh.

'So what do the doctors say?'

'They can't believe it.'

There is a pause between them for a few moments.

'It was good last night,' she says suddenly.

'Yeah.'

'I'm glad he came in the end.'

Quiet moments with Alice are interesting, even though they make him nervous. Time seems to slow right down. It's like he can feel the world's heartbeat under everything. He becomes aware of small things, like his own fingers tapping on the bench or the motes of dust in the air. She's different from other girls he knows. Not just girls actually, *everybody*! Yak yak. Most people want to fill up the quiet spaces. She is the first person he's come across who doesn't seem shit-scared of silence.

'Jonty came around today,' Tom offers, 'out of the blue.'

'Really!' Alice is thoughtful. 'I've been thinking about him. What did he say?'

'We just hung out for a while.'

'That's good,' she said slowly, 'isn't it?'

'I guess so. He seems pretty freaked out about his father. Has your aunt told you anything more?'

'I don't really have anything to do with my aunt,' Alice replies.

'Why not?'

'That's just the way . . . it's always been.'

'Don't you like her?'

She laughs a little. 'You ask a lot of questions, don't you?'

'I like to know the score.'

'Hmmm,' she laughs again. 'Well, the score is I don't really know her. But . . . my cousin,' she continues thoughtfully, 'he interests me. I want him to be . . . okay.'

'Yeah,' Tom sighs. *What about me Alice? Are you interested in me?*

'Last night was a bit of a fizzer,' Tom changes the subject, trying to sound chirpy and on top of everything and then realises that he's just said the opposite to what she said. 'What I mean is, was Eric all right with it?'

'Oh he's okay with anything,' Alice says casually. 'He doesn't care.'

'Is he . . . is Eric your boyfriend?'

She doesn't answer immediately and Tom's words hang in the air, so pathetic and intrusive . . . God he wishes he hadn't asked her that! What business is it of his?

'You want to know the score?' she asks lightly. 'Is that it?'

'I guess so,' Tom tries to sound light-hearted, too.

'No,' she says dryly, 'he's not my boyfriend.'

Well that's something anyway. Still, Tom wishes he hadn't asked.

He wakes early the next morning and lies there listening to the rain. His throat is on fire, and his nose is blocked even though he's constantly blowing it. He needs another one of those strong lemon-juice and honey drinks but doesn't want to get up to get it. It would mean going out to the lemon tree in the rain.

Tom begins to seriously consider heading back to the city. He could just give his notice in to the *Chronicle*, see the week out and leave. It wouldn't be such a big deal. He could tell his lecturers that the work experience stint didn't work out. They're flexible. He'd be able to make it up some other time during his course. On top of the Jonty fiasco, there is Alice. If he hightailed it back to the big smoke, this consuming desire for her would eventually fade away. Sooner rather than later, most probably. *Face it, Mullaney. Getting together with Alice Wishart is never going to happen.*

Tom lies there coughing and spluttering into his wet hanky. He takes some more Panadol and drifts off to sleep again.

He finally surfaces a couple of hours later. The need to take a piss wins out over just wanting to lie there in the warmth. He wraps the doona around his shoulders and heads out to the bathroom and then down to the kitchen. With a bit of luck, his mother might have brought in a few extra lemons from the tree last night before she left. *Yes!* He sees them there, at least six sitting in the fruit bowl. His old man isn't up yet, so Tom switches on the heating and begins to squeeze lemons. He is about to turn on the radio when he hears laughter coming from the spare room. Tom listens to the low murmuring voices and then more laughter. His mother must have stayed after all and Ned must be in there with her.

Tom has a twinge of nostalgia remembering how he used to jump into bed with Anna on Sunday mornings, right up to when he was about Ned's age. His dad would be tooling around in the kitchen, bringing her in a cup of tea and making plans for the day, while she read the papers and talked to Tom. She'd read to him and they'd talk and laugh about nothing much. But there was something special about lying together there under the blankets. Tom is pleased to think of his little brother doing the same thing.

The laughter and talking continue, and Tom is just coming around to thinking that the male voice doesn't sound like Ned's when the door opens and his old man comes out looking all rumpled and sleepy and, when he sees Tom, *embarrassed*. His feet and chest are bare but thankfully he's wearing jeans.

'Hi there, Tom.' Luke saunters past to the bathroom pretending everything is absolutely normal. Tom doesn't answer.

'How is the cold?' he asks casually on his way back. 'Did you manage to sleep?'

'Listen,' Tom says in a low voice, '*this* is fucking irresponsible!'

'What is?'

'What do you think?'

Luke has the grace to be embarrassed as well as perplexed.

'Now, listen here, Tom,' he comes back a few paces. 'No harm has been done so . . . just calm down please!'

'What do you mean *no harm*?' Tom points to his little brother's room. 'What about Ned, eh? You think this is fair on him?'

Luke shakes his head and smiles, as though Tom is the one being unreasonable. 'All right, all right,' he makes a quietening gesture that only makes Tom more furious, 'I know it's all a bit strange but . . . just keep your seatbelt on. There is nothing to get excited about.'

'You both put him through the mill once,' Tom accuses angrily, 'not to mention Nellie and me, and now you're going to do it again.'

'He isn't even here, Tom,' his dad says mildly.

'What do you mean?'

'After you'd gone to bed, Ned went round to his mate's place to stay the night. So he doesn't need to know about this unless . . . you tell him.' This catches Tom off guard. He turns back to the last lemon. 'You're the only one who knows.'

'Okay,' Tom says, not looking at him. 'I still think it's irresponsible unless you're going to . . . I mean, what about Nanette?'

Lukes stares back at him without speaking.

What about Nanette? Is Tom actually worried about Nanette? Not really. It's the whole idea of his parents chucking everything up in the air again! Just when the five of them are all finally getting used to things, the new households and the new partners and the rest of it.

'Listen, don't say anything to Ned, okay?' Luke is busy trying to look as though he gives a rat's arse about what Tom thinks, frowning and rubbing his hands through his hair, and Tom feels like thumping him because he knows it's all an act. He planned this. It's what he's wanted all along, the old bastard! Tom isn't going to let him off the hook that easily though.

'As though I would!' Tom pours in the boiling water then slips a big spoonful of honey into the cup and stirs it around. 'Are you going to tell Nanette?'

'Look, Tom, that isn't actually any of your business,' Luke says, which makes Tom feel like a moron because his father is right. 'And for your information it's . . . nothing serious okay?' he adds heading back to the spare room.

'*What?*' Did Tom actually hear him say that? *Nothing serious?*

'Things aren't necessarily going to change,' his old man adds, his hand on the doorhandle.

'Oh, right!' Tom's voice is thick with sore throat and sarcasm. 'Don't forget to tell me when it gets serious, will you?'

The little darkroom hasn't been used in about three years. It needs airing and it's grimy with dust and spider webs, but the tin roof hasn't leaked and all the equipment seems to be in working order. As Tom checks the lights and bottles of chemicals, the paper and trays, his black mood shifts a little. Yeah, he'll be able to get something happening here! Shouldn't take long either.

An hour later he's printing off a few happy snaps, just to get himself into the swing of it all again. There are some shots of Nellie and Ned taken on the boat and a few of his uni mates that he'd forgotten about. He spends a bit of time working up a nice print of his mum hugging herself on the park bench, looking all bemused and above it all. Tom grins to himself, thinking how his brother is going to love the way his muscles show in this shot where he's hauling the bucket of fish in.

It's good to feel his dormant skills come to life again. Working in black-and-white is a bit like getting behind the wheel of an old car with dodgy gears after a long spell of driving automatic. You wonder if you'll remember how to do it. What are the tricks again? Then the brain boots up and your hands and eyes take over.

Within a short space of time he's got a set of prints drying on the lines he's set up above the sink.

Tom has been working for a couple of hours when there's a sharp rap at the door.

'Hey, Tom!' his father's voice booms. 'You in there?'

'Hang on,' Tom says irritably, 'I'm in the middle of something.'

He's working on a particularly nice shot of an empty fishing boat against some low cloud. The light on the water is beautiful. He is on the point of cropping out the pier, thinking he might be able to use it as background for the big montage he is putting together for his end of term assignment.

'Tom! How long you going to be?'

Shit. 'What do you want?' Tom calls back sourly. 'I'm busy.'

'I have a visitor for you.'

'Who?' Tom sighs.

'Alice,' Luke yells back, 'and we're both waiting.'

Tom quickly throws the unfinished print into the fixer and washes his hands.

'Okay, I'm coming,' he says, switching on the light.

When Tom opens the door, she's standing next to his father, biting her lip. He doesn't quite know what to say. Every time he sees her he's surprised. She has this old-fashioned loveliness and is quite unlike anyone else he has ever thought beautiful or attractive. Her hair is pulled back from her face and she's in a long dark dress with some kind of red cardigan over the top that brings out the colour of her rosy cheeks. He notices that she's also wearing shiny lipstick and . . . she looks nervous.

'I brought these around,' she says, holding out a small yellow package of negatives. 'You said that it would be okay.'

'Oh, sure,' Tom takes them, 'that's fine.'

'I'll leave you to it then,' Luke says, edging away.

'I'll go, too,' Alice says hurriedly. 'I just wanted to drop them off . . . if that is still okay with you?'

'Come in,' Tom smiles at her, 'and I'll do some now.'

'Oh, I didn't expect you to do them *now* . . . I don't want to interrupt!'

'But I'm not doing anything important.'

'You're not too busy?'

'No, of course not.'

'So, what's here?' He opens up her yellow envelope. There are probably about fifty large negatives inside. He pulls one out and holds it up against the light. 'Wow!' He turns to Alice with a smile, 'These are from an old Brownie. The first ever mass-produced camera!' He turns back to the neg. 'These will be good, Alice!' He peers into the image. 'Do you know who they are of?'

'Not really.' Alice is looking around the darkroom curiously, running her finger along the bench. 'I found them in my grandmother's sideboard, behind a whole lot of stuff.'

'Does she know you've got them?'

'No.'

'Have you been in a darkroom before?'

'Not really.'

'We've got to turn the light off,' Tom explains, pulling on the red-light cord. 'if you want to see these printed up.'

'Okay.'

He switches off the overhead light and they're immersed in a dull red light. He pretends not to notice her surprise.

Tom goes over to the enlarger and positions the first negative into the viewfinder. He peers down into the lenses and adjusts the focus. The image is of a woman in the street, all done up sixties-style in coat and hat and gloves. She is pushing a pram, and there is a little girl in a coat standing next to her, frowning into the camera.

'Come have a look,' Tom says. Alice moves closer and stands quietly behind him. 'Do you know who this is?'

'Well, I think that is my mother as a little girl.' Alice says slowly. 'And my Aunt Marie in the pram.'

'Okay.' Tom tries not to show how revved up he is. *She's come.* He wasn't at all sure that she would. 'And that would be your grandmother?'

'Yes,' she says softly.

'You want me to print it up?'

'Could we have a look at some of the others first?'

'Good idea! You can pick the ones you want.'

The next hour goes by in a weird kind of daze. Every now and again Tom almost has to pinch himself. For once fate is on his side! He is in a small room with Alice Wishart, bathed in red light. They're so close to each other now that he

302

can smell her perfume under the toxic chemical fumes. *What next?* In spite of the physical proximity, he feels weirdly shy and unsure, and has no idea what he might say or do to bring them closer.

One after another, he puts the negatives into the viewfinder but because it is dark he can't see how each one affects Alice. She remains silent and even when she does comment briefly she doesn't give much away.

'My grandparents,' she murmurs. 'That's Mum and her sister. That is probably Grandma and her two sisters.'

It's almost as though the dim light has made her forget Tom. She could be talking to herself. Tom doesn't say much, just lets her have a few moments to look at each image before he pulls it out and slots in the next one. Most of the prints are pretty standard: mother and children, mother and baby, a couple standing together near a car. Just amateur snaps, they're sharp enough but nothing special. No close-up shots of anyone's face or even mid-range shots that show anyone in much detail.

They are almost through the pile of negatives when a closer image emerges under the light. It's of a good-looking young couple sitting on a verandah. The woman is holding a baby and they're both smiling happily into the camera. It takes Tom a moment to see that the woman is Lillian and so . . . the baby must be Alice.

'That you?' Tom says lightly, pointing at the baby.

'I guess,' Alice replies guardedly.

'We'll definitely print that one up!' Tom tries to sound jocular because he doesn't want to give away how affected he is by the image of Lillian looking so young and full of happiness. The happy couple with their baby, smiling innocently into the camera. How little they knew then of what would happen! A flash of Lillian lying still on the grass shoots in from nowhere and makes Tom shudder involuntarily. *God!* He wonders if that same image jumps in on Alice, too, when she least expects it. *One day*, he swears to himself, *I'll ask her.*

'That's my father,' she says pointing to the guy in the image.

'He's a good-looking guy,' Tom says sincerely. She makes a low noise of disapproval in her throat. 'You don't think so?'

'He's not like that now.'

'What's he like?' Tom asks lightly.

But Alice doesn't answer. She is peering forward intently, staring into the image as though it might be withholding some secret from her. Tom pulls back from the bench so she can get nearer.

'Have a good look,' he says. 'I'll print it up. It's the best so far.'

'Okay,' she whispers, continuing to stare but not moving onto the now vacant stool.

'They were obviously happy together,' Tom says quietly. 'He still live in Darwin?'

'Yeah.' They are both bending over the image, their faces only inches apart, and the moment drags on.

'How long since you've seen him?'

'About a year.'

What is the picture telling her? Tom feels a sort of dampness developing on his forehead and under his arms. He runs one hand through his hair. It's embarrassing. He can smell himself! The tablets must be wearing off because his head is thick again and his nose is running.

'Okay,' Alice sighs at last, 'that's enough.'

Tom straightens up and pulls the negative out. He puts it down away from the rest and slips in the next one.

Alice lets out a gasp, and although Tom makes no sound, he is similarly affected. It is Lillian, sitting on a fence, about the same age that Alice is now. Her hair is blowing back with a few strands

304

across her face, and she's laughing. Tom doesn't know if it's the cold or Alice being so close, but his sense of reality is blurring around the edges and he loses sense of where he is. *Lillian? Maybe she's back? Maybe she is here standing beside me.* On one level he knows this is crap but . . . it *feels* as though it might be true.

'Alice,' he says, his throat is hoarse and his voice faint. The girl in the picture and the girl beside him! *Where does one end and the other begin?* No. He's sick and that's making him stupid. He might well have a fever. *Or he could be going crazy.* Tom gulps and licks his lips, blows his nose again and tries to clear his mind. But it doesn't clear, one image arrives on top of another. They fly into his mind and . . . underpinning them all is the longing, as intense now as it was in the courtroom. But there is nothing he can do about it. The chasm separating them is as real as a raging river.

'What?' she whispers.

Without asking her if she's finished looking, or if she wants him to change the image, he takes the negative out and puts the last one in. It is Lillian again, probably taken the same day because she has got the same dress on.

'I remember that dress,' Alice smiles. And her saying that somehow releases Tom. The chasm doesn't seem quite so impassable any more. In this new dreamy state he finds himself picking up her hand from where it is sitting, bunched up into a tight fist on the bench. She doesn't pull away as he gently unfurls each finger and locks his own fingers with hers. Then he reaches out his other hand, puts it under her chin and turns her face to him. They look at each other in the weird, blood-red light.

'I've got a cold,' Tom says.

'It doesn't matter,' she whispers.

Tom reaches out for her other hand and she gives it to him and they stand looking at each other. Tom is overwhelmed and can't think of what to say. It is as though he's on the point of diving into a clear sparkling stream of water. Does he dare? Is it deep enough? What if he is imagining it all?

'Alice?' he whispers.

She doesn't say anything but moves ever so slightly towards him, and that's when he knows he can kiss her. So he does. The kiss is as soft and as light as a handful of feathers being thrown up into the air. Down they come again, floating, and he reaches up to cup her face in his hands and kiss her again.

'I love you,' he says. He has never said those words to anyone else in the world, except to his mother when he was a kid. But as daggy and hackneyed as those three little words might be, he knows that they are absolutely true in this case. He's not embarrassed or sorry he has spoken them, and he doesn't want to pull them back. He loves her and no matter where it gets him, he's glad to have said it.

Her eyes open wide in surprise and she laughs a little, then opens her mouth to speak and says . . . nothing. They kiss again. Tom puts his arms around her and draws her close. Then he takes the elastic out of her hair, letting it fall out around her face. Still holding her close, he runs both hands through it.

'Your hair,' he says, kissing it and then her neck, 'it's wonderful.'

'You've got nice hair, too,' she laughs softly.

'Have I?'

'Yes.'

Then he tells her again that he loves her. But this time she stiffens and steps back a little. She frowns and turns her head away and looks down at that image of her mother.

'Why?' she whispers, after a while.

'I don't know,' he says, 'a million reasons. Why does anyone love anyone else?'

'I don't know either,' she whispers.

306

Tom laughs softly.

'I don't really trust myself.'

'Why not?' he whispers and clears his throat. His head is beginning to spin and throb. *Damn it!* He needs all his wits about him.

'And I . . . I don't think I trust you.'

'Why not?' he asks again.

'People say . . . things,' she murmurs.

'People don't know *shit*!' Tom knows he is being defensive, but he doesn't know how else to play it. *Come on, Alice.* He reaches out again to touch her hair, everything in him is aching now. If he can just hold her in his arms again he knows that every little reservation she has about him will resolve itself. Has to. Fate is whispering in his ear, telling him that he's been building up to this moment all his bloody life.

'Whatever happened in the past doesn't matter. It's over,' he says hoarsely, moving closer, but this makes her edge further away. She is looking positively wary now.

'No,' she says quietly, 'everything that happened . . . in the past . . . matters a lot to me.'

'Of course it does but . . .'

'I hated you back then!' she bursts out suddenly, drawing away and pulling the cardigan tightly around her. 'I hated you and my cousin coming around.' She stops to squint at him. 'Did you have any idea of that? I mean . . . any idea of just how much I hated you?'

Tom's breath gives way momentarily. He is truly shocked. He tries to think back but can't remember anything. He can only see her now, those beautiful eyes shining in the red light, the heavy eyebrows and chiselled nose and chin – *so sweet, this girl! Who is she really?* He doesn't know, but he wants her. Badly. He knows that. He shakes his head. 'Why?'

'You and Jonty being there all the time,' her voice breaks, 'it was so weird!'

'But we were just friends . . .' Tom mumbles lamely.

'No, it was . . . weird!' Alice shudders, holding herself in, arms tight across her chest. She backs towards the door and a chill passes through Tom like a gust of icy wind. Part of him can't believe this is actually happening. Moments before he had her in his arms. She wanted him the way he wanted her. But now . . .

'So, tell me it's not true!' she says hoarsely.

What? But he knows. He knows what she means. What can he say? He can't lie to her but he can't tell her the truth either.

Her face accuses him without her having to put it into words. Her mouth tightens and she raises her chin as though pulling even further into herself. Then she turns to open the door.

'Alice, I was just a kid.' Tom sounds pathetic. 'Don't go . . . please.'

'I came for help with the photos,' she whispers sharply.

'Yes,' he replies helplessly.

'That's why I came.' Her eyes are blazing with anger. 'Not for anything else. You said you'd help me do them.'

'I know that!'

Before he can say anything else she has disappeared out the door. He watches her walking determinedly back towards the house. At the back verandah she hesitates for a moment, but doesn't look back.

Water is boiling. *Slip in the spag. Crush the garlic and get it sizzling, then chuck in the chopped bacon. Hmmm. Cream. Where is it?*

'Hey Buzz, cream, mate?'

Buzz brings it over from the fridge and snaffles a bit of Jonty's bacon.

'How many of these you doing?'

'Two.'

'This will feed four,' Buzz says frowning.

'Mind your own business!' Jonty edges him out of the way, throws some diced onions into a wok on one of the other burners and starts shifting them around under the heat.

'So how are you?' Buzz asks quietly.

'I'm here, aren't I?' Jonty pulls a piece of the pasta out with a fork, to test it.

Buzz puts a hand on his shoulder before moving off to the herbs rack. 'And I'm glad about that, Jonno,' he says, 'very glad.'

Good old Buzz! He'd found Jonty virtually hanging off the cliff face the night before. It was a clear sky and Jonty was out there in the dark, staring down into that roiling sea. The funny old bastard must have seen him. Jonty thought that there was no one else left alive on earth but . . . well, it turned out Buzz was still there. The big wire fence was a total joke. It was no trouble for Jonty to climb over it. Took him about three minutes. Maybe he just wanted to prove that he could.

Did he go there to jump? Maybe he did and maybe he didn't. You could say he was sizing up future possibilities. It was actually cool being out there in the wind, listening to the sea smashing against the rocks, being just a few feet from instant destruction.

Jonty needed to get off his head. Badly. When the craving gets like that, there is nothing else in the world. All night he'd been obsessing about getting his hands on something serious. A hit of smack, a line of coke, a few pills, even just a nice strong joint would've done the job. He hadn't felt so crazy since . . . well since he'd got out of remand. Since then he's been able to brush it aside without too much trouble. But last night it had been eating away at his nerves. *Come on! Just one snort, one line one . . . whatever!* Something to take the edge off.

As soon as night fell he'd headed off down to the centre of town to score. That used to be the place, years ago. There was always some dude hanging about selling something. But nothing doing last night. Nothing at all. He started to get frantic. *Shit! What is this? Is every prick in rehab or what?* So he went along to Manning Street, but that whole joint has closed up too. Maddening to know that there would be lots out there, but he didn't know who to call. He was out of the loop now. And that was the truth. In the end, he had to make do with a bottle of Jack Daniels. He bought it and took himself up to the point.

The feeling of having something ugly clinging to the back

of his skull, putting weird pictures in his head, has to be about big bad Jed. *Why did he come back three years on for the big fess up? What does any of it mean?*

Any shrink could tell you what was troubling him, but hey . . . what do those guys know? It's only words in the end isn't it? Big, pillowy words that make everyone else feel comfortable, as though they understand what's really going on. But to Jonty, words aren't the point. What actually happens – what has been done and what is to be done – that's the point. And he isn't sure about any of it.

Anyway, he ended up on the wrong side of the fence getting drunk and looking down at his own death. *Did he want it now or later or . . . not at all?* He was out there for an hour or three and then Buzz was suddenly calling to him from the other side of the mesh wire.

'Come here, Jonno!' he yelled. 'I want to talk to you!'

'Go home, Buzz,' Jonty yelled back, 'I'm okay.' But he wasn't okay, and Buzz must have sussed that out because he didn't go home.

What that old coot did was actually pretty amazing. He climbed the fence! All eight feet of it. Jonty couldn't believe it. Buzz is over sixty, and there he was, pulling his skinny arse up and over like a monkey. By the time he got down the other side, Jonty was standing, laughing with admiration.

'Were you an acrobat in your last life?' he asked.

But Buzz didn't answer. He grabbed Jonty by the arm, pulled him away from the drop and made him sit down on a rock some way back from the cliff face. Then he put his arm around Jonty's shoulders, took the bottle, had a swig and put it in his pocket. They sat there for quite a while, not saying much, and that was okay. Jonty figured there was enough noise going on, what with the sea and all the shit inside his head.

Eventually Jonty told him about feeling like his old man is inside his head, and it turned out Buzz knew the feeling. Knew just how mad that kind of thing can make a person. Because you can't get away from them even if you're a hundred kilometres apart. Even if one of you is locked up and the other one is roaming free as a bird, you can't get away.

'What does he say to you?'

It would have taken forever to answer that question, so Jonty just shrugged.

'Does he threaten you?' Buzz asked after a while.

Jonty shrugged again. The sound of the sea was so loud and the yellow moon was so bright that everything he wanted to tell Buzz had gone blurry and collapsed in on itself. Even trying to concentrate made Jonty feel exhausted.

'What happened back then, Jonno?'

'That's the thing,' Jonty puffed his dark laughter into the cold night, making a fog in front of his face. 'I was on a lot of shit at that time.' Buzz nods but doesn't comment. 'Heaps of it was legal, too. The friggin' doctors got it all wrong, I reckon. Chunks of my life sort of *blur*,' Jonty explained, 'like a movie out of focus.'

'It'll come back one day,' Buzz said quietly.

'You reckon?'

'It will,' Buzz continued matter-of-factly, 'and you'll wish it hadn't.'

Jonty tried to get his head around this. Buzz had never talked about his experiences in Vietnam, yet Jonty knew that's what he meant.

'You remember much of it, Buzz,' he asks eventually, 'the war I mean?'

'Yeah, I remember.'

'Does it . . . get you?'

'Only every night,' Buzz sighs. 'Every fucking night.'

Eventually they get up, climb back over the fence and walk home.

'Come back to work tomorrow,' Buzz orders stiffly when he says goodbye. 'It will do you good.'

'Okay.'

Buzz was right on two fronts. It did him good to be back at work and there *was* enough spaghetti for four. At the end of the night they heat up the leftovers and sit down together to eat.

'It's colder tonight,' Buzz says as he buttons up his coat. 'You going straight home?'

'Nah,' Jonty grins at him, 'thought I might just hang off the point again!'

'I'm going to see you to your door,' the old guy says firmly.

'No need, Buzz.' Jonty switches off the light. 'Don't actually feel like necking myself tonight.'

'That's a relief.' He gives Jonty a wry smile.

Jonty lets himself in through the back door and goes to check that his mum is okay. She is snoring peacefully in the front bedroom. His newly acquired mobile phone suddenly peeps and he sees that he has a message from Tom Mullaney.

Beers and pizzas next Friday? My place.

You're on! Jonty texts back. *Is Alice coming?*

Alice

Tom answers the door.

'Hello, Alice!' He smiles without meeting her eyes, which tells her he's awkward too. 'Come in, why don't you? Shit of a day, eh?' She nods and steps inside. He takes her coat and hangs it on the stand.

'Jonty's here,' he says. 'We're down the back watching a DVD. Thought we'd wait until you got here before ordering.'

Alice nods, hoping her fluttering heart is not on display. It feels a bit like a bird inside her chest, trying to get out.

'It's just us.' Tom shuts the front door behind her. 'Dad has gone to Melbourne for the weekend.'

This piece of news registers as a faint jolt of disquiet inside Alice. She'd been counting on Luke being there to make things easy.

'Straight down there.' Tom points down to the end of the hallway. 'You look nice,' he adds almost curtly as he follows her towards the back of the house.

'Thanks.' Alice is so keyed up that she can hardly get the word out, but the terse compliment pleases her. It took her near enough to an hour to get ready. It wasn't just the bath with special stuff she'd never used before, but working out what to wear. In the end, she'd gone with quite ordinary things – jeans and a white knitted top she'd found in the sale bin of a local store. She worries that she is too fat for jeans, but the top has lace around the neckline and it really suits her. She decided in the end that wearing it with a skirt would make her look like the local librarian's assistant.

Alice looks around at the large generous furniture, the colourful shabby cushions and the general messiness and feels oddly at home. The house at Pitt Street was like this, much smaller but with the same lived-in feel. Tom's house has nothing of the style and opulence of her grandmother's beautiful home but it's way more comfortable.

A few empty beer stubbies sit on the kitchen bench, along with a half-finished one, but nobody is there watching the blaring television. So where is her cousin? She sees the vague shape of someone outside the big glass sliding door on the back verandah. When Tom taps the glass she sees it's Jonty, bending over a dog. Somehow he looks younger than the nervy, battered young man who had turned up at the pub. Tom and Alice watch Jonty come inside and carefully shut the sliding door behind him.

'Hello,' he smiles tentatively, 'Alice!' His eyes move quickly back to Tom. 'She's lame. Got something in her foot.'

'I know,' Tom grimaces. 'I was meant to take her to the vet this morning. The old man will be dark!'

'I might be able to get it out,' Jonty says.

'Okay.' Tom takes a swig from the half-finished stubbie and then turns to Alice with a shy smile. 'You like a drink?'

'I'm okay, thanks.'

'But you've gotta have *one*,' Tom protests. 'We bought champagne for you.'

'Girls like champagne!' Jonty cuts in with a laugh. 'I told him that.'

'Oh!' Alice flushes. 'Okay then. Is it a celebration?' They both seem surprised by her question.

'Always something to celebrate, Alice!' Tom says dryly, not meeting her eyes as he heads to the fridge, pulls out a green bottle and proceeds to tear off the silver foil around its neck.

Jonty turns his attention back to the old dog looking in at them through the glass with big mournful eyes. 'I'll have a go at it now while there's light,' he tells Tom. 'Okay?'

'I'm a dickhead for forgetting poor old Bess,' Tom admits to Alice. 'Take a seat, why don't you.'

'You got any tweezers?' Jonty yells from outside.

The next half hour is taken up with the dog. Alice watches Jonty lift the dog onto an outside bench and proceed to examine her paw. Sure enough, something is embedded in the flesh between two of her pads, making the surrounding area sore and swollen.

'Looks like a long shit of a prickle,' Jonty mutters to himself, reaching for the tweezers in Tom's hand. 'Let's get it out.'

Initially old Bess is suspicious. She whimpers and growls as Jonty probes deeper, even makes a few angry snaps to remind him she has teeth. Unfazed, Jonty gently pulls the offending matter out, piece by tiny piece. In spite of herself, Alice is fascinated. Not just because she loves animals, and this dog seems like such a gentle lovely creature, but seeing her cousin up close like this is . . . oddly illuminating. His hands are lean and strong and capable, and his profile in that late afternoon light is sharp and handsome. Tom is standing close on the other side of Jonty with his hand on the dog's head. He's distracted, whereas her cousin Jonty is totally engrossed.

'You're a good old girl, Bess.' Jonty mumbles the words softly, as though he has forgotten about the other two even being there.

'So brave! You were brave as a puppy too, chasing cars. We're going to get you up and running again, and no one will be able to hold you back.' All the while he's pulling the prickle out, bit by difficult bit. Bess whimpers occasionally but she also wags her tail. Alice can see she trusts Jonty.

'This has been cramping your style, hasn't it?' Jonty whispers as he pulls out the last offending piece, 'but we've got it all now.' He straightens up and shares a smile with Tom and Alice. 'I reckon that's it.'

Tom puts a hand on his shoulder. 'You should have done vet science, Jonty!'

'Man, I *should* have done a lot of things!' he replies, and they both laugh.

A warm glow rushes through Alice. *Watch someone with a child or an animal, Alice*, her mother used to tell her, *and you'll see what kind of person they are.*

'I need a bandage,' Jonty orders. 'A bit of old sheet will do. And have you got any antiseptic?'

'I'll go look.' Tom heads off down the hallway and Alice puts her hand on the dog's head. When Bess turns to lick her, Alice smiles and tickles her behind her big soft ears.

'She likes you.' Jonty bends to pick stray hayseeds out of the dog's long coat. 'You got a dog?'

Alice shakes her head ruefully. 'I've never had a pet, have you?'

'We had farm dogs.'

'Did you love them?' It's a *girly* question, she knows, but she needs suddenly to find out more about her cousin.

'Oh, sure,' he mumbles distractedly, picking at seeds in the dog's coat. 'The dogs were good.'

Tom brings back the bottle of antiseptic, cotton wool and a piece of clean rag. Jonty cleans the wound and bandages up the paw securely.

'I think it will be okay,' he says, lifting the dog down. They all watch her limp off. 'So that will be a hundred bucks, Mullaney, and bring her back for a check-up next week and I'll charge you another hundred.'

'Thanks, Jonno,' Tom grins.

'Did someone mention a drink?'

Tom opens the green bottle. There is a loud pop as the cork flies to the other end of the room, making the overweight grey cat on the couch sit up and growl.

Alice laughs and squats down to entice the cat over for a pat. 'Come here, puss. Come on!'

But the cat looks back disdainfully through half-closed lids, as though she wouldn't dream of it in a pink fit.

'Don't take it personally,' Tom smiles at Alice, 'she plays hard-to-get.' He fills three glasses and hands them out.

Jonty takes his glass and holds it up to the light before gulping down the lot.

'Hey!' Tom pours him another. 'It's meant to be sipped not guzzled, you ingrate!'

'Here's to it, then.' Jonty holds one finger out daintily in the parody of a lady, and raises his glass.

'To what, Jonno?'

'I dunno, to us, I suppose.'

'That'll do.' Tom clinks his glass with Alice's and smiles.

Alice takes her glass over to the couch and sits near the cat. Sensing a new, comfortable seat the cat deigns to get up, stretch and then come to sit on her lap.

'Told you it wouldn't take long.'

Alice smiles. She runs her hand along the cat's sleek, glossy coat and turns to her cousin, who is kneeling in front of the stereo flipping through CDs. 'How's your mother?'

Jonty frowns. 'Not great.'

Alice nods, meets his eyes for two seconds and then looks away. The cat's tail is swishing warningly. *Why did I ask that?*

'Did you . . . know my old man at all?' Jonty asks casually as he slips a disc into the player and adjusts the volume. A wild percussion instrumental track blasts into the space between them. Alice doesn't recognise the music, or like it much, but she's glad of it nevertheless.

'No,' she says stiffly, continuing to pet the cat. She has plunged the conversation into dangerous territory and she's unsure how to get out of it.

'Lucky you.' Jonty plonks himself down into the armchair opposite her.

'But I heard *about* him,' Alice adds. *From my mother,* is on the tip of her tongue, but she stops herself in time. 'Every now and again we'd hear stuff, you know.'

'All good, no doubt?' Jonty says sarcastically.

Alice doesn't know what to say to that, but a heavy, frantic desire simply *to know* hits her without warning. She wants to ask this cousin of hers, *Why?* Why would Jed have done such a thing? Does Jonty know of any reason why his father would kill her mother? She looks up at Tom who is leaning against the bench, champagne in hand, staring thoughtfully at both of them. She has a bizarre feeling that he knows what she's thinking. But just being here with both of these guys is strange enough for Alice. How could she possibly ask more questions?

Tom orders the pizza and the boys talk about football and whether Ned is any good, and Alice sits quietly listening. The champagne has hit her empty stomach with a whoosh and now it's radiating out into her limbs, making her feel relaxed and ready for something to happen. Almost anything would do.

The cat suddenly stops purring, jumps down from Alice's knee, stretches languidly and then saunters over to Jonty.

'I guess I offer a superior service,' Jonty says dryly as it leaps onto his lap. Alice laughs. Holding the cat in one hand, Jonty goes outside for his cigarettes and Tom refills her glass.

'White suits you,' Tom says to her shyly. 'I like that shirt or . . . whatever it is.'

'Thanks.'

He hovers for a moment or two before putting the bottle on the coffee table next to her. 'Way better than the red cardigan.'

Alice laughs, feeling herself flush as she remembers being in that darkroom. So he's thinking of it too? A rush of excitement makes her heart race, but she doesn't dare look at him. Jonty comes back in.

'So, have you seen your father since he got . . . went inside?' Alice asks, not sure why she wants to know. Her voice sounds oddly forced. Too loud and slow, as though she's talking to someone who can't speak the language properly.

'No,' Jonty frowns, 'and nor has Mum. That's one good thing that has happened. My mum isn't going to have anything to do with him anymore.' He looks up suddenly and smiles at Tom, 'Remember when Lillian wanted to kill him?'

There is a moment of panic between the three of them as his words sink in. Alice watches Tom's face drain of colour, and then the swift blush of embarrassment on her cousin's face as he realises that he has said the wrong thing. The comment about *Lillian*, out of the blue like this, *has* shocked her but she's not in the mood to take offence. Her cousin has put his foot in it. So what? Everyone does that. In fact, right at this moment, Alice decides that she really likes him. Her cousin Jonty has an impetuousness about him that feels like honesty.

My mother loved him, so why shouldn't I?

'You mean down at the caves?' Alice says lightly. 'I remember her saying that she'd like to throw your father down one of the caves one day!'

'So she told you, too?' Tom asks.

Alice stares back at him and gulps. *Why does he look so serious?* 'But she didn't *mean* it!' Alice's quick laugh is strained. 'I mean . . . she couldn't mean it!' Neither of them is looking at her now, and it makes her feel like the kid sister who knows nothing.

'Right,' Tom says carefully.

'No,' Jonty adds calmly, 'she wasn't serious.'

But something about the way they are purposefully not looking at each other makes Alice think the exact opposite. Her mother seriously wanted to kill Jed van der Weihl? But that's just too . . . *crazy.*

Thankfully the mood breaks when the doorbell rings.

'Food!' Tom grabs up his wallet and runs for the door. Jonty looks after him thoughtfully, the cat draped around his neck.

'She used to get into moods,' Jonty tells Alice, 'and say some . . . funny things.'

'Yes,' Alice breathes, 'she did.'

'I guess you'd know that better than me,' Jonty adds with a sad laugh.

'I guess I would.'

Within half a minute, Tom is back with four brown boxes. 'Come on you guys!' he grins. 'Where do you want to eat? At the table or in front of the TV?'

'Hey, Tommy!' Jonty is in the kitchen getting a fresh beer. 'Why don't we jump in the car and have 'em out there?'

Tom dumps the boxes on the table. 'Where?'

'The caves!' Jonty's face is suddenly ablaze with enthusiasm. 'It's good out there! Remember? Won't take long. Wrap the pizzas in a blanket or something.'

Tom hesitates and then smiles. 'But it's going to rain.'

'So?'

'And *I'm* too pissed to drive.'

'I'm not.' Jonty turns to Alice. 'What do you say?'

Alice doesn't want to go, but she doesn't want to be the one to throw cold water on the idea either. Maybe she should go with the flow. Maybe all this – whatever the hell it is that is happening here – would be easier outside in the fresh air. They're both looking at her now.

'Okay,' she says.

'We'll need coats,' Tom calls cheerfully, 'and I'll make some coffee for the thermos.'

Alice feels as if she is in a movie. Jonty is driving too fast, but she doesn't care. She is squashed between them in the front seat, the music is up loud and the countryside on both sides is fantastic, a shining green velvet blanket. The cows and little sheds, even the trees are dotted over it like toys. A surge of strange wild joy runs right through her. All those black clouds piling up across the sky are wonderful! It's just like a painted backdrop for some great and momentous drama. *Okay. I'm ready for it!* Alice thinks. *Bring it on. And I want to play the main part.*

Tom begins to sing along with the old Chili Peppers hit 'Californication', and Jonty hums and drums his fingers on the steering wheel, nudging Alice every now and again when he wants her to look at something. First it's half-a-dozen horses galloping along a nearby fence, then a group of beautiful black-and-white cows, with their calves, staring out across the highway. When a mass of tiny birds dip and swoop across the road in front, they both laugh. She feels the champagne swimming in her veins and wishes she knew the words so she could sing along with Tom.

Here she is, scooting along the highway with two guys – both of them good-looking, and one of them fancies her! How did that happen? The delicious smell of pizza is filling up the cabin. They're going out to some pretty spot in the bush to eat and drink, to talk and . . . she is eighteen years old and this is what she's meant to be doing.

Jonty and Tom reminisce about old times: the stuff they got up to with their classmates during excursions and football matches! She wishes she had those kinds of memories herself. Why hadn't she gone out with girlfriends to lonely weird places to climb rocks and hang off edges, to drink and throw pies at each other, to play jokes on teachers and compete over impossible physical feats? Her childhood was made up of sedate netball games, on-and-off friendships and tame little parties where everyone was home by eleven. So damned boring, in comparison! Even her mother would sometimes gently encourage her to branch out a little. *You know I trust you, Alice. Stay as long as you want. You don't have to be home at a certain time.* But she never did stay out late. She never dared do anything much at all.

'Have you been out to the caves before, Alice?' Tom holds out a handful of lollies that he's found in the glove box. She takes a couple and he lifts his arm and puts it around her as though it is the most natural thing in the world, then smiles into her face. Their noses are only inches apart.

'I came with my mother once,' she offers.

'Me too,' Tom laughs. 'What is it about the caves and our mothers? They all love the place. Mine said she could feel the spirits or some crap!'

'So did mine,' Alice says shyly.

'What perfume are you wearing?' Tom whispers so that Jonty, who is still singing and thumping on the steering wheel, doesn't hear.

'*Youth*,' she whispers back.

'It's nice,' he says shyly. 'I usually hate perfume but it's nice.'

'I stole it from my grandmother,' Alice whispers back.

'Did you?' He pretends to be outraged.

'It is so expensive,' Alice starts to giggle, 'and she's too old for it.'

Tom smiles at her giggling. He runs a finger up her arm to her elbow and leaves it there.

'How old is she?'

'Ninety-two!'

Tom throws his head back to laugh. 'You are completely within your rights to steal it.' He picks up a stray strand of hair and pushes it behind her ear. 'No ninety-two-year-old has the right to wear Youth!'

'Glad you agree!'

'Okay you two,' Jonty chimes in, 'what's going on?'

'Shut up and drive!' Tom orders and then peers around Alice to check the speedo. 'You're doing 120, Jonty.'

'So, I'm just the chauffeur am I?'

'In a nutshell, *yes, mate*. And slow down!'

Alice is giddy with all this. It's just happened so quickly and . . . *perfectly* that she can barely keep up. What will the twins say? She has to stifle a laugh, picturing Sylvie's face when she hears the news. *He had his arm where? So . . . how many times did he touch your hair?* What about Eric? She throws her head back and closes her eyes. Definitely. She'll tell Eric. *He likes you,* Eric had told her after that time in the pub. *It's in his eyes.*

'What's funny?' Tom's mouth is almost touching her ear. She turns to look at him and decides that he has the most beautiful eyes she has ever seen. So melancholy! As though he knows about grave and desperate things that she can only guess at. Then, when he smiles it's . . . *wham*! The sadness disappears and they're as bright as the ocean on a good day. They tell her everything might, in fact probably will, go on forever, and it will all be good.

'Nothing,' she mumbles.

'Liar!' he breathes, and they both laugh.

They turn off the main sealed road onto a dirt track. It is slippery because of the recent rain, but Jonty doesn't slow down. After the third skid where the car almost ends up off the road altogether, Tom yells at him, 'For fucksake, slow down, Jonty!'

'It's okay.'

'I don't want my car wrecked!'

'It's a heap anyway!' Jonty laughs.

'Yeah well,' Tom snarls, 'it's my heap.'

When they get out in the little parking place at the boundary of the national park, they are suddenly three individuals again. Alice shivers as she looks around at the few scraggly trees and low-lying hills all around. She remembers it being more spectacular than this . . . scrub. With the music and close warmth of the cabin gone, the stillness is almost overpowering. So chilly, too! As if they have suddenly landed in another world and they might have to learn the simple things all over again.

'Hey, let's eat while the pizzas are still vaguely warm!' Tom is at the car, opening the back door.

Alice helps to carry the food and drink, the rug and the coats. Her cousin stays apart, hands thrust deep into his pockets, scowling distractedly as he looks about. He seems to have dived into some inner, private place.

Then she remembers. It's one of those memories that surface quickly, out of the blue, like a hard whack to the face. This is where he came the night . . . the night her mother was murdered. This place. He was found out here cold and traumatised and when questioned he could only gabble incoherently. What had he talked to her mother about? What had he . . . *seen*? Why did he want to come here tonight?

Once they have everything, Jonty follows them through the small gate and they walk in silence up the little dirt track towards the caves.

'What about here?' Tom suggests when they reach a small grassy enclave sheltered by huge boulders on one side and a couple of scraggly acacias. 'We can lean our backs against the rocks, and it's near enough to the car when the storm starts.' He looks at Alice. 'You okay with this?'

She nods.

'Let's just eat,' Jonty calls. 'I'm starving.'

They throw down the rug and put the boxes in the middle then settle themselves down. Tom hands Jonty a beer and Alice a can of lemonade, then opens the first box – tomatoes, ham, olives and peppers on a still-warm crust.

Alice has never tasted anything so delicious. She has three slices before she can even think or remember where she is. In fact, two whole large pizzas are consumed before anything like a conversation resumes.

Tom and Jonty are half-lying on the rug as they munch away and Alice is sitting between them.

'That's a finch.'

'No! It is a swallow, you idiot.'

'A swallow is a *European* bird, Mullaney!'

'Ever heard of birds migrating to warmer climates?' Tom explains that his grandfather had been a birdwatcher, and tries to impress them with his knowledge of the different types. But he's forgotten most of what he used to know, so the other two tease him about being a fraud. They get onto birdwatching and scenic photography and famous photographers working in the field. Alice listens quietly, wishing she could join in, but she hasn't heard of any of the names.

327

Eventually no one can eat any more. Jonty gets up to stretch. He takes a stroll over to the nearest cave.

'Come check this out!' he yells for them to join him.

They stand on the edge of the first big crater-like hole. In the strange, low, grey light Alice can only just make out the layers of rock, full of cracks and crevices, leading off into tunnels. Moss and grasses grow here and there, down into the depths. Little birds, swallows and wagtails mainly, tweet and hop in front of them. The quietness is actually full of noise.

She can hear the far-off sound of cows, and the occasional sheep or motor. She can hear Jonty's breathing, and the small sniffs and coughs Tom makes when he clears his throat. Every now and then she fancies she can hear her own heartbeat, and she is filled all over again with the weird feeling that they've landed in a new world.

'Want to walk on a bit?' Jonty says.

'Need a coffee first.' Tom looks at Alice, who nods.

'But we'll run out of light,' Jonty protests.

Tom shrugs. 'We didn't come out here to do a fucking *hike*, Jonno.'

Tom and Alice head back to the picnic site, leaving Jonty looking down the hole. The two of them sit down on the rug again and Tom pours the coffee. Sitting on the ground with her chin on her knees, Alice is momentarily uneasy as she watches her cousin's back. He is still squatting over the cave. *What's he thinking about?*

'Top stuff this,' Tom grins, as he hands her a cup of steaming coffee in a red plastic mug. 'Pure instant coffee. You want sugar?'

'You got any?'

'Of course!'

He gives her a spoonful and then stirs three heaped ones into his own cup.

328

Alice smiles. 'What about your teeth?'

'Perfect,' Tom bares his fangs and laughs, 'not one filling. How is the coffee?'

'Perfect,' she says softly, loving the way his eyes drift about but then always come back to *her*. It's like he's hungry to keep looking at her. And the coffee *is* perfect. It warms her all the way down into her core.

'You got lucky then.' He is nearer now, smiling into her eyes. 'I worked for a week making coffees in the University Café on Lygon Street. So I know my stuff. I'm an expert.'

'Only a week?'

'I kept boiling the milk!' he admits with a laugh, throwing back his head.

'They sacked you?' This amazes her for some reason.

'No way,' he grins, 'they *let me go*.'

'Really!' Her surprise is genuine. 'But I thought you'd be *good* at everything. I mean, I thought you'd be one of those people who gets everything right!'

'But . . . *I do* Alice!' Tom laughs and takes her hand, caressing it with his own. 'I was a miserable failure at making coffee, but I'm bloody ace at everything else. Promise!'

Alice turns back toward Jonty, who is still in the same position. Should they call him over for a drink? But it's so nice being here with just Tom, talking about nothing and watching each other. Jonty is still standing in the same spot, looking down into the cave, deep in thought. Is he remembering being out here *that night*? Alice shivers suddenly. *Why was he so keen to come here?*

When she turns back, Tom is lying on his side, propped up on one elbow, facing her, one hand mucking around with some little twigs he's found, building a tiny square structure in the dirt. He looks up briefly.

329

.

'Jonno is a good guy,' he says quietly. She hears the strained tone and waits for him to continue, but he just keeps building his little stick structure. It's a few centimetres high now and so she collects a fistful of her own sticks and passes them over. Tom thanks her with a smile.

'You guess my thoughts sometimes,' Alice ventures shyly. 'I *was* thinking about Jonty just then.'

'He *is* a good guy,' Tom mutters again.

'He let my gran have it once and . . . that takes guts!'

'She's a tough one, is she?'

'Is she ever!'

'Jonno always did have guts,' Tom says thoughtfully. He clears the twigs away with one hand and rolls onto his back, shuts his eyes and smiles. 'Tell me what he said to your gran.'

As Alice talks, Tom edges his body closer. Still on his back, he slides down a bit and leans his shoulder against her arm as she sits, her chin on her knees, describing the scene. She loves the familiarity of this. The closeness it implies. She can look down and see the top of his head, the way the curls spread out from a central point. *I've got a name*, Jonty had said that day. She'd really liked that. He'd refused to be intimidated by his rich bossy old grandmother.

'I watch you closely, Alice Wishart,' Tom muses softly, and turning on his side reaches one hand up and buries it in her hair. Alice smiles down into his face and briefly touches his hand entwined in her hair.

'Do you?'

'I do,' he breathes, 'and I think about you, too.'

'When?' she laughs.

'*When?*' Tom laughs too. 'Try pretty much *all the time*!'

'No you don't!'

'Yes I do.' Tom winds her hair around his fingers. 'I wake up in

330

the morning and you're there. I go to bed and . . .' he withdraws his hand. 'I've said too much already! You'll think I'm a complete dork . . . spinning you a line!'

'You're not a dork,' Alice says shyly.

'I'm not?'

'You're not.'

He takes her hand. This is totally new ground for her. New and wonderful ground! She has never before sat out in the open under a wide, darkening sky holding hands with someone. Nobody has ever told her before that he thinks about her all the time, or kissed her hand. It makes her giddy with happiness, and slightly afraid.

'Sorry about the other day.' Tom rolls onto his side, propping his head up with one hand. 'In the darkroom, I mean.'

'No,' Alice frowns, 'I'm sorry! I just can't . . .'

'You don't have to explain!' Tom says. Jonty is walking back towards them. If he's noticed the hand-holding he doesn't let on.

'Want to go now?' he asks.

'Not really,' Tom laughs.

'You always were a lazy prick!'

Jonty picks up Tom's leather coat lying on the side of the rug. 'I remember this!'

'Luke used to wear it to our footy matches,' Jonty tells Alice as he rubs his hand over the soft leather. 'I can see him on the sidelines yelling out *C'mon the demons* and smoking.' He slips the jacket on. 'How is your old man?'

'He's all right,' Tom says easily, sitting up a bit to look at Jonty. 'Clothes always did fit you better than me, Jonno'.

Alice sees that it's true, Jonty has the better physique. Compared to Tom, who is too thin, Jonty has a good chest and muscled arms. He strikes a few poses in Luke's jacket, making the others laugh. With his fair hair and even, chiselled features he could be a fashion model.

'You can't have it, though!' Tom tells him.

'Sorry, mate,' Jonty grins, buttoning it up, 'mine now.'

'No way! Hey, Jonno, thanks for introducing me to your cousin,' Tom says lightly, grinning at Alice.

'Did I introduce you?' Jonty laughs.

'Well . . . sort of.'

'You've got her blushing, Mullaney!'

'I'm not!' Alice laughs. But she is and what's more, she doesn't care. Tom is squeezing her shoulders and Jonty is shaking his head, trying not to smile, embarrassed but also pleased. She can see that. He is pleased for the both of them.

'Bloody great chick!' Tom jokes and the three of them break up laughing. It is such a lovely moment. Everything seems so clear and . . . sparkling, like that piece of crystal hanging in her grandmother's window. Depending on the sky, the colour is faintly different every time she sees it. So lovely and transparent.

'Come on, you two,' Jonty yells. 'Let's just have a bit of a commune with nature before we go back. Just walk up the hill a bit. I want to see if I can find this particular rock.'

'What rock?'

'Just a rock.'

'It's going to piss down!'

'You're a weakling, Mulla,' Jonty punches Tom's arm. 'Come on, just a few minutes!'

'Okay,' Tom holds out a hand to Alice, 'just to please this idiot we'll go on a quick trek, eh?' She takes his hand and stands up too. Tom looks up at the blackening sky and groans. 'Better put all this stuff away first though,' he says.

Motivated now to get the walk in before the rain, they scramble about, hurriedly packing up their things. Alice grabs the rug. Tom chucks the thermos, cups and sugar into the empty plastic bag, and Jonty grabs the empty pizza boxes. Jonty is first to the car. He opens the back door and throws in the boxes. Suddenly the wind shifts and the temperature falls. They all feel it and turn to each other. The air is now heavy and grey. *Splat!* The first fat drops splatter down.

'I reckon we should go back home now.'

'No!'

'The road out of here will get bad fast,' Tom says.

'Stop being an old woman!' Jonty reaches into the car and throws his own jacket at Tom.

'Put this on. We'll be right.'

Tom sighs and does what he's told. Jonty's jacket is a good-quality waterproof that will keep the wind and rain out. Alice is slipping on one much the same. Tom pulls a cigarette out of his jeans pocket and sticks it in his mouth.

'You got a light?' he asks Alice.

'I don't smoke.'

'Yes you do,' he smiles. 'What about outside the court that time?'

'That was my first ever,' she laughs recklessly.

'Yeah?' he grins at her, then puts one hand under her chin and kisses her nose. 'I'm honoured!'

'Come on you *pathetic* little lovebirds!' Jonty is hopping from one foot to the other anxiously. 'I want to check out this massive rock. There will be a lighter in my jacket.'

They walk off together towards the trees, Tom holding Alice's hand and tapping around the pockets of Jonty's jacket with his other hand for the lighter. The rain holds off, but the wind has begun to blow like the fury.

'So where is it?' Tom shouts above the noise of the wind at Jonty, who is walking on ahead. 'I need nicotine *now*, man.'

333

'Pocket!' Jonty calls back. 'In one of the pockets some-where.'

Tom lets go of Alice's hand as he searches though Jonty's pockets. He grins as he pulls out a hanky, and then a twenty-dollar note and a few train tickets.

'You always did carry a lot of shit, Jonno!' he calls to Jonty's receding back, as a wad of used tissues comes next. Jonty walks back impatiently when he sees the other two have stopped. He and Alice watch Tom dive into the inside breast pocket. Out comes a small address book then a couple of biros.

'Ah!' he cries triumphantly, 'some other little treasure here in the corner!' He opens his hand to see what he has found.

In the middle of Tom's palm is Lillian's necklace, a small diamond heart on a chain of gold. Tom slumps a little. Holding it at one end, he lets it dangle in the air between them.

Alice takes a step backwards and then another, staring at the necklace. The magic stones shine in the rain and quickening dark like something alive.

Jonty stares at the necklace too, as though in a trance. Tom looks at Jonty. The necklace swings a little in slow round circles. Around them the trees creak and bend with the wind.

The knowledge that the necklace has been sitting in Jonty's pocket for the last three years explodes into Alice's life like an inexpertly detonated bomb. Everything is flying up in the air again and not coming down. *It can't be! What does this mean? Oh please no.* She thinks of him with the dog earlier, then settling in behind the steering wheel. *Ya gonna love this, Alice!* Jonty was her brother. The one she never had.

How long do the three of them just stand there staring at the necklace? It feels like forever. When is someone going to say something? When is one of them going to explain?

'That belongs to my mother,' Alice eventually whispers. She

reaches out and takes it from Tom. Alice closes her fist tightly around the necklace and collapses onto her knees, feeling the shock waves race through her. Tom squats beside her, tries to put an arm around her shoulders, but she pushes him away.

'I remember now.' Jonty's voice is devoid of emotion.

'What do you remember, Jonno?' Tom says sharply.

'I was *there*,' Jonty mutters. 'I remember now. I was there.' He begins to stumble off like a drunkard, away from them, up the track leading into the trees.

But Tom gets up and hauls him back. Jonty tries to resist at first. They scuffle a few yards from Alice, but in the end Jonty allows himself to be pushed down onto the ground next to Alice. Tom kneels between them. So it's the three of them on their knees on the dirt in the smattering rain, Jonty breathing heavily, muttering *oh shit* and *jeez* with his eyes closed, picking up handfuls of the soft soil and letting it run through his hands.

'Come on, Jonty,' Tom shouts into his face. 'What do you remember?'

She was sitting at her little wood slat table out in the backyard, smoking a cigarette, drinking from her crystal glass and looking up at the sky.

'Hi, there.'

'Jonno!' Her face jerked around. 'God! You gave me a fright.'

'Sorry,' I walked towards her, 'but I've got news!'

'Well,' she said, 'I hope it's good. Pull up a seat.'

She didn't seem all that pleased to see me but I knew she'd be pleased when she heard the plan. Anyway, Lillian sometimes took time to warm up. I was used to that.

I began to talk but I couldn't stay sitting down. I was so edgy that I kept jumping up and sitting down again, striding up and down in front of her, stopping to lean my hands on the back of the chair, gesticulating to the heavens. She stayed very still as I talked – just sat there stiffly, smoking and listening as I outlined my plan.

'Oh, Jonno!' she said. 'Don't be ridiculous.'

'*What?*' I was stunned.

'I wasn't *serious*!' she said. 'For God's sake!'

'Yes, you were!' I said.

'Darling, I'd been drinking!'

'So?'

'Jonno,' she sighed deeply, as though talking to a very young child, 'I'd drunk rather a lot when I suggested . . . all that.'

'But you weren't pissed!' I cut in vehemently. 'You were spot on.'

'When you wake up in the morning,' Lillian yawned, 'you'll see that it is all quite preposterous.'

I just stood there, shocked and completely winded, staring down at her, hardly able to believe what I'd just heard her say. The business that had been consuming all my waking time had come to nothing. Without her it would basically just *disappear*.

Three nights before, my old man had thrown two buckets of ice-cold water over me while I was sleeping. Once, he'd locked my mother in the old shed all night – in the cold and the dark without even a blanket. I hadn't been there to let her out – I'd been staying at a mate's place in town, stoned out of my head – and I suppose that was playing on my conscience.

He was getting worse. The mad patches were becoming more frequent and more terrifying. The week before, he'd threatened to electrocute me with a dodgy power cord if I didn't start *playing by his rules*. No one would miss me, he said. He'd be doing the world a favour. I was filled with the bad blood of my mother's side of the family.

Something had to be done. The icy water was nothing. I was used to stuff like that. What I wasn't used to was moving on past the anger and powerlessness to something else. The resolve to end him had settled down in me like freshly poured concrete left in the hot sun. Working out how to do it had been so . . . exciting.

'Sit down,' Lillian said again, and when I continued to stand she got up, picked up the bottle and screwed the top on. 'I'm tired, Jonno,' she said, 'I've been working for ten hours straight.'

I opened my mouth to say something, but my head wasn't there anymore. It seemed to have tipped over into some other reality. I could feel myself falling away, and it was the weirdest sensation. Terrifying too. I grabbed the table because it felt as though I was slipping off the world and into an unknown void. And I didn't want to go. Heat was coming up from under the grass and I could feel sweat running down my backbone.

'Listen, Jonty,' her voice was a long way off now, 'I don't want anything to do with what you've suggested. Do you understand me? Go home,' she said stiffly and then peered into my face suspiciously. 'How many bongs have you had tonight?'

'What does it matter?' I snapped childishly.

'And other stuff, too,' she said sharply. 'You're on ice, aren't you?'

'No, no . . . so what if I am?'

'Oh Jonno . . . it does matter! Please, love.'

We stood there looking at each other. I was slipping and sliding from one greasy patch of thought to another. I was thinking about an essay I hadn't done and then my old man and his snow-white shirts . . . The plan to kill him had given me a reason to live. It had sustained me. She had closed the door in my face, pulled away my hope . . . left me swinging on a rope, looking for a place to land.

She fetched a potted plant from under the kitchen window, took it down to the back fence. Then she reached up to take off one of the pots hanging on the fence.

I followed her, thinking that there must be something I could say to change her mind. *Cut the theatrics*, I told myself. I would speak softly this time. I came up behind her while she was trying to unhook another pot plant, but when she sensed me behind her she turned around quickly.

'I mean it, Jonno,' she said sharply, 'I've had enough tonight!'

'But he's spreading rumours about you,' I said, trying to keep my voice easy, 'telling weird lies about you . . .'

'What kind of lies?'

I heard his voice again. *That Mullaney kid is a degenerate. You know he's on with your aunt? Saw them with my own eyes. Caught them hard at it.*

'He says that you've got something going with Tom Mullaney!' I was staring down into her face, waiting for the full shock of what I'd said to sink in. 'He says that he saw you and Tom . . .'

She looked at me blankly for some time. I could see her face clearly in the light coming from the kitchen, and her expression didn't change, which was simply . . . *maddening.*

'Look, Jonno,' she said very quietly after a while, 'your father did happen to come across Tom and me . . .'

'Tom and you?' I didn't understand her meaning.

'Tom and me,' she said again.

'Tom and . . . *you*?' I was just about choking on my own fury by this stage. 'But you . . .'

'Don't jump to conclusions.' She smiled wearily, as though all this was sort of obvious and boring and shouldn't have to be spelt out.

'What!' I was yelling into her face. 'What do you mean "Tom and you" then, for fucksake?'

'Step back, please,' she said putting a hand on my shoulder and giving me a little push. 'Please, Jonno, I want you to just leave me alone tonight, okay? And we'll talk about all this tomorrow. It really isn't anything to . . . worry about.'

But I didn't step back. I had her cornered up against the fence.

'Tell me what you have going with Tom,' I hissed.

'I will *not*,' she said, pushing me back again, this time a little harder. 'Now, please move and . . .'

And that's when the curtain came down. Just blackness at first and then little red and silvery stars shooting upwards in front of my eyes like fireworks.

'Tell me! Tell me!' I picked up both ends of the scarf she was wearing and pulled them tighter and tighter around her neck. 'Tell me about you and Tom Mullaney!'

But how could she tell me anything? There was no way she could talk. She could hardly even make a sound, just these sort of jagged, gasping noises.

She was pulling frantically at my hands. Then her little fingers with the long pretty red nails began to scratch at my face. She was trying to go for my eyes but it was easy to brush her off. Those frantic hands were so weak and pathetic that I began to laugh. The last few obsessive weeks of plotting his death came sailing into my head. All that concentration and pent-up emotion for *nothing*. I felt as though I'd trained hard for a race and now they were telling me that I wasn't even allowed to run.

I let go of the scarf suddenly then pushed her backwards. I deliberately pushed her hard against the back of the fence. There was a dull crunching noise. She gave one deep wild cry before she collapsed.

I stood back, waiting for her to get up, but she didn't. Then in the light coming from the house I saw the pointy spike sticking out of the fence.

That's meant to have a pot plant on it, is what I thought. I looked

341

down and saw that I was holding her necklace in one hand and her scarf in the other. Some part of me knew something terrible had happened, but I couldn't fathom what exactly. The little heart of diamonds twinkled in the half light, so pretty and delicate, and I wondered how the hell I came to be holding it.

I bent down to look at Lillian lying on the grass. Then I moved around to the other side and saw the back of her head. All her long curly hair was wet. I put my hand out to touch it and I felt the stickiness. Did I do this? I crouched down beside her and whispered, *Get up, Lillian. I'm sorry. I didn't mean . . . to lose it like that. It's just that, Tom is my mate and I'm . . . I'm so stoned.*

Someone was going to shout *cut* any minute. The lights would come up and I'd walk out of the theatre with everyone else. I never cry. But I cried then, and I couldn't stop.

Then I heard a noise. Someone was walking up the side of the house. A voice called softly, *Lillian. Are you there? Lillian?* So late at night? My first thought was Tom.

Lillian! Louder now. It was a male voice, but not Tom's. Familiar in a way, but I couldn't place it. Then the figure emerged. It was my father. I remember thinking, *but you're the one who is meant to be lying in the grass bleeding to death.*

He went straight past me to where she was lying. Didn't say anything at first. Just stood over her. Then he squatted down and touched her. After a while he got up to face me.

'You did this?' he asked.

I didn't say anything.

'Just go. Leave now,' he said. He rarely spoke like that to me. His voice was almost gentle. 'Just clear out, Jonty.'

'Where?'

He put one hand on my shoulder and looked closely into my face.

I dream about that moment. I wake up in the middle of the night to his face . . .

'Anywhere,' he said, 'just go. Get away. I'll look after this.'

I'll look after this.

Did this mean that he would call the doctor and get her to hospital? Would I be able to come around the next day with flowers to apologise?

'Will it be okay?' I asked him.

'It will be okay,' he said, 'just go.'

I stuffed the scarf and necklace into my pockets and walked quickly out the side gate, the way I'd come. I didn't realise that the warm sticky stuff over my hands was blood. I walked down to the end of the street and wondered if I should go home or . . . where else could I go? Maybe I should admit myself to hospital. I'd done it before. They'd know what to do with me. I was off my head and they'd give me something to calm me down. But I didn't. In a kind of unconscious daze I walked all the way out here . . . *to these caves.*

When I reached the bridge before the turn-off I wrapped the scarf around a rock and threw it into the water. Then I washed my hands and face. The caves seemed like the one place I could go. I wanted the hollow sounds and the feeling that nothing much matters because . . . time is such a long thing.

Every now and again an image of her lying on the grass would slide into my brain and I'd think . . . well that must be it. I must have done it. But I'd gone there that night to arrange killing *him*. Her lying still on the grass just didn't make sense. I didn't really believe it. All the way out to the caves I was expecting to be pulled up by the police or at least stopped by someone. But no one noticed me.

Jonty says all this with his eyes closed, rocking backward and forward. He stops suddenly and gets up and, without looking at Tom or Alice, runs towards the track leading into the bush.

Have to get away. Those two staring at him like he's some kind of freak. He's making his way uphill through the trees, panting like an eighty-year-old. He knows he's gotta do something about getting fit again! *What is the point of giving up dope and fags if you can't walk up a hill? Footy maybe?*

Thing is, he remembers sitting on some great mother of a rock out here . . . it came to him like a knife in his head when he was sitting back there with the other two. But where exactly is it? Some gut instinct tells him to keep to this track for a while yet. Once he gets to the top of the hill and the trees thin out, everything will be clearer, he'll be able to see around and have a better idea where he is. He feels sure there're more caves down the other side, deeper darker caves if he remembers right, but . . . it was a long time ago.

You'll unravel one day, Jonty. Everyone does. I could lean across the desk and pick a thread from that old jumper you're wearing right now. Just one thread is all I need. Then I'll pull and I'll keep on pulling and we'll both watch it come apart, bit by bit, line by line. Kinda fun, if you think about it! That will be you one day, Jonty . . . You'll start to unravel and there will be no stopping you once you start.

Jonty walks and walks, crashing through the undergrowth, gasping and panting. Big dark sky above and he can see for miles around. And the wind! It's blowing from the south and making the saplings bend over like a crowd of old woman. The pale grey light is blinding him. *You can see right through it. How many shades of grey are there? Pearl-grey, steel-grey, charcoal and lead. Grey so dark it's almost purple.*

To the right of Jonty is the town, and just around from there, if he strains hard, he can see the blue of the sea. He closes his eyes and breathes in the smell. The birds are twittering like maniacs. They must know something is going on. What *is* going on? Maybe it's just the inside of his head. A small gap in the clouds and he sees a patch of white sky. *The eye of God? Hey, that would be cool. If only God would appear now and show him something important.* It won't be long before the stars come out. As a kid out on the farm, he used to love the calm before the storm – the air, soft and heavy around him, waiting to explode. It'll be dark soon and he's got to find that rock.

Since his father came back, Jonty has found looking in the mirror a trial. *Sure looks like me but . . . do I know this person?* He'd tried to explain it to Buzz the other night, but the old geezer had just nodded and changed the subject. As though Jonty had just said something completely normal. *Jonno could tell he knew what he meant.*

He gets these flashes and they're like clues. Every now and again he gets a whole sequence that he'd forgotten about completely. They're like little films rolling behind his eyes. Scary. Some stuff feels completely new. Doesn't ring any bells at all. But he has to assume it happened, doesn't he?

Is there more he doesn't remember . . . yet? What else is waiting out there to ambush and twist his brain into one of those metal pot-cleaners? A mass of dense interconnecting wires that end up where they began.

Jonty is off again, making his way down through the trees to the other side of the valley, feeling pretty easy in old Luke's coat.

'Hey, Jay Van, your lawyer!' the screw would yell. And there would be Luke in the visiting area, sitting at one of the tables like he'd been there forever – overweight, middle-aged and grey-haired, just like anyone's uncle. Jonty was always glad to see him. Apart from his own mum, Luke was his only visitor. They'd shake hands and sit on opposite sides of the table.

'Well, Jonno.' His eyes twinkled as he offered Jonty a cigarette. 'How are they treating you?'

'Not too bad.'

'That's the spirit. You keeping that mouth shut?'

'Yep.'

'Good lad.'

Jonty liked watching Luke smoke. His hands were wide and blunt and meaty, the hands of a road worker rather than a lawyer. But there was something refined about the way he'd pick the cigarette out of the packet, slowly, with those thick fingers. He'd take his time to light it too, seemed to enjoy holding the unlit cigarette a while, flipping it from one hand to the other as he talked. Tom is like that too sometimes. Says he wants a smoke and then takes forever to light the damned thing. *Like father, like son.*

'Now, Jonno, is there anything you need? You seen your mother?' Luke would ask in his nice, easy, deep voice, never harsh or loud. 'You want me to pass on any message to her?' You'd have thought Jonty was in there for pinching a bag of lollies or something. But he'd liked Luke asking after his mother. It's funny the things you like about people. Funny, too, the things you remember.

Even weirder the things you forget.

He is just about on the flat again and it is starting to spit. Jonty does up Luke's coat and hurries on. It's only six, but the dark is starting to close in now. Heavy clouds are piling up like enormous old cushions left behind after a posh party. Someone has sneaked in through the side doors and filled them with poisonous gas or maybe some other . . . dark and dangerous stuff.

He is crashing through the undergrowth. How mad was he to think that he would be able to carve out something new for himself.

It's raining now and Jonty is walking fast. He's puffing and panting, rushing through the bush, trying to find the place. And before long – so easily really, he finds it. Yeah. Here is is. Did he really think it had been hiding from him? He starts laughing. So he can still remember some things okay. His brain isn't completely fried! He lays his hands on this big mother of a rock and looks up. Such a massive round prick of a thing! From this angle it looks like a huge egg. It's been sitting in the same spot for thousands of years, maybe millions, letting the wind and sun and the rain just wear it away. This is where he came that early morning after . . . everything happened.

The rain is light but steady now and the rock is slippery. After falling on his arse a few times he manages to find a few toeholds and haul himself up, apart from a torn fingernail, more or less unscathed. He can't see that much now. But he feels the mountain behind him, the bush all around, and above him the mammoth clouds shifting and rolling in the wind. Lightning streaks across the sky in the west, then a distant roll of thunder.

Down in the gully, nestled between two clumps of acacias, is the long narrow cave in the shape of a fat snake. This he remembers. It's lying there in front of Jonty, black and treacherous.

'Hey Jonty! You there mate? Coooeeee!'

Jonty hears his name but it doesn't really penetrate. His mind is loose, flapping like a flag come away from its pole. It's being swept up by the wind into the cliffs and the trees, down along the dirty ground and then up again. Luke's coat flaps open, but he can't even feel the mean wind blowing straight through him.

'Jonteee!' The voice comes again from a long way off. 'It's getting dark, mate! Come on! Where are you?'

Tom. Tom, who's been his best mate for years but who never even passed on any word or greeting, much less rang or came to see him in detention. Tom who is out there looking for him, but it's all too . . . way too late now. So many times during those months inside, Jonty had been tempted to ask Luke about Tom but pride had held him back.

He is sitting on top of the rock now, watching the heavy sky, feeling the rain drive down his face. He looks down at Luke's soaking leather coat, trying to remember how come he's wearing it. Luke is Tom's father, not his father, so . . . how come he is wearing this coat? Where is *his* father? *Oh yeah, that's right.* Just thinking of old Jed in jail taking the rap makes Jonty laugh. Those sharp black bits in the darkening sky, the stream of pink light coming through the edge of one cloud where the sun is sinking, what do they mean? Where are they going? Is the universe trying to tell him something? Is everything going to be . . . *okay*?

'Jonteee!'

Jonty stands up. The gaping hole down in the gully is starting to move. One end seems to be slowly opening up. It's sliding across the ground like a huge mouth or a . . . *grave*. His eyes are open but he's in a nightmare. *Come on, Jonno! Hold it together, man.* He wishes Buzz was with him. This stuff is bullshit and he knows it is bullshit and yet he can't help it . . . *Strange that now he knows he did it, he also knows that he didn't mean to. Killing her wasn't what he'd had in mind.*

'Jonno!' The voice is louder now. 'C'mon, mate, where are you?'

Jonty turns and there is Tom crashing down through the trees towards him. Tom skids to a halt when he sees him up on the rock.

'What the *fuck*!'

Jonty slides down the wet rock, landing hard on his left leg.

He stands in front of Tom in the semi-darkness, the rain pissing down between them. Tom is wearing his coat. Jonty thinks of the necklace nestled in the inside pocket for three years. Did he really forget? Maybe. Maybe it was more like he didn't want to remember. It was a little secret he had with himself. What he does remember now is the way he nearly threw it into the river along with the scarf, but in the end he couldn't bring himself because . . . *it used to look so nice around her neck.*

When Jonty moves, a blast of pain shoots up his leg from his ankle. His leg gives and he collapses onto the ground.

'Jonno?' Tom crouches down beside him.

'I've fucked my ankle.'

He remembers being out here in Year Ten. When the bus came, he and Tom had been among the pack of kids who hid. The teachers had gone berserk. But when he opens his mouth to ask Tom if he remembers . . . nothing happens. He can't get the words out.

After a while, Jonty lets Tom haul him up and help him over to some shelter under trees.

'We'll stay here,' Tom tells him, 'until the rain passes.'

'I don't want him to save me,' Jonty says eventually.

Tom nods steadily, as though he knows what Jonty means.

'You gonna piss off this time, Tom?'

'No.' Tom puts his arms around Jonty's shaking shoulders. 'I'm here, Jonno. I won't piss off this time.'

Alice

Gripping the necklace tightly, Alice runs back to the car and jumps in. She stares straight ahead though the windscreen. In the distance, she hears a roll of thunder and thinks, *my mother is up there.* Suddenly the sky cracks open with a sharp flash of lightning, right in front of her. Clutching the necklace tight, she closes her eyes.

Alice sits alone in the front cabin for over two hours watching the rain and waiting for them to come back. She doesn't have the keys or she would drive off without them. That's what she tells herself, anyway, because the longer she sits there the more she hates them both. *Tom went after Jonty to bring him back. So what the hell is he doing? Could they have decided to run away together? Jonty's cover is blown so Tom might have switched sides. They're out there, right now, rekindling their old friendship and planning their escape or . . . they could be planning to come back and kill me!* Oddly enough, this last thought doesn't frighten her in the least. *Let them try!*

She rummages around for something to protect herself with and comes across a rusty old pocketknife. She spends a bit of time cleaning up the biggest blade, clips it shut and then slips it into her belt. *Let them try.*

The rain eventually soothes her anger. It pounds down on the roof of the car, splattering on the bonnet like tiny angry insects. She sits watching it, cold but at least dry in the cabin, with her mother's necklace held tightly in her fist. Holding it like a sort of talisman. She tries to imagine travelling back into town with *her mother's murderer* sitting beside her. *How bizarre will that be?* Any minute now they will show up and . . .

But she can't focus. She can't keep her mind on anything at all. The meaning stays hidden, like a slippery fish under the surface of the water, impossible to catch.

Just as soon as she grasps one idea it disappears and something else comes galloping in to fill the space. It is like a disjointed poem made up of beautiful images that no one understands. She remembers this feeling. When she found her mother's body that day three years before, it was exactly like this. Reality seems to be slip-sliding along the surface of her mind, like children skidding up and down a polished floor in their socks.

So they were right all along, Jonty . . . But she doesn't even think about that very much. A cushioning blanket of dreaminess covers everything.

Every so often, she opens her hand and examines the necklace again, touching the three long hairs tangled in the chain in wonder. My mother's hair! She will keep it forever. How heavy the chain is and how delicate. How brightly the stones shine. It is a beautiful thing and she is glad to have it. It used to look so pretty around her mother's neck. Alice pulls the rear-vision mirror around and holds it up against her own throat and pouts her mouth, turning this way and that. Yes, it suits her, too. She is like her mother in so many ways. She wonders, yet again, where the necklace came from.

'But who?' Alice demanded. Her mother had just told her that it was a gift from an admirer. But as much as Alice would like to believe this, she doesn't know of any admirers. Lillian didn't go out with men. There were only those two boys, and Alice knew it was too expensive a gift for either of them.

'Never you mind!' Her mother had gone coy and secretive. 'It will be yours one day.'

And so it is, Alice thinks, gripping the necklace and looking out at the blackness and driving night rain. So it is. My mother was right. It will be mine from this day on.

She hears the boys before she sees them. The doors are yanked open. Tom gets into the driver's side and Jonty gets in the other. Both of them are soaked through and neither of them speak. She doesn't look either right or left. Not so much as a glance at either of them. She will never look at either of them again, never willingly anyway. No one speaks for the whole way home.

Tom pulls up outside Jonty's little house and opens his door.

'You need a hand to get to the door?'

'I'm right. It's just a sprain.'

'Bye then, Jonno,' Tom mutters. 'I'll see you tomorrow.'

'Yeah, okay. Thanks. See you.' Jonty gets out quickly without looking at Tom or Alice.

They watch him limping his way through the rain towards the gate. He turns briefly before heading to the front door. Tom nods but doesn't take his hands from the steering wheel. They watch him go inside.

'You want to come with me, Alice?'

She turns and sees that Tom is still staring after Jonty, his face drawn in the harsh light of the street, drained of all expression.

'Where?' she whispers.

'I'm going to ring Lloyd right now,' he says, 'and tell him we'll be there tomorrow.'

Lloyd? Alice has forgotten who this is and is angry suddenly. *Why is he going off to ring other people when this has happened? Where will he be? What is she meant to do with the necklace? Does she have to go by herself to the police?'*

'Lloyd Hooper, the detective in charge of the case,' Tom sighs. His knuckles are like sharp stones, gripping the steering wheel.

'Oh.'

'I'll take you home now.' He slumps forward and starts to cry.

Alice watches in numb horror as the tears build into terrible racking sobs that go right through his body. Part of her wants to reach out and touch him. His bony back and shoulders, the thin hands covering his face, seem so defenceless suddenly, and oddly young. He could be a boy of fourteen or fifteen instead of a young man in his early twenties. But she can't reach out. She can hardly move. They are sitting only inches apart in this same cabin where only hours before they'd been so close. But something huge has moved into the space between them blocking them from each other.

'Does he know you're going to do that?' she asks coldly.

'Yeah,' Tom groans, searching his pockets for a hanky. He finds one and blows his nose, still gasping.

'I'll go home then,' she says.

'Okay.' Tom shakes his head and starts up the engine.

By the time Alice gets back to her grandmother's house it is nearly midnight and still raining. Tom wants to drive into the grounds and drop her at the door, but Alice insists that being left at the side gate in the street will be fine.

'I'd prefer to see you in,' he says formally.

'This is fine.'

'You don't look too good, Alice.'

'I'm okay.' She reaches for the handle as he brakes the car and hesitates without turning to face him. What can she say that will make things clear? Is she meant to do this in a formal way?

'Thanks, Tom,' she mutters and pushes the door open.

'Speak soon?' he asks, staring miserably ahead.

'I don't think so.' Alice gets out of the car. 'Goodbye, Tom.'

She walks off towards the little side gate and doesn't turn back, not even for one last look or one last wave. Whatever she and Tom Mullaney had, or thought they had, whatever they hoped for, is gone. Over. That much is clear. She probably won't ever talk to him again.

Walking up the paved path towards the lighted front door, Alice feels the big overhanging trees crowding in on her. Two of the lamps leading up to the house are out, so the darkness between the trees seems ominous, as though the deep patches of mottled dark hold strange and terrible secrets.

Alice stumbles up the front steps, praying that she won't come face to face with her grandmother on this of all nights. She feels as though she is only hanging together by a thread. A late-night conversation full of the usual complaints and unwanted advice is the last thing she wants. She fits her key into the lock and pushes the heavy door. All she wants is to get upstairs and into her own room. She wants to crawl under the doona and lie there, possibly forever.

In her room now, with the door locked behind her, Alice sits awhile on the bed. Then she gets up and opens the window and lets in the cold night air. The rain has stopped and the pale yellow moon has drifted out from behind the clouds. Alice thinks that she will remember this night for the rest of her life. It is the night when so many things came together and then . . . fell apart again.

There will be some kind of trial and she might have to testify. Who knows? It will all come out, and the gossips will have a field day, but she is not daunted. *I came home for this,* she whispers into the dark night, hoping her mother can hear. *I came home to find whoever did it . . .*

She picks up the yellow package that Tom had dropped into the office only days before, pulls out the prints and begins to flip idly through them. Here they all are. The one of her mother and her aunt in front of the car, then her mother and father on the verandah with little Alice. Then there is her grandmother as a young mother pushing the pram with a three-year-old at her side. Here is her grandmother as a bride outside the church, brushing confetti off the bodice of her dress and looking straight into the camera. Alice stares hard at that one, trying to find the cantankerous old woman in that young bride. Yes, she is there in the cool expression of delight. Alice's grandfather had been a catch, the most eligible man around, and her grandmother had been smart enough to snare him. Alice smiles. It's all there on her face!

There is one print at the end of the pile that she hadn't seen. Tom must have liked it, because he has mounted it on board. It is of her mother and aunt standing by a fence. Lillian has Alice on her hip in a little smocked dress and with a bow in her hair. And there is her Aunty Marie, smiling into the camera, with little Jonty, about three years old, dressed in shorts and a striped shirt.

He is standing on tiptoes between Marie and Lillian, reaching up to hold hands with baby Alice, who is looking down at him in absolute delight. There they are, two sisters with their babies, all of them looking so delighted.

Alice's eyes sting with sudden tears as she stares at the little boy in the photograph, hearing her mother's voice, so clear and lovely in the cold night air.

Jonty is the nearest you'll have to a brother, Alice.

Sadness has a familiarity about it that joy or excitement, or plain old happiness, simply can't match – a kind of lived-in, homey feeling, like the worn nightie folded up under her pillow or the scruffy slippers under her bed. Who wants to be knocked around by love every day? When you get down to the nitty-gritty of it, who seriously wants to be surprised by life? Not Alice. Not really. This flatness feels like an old friend coming home after being away. He has been waiting outside for everyone else to leave and his arrival is no surprise.

She sighs and slowly goes to shut the window and pull the curtains across. She takes off the lovely white top that she'd bought especially for the evening, peels off her jeans and puts on her old flannelette nightie. She slides under the doona, reaches out to switch the light off and waits for sleep.

TOM

A YEAR LATER

Luke says he likes to let his mind wander when he's driving, that it relaxes him. The classy little European shitbox is flying along like a bat out of hell, way over the speed limit, and it's on the tip of Tom's tongue to ask if he's ever thought about de-stressing some other, less lethal way but he holds back. Classic FM is blasting out into the silence between them, and Tom can't help wondering if Chopin ever thought his sonata might come in useful as filler for two people who are still awkward with each after a big personal drama. Probably not.

'You remember your camera?' Luke asks abruptly.

'Nah.' Tom slumps down in his seat and closes his eyes.

'How come?'

Tom shrugs irritably. He doesn't take photos anymore. He doesn't know why that is, but he sure as hell knows he doesn't want to talk to his old man about it.

Tom's car is in dock getting a new clutch. He'd planned to catch the train back to Warrnambool for his mum's birthday bash, but

Luke had a court appearance in the city and when he found out that Tom didn't have much on, or a car, insisted on picking him up. Tom didn't feel free to say that he'd been looking forward to the long train journey and a little solitary *lead-in* time. But here he is, doing the right thing, travelling home with his father, wondering if they'll get there at all. Luke is such a speedster.

Closer now, and along this stretch of highway new developments rise up out of the landscape: innocuous little moles that look like nothing until you get closer. Then the alarm bells start ringing and you find yourself thinking of melanomas or diseased bone marrow. Hundreds of acres of undulating farmland and bush have been graded and pegged out into blocks. Paved roads eat into land that even last year would have been grass for sheep and cows. The odd display-home near the road, complete with those weird long brick entrances, announces the names of the proposed estates: *Lockhart Downs*, *Sugar Loaf Hills*, *Teppling Mews*. Every one of them is different but strangely similar. There are great stone entrances complete with water features and potted plants, fake pillars and split-level, second-storey extensions. They sit there like bizarre signposts pointing the way to the future.

Tom can't shake the feeling that he's lived most of his life already. He might be only twenty-three but he can tell that from now on there will just be a few split-level diversions and a couple of spiky relationships until he finally drops off the tree. The main game has already been played and . . . he lost.

'You think you'll ever take another photo?' Luke asks in a pointedly casual way that tells Tom he'd like to keep the conversation rolling. 'I mean for pleasure?'

'I don't know,' Tom mutters, figuring that his father's insistence on them travelling back together should let him off the politeness hook.

Hooks . . . spikes, and nails.

Yeah, well, a year might have flown by but a word can bring it all back. And it does. *Vividly.* Skinny, handsome, blue-eyed Tom. Mr Cool Cat, with his camera slung over his shoulder, his smart-arsed ambitions, and his sneaky easy way with girls – except with the one that mattered. It's amazing he didn't twig to himself sooner.

Okay, his mum might be right – he's probably depressed. Eating is mostly a chore and he's got a rash creeping up his neck that is freaking him out. He doesn't sleep too well, either.

He hasn't spoken to Alice Wishart since that night the three of them drove home from the caves. Tom rang her up once when Jonty's name was all over the local paper again and then once more before the sentencing hearing. Both times she said *sorry* and hung up. *It's all over now, Baby Blue.*

He wishes he could have told her that he really did love her. Just in case she thought it was only some weirdo mixed-up stuff about her mother. Tom would like her to know that at least that part was real.

'Hey, slow down,' he says gruffly, pointing at the speedo, 'we're in an 80 zone.'

Luke turns as though surprised to hear Tom's voice.

'You're right,' he says mildly, and keeps going at the same speed.

'You're a newly married man,' Tom jokes weakly, 'so you owe it to your wife to be careful!'

Luke smiles and slows down just a little. But more as a kind of goodwill gesture than anything else. Tom sighs and has to laugh.

'Don't worry,' Luke mumbles. 'All under control.'

'I've got a good chance of getting that job in South Melbourne,' Tom adds.

'Of course you'll get it!'

'Not if I'm dead.'

'Okay,' Luke laughs and lifts his foot off the accelerator this time. 'I'd hate you to miss out on it.'

Tom isn't seriously excited about the job. It's with an advertising agency, for God's sake, and that means frozen peas and pretty models in pretty frocks, lipsticks and airbrushed thighs and the rest of it. But he will have finished his course by the time they want him to start, and he plans to go to the States next year. He wants to buy a pick-up truck and drive from east to west on his own. For that he's going to need money.

Once the court case was over, Luke and Anna's plans to get married again became the new hot topic around town. The number of people who came up to Tom during a break in the court proceedings was phenomenal. *Good to hear about your mum and dad . . . Always thought them splitting up was a shame . . . blah blah.*

Oh yeah. Whatever. Thanks. Tom couldn't get excited. He said congratulations and the rest of it, but basically it went into the way-too-bizarre basket. They'd had the murder and the trial, got that born-again fuckwit Jed out on a suspended sentence, then put Jonty away again for a few years and so then it was time to have a . . . *wedding*?

But on the day, well . . . Tom has to admit that the day went well. His father was obviously so happy and Anna looked great. Even Tom got happy for a few hours. He hung out with Nellie and Ned for most of it, and their exhilaration was contagious. He felt good from the time the ceremony began at five in the afternoon until one the next morning. And he wasn't even drunk. Eight hours of feeling good should never be sniffed at, but particularly when your general level of levity is only this side of morose.

'We made good time,' Luke mumbles, looking at his watch.

'What time is Mum expecting us?'

'One I think.' His father turns to him, 'She's glad you're coming, Tom. We both are.'

'As though I'd miss it!' Tom is embarrassed to think that he has turned into the kind of wanker who might not come to his mum's fiftieth birthday party. Apparently it's going to take the whole weekend, but he's up for it. There is no great social life waiting for him back in town, so why not? There's today's family lunch, followed by a party in the evening, then a garden party being thrown by an old friend of Anna's the next day. Not that Tom is actually *looking forward* to any of it, but he figures he might as well be there as anywhere else.

Jonty had been as white as death in the dock, his voice so faint and low at times that it near-enough broke Tom's heart. Inside that baggy suit he looked like someone else; someone older, tougher and more hardened. And yet at odd moments he could have been a fifteen-year-old, caught for some trivial shop-stealing offence. The suit had obviously been bought off the rack in some department store or specials counter, but Jonty either hadn't tried it on beforehand, or else they'd parcelled up the wrong size by mistake.

But he answered most of the questions put to him and he didn't fudge either, not about his relationship with Lillian or his father, not about the drugs he took, and not about . . . what happened.

Tom had to get up there, too, in front of the whole town, and tell his part in it. He figured that it was the least he could do for Jonty. In summing up, the judge gave them both credit for being honest.

Luke persuaded Jonty to plead guilty to manslaughter. He got ten years with six non-parole. The police prosecutor appealed that it wasn't enough. Most people thought it was a satisfactory outcome *considering* . . . Luke brought in a few shrinks who were able to make a pretty credible case for his head being done-in by a combination of illegal and prescribed drugs and years of sustained abuse.

Alice resigned from the job with Luke the day after they'd been out at the caves. After the trial was over she went back to uni.

Ah . . . but he's sick of thinking about it!

Tom winds down the window for some air and then uses the vanity mirror to check his neck for about the millionth time that morning. The weird rash is itchy and gets hot sometimes and, worst of all, he thinks it might be *growing.* There is a little patch under one ear that wasn't there yesterday. He's got to get some vitamins into him. He's got to eat more. Got to get some sun for Christ's sake! Maybe he should go into rehab and *detox* or what-ever it is that they do there. Can you get detoxed from a state of misery? *What about a broken heart?*

It would be wrong to say that Jonty never met Tom's eyes during the sentence hearing. After both barristers had summed up, two days passed before everyone was called back to court for the sentencing. Jonty was standing in the dock, the judge was at his bench and the public gallery was full of rubbernecking locals. The judgement was read out, and Jonty turned to Tom as the bevy of short-sleeved, stony-faced coppers closed in around him. Jonty looked straight past them to Tom. He seemed to be asking: *How did I get here, Tommo?*

It was hard to explain, but in that instant Tom saw again the young kid he'd first encountered at Wattle Bank Primary – the wild, clever kid with eyes so green and clear and bright that you couldn't help knowing he was up for anything. Within the first hour of knowing Jonty, he'd discovered stuff that he'd never learn anywhere else. More than anyone, Jonty had been someone who lived as though just being alive was enough. That was his gift and . . . he gave it away for free.

Fuck drugs! Fuck the dealers who don't care whose lives they ruin! Fuck the doctors and shrinks who dish out the legal ones like lollies . . . And fuck that moron Jed who thinks you can undo it all by doing some kind of penance.

And fuck Jonty too, for his wild pride . . . and the way he never knew when enough was enough.

Tom's eyes had stung with tears as he watched Jonty being handcuffed and led away. He was crying for Jonty, of course, for . . . the waste. But he was crying for himself, as well, for all those days that he'd never have back and the fact that not one iota of any single thing that happened could ever be changed. *Fuck.* He was crying for Lillian, too, and for Alice, and the way that time marches on leaving everything behind.

'Hey, Dad, can you let me off here?'

'How come?' his old man says sharply, but he has his foot on the brake and they are slowing down.

'I want to walk into town along the beach.'

The Hopkins River bridge is just up ahead. A sign points left, up through blocks of housing to the beach. Logan's Beach is mostly sparse and wide, with a wonderful empty curving grandeur of its own, but this spot, where the river estuary runs into the sea, is a favourite of Tom's. He likes the sheltered nature of it and the outcrop of sandstone rocks, some of them massive and craggy, with hidden crevices and crannies big enough to hide in. The rocks are like old people in overcoats looking out to sea, waiting for lost relatives, sad and hopeful but not expecting too much too quickly. Every million years or so someone might turn up!

'Why?' his father wants to know.

'Just feel like it,' Tom shrugs. 'I'll be home in an hour.'

'Okay. Don't be late. You know what Anna is like.'

'I'll be there.'

Tom gets out, trudges to the end of the road, through the empty car park and onto the rough dirt path that runs down through the rocks to the ocean. He stops a moment before his descent, zips up his jacket, even though the breeze is more a light caress than anything else, and breathes it all in. It is an absolutely brilliant day and he's got it to himself, hardly another person on the beach. The ocean spreads out as far as he can see, clear and bright as shimmering glass, the narrow band of waves along the shoreline like a fine lace trim on a girl's shirt. The sky is a flimsy canopy of duck-egg blue, punctuated only by the occasional swooping gull on a mission to find the next meal.

Far out! Tom's heart lifts as he makes his way down through the rocks onto the sand, glad to be away from his father and the melancholy Chopin. He pulls off his runners, rolls up his jeans, goes right down to the shoreline and wades in, bending to watch the sea sloshing and pulling at his toes, white now with the cold. As the waves suck back out again he feels a small part of himself go too, off into the deep unfathomable world of the deep.

He looks at his watch and sees he'd better hurry . . . There is his family to see and a party to get to. Reluctantly he walks back up to the dry sand and puts on his shoes. Head down, hands stuffed into the pockets of his jacket he begins the walk into town at a sharp pace, only stopping occasionally to throw some bit of driftwood or rubbery seaweed back into the water.

Fifteen minutes into the walk, he notices the hazy dark shape of someone in the distance, rollicking around on the sand halfway between the cliff and the shoreline. *What's going on?* Then he sees the black shape of a scruffy little dog darting about the human

366

figure like a mad thing. Whoever it is is throwing sticks and the wild hairy little ball is careering about, yelping and barking, chasing and retrieving, not letting up for a second.

Soon he sees that the figure is a girl – she's wearing a mid-length dark skirt and flat boots, and her hair is blowing about in the breeze. When she notices him approaching she stops playing so gaily with the dog and retreats further up the sand, still throwing the stick. Tom heads down to the wet sand. *Don't mind me.* But she's obviously embarrassed to have been caught playing so boisterously. He resolves to pass by quickly so she can have the beach to herself again.

As he gets closer it begins to dawn on him that it could be *her!* *Of course it isn't her! She doesn't have a dog for a start.*

He turns away, looks out to sea and tries to think of something else. *Get over it!* he tells himself angrily, *it's been nearly a year since you had anything to do with her.* But when he turns back, the girl has walked down to the shoreline and he can see that it *is* her.

Alice Wishart.

Tom stops dead.

The look of absolute disbelief on her face when she recognises him makes him want to run in the opposite direction. Does he keep walking towards her or . . . *not?* The crazy little dog is circling her, yapping noisily, wanting more games with the stick. But she isn't paying it any attention now. She is staring out to sea, probably trying to pretend that it isn't happening. Tom grabs a nearby stick and throws it towards the cliff face as hard as he can. The dog is off immediately.

Slowly, they edge towards each other, stopping only a few feet apart.

'Alice!'

'Tom.' She isn't smiling.

'Has your grandmother died?'

'No,' she says in surprise, 'at least, not last time I looked.' A faint lift at the edge of her mouth. 'Have you heard something I haven't?'

Why the hell did he say that? 'Sorry!' He picks up the stick that the dog has brought back and throws it again. 'I thought that you might have come home for it,' he mutters stupidly.

'*It* being the funeral?' Alice's smile widens.

'Well . . . yeah, I guess.'

'Last time I saw her she was arranging flowers,' Alice says dryly and looks at her watch, 'about two hours ago actually.'

'Oh, that's good' Tom nods enthusiastically.

Alice laughs.

Tom clears his throat and looks away, knowing the sooner he gets off this ridiculous topic the better.

'You back living here?'

'No,' she shakes her head, 'I'm back for a birthday party. Do you know the twins? Sylvie and Leyla Cassidy?'

Tom frowns trying to think if he does.

'You mean those two weird girls?'

'They're my best friends,' Alice says calmly, 'so watch what you say.'

'Sorry,' he says hurriedly, 'I haven't seen them in years. They've probably changed a lot. Do they still live out of town on a farm?'

'Yep,' she laughs quickly, 'and they haven't changed much at all, actually.'

The dog has dropped the stick at her feet and is yapping manically. Alice frowns thoughtfully as she picks it up.

Tom takes the opportunity to sneak a close-up look at her. She is as lovely as he remembers. Those heavy eyebrows and long dark lashes, the high cheekbones and pretty mouth. He has a sudden rush of memory of putting both his hands into that long shiny hair.

'I'm out here preparing my speech,' she offers. 'I was actually thinking about their *unusualness* and trying to work out how to put it into the speech,' she smiles, 'maybe I should just call them weird.'

'So,' Tom smiles, determined to make up for his clumsiness, 'a party with speeches?'

'Eric is here,' Alice smiles, 'and he's giving one too.'

'Oh, Eric,' Tom says uneasily.

'You didn't like him, did you?' she asks wryly.

'Not much,' Tom shrugs, clears his throat and looks away. He is messing this up big time but can't seem to help himself. Within two minutes he's assumed her grandmother was dead and insulted all her best friends. But when he turns back to her she's smiling a bit as though something is funny.

'What?' Tom colours with embarrassment. 'What did I say?'

'Nothing! It's odd . . . seeing you here.'

'It is.'

'Good though, Tom.'

'Yes.'

There is an awkward moment where neither knows what to say.

'I'm headed that way,' Alice says eventually, pointing towards the rocks that Tom has just climbed down. 'So I guess I'll be off.'

Her words send a shot of panic to his belly and make him game. He simply can't let her go now. Not after . . . so long.

'Can I come?' he asks abruptly.

'But you're going the other way.'

Tom catches the warmth in her voice and her smile, and it sends a succession of tiny blasts of crazy hope into his brain. He squats to pat the little dog so she won't see how nervous he is.

'This yours?' He is caressing the dog's ears.

'Mm-hmm,' Alice nods, 'got her last year.'

369

'So, what's her name?' Tom asks.

'Bess,' Alice says, and then colours up when she sees his surprise. 'I . . . thought I'd pinch the name, that's all.' She is embarrassed. 'I heard your dog died.'

'It's a good name,' Tom agrees softly. He is trying to hide just how pleased he is by this bit of information.

'You don't mind?'

'No,' he laughs, 'why would I?'

'This one is very different, a complete maniac!' Alice offers. 'Not like . . . yours used to be.'

'Ours used to be a maniac,' Tom meets her eyes and smiles 'until she got old. So, Alice . . . I haven't seen you around in a while.' Tom stands up.

'Have *you* been around?' she asks.

'I suppose not . . . not really.'

'So it would be pretty hard to see me if . . . you weren't even here!'

'Okay!' Tom laughs. He knows she is playing him, but he doesn't care because he also knows that she is enjoying herself; that she doesn't want to be anywhere else right now. And nor does he. Right at this moment, *this* is the best place in the world for the both of them. 'Do you and Bess want company or not?'

'Sure.' Alice bends down to pat the dog. 'We like company.'

Slowly they make their way back along the stretch of beach that Tom has just come from. At the estuary they find a rock to lean against as they throw sticks to crazy little Bess. When the wind picks up, they retreat to a place between two bigger rocks and sit down on the sand. After the intial shyness they find they have a lot to talk about.

Tom forgets his mother's birthday lunch. He forgets his rash. He even forgets how pissed off he was feeling about everything only an hour before. But he doesn't forget everything. He remembers

Jonty – Jonty is never far away – and he remembers what happened. And before long he remembers why he fell for Alice Wishart.

Bess sits between them, panting, exhausted at last from all her running around. She looks from one to the other as though she understands and absolutely approves of everything being said.

Anyone watching the three of them walking back along the beach towards town an hour later would see a tall, good-looking guy with his hands stuffed deep into his pockets, walking alongside a pretty, plump girl with unruly curly hair, and a tired little dog trotting behind them. But they pass only one other person – a middle-aged bald man rugged up against the wind, sitting on the sand reading a newspaper. Their talk and laughter cause him to look up but he quickly goes back to the article he's reading and so doesn't see the way their faces light up when they look at each other.

Maureen McCarthy is the ninth of ten children and grew up on a farm near Yea in Victoria. After working for a while as an art teacher, Maureen became a full-time writer. Her novels have been shortlisted for numerous awards and include the In Between series, which was adapted from scripts Maureen co-wrote with Shane Brennan for SBS TV; *Ganglands*; *Cross My Heart*; *Chain of Hearts*; *Flash Jack*; and *When You Wake and Find Me Gone*. Her bestselling and much-loved book *Queen Kat, Carmel and St Jude get a life* was made into a highly successful four-part mini-series for ABC TV. Her most recent novel is *Rose by any other name*. Maureen has three sons and lives in Melbourne.

Rose is all packed up. She's got a van full of petrol and a stack of CDs. She's got a surfboard in the back and a secret that won't go away. But that's okay. She also has enough attitude to light up the night sky. Then her mother decides to come along… and Rose's road trip takes a U-turn, straight to the heart of last summer.

❝ McCarthy is so very good at emotional authenticity… most especially we are drawn to Rose, prickly and delicate as her namesake. *❞ The Age*